D0853316

l

DATE		
NOV 12 1982	APR 2 1 1989	
NOV 28 1985	MAR 29 1990	
APR 15		
MAR 17 '86	MAR 1 1 1991	
APR 1 7 '86	MAR 27 1991	
MAR 23 '87	FAC	
APR 6 '87	MAR 25 '94	
NOV 30 '87	APR 09 '94	
MAR 2 9 1989		
APR 1 2 1989		

SEVEN MODERN AMERICAN NOVELISTS

THE *seven essays which appear in this book were first published separately in the series of University of Minnesota Pamphlets on American Writers and, together with the other pamphlets in the series, are intended as introductions to authors who have helped to shape American culture over the years of our colonial and national existence. The editors of the pamphlet series are Leonard Unger and George T. Wright. Many pamphlets, in addition to the seven represented here, are available.*

SEVEN MODERN
AMERICAN NOVELISTS

An Introduction

EDITED BY
WILLIAM VAN O'CONNOR

The University of Minnesota Press, Minneapolis

Printed in the United States of America at
North Central Publishing Co., St. Paul

 3

Library of Congress Catalog Card Number: 64-18175

ISBN 0-8166-0327-8

SIXTH PRINTING 1972

PUBLISHED IN THE UNITED KINGDOM AND INDIA BY THE OXFORD
UNIVERSITY PRESS, LONDON AND DELHI, AND IN CANADA BY THE
COPP CLARK PUBLISHING CO. LIMITED, TORONTO

Distributed to high schools in the United States by Webster Division
McGraw-Hill Book Company, Inc.
St. Louis   New York   San Francisco   Dallas

Table of Contents

INTRODUCTION, *by* William Van O'Connor   3

EDITH WHARTON, *by* Louis Auchincloss   11

SINCLAIR LEWIS, *by* Mark Schorer   46

F. SCOTT FITZGERALD, *by* Charles E. Shain   81

WILLIAM FAULKNER, *by* William Van O'Connor   118

ERNEST HEMINGWAY, *by* Philip Young   153

THOMAS WOLFE, *by* C. Hugh Holman   189

NATHANAEL WEST, *by* Stanley Edgar Hyman   226

SELECTED BIBLIOGRAPHIES   265

ABOUT THE AUTHORS   281

INDEX   285

SEVEN MODERN AMERICAN NOVELISTS

WILLIAM VAN O'CONNOR

Introduction

W E EXPECT a fiction writer to know his craft, and to help us discover something about the world we did not know before or know in the same way, something we believe to be true and that has relevance to our own attitudes and conduct. We expect a fiction writer to find, as we do in life, themes submerged in action. He must ponder them and make them live, like a vital electrical force. A theme ought to struggle with resistant, recalcitrant, and partly inchoate matter — and overcome it or almost overcome it. He ought not to know in advance what his subject means. He must discover his theme as the story develops. And if, when the book is completed, the theme emerges with perfect clarity probably the writer has hidden some of the evidence, and produced a piece of didacticism or propaganda.

We also expect a strikingly brilliant story — the mad-eyed captain pursuing the white whale and his own death; John Marcher caught in his dream that fate has something special for him; Hester Prynne, with the luminous A on her bosom, living in the guilt-ridden community between the forest and the ocean; Moll Flanders, corklike, refusing to let her experiences sink her; or Joe Christmas, living in a community that refuses to recognize his humanity, finally confronting Joanna Burden, the embodiment of implacable inhumanity, confronting the threat to his own manhood and his own life.

We expect a story to begin well. The undertow begins, or should begin, on the first page, and pull the reader's feet from beneath him, so that soon he is swimming for dear life in the fictional sea

3

the writer has created. Faulkner is good at such beginnings. Lena, at the opening of *Light in August*, is sitting by the road, watching a wagon coming toward her, and she thinks: "All the way from Alabama a-walking. A fur piece." Hemingway is good at it too. The first page of *A Farewell to Arms* pictures soldiers walking along the dusty road, with the dust settling on the leaves, and we are told the leaves fell early that autumn. The opening paragraphs tell us, although not in detail, what will happen:

In the late summer of that year we lived in a house in a village that looked across the river and the plain to the mountains. In the bed of the river there were pebbles and boulders, dry and white in the sun, and the water was clear and swiftly moving and blue in the channels. Troops went by the house and down the road and the dust they raised powdered the leaves of the trees. The trunks of the trees too were dusty and the leaves fell early that year and we saw the troops marching along the road and the dust rising and leaves, stirred by the breeze, falling and the soldiers marching and afterward the road bare and white except for the leaves.

The plain was rich with crops; there were many orchards of fruit trees and beyond the plain the mountains were brown and bare. There was fighting in the mountains and at night we could see the flashes from the artillery. In the dark it was like summer lightning, but the nights were cool and there was not the feeling of a storm coming. . . .

At the start of the winter came the permanent rain and with the rain came the cholera. But it was checked and in the end only seven thousand died of it in the army.

We expect, but rarely find, characters that live in the memory. E. M. Forster says plot and story might be set aside in favor of some other units, but one wants characters "to seem alive." He adds that there are characters who live in the mind long after the book is finished, and those that live only on the page, as one reads, but die once the book is closed. Probably most of Edith Wharton's characters die after the book is closed, but some of these are "alive" and engaging as one reads.

Each memorable character represents a principle, a force, a condition, an essence. The movement of such characters through a story seems inevitable; there is something mysterious, simple, and fateful about them. Lesser characters live thanks to the situation in which they are involved, the verbal skill of the author, or the reader's curiosity about *what happened?* Perhaps Nathanael West's characters belong in this category.

One ought also to be able to "hear" a character, as well as "see" him. Probably Jay Gatsby in his garish clothes would be less memorable if we did not hear him say "Old Sport":

I went in — after making every possible noise in the kitchen, short of pushing over the stove — but I don't believe they heard a sound. They were sitting at either end of the couch, looking at each other as if some question had been asked, or was in the air, and every vestige of embarrassment was gone. Daisy's face was smeared with tears, and when I came in she jumped up and began wiping at it with her handkerchief before a mirror. But there was a change in Gatsby that was simply confounding. He literally glowed; without a word or a gesture of exultation a new well-being radiated from him and filled the little room.

"Oh, hello old sport," he said, as if he hadn't seen me for years. I thought for a moment he was going to shake hands.

"It's stopped raining."

"Has it?" When he realized what I was talking about, that there were twinkle-bells of sunshine in the room, he smiled like a weather man, like an ecstatic patron of recurrent light, and repeated the news to Daisy. "What do you think of that? It's stopped raining."

"I'm glad, Jay." Her throat, full of aching, grieving beauty, told only of her unexpected joy.

"I want you and Daisy to come over to my house," he said, "I'd like to show her around."

"You're sure you want me to come?"

"Absolutely, old sport."

Some authors — Thomas Wolfe and Hemingway are writers in point — use essentially the same protagonists, their own alter egos, and feel other characters only in relation to the protagonists. Therefore they tend to write pretty much the same story in novel after novel. Others, William Faulkner, for example, can create a diversified community of characters, each seeming to live individually and not merely in his relationship to the protagonist.

A truly memorable character has, as Henry James said, been vividly rendered — but the external appearance must be in keeping with his psychic identity, as it is for example, in Dickens' Joe Gargery, Magwitch the convict, and Mr. Jaggers; they are "seen" *and* "felt" and flow inside the action, as in an electric field. What they are and the way they appear affects Pip's feelings and actions, and the plot's development. What each is becomes, finally, a part of Pip, forming him for the rest of his life. James created such a character in Miss Bordereau, the "Juliana" of *The Aspern Papers.* He evokes the old lady's physical presence, set against a chill sense of the past. When we learn in the next chapter that this ancient crone, almost a living corpse, is greedy and has a quick, malicious, and cynical mind, and when we hear her laugh, we realize that James has created a memorable character. Thanks to her, the situation that is the story becomes filled with excitement and suspense. The visiting writer and the sweet, generous, but unattractive niece are soon caught in a downward movement, from which there is no escape. She sets the action in motion, like a strong wind catching a heavy canvas sail, and contributes to the story its rhythmic sweep.

There are many characters in Faulkner's novels whose physical appearance and psychic identity are of a piece. In the final scene of *The Sound and the Fury*, for instance, we see Luster, patient, hard-working, yet childlike, Benjy, lost in his dream of sorrow, and the mean-spirited, cynical Jason. The novel ends with a tableau, in which each character is *in* the story, yet seems to project outwardly into space and time:

They approached the square, where the Confederate soldier gazed with empty eyes beneath his marble hand into wind and weather. Luster took still another notch in himself and gave the impervious Queenie a cut with the switch, casting his glance about the square. "Dar Mr Jason's car," he said then he spied another group of negroes. "Les show dem niggers how quality does, Benjy," he said, "Whut you say?" He looked back. Ben sat, holding the flower in his fist, his gaze empty and untroubled. Luster hit Queenie again and swung her to the left at the monument.

For an instant Ben sat in an utter hiatus. Then he bellowed. Bellow on bellow, his voice mounted, with scarce interval for breath. There was more than astonishment in it, it was horror; shock; agony eyeless, tongueless; just sound, and Luster's eyes back-rolling for a white instant. "Gret God," he said, "Hush! Hush! Gret God!" He whirled again and struck Queenie with the switch. It broke and he cast it away and with Ben's voice mounting toward its unbelievable crescendo Luster caught up the end of the reins and leaned forward as Jason came jumping across the square and onto the step.

With a backhanded blow he hurled Luster aside and caught the reins and sawed Queenie about and doubled the reins back and slashed her across the hips. He cut her again and again, into a plunging gallop, while Ben's hoarse agony roared about them, and swung her about to the right of the monument. Then he struck Luster over the head with his fist.

"Dont you know any better than to take him to the left?" he said. He reached back and struck Ben, breaking the flower stalk again. "Shut up!" he said, "Shut up!" He jerked Queenie back and jumped down. "Get to hell on home with him. If you ever cross that gate with him again, I'll kill you!"

"Yes, suh!" Luster said. He took the reins and hit Queenie with the end of them. "Git up! Git up, dar! Benjy, fer God's sake!"

Ben's voice roared and roared. Queenie moved again, her feet began to clop-clop steadily again, and at once Ben hushed. Luster looked quickly back over his shoulder, then he drove on. The broken flower drooped over Ben's fist and his eyes were empty and blue and serene again as cornice and façade flowed smoothly once more from left to right; post and tree, window and doorway, and signboard, each in its ordered place.

The fiction writer knows he is a friend of the genie. The genie makes a gesture — and smoke rises from the earth. One looks more closely, and sees a tight-lipped young man entering an all-night bar in Spain. A waiter, wiping a tabletop, looks up, and smiles. Ah, we say, Hemingway. The genie puffs his cheeks and blows the cloud away. Another cloud, and again we peer intently. We see a freckled young man with light red hair; he is wearing a striped suit. He has goose-blue eyes, and thick sensual lips. He is sitting in a shabby hotel lobby. He is a drummer. It is a November day, about 1910. The elevator door creaks open, and a young lady wearing a long skirt emerges. She is obviously poor, and probably has come to Chicago to find work. The drummer intends to make advances. Ah, we say, Theodore Dreiser.

Each fictional world is different, and recognizable. Book to book the characters change, and the setting changes — but the individual vision usually remains constant. *Plus ça change, plus c'est la même chose.* It is up to Edith Wharton, Sinclair Lewis, F. Scott Fitzgerald, William Faulkner, Ernest Hemingway, Thomas Wolfe, or Nathanael West to cause us to believe in and to respond to the worlds they have created.

We also expect a fiction writer to master time, to properly describe the color of the sky, the weather and time of day, the stains on an old walnut table, street lighting, carriages, hairstyles, and tiepins. Simultaneously, he has to give his story another dimension — the chronological time of the given action and a universal time, recognizable in 1797, 1832, or 1960. The achievement of universal time in a story is the ultimate test of a writer's lasting power. One can say with some assurance that the early Fitzgerald stories are period pieces, and will eventually interest only the specialist and the cultural historian. Possibly this will be the fate of all, or most, of the novels of Sinclair Lewis. Probably this will not be the fate of Willa Cather's *The Professor's House* or *My Mortal Enemy.*

We ought to ask of American novelists neither more nor less than we ask of European novelists — that they be judged against the great writers who preceded them, a Jane Austen, a Charles Dickens, a Herman Melville, a Nathaniel Hawthorne.

Ever since Henry James and Ford Madox Ford were issuing manifestos, much has been made of "technique," of "rendering," of "impressionism," of "point-of-view." These concepts made it easier to talk about fiction — and presumably aided certain novelists to learn their craft. When, for example, would William Faulkner have found his "impressionism" — his *Sound and the Fury* and his *Absalom, Absalom!* — if he had not studied Joseph Conrad's Marlow? He might, however, have learned a good deal from Emily Brontë's *Wuthering Heights.*

When one is young, it is easy to dismiss the "older generation," but as T. S. Eliot said, in advising against this practice, we should not brag about knowing more than our predecessors, because *they* are that which we *know*. Presumably the observation is valid. Now that the Modernist movement has itself begun to recede into history, it is easier to see that modern fiction, after all, is a part of a long tradition.

For example, Charles Dickens, a generation ago, was held up as a "sentimentalist," which he probably is, but what novel better catches the hallucinatory air of the modern city than *Great Expectations?* Virginia Woolf's London or John Dos Passos' New York can't hold a candle to it — although Joyce's evocation of a paralyzed Dublin is a different matter.

The twentieth-century novelist has been advised to tidy up loose ends in his novels, to be careful to justify his focus of narration. But neither Henry James nor Scott Fitzgerald was more successful in maintaining steadily the steady foci of narrators than was Emily Brontë in *Wuthering Heights.* Her sense of the pre-human or anti-human or cosmic also puts her close to the "discoveries" of D. H. Lawrence.

A writer's world vision, we have often been told, should hang together — the premise of his "world" should give rise to plot, setting, character, diction, and philosophical implication. The "Hemingway world" is self-contained, a revelation of a world always at war, and of man confronted by *nada.* Hardy's "world" is also self contained, as in *Tess of the d'Urbervilles* and *Jude the Obscure* The very stones and chairs and beds are dank, and every twilight glowers.

The point of all this is not that the twentieth-century novelists are less able than their eminent predecessors — some are and some are not — but that genuine art in any period has certain characteristics, and the great novelists have always known how to *tell* a story. Literary conventions come and go. We have been inclined to find George Eliot's intrusion as an all-knowing author rather painful — but we must admit that her knowledge of human characteristics greatly surpasses Virginia Woolf's, or Ernest Hemingway's; in reading her we eventually suppress our annoyance, and say, yes, her insight into human psychology, however heavy-handed she sometimes is, is enormous. The point then is that the great novelists in one period have a lot in common with great novelists in another period. Those contemporary with each other may at first glance seem closer to each other, but for superficial reasons. The great ones leave their contemporaries, and live in another order of time.

All history, including literary history, tarnishes, and enthusiasts for a particular author or novel find it necessary to get out the silver polish and the cloth, to try to show that back of time's tarnish is valuable metal. If the metal is truly valuable other observers will acknowledge it. This presumably is why critics are tolerated — and sometimes thanked.

Edith Wharton

It was the fashion among Edith Wharton's friends, initiated by Henry James, to describe her in terms of glowing hyperbole, to see her in the guise of a great golden eagle swooping down from her high built palace of adventure to stir up the poor old croaking barnyard fowls. The woman is almost lost sight of in their boasts of her activities and possessions: the lovingly clipped and tended gardens, the gleaming, perfectly appointed interiors, the big, fast motor (purchased with the proceeds of the current book) bearing its multilingual owner and her faithful band over the roads of Europe to seek out in every nook and cranny the beauty that must redeem a modern wasteland. One imagines rooms refurbished and gardens relandscaped, all over Europe and the American East Coast, to conform with the mandates which she laid down in *The Decoration of Houses* and *Italian Villas and Their Gardens.* Indeed, there are moments when the lady whom Percy Lubbock describes in her Paris garden, fresh and trim, basket on arm, clippers in hand, ready for the daily task of shearing the heads of yesterday's roses, seems but the symbol of a larger self dedicated to sprucing up our very planet.

This is a long way from the picture in the minds of some American critics of a precious and snobbish old lady. Yet one can see how both pictures came into being. Perfection irritates as well as it attracts, in fiction as in life. As some of Mrs. Wharton's acquaintances complained that her taste in furnishing was too good, her French too precisely idiomatic, so have some of her critics found her heroes and heroines too exquisite, too apt to exclaim in rapt unison over little known beauties in art and literature with which the majority of her readers may not be equally familiar. The glittering structure of her cultivation sits on her novels like a rather showy icing that detracts from the cake beneath. That same majority may be put off by descriptions, however vivid, of physical objects and backgrounds that obtrude on the action, by being made to notice, even in scenes of tensest drama, a bit of red damask on a wall, a Jacqueminot rose, a small, dark Italian primitive. As Edmund Wilson points out, Mrs. Wharton was not only the pioneer but the poet of interior decoration.

Such cultivation was certainly not typical of her generation. Ladies of the New York and Newport of her day, educated by tutors, may have acquired a sound basis in German, French, and Italian, but they used these languages, if at all, more for dinner parties than for books. They did not spend their spare time, like Edith Newbold Jones, in their father's library, nor did they publish, at the age of sixteen, privately printed volumes of poetry. In fact, the very rarity of such intellectual achievement in the family of George Frederic Jones has lent comfort to the bearers of an old legend, totally without foundation, that Edith was the daughter of her brothers' English tutor, a clever young man with a mild painter's talent who was killed in the West by Indians. The theory seems to spring from the same kind of thinking that cannot conceive a Shakespeare born in Stratford. But I find it easier to believe that Lucretia Stevens Rhinelander Jones, granddaughter of a Revolutionary patriot and a conventional society matron in a then small-town New York, should have had a brilliant daughter than an illegitimate one, and the fact that Edith, being so much younger than her brothers, was brought up like an only child seems adequate explanation for the hours that she spent alone in her father's library in West 23rd Street.

In her memoirs she describes as her good fortune that she was forbidden, on moral grounds, to read the ephemeral rubbish of the day and so was not distracted from the classics on the paternal shelves. It was obvious, she tells us, though I am not sure how quickly we agree, that a little girl "to whom the Old Testament, the Apocalypse and the Elizabethan dramatists were open, could not long pine for Whyte Melville or even Rhoda Broughton." In the sternly impressive list of her early reading, with its heavy emphasis on history and poetry, the only American names are Prescott, Parkman, Longfellow, and Irving. The other Melville, Herman, "a cousin of the Van Rensselaers, and qualified by birth to figure in the best society," she never, as a girl, even heard mentioned. Culture and education, to the Joneses and to their group, still meant Europe.

Europe, however, was not only the fountain of arts; it was also good for one's health and pocketbook. The Joneses were badly hit by the inflation that followed the Civil War and took their little daughter for long, economizing visits to Italy and France. It was a life of hotels and watering places, seeing only fellow Americans and their servants, but there were compensations for a sensitive child in driving out to the Campagna and wandering among the tombs of the Appian Way, in collecting fragments of porphyry and lapis lazuli on the slopes of the Palatine, and in such Parisian sights as the Empress Eugénie in her *daumont,* with the little Prince Imperial at her side and a glittering escort of officers. At the same time the young Henry James was knocking about the Continent, staying in pensions and picking up material for his first international tales. On both, the European experience was to have a lasting effect. But what was to have a much greater influence on Edith Jones as a writer, and to supply her with the subject material for her most important work, was neither her father's library nor her early impression of Europe, but her own clear, direct, comprehensive little girl's vision of the New York society in which her parents lived.

In 1862, the year of her birth, and for perhaps two decades thereafter, this was a small, sober, proper, tightly knit society, of Dutch and English descent, which lived in uniform streets of chocolate house fronts on income largely derived from municipal real estate. It was wary of the arts, beyond a dip into Longfellow or Bryant, or an evening of *Norma* at the Academy of Music, and disdainful of politics and any business that smacked of retail. The men practiced law in a listless sort of way and sat on charitable boards and had the leisure and taste to appreciate with their wives long meals of good food washed down by the "Jones Claret" or the "Newbold Madeira." Young Edith, sharply aware of their indifference to beauty in the arts, found their society stifling and stultifying, but as an elderly woman, surrounded by a world that seemed to her to have lost its values, she decided ruefully that the merit of those "amiable persons" had been to uphold standards of education and good manners and of scrupulous probity in business and private affairs.

As a young girl and as a debutante, she was miserably shy, a quality that was to dog her all her life, and that she was later to encase behind the enamel of formality, but by the time of her marriage, at the age of twenty-three, she had become at least outwardly reconciled to the observances of social life. Edward Robbins Wharton was an easygoing, friendly Bostonian, of no intellectual pretensions, who adored his much younger wife and always kept a thousand dollar bill in his purse in case "Pussy" wanted anything. They lived in New York and Newport and went every year to Europe, and no children came to interrupt their social and sightseeing routine. Obviously, it was not an existence to satisfy indefinitely a mind rendered immune to Rhoda Broughton by the beauties of the Apocalypse, and gradually the young wife started to write, here and there a poem, then a sentimental short story with an uplifting conclusion, then a serious book on interior decoration, then travel pieces, at last a historical novel. In her memoirs she describes her writing as the natural sequence of a childhood habit of "making up" on bits of brown wrapping paper, but Edmund Wilson suggests that she took it up because of the tensions of an incompatible marriage and at the advice of Dr. S. Weir Mitchell, an early pioneer in female neuroses and himself a novelist. Fragments of her diary, recently published by Wayne Andrews, in which she notes that she could endure the "moral solitude" of her marriage only by creating a world of her imagination, certainly seem to substantiate Wilson. At any rate, there was the gap of a generation between those brown paper scribblings and the publication of her first volume of fiction at the age of thirty-seven.

The tales in *The Greater Inclination* (1899) and in its successor, *Crucial Instances* (1901), have some of the flavor of James's stories of artists and writers of the same period. They are apt to be set against European backgrounds and to deal with such themes as the temptation to the serious artist of commercial success or the bewildering influence upon him of the art of an older, richer civilization. They are clever and readable, if a trifle thin, and in three of them, "The Pelican," "The Rembrandt," and "The Angel at the Grave," Mrs. Wharton shows herself already in full command of the style that was to make her prose as lucid and polished as any in American fiction. It is a firm, crisp, smooth, direct, easily flowing style, the perfect instrument of a clear, undazzled eye, an analytic mind, and a sense of humor alert to the least pretentiousness. We may later wonder if her style was adapted to all the uses to which she put it, but at this point it perfectly presents to us, in all their pathetic and confused dignity, the brave little lady who lectures with an ignorant boldness to women's groups on every aspect of arts and letters, first for the love of her baby and ultimately for the love of her own voice, the proud and splendid widow who is induced only by direst poverty to part with her false Rembrandt, and the dedicated spinster who devotes a lifetime to maintaining her grandfather's house as a shrine for a public that has forgotten him. The defect in Edith Wharton's poetry, of which she published three volumes, is that this same style, consciously ennobled and stripped of laughter, becomes as dull and over-ornamented as the privately printed verse of any number of aspiring ladies who sought refuge from the distraction of social life. But poetry is subjective, and Mrs. Wharton, like many persons of wide reading and disciplined exterior, was inclined to be mawkish in subjective mood.

Her first novel, *The Valley of Decision*, appeared in 1902, when she was forty, and its scene is laid in Italy, that charnel house of English and American historical fiction. It is Edith Wharton's

Romola, except that it is a better book than George Eliot's, for the fruits of her research are strewn attractively through the pages and not spooned into the reader like medicine. But although she captures remarkably the spirit and color of the eighteenth century, nothing can save the novel from its pale and lifeless characters. It is like a play with perfect settings in which the actors stand stiffly in the middle of the stage, their eyes fixed on the prompter. Only when Odo as a boy visits his grandfather's castle in the mountains, and later in the grand ducal gallery when he faces the portraits of his interbred ancestors, is there any true linking of characters and sets. The theme, however, is of some interest to the student of Edith Wharton, for it presages the political and social conservatism that was later to enchain her. Odo brings reform to Pianura only to find himself the harbinger and later the prisoner of the Reign of Terror. His creator was always afraid that even a needed cleaning of sewers might cause the collapse of the civilization above them.

The next two years find Mrs. Wharton still experimenting. *Sanctuary* (1903) demonstrates, a bit comically, the combined influence of Paul Bourget and James. In the first part of this absurd but charming little tale Kate Peyton marries a cheat and a liar in order to become the mother of the moral defective whom he might otherwise sire upon a woman less capable of raising such offspring — surely almost a parody of a Bourget theme — and in the second, twenty-five years later, she contrives to keep this offspring from committing an odious fraud by radiating sympathy to him in silent Jamesian waves. *The Descent of Man* (1904) is another volume of short stories, similar in tone to the earlier ones except for "The Dilettante," which marks an advance in the development of a male character who is to pervade all of Mrs. Wharton's fiction, the cold, cultivated, aristocratic egoist who feeds on the life and enthusiasm of simpler souls. The story has a clever twist at the end when the dilettante's betrothed jilts him on discovering that the lady who has been his intimate friend for years has *not* been his mistress. It is a theme that we shall meet again.

The House of Mirth (1905) marks her coming of age as a novelist. At last, and simultaneously, she had discovered both her medium and her subject matter. The first was the novel of manners and the latter the assault upon the old Knickerbocker society in which she had grown up of the new millionaires, the "invaders" as she called them, who had been so fabulously enriched by the business growth following the Civil War. New money had poured into New York in the 1880's and 1890's and turned the Joneses' quiet old Fifth Avenue into a dizzy parade of derivative façades from Azay-le-Rideau to the Porch of the Maidens. The Van Rensselaers and Rhinelanders might purse their lips at the ostentation of the Vanderbilts, but in a dollar world the biggest bank balance was bound to win out. A Livingston would marry a Mills, as in an earlier day a Schermerhorn had married an Astor. For what, really, did that older world have that was so special? It was all very well for James to describe the Newport of his childhood, surviving into this gilded age, as a little bare white open hand suddenly crammed with gold, but the fingers of that little hand closed firmly enough over the proffered bullion. The sober brown stucco of Upjohn's country villas concealed a materialism as rampant as any flaunted by the marble halls of Richard Morris Hunt. Mrs. Wharton saw clearly enough that the invaders and defenders were bound ultimately to bury their hatchet in a noisy, stamping dance, but she saw also the rich possibilities for satire in the contrasts afforded by the battle line in its last stages and the pathos of the individuals who were fated to be trampled under the feet of those boisterous truce makers.

Lily Bart, the heroine of *The House of Mirth*, stems from both worlds. Her father is related to the Penistons and the Stepneys, but is driven by her mother, a more ordinary creature, to make a fortune which, not being of invader blood, he is bound to lose. Lily, orphaned, is loosed on the social seas with only her beauty and charm for sails and no rudder but a ladylike disdain for shabby compromises and a vague sense that there must be somewhere a better life than the one into which she has drifted. Her rich friends, who use her as a social secretary to write notes and as a blind to shield them from importunate and suspicious husbands, cannot understand the squeamishness which keeps her, at the critical moment, from extracting a proposal from the rich bachelor whom she has not been too squeamish to pursue. Her respectable relatives, on the other hand, of an older society, cannot understand her smoking or gambling or being seen, however briefly, in the company of married men. Lily falls between two stools. She cannot bring herself to marry the vulgar Mr. Rosedale for all his millions, or the obscure Lawrence Selden, for all their affinity. She postpones decisions and hopes for the best and in the meanwhile seeks to distract herself. But we know from the start that she is doomed. She has only her loveliness, and what is that in a world that puts its store in coin and hypocrisy? The other characters, of both new and old New York, seem strangely and vindictively united in a constant readiness to humiliate her: Grace Stepney to tell tales on her, Mrs. Peniston to disinherit her, Bertha Dorset to abandon her in a foreign port, Gus Trenor to try to seduce her, his wife to say he has. We watch with agonized apprehension as Lily turns and doubles back, as she keeps miraculously rehabilitating herself, each time on a slightly lower level. For no matter how hard she struggles, without money she is unarmed in that arena. And in the end when she finally compromises and is willing to marry Rosedale, it is too late. He will not have her, and she falls to the job at the milliner's and the ultimate overdose of sleeping tablets. But we finish the book with the conviction that in the whole brawling, terrible city Lily is the one and only lady.

The different levels of society in *The House of Mirth* are explored with a precision comparable to that of Proust whom Mrs. Wharton was later so greatly to admire. We follow Lily's gradual descent from "Bellomont" on the Hudson and the other great country houses of a world where the old and new societies had begun to merge, to the little court of the Gormers, who, although rich enough to be ultimately accepted, are still at the stage of having to fill their house with hangers-on, to the bogus intellectual world of Carry Fisher who pretends to like interesting people while she earns her living helping climbers up the social ladder, to the final drop into the gilded hotel of the demimondaine Norma

Hatch. Lily learns that money is the common denominator of all these worlds and that the differences between them consist only in the degrees of scent with which its odor is from time to time concealed. Van Wyck Brooks accused Mrs. Wharton of knowing nothing of the American West, and perhaps she did not, but she had a firsthand knowledge of where the profits of the frontier had gone. Lily Bart, weary on foot, watching the carriages and motors of her former friends ply up and down Fifth Avenue, Mrs. Van Osburgh's C-spring barouche, Mrs. Hatch's electric victoria, is seeing the natural successors of the covered wagon.

I do not suppose that Mrs. Wharton intended Lawrence Selden to constitute the last and greatest of Lily's trials, but so he strikes me. He is a well-born, leisurely bachelor lawyer, with means just adequate for a life of elegant solitude, who spends his evenings, when not leafing through the pages of his first editions, dining out in a society that he loves to ridicule. Lily knows that he is a neutral in the battle of life and death in which she is so desperately engaged, and she asks only that he hold her hand briefly in moments of crisis or brush her lips with a light kiss. He does, in the end, decide to marry her, but as she has been too late for Rosedale, so is he too late for her, and he can only kneel by her bed and give to her lifeless lips the last of his airy kisses. Mrs. Wharton's attitude toward Selden's type of man is enigmatic. He may be a villain in "The Dilettante," or he may at least pose as a hero in *The House of Mirth.* She is careful in the latter to point out for his sake, whenever he condemns Lily Bart, that appearances have been against her. Perhaps she conceived him as an abused lover in the Shakespearean sense, as an Othello or a Posthumus. But Othello and Posthumus are quick to believe the worst because of the very violence of their passions. An eye as dry as Selden's should be slower to be deceived. I incline to the theory that Mrs. Wharton really intended us to accept this plaster-cast figure for a hero, but that she had a low opinion of heroes in general. When Lily suddenly retorts to Selden that he spends a great deal of his time in a society that he professes to despise, it is as if the author had

19

suddenly slipped into the book to express a contempt that the reader is not meant to share.

The enigma of Selden inevitably leads to a consideration of the deepest friendship of Edith Wharton's life. "The year before my marriage," she relates in her memoirs, "I had made friends with a young man named Walter Berry, the son of an old friend of my family's (and indeed a distant cousin)." Despite the note of kinship thus cautiously sounded, there is a legend that he proposed to her and was turned down as a not good enough match. This might, if true, explain in the light of revenge some of his acts of coldness to her in later years. At any rate, he became a friend of the young Whartons, and it was during one of his visits to their house in Newport that she showed him the "lumpy pages" of an early manuscript and had the mortification of hearing his "shout of laughter," a peal that was never quite to cease ringing in her ears. But a minute later he said good-naturedly, "Come, let's see what can be done," and settled down beside her to try to model the lump into a book. In that modeling process she claimed, decades later, that she had been taught whatever she knew about the writing of "clear concise English."

I do not believe it, though I am sure that she did. There seemed no limits to her admiration of Berry. "He found me when my mind and soul were hungry and thirsty, and he fed them till our last hour together." Evidently, he supplied her with the intellectual and spiritual companionship that she had never found with Edward Wharton. The latter, as her writing and fame developed, had shrunk to a kind of cipher in her life. In her memoirs, Consuelo Vanderbilt Balsan recalls him "as more of an equerry than an equal, walking behind her and carrying whatever paraphernalia she happened to discard." It was only to be expected, under the circumstances, that she should fall in love with Berry, yet it is not until 1908, when she was forty-six, that her journal begins to evidence it. "I should like to be to you, friend of my heart, like a touch of wings brushing by you in the darkness, or like the scent of an invisible garden that one passes by on an unknown road." The tone of this and other entries would seem to confirm the opinion of many of those close to her that she received only friendship in return. Berry, according to them, was perfectly willing to let her play her chosen role of the touch of wings or the invisible garden. But these, of course, had been only phrases. Like any woman, she wanted more: "You hurt me — you disillusioned me — and when you left me, I was more deeply yours." When he went to Cairo to be a judge of the International Tribunal, she could hardly endure it: "Oh, my adored, my own love, you who have given me the only moments of real life I have ever known, how am I to face the long hours and days?" But she did face them, and one wonders if correspondence with so tepid an admirer might not have been simpler in the end than talks and scenes.

What sort of man was he? James seems to have liked him and to have enjoyed their faintly catty old bachelors' correspondence in which Mrs. Wharton, because of her raids into the secluded retreats of friends, is described as "the angel of devastation." But to others of her circle Berry was less sympathetic, and to Percy Lubbock he was a dogmatic and snobbish egotist, the evil genius, indeed, of her life. "None of her friends," he put it bluntly, "thought she was the better for the surrender of her fine free spirit to the control of a man, I am ready to believe, of strong intelligence and ability — but also, I certainly know, of a dry and narrow and supercilious temper."

Mrs. Wharton's attitude toward evasion of the marriage vow was always ambiguous. Divorce (though she was to come to it herself) she considered crude and antisocial, and the facile forming of new marital ties unspeakably vulgar. On the other hand, the dishonesties and evasions of concealed adultery struck her as offensive and degrading, while any open disregard of the conventions led to a slow, sordid end in those shabby European watering places with which the minds of her contemporaries seemed always to identify extramarital passion. Perhaps, finally, the latter course seemed best to her. At least the spirit that was capable of facing it seemed the finest spirit. Paulina Trant in "The Long Run" (included in *Xingu*, 1916) has all her creator's sympathy when she offers to give up her husband and home for love, and Halston

Merrick, who logically and sensibly tries to reason her out of it, appears as the shallowest of lovers. There must have been womanly moments, for all of Edith Wharton's admiration of Berry, when he struck her as a bit of a Halston Merrick, when she saw him with eyes that made even Lubbock's seem charitable by comparison. It is perhaps to such moments that we owe the curious ambivalence in her treatment of heroes.

Despite the great critical and popular success of *The House of Mirth*, Mrs. Wharton did not return to her New York subject matter for another eight years. Perhaps she was afraid of exhausting it too quickly. *Madame de Treymes* and *The Fruit of the Tree*, so radically different from each other, both appeared in 1907. The first is a true Jamesian tale of innocents abroad, as subtle and fine as any of James's own but with more liveliness and humor. It portrays the duel between John Durham, an American hero in the tradition of James's Christopher Newman, and a wily, charming Parisian aristocrat, Madame de Treymes, over the latter's sister-in-law, poor little Fanny Frisbee of brownstone New York, who has found only misery in her French marriage. Principles and ideals, for the last time in Edith Wharton's fiction, are found on the side of the Stars and Stripes, and Madame de Treymes ruefully recognizes the moral superiority of the Yankee in her final sob: "Ah, you poor, good man!" In later years, unhappily, Mrs. Wharton's Americans abroad were to become the corrupters and not the corrupted.

The Fruit of the Tree is an experiment in a totally new field, the novel of reform. Mrs. Wharton began her task of research conscientiously enough with a tour of a factory near her country home in Lenox, Massachusetts, but she soon lost interest in her theme and succumbed to an unworthy compromise. In order to be able to draw her factory manager and trained nurse from models in her own world, she endowed them both with old and distinguished families which had only recently lost their money, thus giving to these parts of her book a curious air of social masquerade. Even so, the reader's interest is caught when Amherst, the priggish manager, marries the widow owner of the factory, having misconstrued her passion for himself as a zeal for the cause of the workers, and settles down in blithe ignorance to what he imagines will be their shared task of reform. But at this point Mrs. Wharton changes her theme altogether. Bessie Amherst, bored with the workers and interpreting, perhaps correctly (again the enigma of the Wharton hero), her husband's interest in reform as indifference to herself, goes galloping over icy roads until she falls from her horse and receives an incurable back injury, which condemns her to a long period of hideous and futile agony. The novel now turns abruptly into a problem novel about euthanasia in the manner of Bourget, for Bessie's sufferings are abbreviated by the needle of the trained nurse with the social background. Mrs. Wharton handles both themes competently, but the book simply collapses between them. The failure of *The Fruit of the Tree* is just the opposite of that of *The Valley of Decision*; the settings, and not the characters, fade away. It is, however, a less disastrous fault. Bessie Amherst, indolent, selfish, but quite ready to be led by any man who will take the trouble to understand her, is interesting enough to make the novel readable even today, when industrial reform of the type in question has long since been effected and when euthanasia, if still illegal, has ceased to be morally shocking.

The Hermit and the Wild Woman (1908) is another volume of slender, contrived Jamesian stories of artists and dilettantes, but *Tales of Men and Ghosts* (1910) contains some superb chillers. A tricky ending to a serious short story will sometimes detract from the total effect and make it seem superficial or sentimental, or both, but in a ghost story it has a valid, even an indispensable, function. The egotism of Mrs. Wharton's constantly recurring bachelors is brought out more effectively in "The Eyes" than in any of her other short stories or novels. Culwin tells a listening group about a fire, which includes his young protégé, of the eyes, the old eyes with sunk orbits and thick, red-lined lids and look of vicious security, that haunt him at night whenever he has performed what he deems an unselfish act, which the reader, of course, knows to have been just the opposite. As he finishes his tale he marks the horror on the features of the protégé, with whose youth and bloom

23

he has tried to water his own dry nature, and turning to look in the mirror behind him, he sees at last whose eyes they are.

Mrs. Wharton's other ghost stories may be considered out of chronological order because their style and effectiveness do not vary, except to improve, with the years. This kind of tale requires a skill that never left her, the skill of telling a story reduced to its bare bones, without the aid of social problems or manners or mores or even of human nature, except in its most elemental sense. She always believed that the storytelling faculty was basic in any writer. She was like a representational artist who looks askance at an abstract painting and wants to know if the man who executed it can really draw. At times she would try her hand, almost as one might try a puzzle, at a story that was nothing but technique, like "Roman Fever," where the interest and excitement are concentrated in the last line that gives the whole meaning to what has gone before. Her technique in ghost stories is to keep the supernatural to the minimum that will still irradiate the tale with horror. Character can be important as in "The Eyes," but it is by no means essential. As long as there is one plain human being, as in "All Souls," to register terror for the reader, there is an adequate cast.

Time, as we shall see, brought to Mrs. Wharton an attitude of disapproval toward the changing social scene which was to sour her later work, but the ghost stories, by their very nature, escaped this, and her grasp of the secret of chilling her reader continued to improve to the end. "The Lady's Maid's Bell," an early venture, suffers from a slight overdose of the eerie. There is not only the bell; there is the constantly reappearing ghost of Emma Saxon. "Pomegranate Seed," a later tale, corrects this. A second wife's happiness is destroyed and her life turned to nightmare by the appearance, at irregular intervals, on the hall table, addressed to her husband in a faint, female handwriting, of envelopes which unnerve him but which he refuses to discuss. The conviction that these missives come from the dead wife begins to dawn on the reader at the same time that it dawns on her successor, and in the mood of horror that we share with her we completely accept her husband's final disappearance. The ghost of the first wife never comes on the scene to derogate from her letters as Emma Saxon does from the bell.

In the compilation *Ghosts* (1937), published in the last year of Mrs. Wharton's life, two of the best of the eleven stories, "Miss Mary Pask" and "Bewitched," deal, not with the supernatural, but with the appearance of it. Here Mrs. Wharton sets herself the difficult task of scaring the reader in a ghost story without the aid of a ghost. The atmosphere has to be made correspondingly more ominous; Mary Pask must be whiter and more wraithlike on that foggy night in Brittany than if she were a true spirit, and the New Englanders of "Bewitched" must be gaunter and grimmer than the characters of *Ethan Frome* to make sufficiently terrible the ending that proves Venny Brand to have been masquerading. The last story of the collection, and its masterpiece, "A Bottle of Perrier," is not really a ghost story at all, but a tale of hatred and murder in the African desert where an eccentric Englishman lives in a lonely castle with his butler and a host of Arab servants. Mrs. Wharton's style is at its richest as she sets her African scene: "The afternoon hung over the place like a great velarium of cloth-of-gold stretched across the battlements and drooping down in ever slacker folds upon the heavy-headed palms. When at length the gold turned to violet, and the west to a bow of crystal clasping the dark sands, Medford shook off his sleep and wandered out." And the final sentence which reveals for the reader where the body of Almodham has all the time been rotting is like one of those screaming chords at the end of Strauss's *Salome*: "The moon, swinging high above the battlements, sent a searching spear of light down into the guilty darkness of the well."

In 1911 Mrs. Wharton published the short novel with which her name has ever since been linked and which sometimes threatens to preempt the whole of her niche in the history of American literature. She says in her memoirs that in writing *Ethan Frome* she felt for the first time the artisan's full control of his implements. In later years its continuing success was to plague her, as the success of "Daisy Miller" plagued James, for she could never agree with the critics who claimed that it was her best work. Yet it is surely among her best. When I think of it, I visualize a small painting, perfectly executed to the last detail, of three silent figures in a small dark cottage kitchen, with snow glimpsed through a window, the terrible Zeena in the center, white and pasty and gaunt, and, scattered on the table, the pieces of a broken dish. But I could never put the story as fiction in the same class with *The House of Mirth* on the very ground that to me it *is* a picture and, as such, one dimensional. Lily Bart and the society in which she lives are turned around and around and studied from different angles. It is not fair, of course, to compare a long novel with a novelette, but the tremendous reputation of *Ethan Frome* evokes such a defense.

There has been some disposition in critics to view with distrust Mrs. Wharton's excursions into life among the needy, as evidenced by *Ethan Frome*, "The Bunner Sisters," and *Summer*, to see her as the great lady from "The Mount" in Lenox, peering at Ethan and his womenfolk from the back seat of her big motor. I doubt if these comments would have been made had the stories been published under another name, for the keenness of Mrs. Wharton's observation was not affected by the social status of her models. Only, in later years, when she attempted to describe persons and places that she had never seen did she fail in her job. I am totally persuaded of the reality of that notions shop kept by Ann Eliza Bunner and her sister and by the dank public library where Charity Royall dreams away her listless days. The reason why *Summer* and "The Bunner Sisters" are less convincing than *Ethan Frome* does not lie in any failure of observation or imagination on the part of the author, but in the fact that one feels her presence, which in *Ethan Frome* the device of a narrator has successfully eliminated. When Charity Royall sees her mother's kinfolk on the mountain "herded together in a sort of passive promiscuity in which their common misery was the strongest link," and when Evalina Bunner, contrasted to the Hochmullers, is described as "a faintly washed sketch beside a brilliant chromo," we see clearly enough what is meant, but we are standing on that mountain and at Evalina's wedding with Mrs. Wharton herself, and we feel with a touch of constraint the incongruity of our presence.

The Reef (1912) was greeted with a burst of congratulation from all the Jamesian circle. "Racinian" was the adjective used by the master, and indeed a Racinian unity of mood is achieved by centering the action in an old, high-roofed chateau of brick and yellowish stone, bathed in the pale light of October afternoons. The rooms in which the characters tensely talk are like a series of paintings by Walter Gay. It is a quiet, controlled, beautiful novel, but its theme has always struck me as faintly ridiculous. Mrs. Leath, a widow, is at last about to marry George Darrow, her old bachelor admirer, and her stepson, Owen, is entertaining a similar plan with respect to the beautiful young family governess, Sophy Viner, when the discovery that Darrow and Sophy have once been lovers reduces all the characters to a state of quiet desperation. Even conceding that in 1912 such an affair might have disqualified Sophy as a bride for Owen, would Mrs. Leath, a woman who had lived all her adult years in France, consider that her own happiness had to be sacrificed as well? Of course, Mrs. Wharton's answer would be that Mrs. Leath is a woman of the finest sensitivities and that the affair occurred at a time when she had every reason to believe Darrow attentive to herself, but I still cannot get away from the suspicion that at least part of the horror of the situation lies in the fact that Sophy is a governess. The final chapter, so jarringly out of tune with the rest of the book, tends to confirm this suspicion. When Mrs. Leath goes to Sophy's sister's hotel to tell Sophy that she has given Darrow up, she is received by the sister in a dim, untidy, scented room, complete with lover and masseur. Coarse and bloated as the sister is, Mrs. Leath can nonetheless see in her what the beautiful Sophy will one day become, and when she discovers that the latter has departed for India in the company of a disreputable woman, she takes her hasty leave, presumably to return to Darrow and happiness.

The only moral that I can make out of this is that Sophy Viner, a paid dependent who is an appendage rather than a true part of the social pattern, may be expected, under the first bad influence, to drop to a life of semi-prostitution. If the problem to which the book is addressed be justified as a problem common to the era, there remains to be justified the point of view of the author, which for once seems as narrowly prudish and class-conscious as her bitterest critics have ever accused it of being.

The Custom of the Country, happily, in the following year, 1913, is a return to the rich, sure ground of New York and the novel of manners, only this time the central character in the conflict of social groups is not a victim but an invader. Undine Spragg is a creature of alloy, as sentimental in her judgments of herself as she is ruthless in her judgments of others. A father is only a checkbook, a husband a means of social advancement, a baby a threat to the figure. No amount of association with cultivated persons or of exposure to the art of Europe can ripple the surface of her infinite vulgarity. She never knows the toll in human misery of her advance to the social heights, for it never occurs to her to look back. The story of how she hews her way through the old New York ranks of the Marvells and Dagonets, already weakened by prior compromises with the invaders, and even into the society of the Faubourg Saint-Germain from which James's "American" was barred, is vivid and fascinating. Undine gets into as many dangerous corners as Lily Bart, but by miscalculation rather than by inertia, and the same shrewd, restless cerebration that gets her in can be counted on to get her out. In *The House of Mirth* our compassion goes out to Lily; in *The Custom of the Country* it goes out to the society which Undine is trying to crash.

The flaw in the novel that keeps it from ranking equally with its predecessor is that Mrs. Wharton hates Undine too much. She sees in her incarnate the devil of the modern world, that world where all fineness of soul and graciousness of living have been submerged in a great tide of insipid and meretricious uniformity whose origin seems to lie vaguely in the American Middle West. New York has been lost to the flood, and even Europe is no longer safe. The family of the Marquis de Chelles are not sufficiently humiliated by his marriage to Undine; they must also see their tapestries stripped from their walls by her next husband, Elmer

Moffatt. What would the wiles of even Madame de Treymes have accomplished against Elmer? James complained to Mrs. Wharton that she had not sufficiently developed the theme of the relationship between the Chelleses and Undine. Surely, he was wrong. Surely, as the book indicates, no such relationship could have even existed. What Mrs. Wharton fails to prove is that Chelles would have married Undine at all. For she is really too awful to be quite so successful with quite so many men. Her vulgarity destroys the allure that such a woman would have been bound to have and that her creator was not to understand until her last, unfinished novel.

Lily Bart takes only one trip to Europe in the course of her saga, but Undine spends half of hers there. It was abroad, indeed, that Mrs. Wharton must have observed her prototypes, for in these years she had been spending less and less time in her own country. She had always been attracted by the order and grace of French living and by the assured social position of intellectuals in France, so different from what she had experienced in New York. She had a deep respect for traditions and ceremonials that gave her some assurance that the existing form of society had a basis in the past, and, by a like token, a hope for preservation in the future. The New York of her younger years had had traditions, but she had found them merely restricting. The dead hand of a Manhattan past had seemed to her simply dead. Her writing, for example, had never been recognized by her friends and relations as anything but a vaguely embarrassing habit that was better not mentioned. Her husband, it was true, took a rather childish pride in her growing fame, but in all intellectual matters he was as bad as the others. "Does that sort of thing really amuse you?" he asked when she showed him a striking passage in R. H. Lock's study of heredity and variation. "That is the answer to everything worth-while!" she moaned in her journal. "Oh, Gods of derision! And you've given me twenty years of it! *Je n'en peux plus.*"

This cry of the heart is dated 1908 when she was forty-six. Release was on its way. In 1910 the Whartons sold the house in Lenox and moved permanently to France. In the same year Edward

Wharton had a nervous collapse and was placed in a sanatorium. In 1913 they were divorced. She had found at last a world where everything blended: beautiful surroundings, intellectual companionship, a society that combined a respect for the past with a vital concern for the present. London was within easy reach, and she could be in constant touch with writers whose conversation was as polished and civilized as their prose: James, Bourget, Lubbock, Howard Sturgis. It is easy to comprehend the charm of such a life, but what did it have to do with the contemporary American scene that it was her profession to study? James in his later years built his characters into an exotic world of his own imagination. It was not necessary for the creator of Maggie Verver or Milly Theale to have an up-to-date knowledge of life on the other side of the Atlantic. It was enough that he had been born American. But Edith Wharton was concerned with representing the life and manners of New York, and for this she needed more than the chatter of tourist friends.

In a surprisingly insipid little book, *French Ways and Their Meaning* (1919), made up of articles originally written to acquaint Americans coming to France during the war with the character of their allies and hosts, Mrs. Wharton descants on the Gallic qualities of taste, reverence, continuity, and intellectual honesty. The picture that emerges, quite unintentionally, is of a nation chained to ancient forms and observances which could hardly have survived four years of trench warfare with the first military power of Europe. Mrs. Wharton was paying France what she deemed the greatest compliment she knew in describing as national virtues the qualities that most attracted her in her own polite, intellectual circle. There is some of the self-justification of the expatriate in the attitude that her adopted country had to possess to the fullest degree, and her native land to the least, the civilized atmosphere which she found so indispensable in daily life. As a result, there was always a presumption in favor of France in her thinking, just as there was one against America, an injustice that is everywhere reflected in this misleading little book. When she speaks of French culture, Richelieu and the Academy are invoked, but when it is a question of American, she cites only the middle-western college girl who "learnt art" in a year.

When crisis came, at any rate, she had proved a true, if not a legal, citizen of France. She scorned the expatriates who scuttled home at the first rumble of danger in the summer of 1914 and whom she later described in *The Marne*. She was passionately involved from the beginning with the land of her adoption and threw herself into work for the refugees and the wounded with a fervor and efficiency which resulted in her being decorated by President Poincaré and named an officer of the Legion of Honor. She regarded the war from a simple but consistent point of view: France, virtually singlehanded, was fighting the battle of civilization against the powers of darkness. It was the spirit that made men fight and die, but it has never, unfortunately, been the spirit of fiction. Reading *The Marne* (1918) and *A Son at the Front* (1923) today gives one the feeling of taking an old enlistment poster out of an attic trunk. It may be a significant comment on the very nature of Armageddon that the only literature that survives it is literature of disillusionment and despair. Mrs. Wharton knew that the war was terrible; she had visited hospitals and even the front itself. But the exhilaration of the noncombatant, no matter how dedicated and useful her services, has a shrill sound to postwar ears.

The corrosive effect of war on a civilization already vulgarized by American money induced in Mrs. Wharton a mood of nostalgia for the old quiet New York world of her childhood that she had once found so confining. Much later she was to write: "When I was young it used to seem to me that the group in which I grew up was like an empty vessel into which no new wine would ever again be poured. Now I see that one of its uses lay in preserving a few drops of an old vintage too rare to be savoured by a youthful palate."

There was no rose color, however, in the glasses through which she viewed the past. She did not flinch at sight of the old prejudices; she simply reinterpreted them. Mrs. Lidcote, in "Autre Temps" (*Xingu*), has been ostracized for leaving her husband for a lover, but when she returns to New York, a generation later, to take her stand by her daughter who has done the same thing, she discovers that times have changed and that her daughter can now marry her lover and be received by the very people who have cut Mrs. Lidcote. The times, however, have changed only for the daughter's generation. Society will not revise its judgments of individuals, and Mrs. Lidcote must dine upstairs on a tray in order not to embarrass a dinner party gathered to beam on the young lovers. But there is another, subtler moral in the story, and that is in the suggestion that Mrs. Lidcote, with all her suffering, has had a richer life than her daughter with her easy divorce and remarriage. She may feel like a lonely anachronism as she returns to her exile in Europe, but there is no envy in her reflections: "Where indeed in this crowded, topsy-turvey world, with its headlong changes and helter-skelter readjustments, its new tolerances and indifferences and accommodations, was there room for a character fashioned by slower sterner processes and a life broken under their inexorable pressure?"

But this is nostalgia for the very brand that did the burning! Ten years later, in *Twilight Sleep*, Mrs. Wharton was to go even further in her stand against the vapid painlessness of the postwar world by ridiculing the heavy doping of mothers in childbirth. The past came to have a certain validity to her simply by being the past. The New York of her childhood, that "cramped horizontal gridiron of a town without towers, porticoes, fountains or perspectives, hide-bound in its deadly uniformity of mean ugliness," having vanished, became as fascinating as Atlantis or Troy. It is to this attitude of apology toward her parents' generation that we owe her finest novel.

The title, *The Age of Innocence*, refers to the New York of the 1870's in the girlhood of Edith Jones and gives to the book the flavor of a historical novel, as is often pointed out by critics. The fact not always recognized by critics is that it was a habit of Victorian novelists to set their stories in the era of their childhood. The novelist of manners has since shown a tendency to revert to a usually recent past where social distinctions, which make up so much of his subject matter, were more sharply defined, or at least where he thinks they were. *The Age of Innocence* (1920) is written in a Proustian mood of remembered things that evokes the airless atmosphere of an old, ordered, small-town New York as vividly as a conversation piece by Eastman Johnson. Here the dilettante bachelor, Newland Archer, as usual a lawyer, is at last placed in a story adapted to bring out the best and the worst in him. For he must have enough passion and imagination to aspire to break through the barriers of convention that surround him and yet be weak enough so that he cannot finally escape the steely embrace of an aroused tribe. Newland knows that he never really has a chance from the beginning; that is his pathos. He is engaged to May Welland, and he will marry May Welland and spend a lifetime with May Welland, and that is that, and both he and May's beautiful, Europeanized, disenchanted cousin, Ellen Olenska, realize it and accept it.

We have a suffocating sense of a creature trapped and doomed as poor Newland comes to the awareness, from the exchanged glances, coughs, and silences that surround him, that all of his vast family and family-in-law, including his own wife, are convinced that he is enjoying the very affair that he has failed to achieve and are united in irresistible tact to cut it short. But Mrs. Wharton is not suggesting that Newland and Ellen, in their renunciation of each other, have condemned themselves to a life of unrewarding frustration. Rules and regulations have now their validity to her, no matter what passions they crush. "It was you," Ellen tells Archer, "who made me understand that under the dullness there are things so fine and sensitive and delicate that even those I most cared for in my other life look cheap in comparison." And a generation later Archer sees no cause to repine in thinking back over his married life with May: "Their long years together had shown him that it did not so much matter if marriage was a dull duty, as long as it kept the dignity of a duty: lapsing from that, it became a mere battle of ugly appetites. Looking about him, he honored his own past, and mourned for it. After all, there was good in the old ways."

It is Edith Wharton's tribute to her own background, this affirmation that under the thick, smoky glass of convention bloom the fine, fragile flowers of patient suffering and self-sacrifice. To run away from society may be as vulgar in the end as to crash it. Newland Archer builds a shrine in his heart around the image of Ellen from which he derives strength to endure his uneventful and moderately useful life, a life where civic and social duties are judiciously balanced and where the impetus of Theodore Roosevelt even gets him into the state legislature, if only for a single term. We see him more completely than any other of Mrs. Wharton's heroes, and the reader who doubts that such a type existed has only to turn the pages of the voluminous diary of George Templeton Strong, published long after Edith Wharton's death.

The comparison with Strong's diary is also relevant in that *The Age of Innocence* is the first of Mrs. Wharton's novels to have all the action seen through the eyes of one character. The interest is thus centered in Newland Archer, as the interest in the two later books where she used the same method, *The Mother's Recompense* and *The Children*, is centered in Kate Clephane and Martin Boyne. Unlike James, however, she refused to be limited in her own comments to her central character's point of view. Archer's conventional way of looking at life, at least in the first half of the book, is too dull a lens for the reader, and his creator never hesitates to peer over his shoulder and point out all kinds of interesting things on the New York scene that we would otherwise miss. James would have objected to this. He would have argued that the spiritual growth of Archer, like that of Lambert Strether in *The Ambassadors*, would have a richer significance if viewed entirely through Archer's mind. It was one of their principal points of division. Mrs. Wharton refused to subordinate to any rule of design the "irregular and irrelevant movements of life" that to her made up the background of her stories.

It is interesting that her name should be so constantly linked with James's, considering how different were their approaches to their art. His influence is visible, superficially, in her early work, and, of course, they were both interested in Americans in Europe, but there the resemblance ceases. James was subtle, speculative, and indirect; Edith Wharton was always clear and to the point. Percy Lubbock speaks of her aversion to the abstract, to any discussion of the conundrum of life's meaning. She dealt with definite psychological and social problems and handled them in her own definite way. Her sentences never have to be read and reread, like James's, for richer and deeper disclosures. Furthermore, she and James, although good friends, never appreciated the best in each other's work. He found her most successful when most under his influence, as, for example, in *The Reef,* while she distrusted the whole artistic bent of his later years, feeling that he was severing himself more and more from "that thick nourishing human air in which we all live and move." If she must be regarded as anyone's disciple, it would be more accurate to note her relation to George Eliot, whose clear, strong style, broad canvas, and obsession with moral questions always fascinated her.

As long as Mrs. Wharton had elected, after the war, to continue writing about the social life of a city that she had given up even visiting, she would have done better to restrict herself to the eras of its history with which she was acquainted. The four stories that make up *Old New York* (1924) evoke the atmosphere of the last century as successfully as anything in *The Age of Innocence.* But she was too concerned with the world around her to write only of the past. She wanted nothing less than to interpret the age in which she lived and to seek out the origin and cause of the increasing number of things in it that angered her. Also, her way of life had become expensive — a house north of Paris, another on the Riviera, twenty-two servants — and she needed a wider audience. To take advantage of the big pay of the American women's magazines, it was necessary for her to write about Americans of the moment.

The Glimpses of the Moon (1922) was first serialized in the *Pictorial Review,* which may give the clue to its author's remarkable lapse of style and taste. The jacket of the book depicts an Italian villa on Lake Como by moonlight to evoke the mawkish, gushing mood of an opening chapter which makes the reader rub his eyes and look again to be sure that he is dealing with Edith Wharton. Nick and Susy Lansing, two bright young penniless hangers-on of the international set, have married on the understanding that their bond may be dissolved at the option of the first to find a richer spouse. Nick is again the dilettante hero, writing a novel about Alexander the Great in Asia because it takes less research than an essay, but now, for the first time, reader and author see him from radically different points of view. To the reader he is, quite simply, an unmitigated cad, perfectly content to live in the borrowed houses of rich friends so long as his wife agrees not to steal the cigars or to take any overt part in the blindfolding of their hostesses' deceived husbands. On these two commandments hang all his law and his prophets, and when Susy has violated both (in each case, for his sake), he abruptly abandons her to pursue an heiress. It is impossible to imagine how Mrs. Wharton could have picked such a man as the hero of a romance unless she seriously believed that he represented what a gentleman had sunk to in the seventeen years which had elapsed since the publication of *The House of Mirth*. But could even Lawrence Selden have degenerated to a Nick Lansing? And could Lily Bart ever have stolen cigars? Surely the world had not been entirely taken over by the Lansings and their dismal set of international drifters who blur together in a maze of furs and jewels and yachts. Mrs. Wharton's preoccupation with vulgarity had for the moment vulgarized her perceptions.

The lapse in her style can be illustrated by contrasting three descriptions of ladies of fashion. The first is from *The House of Mirth*. Lawrence Selden is taking his shrewd, leisurely note of the person of Lily Bart, and his speculations provide our first insight into the central problem of her character:

Everything about her was at once vigorous and exquisite, at once strong and fine. He had a confused sense that she must have cost a great deal to make, that a great many dull and ugly people must, in some mysterious way, have been sacrificed to produce her. He was aware that the qualities distinguishing her from the herd of her sex were chiefly external: as though a fine glaze of beauty and fastidiousness had been applied to vulgar clay.

The second is from the scene in *Madame de Treymes*, published two years later, where John Durham contemplates Fanny de Malrive after her call upon his mother and sister at their hotel and discerns in her fluster a ground for hope as to his future. The passage, with a faint Jamesian ring, is finely conceived:

The mere fact of her having forgotten to draw on her gloves as they were descending in the hotel lift from his mother's drawing-room was, in this connection, charged with significance to Durham. She was the kind of woman who always presents herself to the mind's eye as completely equipped, as made of exquisitely cared for and finely-related details; and that the heat of her parting with his family should have left her unconscious that she was emerging gloveless into Paris, seemed, on the whole, to speak hopefully for Durham's future opinion of the city.

Turning to *The Glimpses of the Moon*, we see one of Susy Lansing's friends, not only through Susy's eyes, but through the angrily disapproving eyes of Mrs. Wharton. The idea to be conveyed is that the lady described is as banal as her motor and her motor as banal as a magazine advertisement, but as the style is literally the style of a magazine advertisement, we can only wonder what reason the author has to sneer:

But on the threshold a still more familiar figure met her: that of a lady in exaggerated pearls and sables, descending from an exaggerated motor, like the motors in magazine advertisements, the huge arks in which jeweled beauties and slender youths pause to gaze at snow-peaks from an Alpine summit.

Fortunately the novels that followed *The Glimpses of the Moon* are not all quite as slick. If they are not good novels, neither are they potboilers. But it seems a pity that Mrs. Wharton should have chosen to lay all the blame for the shapelessness of the postwar world on her native land. In book after book her complaints grow shriller and shriller until at last everything across the Atlantic is tainted with the same grotesque absurdity. She gives to her American towns such names as Delos, Aeschylus, Lohengrin, and Halleluja, and to their inhabitants, in their brief hours away from money-making, a total gullibility in dealing with religious and medical charlatans. Their fuzzy zeal for good causes envelops their hideous skyscrapers in a stifling cloud of euphoria. And the American face! How it haunts her! It is as "unexpressive as a football." It might have been made by "a manufacturer of sporting goods." Its sameness encompasses her "with its innocent uniformity." How many of such faces would it take "to make up a single individuality"? Years before, she had written to an English friend about James: "America can't be quite so summarily treated and so lightly dismissed as our great Henry thinks." Yet, reading her later novels, we can only wish that she had dismissed America altogether.

Kate Clephane in *The Mother's Recompense* (1925) returns to a society in New York which has ostracized her, as it ostracized Mrs. Lidcote in "Autre Temps," to find, unlike Mrs. Lidcote, that it *can* revise its judgments. She is completely accepted by the people who once cut her and thinks the less of them for their tolerance. She finds only one person in New York who seems to have any real moral fiber, and that is her daughter who, perhaps for the same reason, strikes the reader as a rather wooden girl. When Kate discovers that Anne is ignorantly about to marry her own former lover, she tries desperately to break up the match without telling the girl why and finally surrenders to the situation in order to avoid "sterile pain." But having renounced sterile pain for her daughter, she elects it for herself by refusing the offer of marriage from a devoted old admirer who has been shocked, but only momentarily, by her confession.

Mrs. Wharton resented the critics who deplored the ending of the book and spoke of the "densities of incomprehension" with which she now felt herself surrounded. The clue to Kate's sacrifice, she hinted, lies in the quotation from Shelley on the flyleaf: "Desolation is a delicate thing." My own interpretation is that Kate, imbued with the sensitivity of one who, like Mrs. Lidcote, has been broken on the wheel of a sterner age, feels more keenly than anyone else the horror of Anne's marriage. What she hates in the modern world is not so much that such things can happen as that people no longer really care that they do. Anne is caught in the situation of marrying her mother's lover because her mother has *had* a lover, and for that there must be expiation on the mother's part, alone in her shabby Riviera village, without the comfort of her old admirer. For Kate to go from the litter of fallen rose petals and grains of rice of her daughter's wedding to her own would be joining forces with the noisy, thoughtless world of vacuous toasts in which all delicacy of feeling has vanished. Those who believe in the old, harder standards must be willing to suffer alone, without sympathy or even comprehension. But this, evidently, is not sterile pain. Kate Clephane is intended to inhale a finer aroma from the bouquet of her loneliness than her daughter will ever know.

So far Mrs. Wharton had only skirmished with America. The story of the Lansings takes place in Europe, and Kate Clephane's drama is too much of the heart to have the locality of first importance. But she was preparing herself for a closer study of what had happened to America, and she had now spotted a type that she considered a representative victim of the disease of modern vulgarity, if, indeed, it was not the virus itself. Pauline Manford in *Twilight Sleep* (1927) is the daughter of an invader from "Exploit" who has first been married to a son of the age of innocence, Arthur Wyant. But time has profoundly altered both types. The invader's daughter is no longer prehensile or even crude; she has become bland and colorless and pointlessly efficient, building a life of public speeches and dinner parties around causes that she does not even try to understand, while Wyant, no longer the cool, well-dressed New York gentleman with a collector's eye for painting and porcelain, has degenerated to a foolish gossiping creature whom his wife has understandably divorced for a sneaky affair with his mother's old-maid companion. That is what has come of the merger of the old and new societies; it has cost each its true character. Pauline Manford, with invader's blood, has survived better than has Wyant, but hers is a lonely and precarious survival in a rosy cloud floating on an ether of fatuity from which she views with frightened eyes the moral collapse of her family. The invaders and their daughters have in common the faculty of immense preoccupation, the former with their businesses, the latter with their causes. But both are blinded to all that is beautiful or significant in the world around them by the dust stirred up by their febrile activities.

In Mrs. Manford Edith Wharton was groping at the outline of a well-known American phenomenon, the committeewoman who, married to a man who cares only for his business, seeks refuge in bogus Utopias where beauty is expected to spring like a phoenix from the ashes of pain. If Mrs. Wharton had only stayed in America, how quickly she would have comprehended such a woman! But Mrs. Manford is nothing but a caricature, mixing up her speeches to the birth control league and the society for unlimited families, going to the "Busy Man's Christ" for "uplift" treatments and seeing her children only by secretarial appointment. Mrs. Wharton seems to have no sense of the violent resentment that may underlie such a woman's placid stare or of the hatred of spouse and possessive passion for offspring that her false air of good sportsmanship may conceal. The American committeewoman is not apt, like Mrs. Manford, to be surrounded by a family who regard her goings-on merely with a cheerful, amused tolerance. *Twilight Sleep* is a rather formidable battering ram used on a straw woman.

There was to be one more last grim sketch of the final decadence resulting from the now ancient merger between old New York and the invaders. In the short story "After Holbein," a senile Mrs. Jaspar sits down alone every night at the end of her great dining room table, imagining that she is still the hostess at a dinner party, while her smirking servants go through a pantomime of serving guests. Anson Warley, a veteran bachelor, dilettante, and diner out, who has scorned her parties in the days of her greatness, suffering now himself from loss of memory, goes to her house by mistake, and the two old broken-down creatures squeak and gibber together, drinking the soda water which they take for Perrier-Jouet and admiring flower vases stuffed with old newspapers. It has been said that there is no compassion in this story, but how much compassion does a short story need? It is a chilling, cleverly executed little piece, a sort of dance of death, pointing a grim moral in the ultimate inanity of two lives dedicated to the ceremonial of the dinner party.

American mothers she had now done, together with their husbands, both of the invader and dilettante variety, but what about children? They had never played much of a role in her books, as, indeed, they had played little in her life. Mrs. Winthrop Chanler, a long-time friend of Mrs. Wharton's, has written that she was actually afraid of them. But if she was ignorant of American nurseries and schools, she was very much aware of those pathetic little waifs, the products of multiple marriages, who were dragged about Europe in the wake of rich, pleasure-seeking parents and finally abandoned with governesses in seaside hotels. The various Wheater offspring in *The Children* (1928) have sworn to remain together under the lead of Judith, the eldest, in spite of what other custody arrangements their various parents and "steps" may make. The children are sometimes amusingly, sometimes touchingly drawn, but the sketches are still superficial and "cute," and the background of rich expatriate life in European resorts is filled in with the now heavy hand of her satire.

The more interesting though secondary topic of the book is the relationship between Rose Sellars, the quiet, gentle widow of exquisite tact, with whom I suspect Mrs. Wharton may have a bit identified herself, and Martin Boyne, again the tasteful middle-aged bachelor, who has made a fortune, like other Wharton heroes, offstage and has now plenty of time to idle abroad. Rose Sellars immediately understands and accepts the fact that Boyne's preoccupation with the Wheater children is, unknown to himself, a manifestation of his hopeless passion for little Judith. The novel was published in the year that followed Walter Berry's death, and the relationship between the two characters seems analogous to what may have existed between their creator and Berry: she, loving and eager, but restrained by the fear of embarrassing them both by a scene that might expose the small beer of his feeling, and he, detached but admiring, half-disappointed and half-irritated at his own inability to respond to a gratifying if sometimes cloying affection. It is tempting to speculate that Martin Boyne's fate is the author's revenge on his deceased counterpart. We leave him in the end, old and desolate, staring through a ballroom window at the beautiful Judith who, dancing with young men, is no longer even aware of his existence.

After *The Children* Edith Wharton embarked, although then in her late sixties, on the most ambitious experiment of her literary career: the fictional biography of a young middle-western American writer, Vance Weston, told in two novels: *Hudson River Bracketed* (1929) and *The Gods Arrive* (1932). She opens his story in a town which is, typically enough, called "Euphoria" and plunges fearlessly into details of middle-western life, as if Sinclair Lewis by dedicating *Babbitt* to her had given her some special insight into an area of America that she had never even seen. The result is as bad as might be expected, but Vance Weston soon leaves his home town and comes to New York and an old house on the Hudson where his creator is on more familiar ground and where he meets a highly accomplished young lady, Halo Spear, who recites German poetry to him. "Just listen to the sound of the words," she says, when he protests his ignorance of the tongue.

It is easy to ridicule this long saga with its distorted picture of the New York publishing world, its uncouth young writers and artists ("Zola — who's he?" somebody yawned. "Oh, I dunno. The French Thackeray, I guess."), its irritatingly efficient heroine who can change travel accommodations and rent villas as easily as she can spout Goethe, its insensitive hero whose obsessive egotism becomes ultimately tedious, its ponderous satires of popular novelists and literary hostesses, but it nonetheless contains a strong picture of a young genius who educates himself and fights his way to literary success with a ruthlessness of which he is too preoccupied to be more than dimly aware. We sympathize when he is stifled in the ignorant, carping atmosphere of his invalid first wife's home and with his artist's need to rip away even at the most basic family ties. Here at last in Edith Wharton's fiction is a picture of a man. It may have all kinds of personal significance that he is neither a New Yorker nor a gentleman. As he develops cultivation in Europe, however, he develops some of the hardness of the older

Wharton heroes, and when he leaves Halo at last for a round of parties in London, there is not much to choose between him and Martin Boyne. But that is in the second volume which, like so many sequels, should never have been written. Both reader and author have become bored with Vance. Yet one cannot but be impressed by the fund of creative energy that could produce such a book on such a subject in the author's seventieth year.

At the very end of her life Edith Wharton turned back once again to the rich field of her childhood memories, and immediately the shrill bitterness disappears, and the old, clear, forceful style is back to the aid of its mistress. If she had finished *The Buccaneers* (1938) it might well rank among the best of her work. The little band of social-climbing maidens who find New York too difficult and leave it to triumph in London are unique in her fiction as possessing both her approval and affection. Old New York seems merely petty and narrow now in the person of Mrs. Parmore, while the parvenu is actually given charm and vitality in that of Colonel St. George. The author's point of view is expressed by the English governess of the St. George girls, Laura Testvalley, an erudite but romantic spinster of Italian descent, a cousin of the Rossettis, who adores her covey of Daisy Millers and guides them up the slippery rungs of the London social ladder. Until the girls have achieved their titles the mood of the book is light and amusing; thereafter it becomes more serious. For they have, after all, missed happiness, and Nan, as the author's notebooks reveal, will find hers only by leaving the Duke of Tintagel for Guy Thwarte.

Mrs. Wharton had not only cast aside for once her disapproval of those who are discontented to remain in the social grade of their origin; she had even cast off four decades of classicism in taste and morals to plot an ending that was to celebrate the triumph of "deep and abiding love." Yet how many times in her stories and novels have we not been told that no love can survive the cold shoulder of society, the disintegrating shabbiness of a life in second-class watering places! And is Nan now to get away with it, to escape the fate of Anna Karenina?

But if Mrs. Wharton, at the end, permitted herself to indulge in the vision of a love that was to make up for everything, the love that Ellen Olenska and Newland Archer had renounced, she was still enough of a Yankee puritan to stipulate that such a love had to be paid for. If Nan and Guy are to have their happiness, Laura Testvalley must lose hers. Her engagement to Guy's father will not survive her role in his son's elopement. Laura, the author's representative and a bit her alter ego, must be sacrificed to the gods of order. One wonders if at the last those gods did not, to Laura's creator, show some of the lineaments of the gods of derision whom she had so bitterly apostrophized in her journal thirty years before.

With her posthumously published works, *The Buccaneers* and *Ghosts*, the total of Edith Wharton's fiction comes to thirty-two volumes. Obviously, her ultimate reputation in American letters will rest upon only a fraction of this list. *Ethan Frome*, I have no doubt, will always be read, but it is out of the main stream of her work. I believe that she will be remembered primarily for her two great novels of manners: *The House of Mirth* and *The Age of Innocence*. In these she succeeded in re-creating an unadventurous and ceremonious society, appropriately sheltered behind New York brownstone, looking always to the east rather than to the west, and the impact upon it of the winds that blew from both directions. There were plenty of minor writers who attempted to delineate this society, but among those of the first rank Mrs. Wharton, at least in the first decade of our century, had it to herself. It is true, of course, that some of James's characters come from the same milieu, but they are rarely considered in relation to their native land or cities. The reason Mrs. Wharton succeeded where so many others have failed is that in addition to her gifts as an artist she had a firm grasp of what "society," in the smaller sense of the word, was actually made up of. She understood that it was arbitrary, capricious, and inconsistent; she was aware that it did not hesitate to abolish its standards while most loudly proclaiming them. She knew when money could open doors and when it couldn't, when lineage would serve and when it would be merely sneered at. She knew that compromises could be counted on, but that they were rarely made while still considered compromises.

She knew her men and women of property, recently or anciently acquired, how they decorated their houses and where they spent their summers. She realized that the social game was without rules, and this realization made her one of the few novelists before Proust who could describe it with any profundity. In American fiction her nearest counterpart is Ellen Glasgow.

Edith Wharton died in her house near Paris of a stroke in 1937, at the age of seventy-five. Her private papers were given to Yale and may not be published before 1968, which is probably the reason no biography has yet appeared. A great deal has been written about her in articles and memoirs, but almost always about the great lady, rarely the writer. This is nobody's fault, for Mrs. Wharton took a certain pride in keeping her writing behind the scenes, in presenting herself to the world, so to speak, on her own. One short piece, however, by Iris Origo, describes a weekend on Long Island that Mrs. Wharton spent with old friends during a brief visit to America to receive a degree from Yale. It is one of the rare recorded occasions when the survivor from New York's age of innocence, the real figure behind the novelist, predominated over the brilliant and formidable lady of perfect houses and gardens. Iris Origo relates how Mrs. Wharton refused to be led into any discussion of persons or events in France, of Carlo Placi or Madame de Noailles, and how, at each such attempt, she gently and firmly steered the conversation back to old friends and old memories in New York. The W's house on 11th Street, had it really been pulled down? Did her hostess remember the night they had dined there before the Colony Club ball? The X's daughter, the fair one, had she married her young Bostonian? Had Z indeed lost all his money?

"For the whole evening, this mood continued. At one moment only — as, the last guest gone, she turned half-way up the stairs to wave good-night — I caught a glimpse of the other Edith: elegant, formidable, as hard and dry as porcelain. Then, as she looked down on her old friends, her face softened, even the erectness of her spine relaxed a little. She was no longer the trim, hard European hostess, but a nice old American lady. Edith had come home."

45

Sinclair Lewis

Harry Sinclair Lewis was the youngest of the three sons of a country doctor, Edwin J. Lewis. He was born on February 7, 1885, in the Minnesota village of Sauk Centre, a raw little town less than thirty years old. No one now knows where the name Harry came from, but the name Sinclair, which was to become famous, was the surname of a Wisconsin dentist who was Dr. Lewis' good friend. The boy's mother was an ailing woman who had to spend much of her time away from home, in the South and Southwest, and when Harry was five, she died. In a year the doctor was married again — to a good, brisk, busy woman well suited to the hard-working doctor's unbending, frugal temperament. Harry Lewis' boyhood was curiously loveless, vexatious.

He was homely, ill-coordinated, astigmatic, redheaded, a stumbling, noisy, awkward boy. He was inept at hunting and fishing, could hardly swim, was shunned in boys' games and sports, derided by his fellows and patronized by his elders. He was nearly friendless and was early given to solitary tramps about the countryside and to wide, indiscriminate reading. He yearned to be in some place both more colorful and more kindly than Sauk Centre.

When he was seventeen, his father, whose forebears had lived near New Haven, Connecticut, allowed him to enroll in Yale College after six months of necessary preparation in the Oberlin Academy. The college experience dashed his hopes for a happier life: at Yale he was again friendless and lonely, more the outsider than ever, even though a number of his professors, recognizing his lively intelligence, were good to him. In high school he had written

46

occasional verses, and now at Yale he began to write regularly. Writing was not only a substitute for those social amenities that were denied him but also, he saw, the one means available to him whereby he might win the recognition and the respect of his fellows.

His early verse and prose alike bore almost no resemblance at all to either the subjects or the manner for which he would ultimately become famous. The poetry was imitative, occasionally of Kipling but generally of Tennyson and Swinburne, and he was much given to medieval subjects as he conceived them. His prose was archaic and floriated and its subject matter fantastic and melodramatic. Still, in 1904, he was the only freshman at Yale to appear (with a poem called "Launcelot") in the *Yale Literary Magazine*. That poem is not without a certain imitative charm and almost certainly represents the highest poetic achievement of H. Sinclayre Lewys (as, at sixteen, he had thought of his literary persona).

LAUNCELOT

"Oft Launcelot grieves that he loveth the Queen
But oftener far that she cruel hath been."

> Blow, weary wind,
> The golden rod scarce chiding;
> Sir Launcelot is riding
> By shady wood-paths pleasant
> To fields of yellow corn.
> He starts a whirring pheasant,
> And clearly winds his horn.
> The Queen's Tower gleams mid distant hills;
> A thought like joyous sunshine thrills,
> "My love grows kind."

> Blow, weary wind,
> O'er lakes, o'er dead swamps crying,
> Amid the gray stumps sighing
> While slow, and cold, and sullen,
> The waves splash on the shore.
> O'er wastes of bush and mullen,
> Dull crows flap, evermore.
> The Autumn day is chill and drear
> As yon knight, thinking Guenevere
> Proves most unkind.

Once this poem was accepted, the way was open for him on the *Lit*. In the following years he became a regular contributor to this and other undergraduate periodicals and in his third year the number of his contributions won him a place on the *Lit*'s editorial staff.

During two of his summers he made cattleboat trips to England and on these trips he began to take systematic notes for fiction. One summer he returned to Sauk Centre where excruciating boredom led him to conceive of a novel to be called *The Village Virus*. (When this novel was at last written, it was called *Main Street*.) In spite of his literary success at college, life at Yale grew increasingly exasperating for him, and at the beginning of his senior year he abruptly fled from New Haven to become a janitor and general handyman at Helicon Hall, the odd experiment in communal living that Upton Sinclair had just established near Englewood, New Jersey, on the Palisades. He sustained that effort for about a month.

Since in this recusant period his father was not giving him any money at all, the young man went to New York determined to live by his pen, but after several months of near starvation he left for Panama where he hoped to find work on the canal then under construction. That failing too he suddenly decided to return to New Haven and finish his education at Yale. He was readmitted to the College and he was graduated in June of 1908, a year behind his class.

There followed a number of years of miscellaneous adventure all over the United States, a time in which he tried to be a newspaperman without success, and continued to try to publish without much success. Iowa, New York, San Francisco, Washington, New York again. For a brief period he lived in a newly established bohemian colony in Carmel, California, where his associates were such writers as George Sterling and Jack London. Failing to sell his own stories, Lewis sold a number of plots (from the enormous plot file that he had put together) to London for sums ranging from five to fifteen dollars, but even this munificence on the part of the older writer could hardly be expected to support the younger and more inventive writer. From the end of 1910 until the end of 1915, he worked in publishing houses in New York and on a number of periodicals. During his vacation in one summer he wrote a boys' book, *Hike and the Aeroplane*, on commission for Frederick A. Stokes Company and published it under the pseudonym of Tom Graham.

More important, Lewis was all the time working on what would be his first novel, and although his friends in publishing circles discouraged him in his effort to be a serious novelist, he continued to work at it until he had what he thought was a publishable manuscript. After it was rejected by several publishers, it was accepted at last by the firm of Harper and published in February of 1914. Two months later, on April 15, Lewis was married to his first wife, a young woman named Grace Livingstone Hegger who now gave up her employment in the office of *Vogue* to establish the first Lewis ménage in the Long Island community of Port Washington. Lewis was still working in Manhattan, writing furiously at home before and after work and on commuting trains, but he was always pining for the time when he could afford to live by writing alone.

Our Mr. Wrenn had a reasonably good press but very small sales. The second novel, *The Trail of the Hawk*, published in 1915, enjoyed the same fate. At work on a third novel, Lewis found suddenly that his whole situation was altered when the *Saturday Evening Post* accepted his story called "Nature, Inc." This acceptance was quickly followed by three more, and Lewis was being paid $1000 for each story. With money in the bank for the first time in his life, he resigned his position at the Doran publishing house and in December of 1915 set out with his wife on what would be a life of wandering throughout their marriage. Traveling once more all over the United States, briefly setting up one residence and then another, he was writing literally scores of stories, almost all of them to be published in the slick periodicals, and he was also working at a number of books. The first of these, called *The Innocents*, was in fact planned as a magazine serial, and is one of the worst books he ever wrote. The next, though the first to be published as a book—both it and *The Innocents* appeared in

1917 — was titled *The Job*; it is one of the best of his early books. The fifth of his novels, called *Free Air*, is a sentimental fictionalization of the Lewis trip across the continent in a Ford, and was published in 1919. At the same time that he was finishing *Free Air*, Lewis was working at what would be *Main Street*, finished in Washington early in the summer of 1920 and published in the fall of that year. Now the apprenticeship was abruptly ended, and ended in a positive storm of vilification and applause. Suddenly Sinclair Lewis was a famous man.

When *Main Street* appeared, plunging literary America into a rare and heated controversy, it seemed that nothing like it, with its shrill indictment of village life, the middle class, provincial America, had been published before. For many years popular American fiction had been picturing village life as sweet and good, the middle class as kindly when not noble, the provinces as aglow with an innocence in sharp contrast to the cruelty and corruption of the cities. In the fifty years before 1920 there had, to be sure, been exceptions — novels a good deal more critical of village life than was the rule; but the prevailing view was that of Friendship Village, and it was this view that *Main Street* abruptly and perhaps forever ended.

Main Street seemed to those readers who had known Lewis' earlier work to be a complete rupture with everything he had done before. A look at those earlier novels now shows this not to have been the situation at all. All five works had essentially the same pattern: the impulse to escape the conventions of class or routine; flight; a partial success and a necessary compromise with convention. Realistic in detail, these novels were optimistic in tone in a way that was not generally associated with what was then thought of as the school of realism, and it was the combination of the optimistic view of human character with the body of observed social detail that critics remarked and some readers enjoyed.

There had been satirical flashes in the earlier books if not the generally sustained and less good-tempered satire of *Main Street*, but satire nevertheless and satire directed against the same general objects. Furthermore, when those earlier novels were effective, they were so because of the body of closely observed physical detail, but it was detail more impressionistically, less massively presented than in *Main Street*. Certain character types that were to be made famous by *Main Street* had already appeared — the hypocritical bigot, the village atheist, the aspiring idealist, and so on. And the basic pattern of *Main Street* was exactly the same pattern that has already been described: a young creature is caught in a stultifying environment, clashes with that environment, flees from it, is forced to return, compromises.

Carol Kennicott, the heroine of *Main Street*, has no alternative to compromise. Her values, her yearning for a free and gracious life, had only the vaguest shape, and when she tried to put them into action in Gopher Prairie, Minnesota, she found only the most artificial and sentimental means. To some readers even then (when thousands of women were identifying themselves with her) she seemed like a rather foolish young woman, and so today she must seem to every reader. In the end, the true values are those of her husband, "Doc" Kennicott, who, for all his stolidity, is honest, hard-working, kindly, thrifty, motivated by common sense — altogether like Lewis' brother, Dr. Claude, and even rather like his father, Dr. E. J. It is Kennicott who has the last word. In the end, then, it is the middle class that triumphs and the Middle West, and the middle-brow. And so it would always be in fact in the novels of Sinclair Lewis.

It is more accurate to say that the triumph is given to the *best* qualities of the middle class and that it is its worst qualities that the novel castigates: smugness, hypocrisy, a gross materialism, moral cant. These are the qualities that Lewis' satire, even when the focus begins to blur as it does with *Dodsworth*, would continue to assail. Thus, immediately after *Main Street*, he plunged into his research in that section of American life where those qualities were most obvious and therefore most readily lampooned — the commercial world of the middle-class businessman in a medium-sized city. "Research" is the correct word if one thinks of a novelist operating in the fashion of a sociologist preparing to make a field report. It is the novel *Babbitt* that established what would hence-forth be Sinclair Lewis' characteristic method of work, a method toward which he had been moving ever since his cattleboat note-taking days.

To begin, he chose a subject — not, as for most novelists, a character situation or a mere theme, but a social area that could be systematically studied and mastered. Ordinarily, this was a subclass within the middle class, a profession, or a particular problem of such a subclass. Then, armed with his notebooks, he mingled with the kind of people that his fiction would mainly concern. In Pull-man cars and smokers, in the lobbies of side-street hotels, in ath-letic clubs, in a thousand junky streets he watched and listened, and then meticulously copied into his notebooks whole catalogues of expressions drawn from the American lingo, elaborate lists of proper names, every kind of physical detail. He drew intricately detailed maps, and maps not only of the city in which his story was set but of the houses in which his actions would take place, floor plans with furniture precisely located, streets and the kind and color of dogs that walked on them. Mastering this body of material, he would then write out a summary of his story, and from this, a much more extended "plan," as he called it, with every scene sketched in, the whole sometimes nearly as long as the book that would come from it. A first draft would then follow, usually much longer than the final version, and then a long process of revision and cutting, and at last the publishable text. Although he traveled the length and breadth of the United States in 1920 and 1921, always listening and looking with *Babbitt* in mind, it was, in fact, Cincinnati, Ohio, that provided the chief scene of his researches for this novel about a place called Zenith.

Again, *Babbitt* (1922) plunged the nation into literary contro-versy. Again, the novel seemed absolutely new, unlike anything that had come before it. Again, to many the assault on American virtue seemed brutal, uncompromising, and unfair. All over the United States Sinclair Lewis was denounced as a villain and a traitor, and all over the United States thousands and thousands of people bought his novel. In Europe it seemed that someone in

America was finally telling the whole truth about the appalling culture of that deplorable country. A class had been defined, as it had been given the name that stays with it still. H. L. Mencken's abstraction of *boobus Americanus* had been given a body, a body that lives still in the American imagination.

Lewis' original intention in *Babbitt*, he later said, was to recount twenty-four hours in the life of his character, "from alarm clock to alarm clock." That original structural conception remains in the first seven chapters as the book stands. The twenty-seven chapters that follow are systematically planned if rather aimlessly assembled set pieces that, taken together, give us the sociology of middle-class American life. These pieces have as their topics such matters as Politics, Leisure, Club Life, Trade Association Conventions, Class Structure and Attitudes, Conventional Religion, "Crank" Religion, Labor Relations, Marriage and the Family, and such lesser topics as The Barbershop and The Speakeasy. There is no plot to contain and unite these interests, but their fragmentariness is in part overcome by the fact that George Babbitt moves through all of them in the course of his rising discontent, his rebellion, his retreat and resignation. Each of these three moods, in turn, centers in a more or less separate narrative: the first in the imprisonment of Paul Riesling after he shoots his wife; the second in Babbitt's attempt to find sympathy in Tanis Judique and "the Bunch"; the third in the pressures brought on him by the Good Citizens' League and his wife's happily coincidental emergency operation. It is not surprising that the general thematic and narrative movement, like the central figure himself, is sometimes lost to sight in the forest of marshaled mores.

Had the early optimist vanished in the Menckenian pessimist, as it seemed to so many readers in 1922 and 1923? In fact, the essential narrative pattern had not changed in *Babbitt*: the individual trapped in an environment, catching glimmerings of something more desirable beyond it, struggling to grasp them, succeeding or failing. Babbitt fails — or nearly does — with the result that the comic-satiric element here is both heightened and broadened over that of the earlier novels. Clifton Fadiman, writing later, defined the essential pattern when he wrote of Dodsworth as a man who "can neither give himself wholly over to the business of *being* a businessman nor give himself wholly over to the more difficult business of being a man. His vacillation between the part and the whole forms the basic theme of all of Sinclair Lewis's finest novels." Similarly, Frederick Hoffman suggested that there are two Babbitts, one the perfect Menckenese "boob," the other the "doubting Babbitt." A double question follows: can the doubting Babbitt conceive of the qualities that make a man as well as a businessman, that create a society as well as a mere association of "joiners"; and, can Sinclair Lewis?

The novel makes it easy enough for one to name the values that would save Zenith and Babbitt with it. They are love and friendship; kindness, tolerance, justice, and integrity; beauty; intellect. For the first two of these Babbitt has a throbbing desire if no very large capacity. Of the next four he has intimations. The seventh he can approach only in the distortions of his reveries, as in his morning dream of the "fairy child." To the last he is a total stranger. Of Lewis one may say he was much like Babbitt in the first two, with no greater capacity; that the next four constitute the core of his character and of his demand on life; of the next, that it is too readily softened by sentiment, as is Babbitt's; and of the last one can only say that on the evidence of the novels the matter remains enigmatic.

Omitted from this list is the power of observation, which, in its full sense, may depend on all the other qualities taken together and become the highest form of intuition; but in the more limited sense in which we commonly use the term in both social intercourse and literary discourse, it is this quality that differentiates Lewis from his creature. It is this quality that enabled John O'Hara, many years later, to say that "Lewis was born to write Babbitt's story. . . . All the other novelists and journalists and Babbitt himself were equally blind to Babbitt and Zenith and the United States of America until 1922."

The novel was, in fact, the first of its kind in two striking ways. American literature had a full if brief tradition of the business novel. James, Howells, London, Phillips, Herrick, Sinclair, Wharton, Dreiser, Poole, Tarkington — all these writers had been centrally concerned with the businessman; and, after James and Howells, only Tarkington was to find in him any of the old, perdurable American virtues. Business was synonymous with ethical corruption; the world of business was savagely competitive, brutally aggressive, murderous. The motivation of the businessman was power, money, social prestige — in that order. But the businessman in almost all this fiction was the tycoon, the powerful manufacturer, the vast speculator, the fabulous financier, the monarch of enormous enterprises, the arch-individual responsible only to himself. And his concern was production.

After World War I, the tycoon may still have been the most colorful and dramatic figure in the business myth, but he was no longer the characteristic figure, and *Babbitt* discovers the difference. This is the world of the little businessman and, more particularly, of the middle man. If his morals are no better, his defections are anything but spectacular. Not in the least resembling the autocratic individualist, he is the compromising conformist. No producer himself, his success depends on public relations. He does not rule; he "joins" to be safe. He boosts and boasts with his fellows, sings and cheers in praise of the throng, derides all difference, denounces all dissent — and only to climb with the crowd. And with the supremacy of *public* relations, he abolishes human relations. All this Sinclair Lewis' novel was the first to give back to a culture that was just becoming aware that it could not tolerate what it had made of itself.

And it did it with a difference. The older novels, generally speaking, were solemn or grandly melodramatic denunciations of monstrous figures of aggressive evil. *Babbitt* was raucously satirical of a crowd of ninnies and buffoons who, if they were malicious and mean, were also ridiculous. And yet, along with all that, Babbitt himself was pathetic.

With *Babbitt*, Sinclair Lewis' extraordinary gift for satirical mimicry of American speech found a fuller and more persistent expression than in any previous work. Nowhere is it more successful than in Babbitt's address at the annual meeting of the Zenith Real Estate Board:

"Some time I hope folks will quit handing all the credit to a lot of moth-eaten, mildewed, out-of-date, old, European dumps, and give proper credit to the famous Zenith spirit, that clean fighting determination to win Success that has made the little old Zip City celebrated in every land and clime, wherever condensed milk and paste-board cartons are known! Believe me, the world has fallen too long for these worn-out countries that aren't producing anything but bootblacks and scenery and booze, that haven't got one bathroom per hundred people, and that don't know a loose-leaf ledger from a slip-cover; and it's just about time for some Zenithite to get his back up and holler for a show-down!"

And so the stream of clotted argot and cliché floods on and on.

With this book, Sinclair Lewis seemed to most readers to have become America's leading novelist. The reviews were extravagant, and the one that seemed to mean most to Lewis himself appeared in the *New Statesman* and was written by Rebecca West. "It has that something extra, over and above," she wrote, "which makes the work of art, and it is signed in every line with the unique personality of the writer." After quoting from one of Babbitt's public speeches, she continues: "It is a bonehead Walt Whitman speaking. Stuffed like a Christmas goose as Babbitt is, with silly films, silly newspapers, silly talk, silly oratory, there has yet struck him the majestic creativeness of his own country, its miraculous power to bear and nourish without end countless multitudes of men and women. . . . But there is in these people a vitality so intense that it must eventually bolt with them and land them willy-nilly into the sphere of intelligence; and this immense commercial machine will become the instrument of their aspiration."

There were dissenting voices among the reviewers. There were those who argued that the vitality of the novel was only the aimless if "unique" vitality of the author himself, and what a critic like Gilbert Seldes, even when praising the book, was really saying was that the imaginative vitality of Sinclair Lewis failed to find any satisfactory aesthetic organization. The whole book should have been rewritten, he argued, after Lewis had taken a long look into himself. The implication was — and it was made explicit by others — that the book had no values beyond Babbitt's own, and that satire, comic and critical as it may be, must found itself on positive standards that are clearly there even if they are not stated. Some critics personalized this view by saying that Lewis himself was Babbitt, and ascribed the success of the novel to the fact that the audience that Lewis satirized recognized in the author not an enemy but an ally, not a teacher but a brother. And, indeed, many of the most loosely enthusiastic reviews that the book received came from the newspapers of those middle-sized middle-western cities that most resembled Zenith and that took pride in having served, as they thought, as the model for that modest metropolis.

If his environment is too powerful for George Babbitt, Lewis' next hero was to prove more powerful than his, and, after the preceding two novels, critics thought again that a "new" Lewis had emerged. In fact, *Arrowsmith* (1925) merely permitted the idealism that had always been present to prevail. The idealist is no longer a solitary figure, for, besides Martin Arrowsmith, there are also Gottlieb, Sondelius, Terry Wickett, and others. These are the dedicated truth seekers, the pure scientists who will not compromise with commercial standards or yield to institutional pressures. If, in the end, in order to maintain their own standards, they are forced to withdraw entirely from institutions, their standards are nevertheless victorious.

After *Babbitt*, Lewis had not intended to write a novel about the medical profession. Returning to the Middle West, he was pursuing his intermittent researches for a "labor novel" which he had had in mind ever since his youth. In Chicago he quite accidentally met a young medical research scientist recently associated with the Rockefeller Institute in New York, Paul de Kruif, and together the two discussed the possibility of a novel about the corruptions of the medical profession and of medical research. The idea seized upon Lewis' imagination. His father and brother were both doctors and two of his uncles had been doctors, and while he had already treated the type of the country doctor, he had not dealt with medical science in its grander aspects, and this subject too had long interested him. With De Kruif, he arranged a tour of the Caribbean, where much of the action of *Arrowsmith* was to take place, and then they proceeded to England where Lewis, with De Kruif always at his elbow, began to write the novel. The writing of this novel probably gave him more personal satisfaction than any other that he had already published or that he was to publish. It released a latent strain of idealism that was very powerful in his character but that his other subject matter had not permitted full expression.

The other side of this idealism continued the same as before, and involved the same subjects for satire. A narrow provincialism, hypocrisy, complacency, the "security" of organizational activity, pomposity, the commercial spirit, and the ideal of cash — all these were present again. Their presentation differed not only in that their opposites were given more substantial representation but also in that they were woven into a story that was itself more exciting than any other that Lewis had devised and in that this story included a heroine, Martin's wife Leora, with whom everyone could sympathize, as not everyone could with Carol Kennicott.

The praise for *Arrowsmith*, except for the disgruntled remarks of a few doctors, was universal. In Evanston, Illinois, an obscure young English teacher named Bernard De Voto was able to say what the book was not: it was not urbane, sophisticated, ironical, symmetrical, concise. If it was in some ways naive, so were Hawthorne, Whitman, Mark Twain. And this is what *Arrowsmith* is — America! — in its naiveté no less than its splendor. And thus, trying to tell us what Sinclair Lewis' true quality is, the young critic, as critic, gives up; but not the enthusiastic reader: "It is the most American novel of the generation; and if it is not the best, at least it can never hereafter be out of mind when the few, diverse novels entitled to compete for such an epithet are considered. . . . It goes down to the roots of our day. It is the almost inconceivable pageant of our America. . . . And that will . . . put *Arrowsmith* safely among the permanent accomplishments of its generation — to endure with a few other great novels of America, none of them quite innocent of defect." The voice grows hoarse; it was, the young De Voto confessed within the review, "the most extravagant praise" he had ever written. And he was by no means alone but only a part of the booming chorus. It came as no surprise that this novel, unlike the controversial works that had preceded it, should command the interest of the donors of the Pulitzer Prize. Sinclair Lewis had by this time become a public figure of such quixotic reputation that it came as no great surprise either when he declined to accept the honor. His grounds, not very well argued, were that such prizes tended to legislate taste. Whether or not he was being disingenuous, attempting to punish the Pulitzer people for not having given him the prize for *Main Street* or *Babbitt*, the fact remains that the attendant publicity was worth infinitely more to him than the prize itself or the publicity that he would have received had he accepted it. With this gesture and his next two books, he swiftly reversed the augmented reputation he had won as an idealistic novelist.

The first of these two novels was a piece of hack work, a ridiculous account of adventures in northwest Canada called *Mantrap* (1926), and the second, *Elmer Gantry* (1927), was another explosion, the most controversial of all his books, the most brutal attack on American standards.

Elmer Gantry deals with the shabby area of evangelical religion. Lewis chose Kansas City as the field for his research, and there he cultivated ministers of every denomination and faith. The result was the broadest and the most slashing satire that he was ever to write and the satire least concerned with the presentation of positive values.

Like most of Lewis' novels, *Elmer Gantry* is a loosely episodic chronicle which involves no primary conflict about which all the action is organized, in which value can achieve a complex definition, and by which at least two orders of value are dramatized. The chronicle, like *Babbitt*, breaks down into three large parts, each pretty nearly independent of the others. In each event Elmer's progress is colored and in two of them threatened by his relations with a woman, but from each Elmer emerges triumphant. The first part takes us through his Baptist education, his ordination, his first pulpit, and his escape from Lulu; the second takes us through his career as an evangelist with the fantastic Sharon Falconer; the third takes us through his experience of New Thought and his rise in Methodism, together with the decline of his marriage to Cleo and his escape from Hettie, who threatens to bring him to public ruin but who is herself routed as, in the final sentence, Elmer promises that "We shall yet make these United States a moral nation!"

It should not be supposed that the frank prominence in *Elmer Gantry* of sexual appetite — a rare enough element in a Lewis novel — or the fact that it several times threatens Elmer's otherwise unimpeded success, in any way provides the kind of dramatized counterpoint on the absence of which we are remarking, or that it in any way serves to introduce an element of human tenderness that modifies Elmer's brutality. On the contrary, it is an integral part of his inhumanity and an integral part of the inhumanity of the religious environment within which he exists. Indeed, of all the forms of relationship that the novel presents, the sexual relation is most undilutedly brutish, and it is perhaps the chief element in that animus of revulsion that motivates the author's creation of this cloacal world.

Hovering on the fringes of the plot are a few figures of good like Frank Shallard, honest clergymen of sincere religious conviction, but these figures, all minor, are never allowed to enter the action or to oppose effectively the major characters, notably Elmer Gantry himself, one of the great beasts of all literature. The minutely detailed history of Elmer Gantry involves an extraordinarily full account of every form of religious decay in American life, an account in which nothing is missing except all religion.

The world of *Elmer Gantry* is a world of total death, of social monsters without shadow. And in some ways therefore the novel gives us the purest Sinclair Lewis. More than this, one may say that, although it caused the greatest furor of all Lewis' novels at the time of publication and although it provided a script for a widely shown film quite recently, it remains the most neglected and perhaps most underestimated of Lewis' major works. For the subject animated in Lewis a latent strain of extravagant fantasy on the one hand, and, on the other, a devastating sense of the possible poverty of human experience. The two moods, nearly opposite and yet clearly counterparts, can be very readily illustrated.

The first is best observed in the phantasmagoric scene in which Sharon capitulates to Elmer before an altar where she associates herself, in a ritual invocation, with all goddesses of fertility:

"It is the hour! Blessed Virgin, Mother Hera, Mother Frigga, Mother Ishtar, Mother Isis, dread Mother Astarte of the weaving arms, it is thy priestess, it is she who after the blind centuries and the groping years shall make it known to the world that ye are one, and that in me are ye all revealed, and that in this revelation shall come peace and wisdom universal, the secret of the spheres and the pit of understanding. Ye who have leaned over me and on my lips pressed your immortal fingers, take this my brother to your bosoms, open his eyes, release his pinioned spirit, make him as the gods, that with me he may carry the revelation for which a thousand thousand grievous years the world has panted. . . . O mystical rose, O lily most admirable, O wondrous union; O St. Anna, Mother Immaculate, Demeter, Mother Beneficent, Lakshmi, Mother Most Shining; behold, I am his and he is yours and ye are mine!"

The absurd extravagance of this scene is somehow emphasized by the absence in it of any honest recognition of human need or of human fulfillment. The travesty that it makes of both the sexual and the religious experience is of course to be associated with the temper of evangelistic orgy that permeates the novel. Dramatically, however, it should be juxtaposed with such an earlier scene, as blankly homely as this one is hilariously horrible — a scene in which a deaf old retired preacher and his wife are going to bed after fifty years of marriage, and the whole of that marital experience is finally equated with the memory of an "old hoss":

"I would of liked to had you try your hand at politics. If I could of been, just once, to a senator's house, to a banquet or something, just once, in a nice bright red dress with gold slippers, I'd of been willing to go back to alpaca and scrubbing floors and listening to you rehearsing your sermons, out in the stable, to that old mare we had for so many years — oh, laws, how long is it she's been dead now? Must be — yes, it's twenty-seven years —

"Why is it that it's only in religion that the things you got to believe are agin all experience? Now drat it, don't you go and quote that 'I believe because it *is* impossible' thing at me again!
. . .

"Twenty-seven years! And we had that old hoss so long before that. My how she could kick — Busted that buggy —"

They were both asleep.

The two scenes supplement one another; they represent the extremes of the nightmare image of a world that, totally empty of human value, monstrously, and without relief, parodies the reality.

The book, to the great advantage of its sales, was immediately banned in Boston, and bans of one kind or another — from the simple refusal of public librarians to put it on their shelves, to announcements by booksellers that they would not stock it, to wholesale municipal bans — extended from Kansas City to Camden, from Boston to Glasgow. Every ban provided the publishers with the least expensive form of promotion.

News stories of every kind developed out of the publication of the book and the character of the author. The Boston *Transcript* announced that "it is neither wrong nor unjust to accuse Lewis of being one of the greatest egoists in the world today." He was invited to a lynching party in Virginia; one cleric suggested that a prison sentence of five years was clearly in order. Letters of abuse cluttered his mail.

In a resolution supporting the Anti-Saloon League of New York State, one Methodist minister declared before the annual assemblage of the New York East Conference, "The Methodist Church is cordially hated, not only by the class represented by Mr. Sinclair Lewis and the rum organizations, but also by every evil organization of every kind whatsoever," while only a few weeks later the graduating class of New York University voted Sinclair Lewis its favorite author. An item in an Ohio newspaper ran as follows: "Trouble in the home of Leo Roberts, general manager of the Roberts Coal and Supply Company, began when his wife brought home a copy of *Elmer Gantry* and he burned it as undesirable reading matter, according to Mrs. Roberts at a hearing Wednesday before Judge Bostwick of Probate Court, when Roberts was ordered to a private sanitarium for a short rest, after his wife, Mrs. Margaret Roberts, 1671 Franklin Park South, charged him with lunacy." Very soon ministers' wives were seeking divorces on the grounds that their husbands were Elmer Gantrys, i.e., adulterers; and ministers themselves were demanding that colleagues too attentive to their choir singers be investigated. In less than six weeks, even the least literate of churchgoers had heard of the novel as it was denounced from the pulpit of his church.

Never has a profession cooperated so zealously with a publisher as the clergy, of all denominations and faiths, in 1927. Generally, of course, the novel was the subject of denunciation: "slime, pure slime," "sordid and cowardly," "venomous," "unprincipled," "an insult," "filthy" — these were some of the terms of abuse. The evangelist Billy Sunday called Lewis "Satan's cohort." He was not only "Mencken's minion," he was Judas. Yet here and there, quieter clerical voices suggested that, while Elmer Gantry was a monster, the novel itself was a useful tonic in a situation not entirely healthy.

Reviewers praised the novel and abused it with equal vigor. Again, thousands of people bought it. H. L. Mencken thought it one of the great satires of all time and compared Lewis with Voltaire. The novel could not have been more appropriately dedicated than it was — to Mencken, "with profound admiration."

There were to be further reversals. Lewis' first marriage had by now fallen into decay and he was wandering about Europe, alone, looking for new subject matter while the furor over *Elmer Gantry* raged at home. He found his subject matter in the story of a wealthier, more powerful, somewhat more sensitive Babbitt named Samuel Dodsworth, unhappily married, wandering about Europe and discovering a superior woman who would become his second wife. So, stumbling into Berlin, Sinclair Lewis met a superior woman, the handsome Dorothy Thompson, best known newspaperwoman in Europe, and presently she would become his second wife.

He interrupted the writing of *Dodsworth* to expand into a book-length work a short story he had recently published in the *American Mercury* — "The Man Who Knew Coolidge" — the monologue of an idiotic, sub-Babbitt type named Lowell Schmaltz. Exercising here once more his remarkable gift for imitating the speaking American voice, he nevertheless added very little to his stature with this work. Then, after his marriage in London on May 14, 1928, he returned to the United States with his new wife and there finished *Dodsworth* (1929). This work once more assured Lewis' readers that he was a generous man, for while it again had its share of satire, the satire was directed largely at the frenetic pretentiousness and snobbery of Dodsworth's first wife, and it presented Dodsworth himself, with all his solidly American middle-class virtues, in full sympathy. Here there was no occasion at all for controversy. And what Sinclair Lewis himself believed in, at the bottom of his blistered heart, was at last clear: a downright self-reliance, a straightforward honesty, a decent modesty, corn on the cob and apple pie.

The terms of the novel are much the same as they had always been, and the pattern is the same, of the man who glimpses a dream beyond the trivial actualities and stifling habits of his life, and who, now, can make it real. Only the emphasis had been shifted, and the object of satire drastically reversed. Whereas in earlier novels he had satirized the stuffy middle-western citizenry, with its smugness, materialism, and aggressive provinciality, and approved of the "outsiders," Carol and Paul Riesling and Martin Arrowsmith and Frank Shallard, now he satirizes the poor critic of Babbittry that he chooses to give the reader in the character of Fran Dodsworth, and approves the middle-western citizenry in the person of Sam, who has more money than Babbitt and needs, therefore, to think less about it, but who is hardly less aggressive in his own kind of provincialism.

For nearly the first time in his major novels he was handling material that was by no means new — for generations there had been novels about Americans in Europe; but what he was doing, or so it seemed, was new to him: approving the substantial middle-class, middle-western virtues, the best of Babbitt. He had, of course, been doing this all the time and very explicitly in the early, little-read books; but after *Elmer Gantry* and *The Man Who Knew Coolidge,* it seemed a sharp reversal.

No critics observed the larger significance of *Dodsworth* in the career of Sinclair Lewis and in modern American writing. Between the end of the war in 1918 and the beginning of the depression of the 1930's, a revolution had overtaken American life in manners and morals and all intellectual assumptions, and *Main Street, Babbitt, Arrowsmith,* and *Elmer Gantry,* whatever their aesthetic limitations, had played a major part, probably the major literary part, in this transformation. At the end of the 1920's, writers were left either in the situation of Scott Fitzgerald, trying "to hold in balance the sense of futility of effort and the sense of the necessity to struggle," or in the situation of young radicals who tried to turn their writing into social action on behalf of a hypothetical "proletariat." Only extremes of attitude presented themselves as possible: the jaded "aristocratic" attitude implied in the work of Fitzgerald (and implicit in such a school of criticism as the New Humanism, however far this school may have been from him) and the revolutionary "working class" attitude exemplified by the *New Masses* and any number of "proletarian" writers. In *Dodsworth,* Lewis refused the extremes and turned back to a reassertion of those very middle-class, middle-brow, and middle-western values that the decade of the twenties seemed to have destroyed forever, and that it had most emphatically modified at least; and with those values he, who would henceforth seem to be the most old-fashioned of modern American novelists, would henceforth abide.

Yet it was the Lewis of *Babbitt* rather than the Lewis of *Dodsworth* that led the Swedish Academy, at the end of 1930, to award him, the first American writer to be so honored, the Nobel Prize for Literature. That event followed on the birth of Lewis' second son, Michael, to his second wife, in the middle of that year, and it was probably a considerably less expected event for him. But for some time European readers had been looking with increasing favor on American novelists, and especially on those who, like Sinclair Lewis, were critical of American culture. Other American novelists who were popular in Sweden — Jack London, Upton Sinclair, Edith Wharton, Theodore Dreiser, Sherwood Anderson — were read in much the same spirit as he was, as social critics of the same materialism and chauvinistic complacency, and with no important aesthetic discriminations to be made between them.

Under these circumstances, it is not surprising that Lewis, who was the sharpest and the most detailed critic and who yet wrote out of what seemed to be love of his country, should have come to seem the leader. He had come to seem the leader, however, of a body of literature that was in itself as exciting as any in the world, and a body of literature that, in its very criticism of American culture, demonstrated its maturity.

That criticism Lewis brought to its climax in his famous address delivered in Stockholm on December 12, 1930, and known now under the title "The American Fear of Literature." An attack on the atrophied tradition of gentility and academicism in American critical values, it announced that "Our American professors like their literature clear and cold and pure and very dead." Rather unfairly, it placed the blame on the continuing prestige of William Dean Howells (who had, in fact, been gracious to the still unknown young Lewis in their single encounter in 1916), and, defying "official" custodians of American literary culture, such as the American Academy of Arts and Letters, it praised such dissident novelists as Theodore Dreiser and Sherwood Anderson, and brought to the attention of its European audience the names of a whole group of young American writers who were still almost entirely unknown abroad. There are fallacies as well as injustices in the address, but it was composed in an authoritative spirit that made Lewis, on that day, in that year, the spokesman — what Walt Whitman had called the "literatus" — for the literary culture of the United States.

If Sinclair Lewis' reception of the Nobel Prize was the historic event — and his spokesman-like acceptance of it only the marker of the event — its historic import was not merely in its putting American literature on a par with any other literature in the world, but also in its acknowledging that in the world America was a power that twenty years before it had not been, and that, until now, Europe had been reluctant to concede that it was. In December 1930 Sinclair Lewis was bigger than America knew; proud as he may have been — and he was proud, above all, because he was regarded as of equal importance with three eminent scientists — he was bigger than even he himself knew, or would ever know. Or should we say that he was a smaller writer than he thought and a much larger symbol?

In Berlin early in 1931, in a fit of pique that climaxed long brooding, Lewis wrote his publisher, Alfred Harcourt, of Harcourt, Brace, and Company in New York, to tell him that their connection was severed. For a long time, he wrote Harcourt, he had felt that the firm had lost real interest in his books, and its failure to rise to the occasion of the Nobel Prize had made its indifference all too clear. With proper advertising of the event, all his novels would have leaped into soaring sales figures again, Lewis announced. Worse than that, Harcourt had done nothing, even though he had the whole European press at his disposal, to counteract the supercilious and denigrating remarks about Lewis in the American press. "If you haven't used this opportunity to push my books energetically and to support my prestige intelligently, you never will do so, because I can never give you again such a moment."

Alfred Harcourt released him from his contractual obligations without any attempt to meet his charges. He may very well have felt that the separation came at a logical time. The decade through which Harcourt, Brace, and Company had helped to make Sinclair Lewis an international reputation, and in the course of which Lewis' novels had helped to make of Harcourt, Brace, and Company a substantial firm, was over. Throughout that decade Lewis had promulgated his version of the American reality, and his effort had been brought to a climax with the great honor. But the decade was over, and Lewis' sense of reality was no longer central to American history. He would never be able to change that sense, but history had already changed and would continue to change in his time, leaving him uneasily behind. His own discomforted sense of the change and of his inability to cope with current history as confidently as he had coped with the past may very well have been the major ingredient in his dissatisfaction with his publisher. His novels would continue to make money, and there would be many more of them, but they would never again bring distinction to a publisher's list as, in a succession of five smashing titles, they had brought to Harcourt, Brace, and Company. The Nobel Prize had come to him at precisely the right moment: it was the moment at which Lewis, the serious novelist, was finished.

He was now forty-six years old and the author of twelve published novels. There were to be twenty more years and ten more novels. The beguilements of alcohol, which had for some time been a problem for him, would become an increasingly acute problem as these twenty years passed. His second marriage would fall into even more sordid decay than had his first. His first son would be killed in World War II. His second son, even taller than his father, solider, and handsome, would grow up to be an actor, successful in that world that would presently captivate the father but in which the father was never to find a real place. Lewis, an increasingly restless man, would move from one establishment to another, from one city to another, all over the world, briefly occupying magnificent houses which, after a few months or a year or two at most, he would sell at great financial loss, when he would move on again in the hope of finding a better place. Precisely like his characters, he was always pursuing some vague and undefined glimmer of a happier place, a richer life.

How far he had moved, in these splendid establishments, from his humble beginnings in Sauk Centre! And yet there was always something bleak and unlived-in about even his most lavish houses that suggested all too clearly that the bleakness of Sauk Centre still clung to him and lived on deep within him. How far, too, his international literary reputation had removed him from those taunts and jibes that had plagued him in his youth and young manhood, and yet he felt himself still the victim of taunts and jibes, never really taken seriously as an artist, he felt, by other artists. In a kind of mounting frenzy he sought out the comforts of women much younger than he, especially young actresses, during a period when he was infatuated with writing for the stage and even took to acting himself, and finally, at the end of the 1930's and for a time in the 1940's, he did find a young actress who was willing to try to comfort him. But in some profound way he was not to be comforted or consoled, and after the young woman abandoned him to marry a man more nearly her own age, Lewis began a series of restless wanderings in Europe, and there, finally, in 1951, he was to die alone, among strangers, in Roman ostentation. But all through those maddening years of decline, he continued, with a kind of mechanical regularity and even ruthlessness, to produce his novels.

The first of these was *Ann Vickers*, published in 1933 — the story of an American career woman, and already, so soon after his second marriage, shot through with all his ambiguities of feeling about the career of his new wife, which was to be phenomenally successful through all that decade and into the next. The novel attempts, through a large part of the life of a single character, to sketch in the chief interests in a whole period of American social history from before World War I into the Great Depression. For this history, Lewis drew largely on the background of his new wife's life but partly as well on that of his own earlier years — prewar Christian socialism, feminism and settlement house work, charity organizations, liberal and radical thought, prison reform, sexual emancipation, the crisis of the depression, careers for women, equal rights, and so on. Through it all is the recurrent theme of a woman who is trying to find herself as a woman, not only as a Great Woman, just as *Dodsworth* was the story of a man trying to find himself as a man within the Businessman.

What is probably most interesting about the novel is the author's own ambiguous feeling about his heroine — exactly the feeling that he was already developing about Dorothy Thompson. Having chosen her as the prototype of Ann Vickers, he put himself in the position of describing sympathetically qualities that he was already resenting in life. His approval of Ann's dedication to "do-good" principles is at least uneasy; he resents the liberal and radical causes that his own characterization of her committed him to approve; the satiric touches are sporadic and sprawling, settling on her, on him, on them, but never pulling these together into real satire at all. Most interesting is the portrait of Ann's husband, a feeble fellow who is jealous of her expansiveness and prestige. Ann is rescued from this marriage by a man with red hair. Sinclair Lewis was famous for his red hair and was nicknamed "Red," but the character bears no other resemblance to Sinclair Lewis, is, rather, quite his opposite — a kind of dream figure of warm tolerance and relaxed sensuality that Lewis would have liked to be but had never been and would never be able to be.

Work of Art (1934), the next novel, was probably the first of Lewis' serious novels since *Main Street* to be completely without distinction. (By "serious" one means work that he himself took seriously.) This novel brings to a climax, certainly, his old, uneasy suspicion of intellect and art, and his deep respect for middle-class virtue, for effort. A novel about the hotel industry in America, it deals with two brothers, Myron and Ora Weagle. Myron is steady and reliable and, even as a boy, dreams of someday owning a perfect hotel. Ora is "literary" and spends his good-for-nothing days mooning in romantic fantasies and in writing verse of much the same sort as Sinclair Lewis wrote as a boy and a young man, and this portrait, a fantastic caricature of the Poet, is Lewis' belated act of exorcism. Ora grows up to be a commercial success and a hack, always self-deluded and scornful of his downright brother. But Myron is the true artist, and Lewis makes nearly his every effort analogous to an act of artistic creation. Ultimately, Myron even keeps a notebook, "what must, in exactness, be called 'The Notebook of a Poet,'" in which he jots down ideas for improving hotel management and reflections upon his experience as a hotelkeeper. Myron, too, has great success, then through the chicanery of others falls to low estate, and recovers when he concludes that no hotel can be perfect but that he can still make a "work of art" of a tourist camp in Kansas. If one wishes to learn about hotel management the novel is no doubt an admirable handbook, and no duller than a handbook; if one wishes to learn anything about art, and especially the art of the novel, there is nothing here at all. *Work of Art* is the fantasy of the perfect Rotarian. It is almost as if George F. Babbitt had suddenly produced a novel.

It was no longer the best of the middle-class character that Sinclair Lewis was praising, but the very middle of the middle. His wife, in a few years, had gained a tremendous reputation on the international scene as a political commentator, and the greater her authority grew and the brighter the glamour that clung to it, the deeper Lewis drove himself back into the defensive but pathetic aggressiveness of Sauk Centre. If he ever divorced his wife, he is reputed to have said, he would name Adolf Hitler as corespondent. But he could not have written his next novel, *It Can't Happen Here* (1935), if he had not been intimately exposed to her intense interest in international affairs, a subject the discussion of which, he continually complained, would drive him out of his wits.

At least one of Lewis' novels after *It Can't Happen Here* was to make more money for him, but no other was to cause such excitement. In this book, it seemed, he was at his greatest: denouncing the fascist elements in American life, praising the independent spirit, holding out for freedom. In 1935 the United States was being heckled on every side by absurd demagogues like Huey Long, and Lewis, seizing on this proliferation of the totalitarian impulse, which did seem to pose a serious threat to the democratic traditions and promises of American life, translated it into the terms of political establishment. The horror of fascism in Europe and local imitations were enough to persuade many readers that Lewis had written an impressively prophetic work.

What he had in fact written was a tour de force in which he simply documented the transformation of traditional American political and social customs into their opposites. Doremus Jessup, the hero, driven into his heroic stance at the end of the novel, is not really very different from Lewis' next hero, Fred Cornplow, of *The Prodigal Parents*. *It Can't Happen Here* elicited considerable excitement among left-wing sympathizers who could, from this novel, be assured that Lewis was not a fascist; but *The Prodigal Parents* — a miserable novel — gave these sympathizers small comfort, for in this book Lewis defended the stuffiest middle-class attitudes against the silliest "proletarian" views.

Considered as a whole work, *It Can't Happen Here* differs from other examples of the genre in having neither the intellectual coherence of Aldous Huxley in *Brave New World* nor the persuasive vision of a nightmare future of George Orwell in *1984*. But in 1935 readers in the United States, like readers in Britain and in France (*Impossible Ici!*), were sensitive to their immediate history, and it was to the immediate possibility of that history that Lewis' novel shook their attention. Yet to have seen the novel as committing Sinclair Lewis to what was then called the United Front — the collaborative effort of all liberal and radical parties against the threat of fascism — was an error; for Lewis, while once a socialist and still a liberal of sorts, was certainly in no sense a political radical. This fact became abundantly clear in the next novel, that sad effort of *The Prodigal Parents* (1938). This story of Fred Cornplow and his wife Hazel, in revolt from their foolishly radical and irresponsible children, brings to a lame end, no doubt, Lewis' one-time ambition to write a novel about political idealism. Radical politics are parodied in the figure of a comic-strip Communist and through the vagaries of undergraduates whose absurd concern with the problems of labor is apparently the net result of Lewis' observation of liberal student attitudes in the United States during the 1930's, when he lived in the neighborhood of Dartmouth College. Against these feeble antagonists is set the good American, Cornplow, a stodgy bundle of received opinions, the stereotype approved.

Now, at the end of the fourth decade of the twentieth century, with the United States about to plunge into another world war and a rather different kind from the first, Sinclair Lewis was only a confused man. Retreating into the absorbing life of the theater and devoting himself to the pursuit of young actresses, he turned, not surprisingly, to frivolous subjects in a half-dozen unsuccessful plays and in his next novel. *Bethel Merriday* (1940) is a novel about a young actress. Less embarrassing than *The Prodigal Parents*, it is hardly more important as fiction. Through the education of his young heroine in summer stock and touring companies, Lewis was able to include everything that he had learned about the theater; attached to rather than incorporated in this handbook material is a pale romance. Learning as much as one does of the theater, one learns nothing of the impulses that drive an actor or of the kind of satisfactions that an actor finds in his profession; and while the novel at one point glances at a May and December relationship, one learns no more of Sinclair Lewis' passion for young women than of that for the stage.

Gideon Planish (1943), the novel that followed, seemed to promise something of a return to the old Lewis. While he apparently intended, in this satiric attack on organized philanthropy and the activities of liberal "do-gooders," a return to the savage mode of *Elmer Gantry,* he achieved in fact little more than a crude parody and none of the solidity of that earlier novel. A splenetic attack, arising from the narrowest channels of a provincial mind, on the efforts of the professional "intellectual," its satire deteriorates into farce very soon after the novel gets under way. One figure in the book, Winifred Homeward, "the Talking Woman," a cartoon-like take-off of his newly divorced wife, only underlined the essential lack of seriousness that characterizes this novel. And yet, self-deluded, Sinclair Lewis was able to autograph a copy of this work with the inscription "My most serious book — therefore, naturally, not taken too seriously."

That he intended to be serious in *Gideon Planish*, at least at the outset, one cannot doubt; but it is something of a relief to turn to the next novel, *Cass Timberlane* (1945), with its much less serious subject. A novel about American marriage, it is half-sentimental, half-splenetic. It is his own thinly veiled love story, or rather, an extrapolation of such little love story as he had to tell; and from this situation arose his chief novelistic difficulties. Cass Timberlane is presented as forty-one years old, in love with a girl of twenty-three; but he behaves in some ways like a man of sixty, which Lewis now was, and in others like a fumbling boy of sixteen, which he also was. Cass's most remarkable quality — which goes unremarked in the novel itself — is his sexual naiveté, and when the young Jinny Marshland leaves him and enjoys an adulterous affair with his contemporary and best friend, it is not, the reader can only assume, his age that has been his problem.

The story of Cass and Jinny is treated with a kind of sentimental affection, with only the faintest overtones of irony, and its treatment marks it off very sharply from the treatment of marriage in a whole group of surrounding sketches which the novel presents under the heading of "An Assemblage of Husbands and Wives." In these often brutally conceived accounts of female willfulness, tyranny, and lechery, the recognition of the American matriarchy is as clear as the method is uncompromisingly satirical. It is as if the novelist is trying to say two things at once, that all these are American marriages in general, including his own two marriages, but that this one at the center, of Cass and Jinny, is another matter, the marriage that he would now make if he could. With the slightest change of method — that is to say, with the slightest shift in perspective on his own situation — that central marriage would become only another in the great assemblage of miserable marriages at large. But one must remember that even Lewis' best novels were not notable for their clarity of point of view or for their power of self-evaluation. Should one expect these of him at sixty, infatuated?

And so he staggered toward his end. In *Kingsblood Royal* (1947) he made his last strenuous effort to re-enter American realities by addressing himself to the problem of the Negro minority in American life. The book aroused some excitement as a social document but none whatever as a literary performance, and even its social usefulness, it is now clear, is minimized by Lewis' mechanical oversimplification of what is, of course, one of the most complex, as well as one of the most pressing, issues in the national life of the United States. From this attempt to deal with the immediate present, Lewis retreated into the historical past of Minnesota. *The God-Seeker* (1949) is apparently the first part of what was projected as a trilogy about labor in the United States. But it is a wooden, costumed performance about which even Lewis' publishers despaired. And his last novel, *World So Wide*, published posthumously in 1951 (he died on January 10 of that year), is a thin attempt to write another *Dodsworth*. It is the final self-parody. As Malcolm Cowley wrote, his characters sound now "like survivors from a vanished world, like people just emerging from orphanages and prisons where they had listened for thirty years to nothing but tape recordings of Lewis novels."

As Sinclair Lewis had experienced a long and unrewarding apprenticeship before his phenomenal, ten-year success, so he suffered a long and sad decline. This beginning and this end do not make easy the problem of delivering any final literary judgment on him. The estimate of his literary contemporaries, which became so apparent at the time of the Nobel award, does not make the problem any easier.

The aggressively enlightened had, of course, almost never taken him seriously. The experimentalists and the expatriates thought of him as a commercial hack. The academic critics — whether simple literary historians like Fred L. Pattee, or dogmatic authoritarians like Professor Irving Babbitt and his followers in the New Humanism, or old-fashioned conservatives like Henry Van Dyke in the American Academy of Arts and Letters — were united in their displeasure with the award. "Nothing [Lewis] can write can matter much now," Professor Pattee had just pontificated in *The New American Literature*, and the brilliant young liberal critic T. K. Whipple had just published his damaging estimate (one of the few genuinely critical appraisals of Lewis up to that time, and up to this) in his book called *Spokesmen*. Young radicals found Lewis politically illiterate. Older writers of no particular allegiance, like Sherwood Anderson, spoke out against him on the grounds of art. A younger writer, Ernest Hemingway, writing to a friend, called the award a filthy business whose only merit was that it had eliminated the "Dreiser menace." Dreiser held Lewis in gross and sullen contempt.

This is all rather cruel because Lewis himself was among the most generous of men in his relations with other writers. He encouraged the young and struggling with praise and with money. He habitually put the men who had chosen him as their enemy, Dreiser and Anderson, at the very head of his list of the greatest modern American writers. He recognized early the brilliant quality of the young Ernest Hemingway and he was instrumental in getting an award for the mature Hemingway as he was for getting a large cash prize for Theodore Dreiser. He in effect "discovered" Thomas Wolfe for the world when, only a year after the publication of *Look Homeward, Angel*, Lewis spoke of this book at a press conference before departing for Sweden and mentioned Wolfe again in the Nobel speech itself.

And it is quite true, of course, that even his most famous novels have crass defects. He was, in the first place, the kind of writer who found it temperamentally impossible to objectify his own anxieties, the tensions of his inner life, or even to draw upon them except in the most superficial way, in his own writing, and the writer, after all, is not different from the man who contains him. Shunning the subjective, he often fell into the sentimental. Yet there are other realities than those that pertain to the subjective life. His twenty-two novels, so uneven in quality, do share in one likeness: they are a long march all directed toward a single discovery, the "reality" of America. This aim was Lewis' inheritance as a novelist who was formed in the second decade of this century, when the discovery of the "real" America, an America beyond the chauvinistic nonsense and the merely sentimental optimism that had formed the image of an earlier generation, became the aim of nearly every writer who took himself seriously. It was a period that, however briefly, put its trust in the democratic promise of American life. For Sinclair Lewis, America was always promises, and that was why, in 1950, he could say that he loved America but did not like it, for it was still only promises, and promises that nearly everyone else had long ago given up. Sinclair Lewis had nothing else to turn to.

There is a personal as well as a cultural basis for this situation. For what were these promises? They were promises, first of all, of a society that from his beginning would have not only tolerated but treasured *him*. That is the personal basis. Generalized, it becomes an idealization of an older America, the America of the mid-nineteenth century, an America enormous and shapeless but overflowing, like a cornucopia, with the potentialities for and the constant expression of a wide, casually human freedom, the individual life lived in honest and perhaps eccentric effort (all the better for that), the social life lived in a spirit that first of all tolerates variety and individual difference. It was the ideal America of Thoreau, of Whitman, of the early Mark Twain, of the cracker barrel in the village store and of the village atheist, of the open road and the far horizon and the clear, uncluttered sweep of prairies. Like Thoreau, Whitman, Twain, Lewis too could see the difference between the idealization and the actuality. It was Thoreau who wrote this indictment: "With respect to true culture and manhood, we are essentially provincial still, not metropolitan — mere Jonathans. We are provincial, because we do not find at home our standards; because we are warped and narrowed by an exclusive devotion to trade and commerce and manufacture and agriculture and the like, which are but the means, and not the ends."

Sinclair Lewis was always carrying around the works of Thoreau. When he claimed him as the major influence on his work, it could have been only this basic element in his own thought, the Thoreauvian ideal of individual freedom and native integrity, that he had in mind.

Of Thoreau, R. W. B. Lewis has written in *The American Adam* as follows: "Probably nobody of his generation had a richer sense of the potentiality for a fresh, free, and uncluttered existence; certainly no one projected the need for a ritual burning of the past in more varied and captivating metaphors. This is what

Walden is about; it is the most searching contemporary account
of the desire for a new kind of life . . . the total renunciation of
the traditional, the conventional, the socially acceptable, the well-
worn paths of conduct, and the total immersion in nature." All
of this, item by item, even to the last, not only appealed to Sinclair
Lewis but in fact formed the positive element in his largely nega-
tive presentation of American life. And into that idealism it was
not difficult to weave the more diluted optimism that he had
found in the novels of the other literary figure who profoundly
influenced him, H. G. Wells — the happy belief that the little man,
the obscure man, the middle-class man, the outsider like the young
Lewis, could break into such freedom as Thoreau envisaged. This
was the motive of Lewis' life as it was of his fiction. Deep under
the quixotic social conduct, and deep under the satire of social
surfaces, lay this ambition and this yearning.

The American defection from the American potentiality for
individual freedom is the large subject of Lewis' satire. When he
excoriated Americans it was because they would not be free, and
he attacked all the sources by means of which they betrayed themselves into slavery: the economic system, intellectual rigidity, theo-
logical dogma, legal repression, class convention, materialism,
social timidity, hypocrisy, affectation, complacency, and pomposity. These two, the individual impulse to freedom and the social
impulse to restrict it, provide the bases of his plots in novel after
novel. Even when he used Europe as his point of contrast, the
conflict was not so much between American and European values
as between the true America as Lewis saw it — that is, individual
Americans true to their individuality — and the false America,
or Americans who yield to values not their own or to values of less
amplitude than their own should be. The result in the novels is
often an apparent praise of provincialism, even of a deplorable
philistinism, but in its impulse the praise is of something much
larger and of something rather noble.

But he was himself sentimental and a philistine, and often these
led him to settle for the very stolidity in American life that he
flayed. "Sinclair Lewis is the most successful critic of American

society," T. K. Whipple said, "because he is himself the best proof that his charges are just." If he was the village intellectual, the village atheist, the rebel, the nonconformist crank for whom the dialect, the cracker barrel, and the false whiskers served as counterpoise to the stuffed shirt in his defense of what Lloyd Morris called "the old, free, democratic, individualistic career of the middle class," he was at the same time the pontifical village banker, the successful manufacturer of automobiles, the conservative, the very middle of the middle. His trust in "culture" was equaled by his trust in "things." His respect for science was certainly greater than his respect for art. Brought up in an environment that condescended to art and reverenced success, he managed, in that America, to make a success of "art." Often and increasingly it was bad art, and the success was in many ways abrasive and self-destructive. In his novels, he loved what he lamented; in his life, he was most secure and content with the kind of people who might have been the prototypes for his own creatures.

Ten years before his death, in a mock obituary, he said of himself that he had "affected but little the work of younger writers of fiction," that his style and his conception of the novel had in no way altered the contours of the American literary tradition. One can only wonder whether he had any sense at all of how increasingly old-fashioned he came to sound, or that the generation immediately following upon his own — Fitzgerald, Hemingway, Faulkner — was in fact quite a different generation which his work could in almost no way impinge upon, that he spoke for an older American experience than theirs. But in a larger sense than is suggested by the most familiar words in our critical vocabulary, *style* and *structure, symbol* and *strategy, tone* and *tension* and *intention*, he was an extraordinary influence, the major figure, probably, in what is called the liberation of modern American literature.

He had other impressive qualities, among them the ability to create a gallery of characters who have independent life outside the novels, with all their obvious limitations — characters that live now in the American historical tradition. A number of them have become gigantic, archetypal figures that embody the major traits of their class. Lewis' novels, as a result, are perhaps the last important American novels that are primarily concerned with social class. Or are John Marquand and John O'Hara and James Gould Cozzens of his stature? If Lewis' novels often depended more heavily than theirs on the mere report of social minutiae and of the details of the American lingo and more often failed to realize that material imaginatively, they nevertheless — as Joseph Wood Krutch has said — "recorded a reign of grotesque vulgarity which but for him would have left no record of itself because no one else could have adequately recorded it."

He performed a function that has nearly gone out of American fiction, and American fiction is thinner for the loss. Many American novelists today tell us about our subjective lives, and on that subject Sinclair Lewis could hardly speak at all. Fitzgerald, Hemingway, Faulkner — they all had some sense of the tragic nature of human experience that was denied to Lewis. Lyric joy, sensuous ecstasy — to these, too, he was apparently a stranger. But he had a stridently comic gift of mimicry that many a more polished American writer does not have at all. And a vision of a hot and dusty hell: the American hinterland. He gave Americans their first shuddering glimpses into a frightening reality of which until he wrote they were unaware and of which he himself may also have been unaware. As Alfred Kazin wrote: "There is indeed more significant terror of a kind in Lewis's novels than in a writer like Faulkner or the hard-boiled novelists, for it is the terror immanent in the commonplace, the terror that arises out of the repression, the meannesses, the hard jokes of the world Lewis had soaked into his pores." With that America "soaked into his pores," he could document for an enormous audience the character of a people and a class, and, without repudiating either, criticize and laugh uproariously at both. In any strict literary sense, he was not a great writer, but without his writing one cannot imagine modern American literature. No more, without his writing, could Americans today imagine themselves. His epitaph should be: *He did us good.*

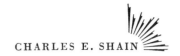

F. Scott Fitzgerald

THE general acceptance of Scott Fitzgerald into the ranks of serious and ambitious American novelists had to wait until his death in 1940. He was forty-four when he died and the story of the early rise and abrupt fall of his literary reputation — as well as his personal fortunes — can be fitted with neat symmetry into those two dramatic decades of the American twentieth century, the twenties and the thirties. The twenties were less than three months old when Fitzgerald's first novel, *This Side of Paradise,* arrived and immediately became a famous American book. Within weeks of this first success a second brand-new postwar product, his stories of the flapper and her boy friends, made it clear that the twenties would be his oyster and that he, handsome, clever, and lucky Scott Fitzgerald, would be one of the brightest figures of the new age. The climax of his fortunes arrived, we can see now, very rapidly. In 1925 came the splendid artistic success of *The Great Gatsby,* and then in the second half of the twenties the days and months of his private world began to descend into tragedy. He could not bring the order into his life that would allow him to write his next novel. By the end of the twenties he was living too high and drinking too much. In April 1930 Zelda Fitzgerald had the mental breakdown that ended the romantic life they had built together over the preceding ten years. During the thirties Fitzgerald's life encompassed enough pathos, irony, and final agony to make his biography by Arthur Mizener one of the saddest records of an American literary life since Edgar Allan Poe. Before he died he was dead as a writer. No one was buying his

81

books though seven were still in print. What has become clearer since his death in 1940 is a final irony, at the expense not of Fitzgerald but of American literary culture: the neglect he suffered during the 1930's was hugely undeserved. It took two posthumously published works to reveal to America how much serious work he had accomplished against great odds during the last ten years of his life.

The critical neglect of Fitzgerald had of course the effect of making the popular neglect seem deserved. That he shortened his own life by dissipation and wasted his fine talent all along the way was the judgment passed by most of the critics at the time of his death. The severity of their judgments may have been justified, but this did not excuse the failure to see how hard Fitzgerald had written all his life, or the failure to distinguish his best work from the rest and to recognize how much good work there was. It will perhaps become less of a temptation as the decades pass to be preoccupied with Fitzgerald as a person, and with his life as a cautionary tale, at the expense of a close concentration on his stories and novels. He used himself so mercilessly in his fiction, there is often such a complete fusion between his life and his stories, that conscientious criticism will always have to remember D. H. Lawrence's warning to biographically-minded critics: don't trust the artist, trust the tale. There is, however, another order of difficulty in appreciating Fitzgerald's best work. His attitude toward money and moneyed people has been much misunderstood.

One way to begin a consideration of Fitzgerald's attraction to the American rich as the prime subject matter of his fiction is to look at the most famous Fitzgerald literary anecdote. As Ernest Hemingway originally wrote it into his story "The Snows of Kilimanjaro," published in *Esquire* in 1936, it went this way. Hemingway's writer-hero is musing on his own life among the American rich. "He remembered poor Scott Fitzgerald and his romantic awe of them and how he had started a story once that began, 'The very rich are different from you and me.' And how someone had said to Scott, Yes they have more money. But that was not humorous to Scott."

F. Scott Fitzgerald

Although the exchange never actually took place it has become part of the story of our two most legendary modern novelists. The moral implications of the anecdote, political, personal, and artistic, have usually been chalked up to Hemingway's score. It is significant for understanding the distance that separated the two men at this point in their friendship that Hemingway could make such demeaning use of Fitzgerald as a character in a piece of magazine fiction. The anecdote concludes with this comment, "He thought they were a special glamorous race and when he found they weren't it wrecked him just as much as any other thing that wrecked him." This was the public burial of a has-been writer, and Fitzgerald was deeply offended.

Hemingway's rebuke belongs to the general charge against Fitzgerald made frequently in the thirties that he was captivated by the rich and their expensive manners, and forgot that too much money in America is always supposed to be a sign of vulgarity and wickedness. Applied to Fitzgerald's fiction this moralism is simple-minded. To disprove it there is exhibited in the novels and stories all the moral energy that Fitzgerald spent "fixing" the rich. Since we read Fitzgerald's stories of the rich in a more affluent American society, in which the rich have become less shocking because they are now less removed from middle-class mores, we should more easily detect the moral and cultural confusions in Fitzgerald's fiction if they are really there. Americans living through a new postwar society can no longer feel superior to Fitzgerald's interest in the American greed for fine cars, the right clothes, and the pleasures of the best hotels and offbeat entertainment. The American people now seem to be less embarrassed than they once were at the snobbery of large parts of their social system. Contemporary social analysis has shown them how far ahead of his times Fitzgerald was in describing the rigorous systems of status that underlie that rather contradictory American term, the Open Society.

We may in fact be today more responsive readers of Fitzgerald's stories of money and display and expensive charm than many of his contemporaries were. He wrote during two decades when an

American social revolution seemed more probable to thoughtful people than it does today. Nowadays we may be more ready to accept as he did the final complexity of our society and to recognize that we create a large part of our moral selves as we become engaged in that society. This is the theme that runs through his fiction — and through his life. We do him an injustice if we assume at the start that in order to understand the dreadful sanctions of social prestige — that is, money — Fitzgerald had to make a fatal submission of himself to the glamorous rich.

The story of the legendary Fitzgerald of the twenties usually begins with the picture of newly married, handsome Zelda and Scott Fitzgerald dancing around or jumping into the fountain of the Plaza Hotel. This pastoral scene may be useful in reminding us that the Fitzgeralds were not native New Yorkers. She was from the deep South, from Montgomery, Alabama. He was a middle westerner. Edmund Wilson, one of Fitzgerald's closest literary friends, insisted on the important influence of St. Paul, Minnesota, in forming Fitzgerald's literary personality. In 1922 when Wilson did a literary profile of Fitzgerald he wrote, "Fitzgerald is as much of the middle west of large cities and country clubs as Lewis is of the middle west of the prairies and little towns." The culture that formed him, Wilson went on in a superior eastern manner, was characterized at its best by "sensitivity and eagerness for life without a sound base of culture and taste; a brilliant structure of hotels and exhilarating social activities built not on the eighteenth century but simply on the prairie." Wilson then took the occasion to advise Fitzgerald — his friends were always giving him advice in public — to exploit the "vigorous social atmosphere" of his native state, "to do for Summit Avenue what Lewis has done for Main Street." Fitzgerald never followed Wilson's suggestion to write a middle-western novel — despite all that public advice one of Fitzgerald's most surprising attributes was a capacity for making up his mind in private — but he made his own kind of use of his Minnesota background. It was not at all like Sinclair Lewis' exploitation of that same territory.

Francis Scott Key Fitzgerald was born in St. Paul on September 24, 1896. On his mother's side he was the grandson of an Irish immigrant who did well in the wholesale grocery business. His grandfather's estate was worth $300,000 to $400,000 when he died at the age of forty-four. This McQuillan money gave young Scott Fitzgerald the advantageous background of his grandmother's large house on Summit Avenue, the most aristocratic street in St. Paul, and it gave him eventually his expensive education in private schools and at Princeton. But he was always sensitive to the McQuillan beginnings as being what he called "straight 1850 potato famine Irish." The other half of his inheritance was much more pleasing to his keen sense of himself. His admiration for his gentlemanly but ineffectual father, who was descended from a seventeenth-century Maryland family, he put into both *The Great Gatsby* and *Tender Is the Night*. He was named for Francis Scott Key, a distant cousin of his paternal grandmother's. In the thirties he wrote that he had early developed an inferiority complex in the midst of a family where the "black Irish half . . . had the money and looked down upon the Maryland side of the family who had, and really had, that . . . series of reticences and obligations that go under the poor old shattered word 'breeding.' "

Fitzgerald's Catholic background was also oppressive to him as a boy. He wrote in his notebook later in his life that when he was young "the boys in my street still thought that Catholics drilled in the cellar every night with the idea of making Pius the Ninth autocrat of this republic." But Fitzgerald never wrote these feelings of social displacement directly into his fiction or into the confessional essays of the mid-thirties. None of his important protagonists is noticeably Irish or Catholic and none of the agonies they suffer is religious. He was not, apparently, a very devout schoolboy, even in a Catholic boarding school and under the influence of a sophisticated and cultivated priest, Monsignor Fay, who was devoted to him and to whom he dedicated his first novel. (*This Side of Paradise* is not at all a Catholic novel.) In 1919 at the end of his college career at Princeton and his war service he wrote to Edmund Wilson that his Catholicism was scarcely more than a memory. The autobiographical essays in *The Crack-Up* tell us a great deal about Fitzgerald's sense of sinning against himself, against his gift of life and his gift of talent, but none of the sources of his despair take us directly back to his early years in the midst of a dubiously genteel Irish Catholic family in St. Paul.

His loyalty to his father may have been partly a way of defending his father against failure in business. As a boy of eleven Fitzgerald shared intensely the embarrassment of his father's being fired as a salesman for Procter and Gamble in Buffalo and the family's subsequent return to St. Paul to live under the protection of the McQuillan money. As if his family were restive under the pressures of feeling dependent, they moved from one house to another in the Summit Avenue neighborhood, circling the social strongholds but never able to afford more than "a house below the average/Of a street above the average" as Fitzgerald once put it. One of his best known stories, "Winter Dreams," a Jazz Age version of the Horatio Alger fable, is based on St. Paul and its summertime suburb White Bear Lake. The hero at fourteen is a grocer's son who must earn his spending money as a caddy at the country club to which many of Fitzgerald's Summit Avenue friends belonged. Fitzgerald was never a caddy, but it was easy for him to project a poor boy's social insecurity. His mother was a further embarrassment. She dressed oddly and sometimes behaved oddly in public. He was always aware that she had spoiled him and helped him to be the little show-off who could easily get on the nerves of his teachers and contemporaries. But the young Fitzgerald is also remembered in St. Paul as an imaginative, vital, and attractive boy. Plenty of social success came his way before he was sent off to boarding school in New Jersey at the age of fourteen.

Fitzgerald mined his boyhood years, as he did every stage of his life, for story material. The *Saturday Evening Post* stories of his youth in St. Paul and at Newman School that he wrote at the end of the twenties are delightful and show what a competent writer of magazine fiction he was by this time. But the moments in the stories that distinguish them as Fitzgerald's are those that show how exactly he could recall a moment of a boy's deep feeling about a person, or a place, or "the way it was." One of the safest generalizations that can be made about Fitzgerald is that he is America's most sentient novelist of manners. He was deeply interested in recording the history of his own sensibility at the same time that he wanted to describe a typical American boyhood. The *Post* stories of his young hero, Basil Duke Lee, are full of events that have their meaning in social distinctions, envious comparisons, and the important implications for young Americans of manners and possessions. But as Basil moves from one emotional crisis to another in his search for who he really is and who he wants to be, Fitzgerald would have us believe that Basil deliberately penetrates each moment of passion for its absolute emotional significance, and then passes on. On one magical late summer afternoon in a St. Paul backyard — the story is called "The Scandal Detectives" — fourteen-year-old Basil really looked into a girl's beautiful, "gnome-like" face for the first time. He had scarcely begun to drink his fill of his response to her, "a warm chill of mingled pleasure and pain," when, Fitzgerald writes, he realized it was "a definite experience and he was immediately conscious of it." Then, as the swift moment of excitement filled him to the brim the boy consciously let it go, "incapable of exploiting it until he had digested it alone." The emotional plot of the story is about a writer-to-be, as well as, we are almost persuaded, a typical American boy.

Fitzgerald's first boyish successes were literary and they were important to both his emotional and his social life. In an autobiographical essay written in the mid-thirties he recalled a piece of schoolboy writing and remembered how necessary it had been to his ability to meet the world. At Newman School the football coach had taken him out of a game unfairly, according to Fitzgerald. The coach thought he had been afraid of an opposing player and had let the team down. Fitzgerald was able to dominate the whole situation, the coach, his lack of success at football, and probably his own cowardice by writing a poem about the experience that made his father proud of him. "So when I went home that Christmas vacation it was in my mind that if you weren't able to function in action you might at least be able to tell about it, because you felt the same intensity — it was a back door way out of facing reality." The need to feel the same intensity of social success that more popular, better balanced schoolboys felt kept Fitzgerald writing stories, poems, and plays. His academic record always suffered, but as a young poet, editor, and playwright he could express his considerable ego and win the kind of public acclaim that was necessary to him. By the age of sixteen he had written and produced two melodramas that had public performances in St. Paul and earned over $200 for a local charity. He was learning to depend on his literary talent very early in his life. When it came time to choose a college he chose Princeton because he learned that you could be a big man at Princeton if you could provide librettos for its musical comedy organization, the Triangle Club. He entered college in the fall of 1913 when he was still sixteen years old.

Princeton's contribution to Fitzgerald's education as an American writer can be best discovered in his autobiographical first novel, *This Side of Paradise*. For the writer as a person it was, from the first moment, a lovely place, an atmosphere full of poignant emotions. ". . . the sense of all the gorgeous youth that has rioted through here in two hundred years" — that was one of the feelings written into the novel, and as Fitzgerald's young men left Princeton for the army camps of World War I they wept for their own lost youth. Through most of the pages of the novel Princeton is primarily a richly complex American social order with very attractive possibilities for a bright young man on the make. The world you aspired to, as soon as you learned your way around, was composed of admirable, even glamorous men, in the classes above you, who could be envied and imitated both for themselves and for their functions in this specialized society. They were the athletes, writers, campus politicians, or just the Men with an Aura. As a freshman you chose your models, entered the intense but secret social competition, and with good luck and much clever management you would be accepted, by the middle of your second year when you joined an eating club, as one of the best of your generation. This was the Princeton that first consumed Fitzgerald's imagination.

What Fitzgerald as an educated man owed to Princeton is harder to discern. Arthur Mizener believes that the group of literary friends that he was lucky to find there — Edmund Wilson and John Peale Bishop were two of them — gave him "the only education he ever got, and, above all, they gave him a respect for literature which was more responsible than anything else for making him a serious man." The narrowness of his educated mind, in one sense the failure of his Princeton education, can be fairly deduced from letters he wrote to his daughter studying at Vassar during the last year of his life.

Twenty-five years after his Princeton career he still recommends what were evidently his own college practices to his daughter. To form a prose style she must read the poets over and over. If she has anything of an ear she will soon hear the difference between poetry and non-poetry and thus have an advantage over most English professors. She must have "some politeness toward ideas," but about adjectives, ". . . all fine prose is based upon the verbs carrying the sentences. . . . Probably the finest technical poem in English is Keats' *Eve of Saint Agnes*. . . . Would you read that poem for me, and report?" Looking back at his own beginnings in college, he identifies himself as a poetic talent. It is the prose talents, he believes, who need the benefits of a formal education; they depend upon "other factors — assimilation of material and careful selection of it, or, more bluntly: having something to say and an interesting, highly developed way of saying it." As for the education of poets, if she will try to give ". . . not the merely *reported* but the *profound* essence of what happened at a prom or after it, perhaps that honesty will come to you — and then you will understand how it is possible to make even a forlorn Laplander *feel* the importance of a trip to Cartier's!"

It was one of the great blows of Fitzgerald's life that his formal Princeton career as he had carefully plotted it and at first began to achieve it was in the end a failure. By the close of his second year he seemed to be well on his way to the first great public display of his personality. He had made the right club, had written the book for a Triangle show, and was an editor of a magazine called *The Tiger*. The aura was beginning to form. But he had overextended himself. Too many academic deficiencies piled up, and under cover of an illness he left college at the beginning of his third year. A year's absence meant forfeiting all the tangible prizes he had aimed for, and he could still relive the pangs of his disappointment twenty years later. When he returned to college in the fall of 1916 he had improved his notion of the superior Princeton type. He began to see more of "literary" men and to fill the literary magazine with his poems and stories. This was the only year of serious education for him at Princeton, and what he learned came chiefly through private reading. He read especially Shaw and Butler and Wells, and read and then imitated Tennyson, Swinburne, and Rupert Brooke. He discovered the prototype for his first hero and novel when he read Compton Mackenzie's *Sinister Street*. Then between his third and fourth years he applied for a commission in the army. What should have been Fitzgerald's last year at Princeton was only two months long and on November 20 he left the campus for Fort Leavenworth.

Before Fitzgerald left Princeton for what was to be fifteen months of service in American training camps — he was never sent overseas — he finished the first of three versions of *This Side of Paradise*. Professor Christian Gauss read the manuscript and returned it saying it was not ready for publication. During Fitzgerald's first six months as an officer in training he struggled not with army manuals and training exercises but with his manuscript. In the summer of 1918 *The Romantic Egotist*, as he first called the novel, was sent to Scribner's, and in the fall that house rejected it by a vote of two editors to one. Meanwhile he had been transferred to Camp Sheridan near Montgomery, Alabama, and there, on the seventh of September, as he noted precisely in his journal, he fell in love. The girl, barely eighteen, was Zelda Sayre, the daughter of a judge.

The close resemblance between Zelda Sayre — who was going to

become Zelda Fitzgerald after a courtship of a year and a half —
and the heroines of Fitzgerald's fiction makes it important to try
to see her clearly as a person. It is not a simple thing to do. Since
her death she has always been referred to unceremoniously as
Zelda, even in formal literary essays. But this informality is really
a continuing acknowledgment that the combined destinies of Zelda
and Scott Fitzgerald are finally one and indivisible. He transmuted
their twin biographies into fiction, and we shall probably never
find it easy to distinguish between the historical person and Scott
Fitzgerald's Zelda.

When Fitzgerald first met Zelda Sayre he was just recovering
from the collapse of a college love affair, the central story of his
novel in manuscript. The romantic egotist of his novel was free
to make another absolute commitment, to invest another beautiful young lady with the aura of "the top girl." (He wrote later
into his notebook, "I didn't have the two top things: great animal
magnetism or money. I had the two second things, though: good
looks and intelligence. So I always got the top girl.") Zelda was
beautiful and desirable for herself, but she was also a prize to be
won against very worthy competition, all the other presentable
young officers in the two army camps near Montgomery. At the
moment of triumph when at last he made her his girl we must
assume that he felt the same ecstatic joy that filled Jay Gatsby's
ineffable moment in the love scene he was going to write five years
later. The persons of the drama were the same: the anonymous
young lieutenant from the North and the belle of a southern city.
The language of the Gatsby passage is as florid and brilliant as
anything in modern fiction since Meredith's early novels. "He
knew that when he kissed this girl, and forever wed his unutter-
able visions to her perishable breath, his mind would never romp
again like the mind of God. . . . At his lips' touch she blossomed
for him like a flower and the incarnation was complete." In *The
Great Gatsby* Fitzgerald was in full control of the language of the
religion of love spoken by a modern but strangely old-fashioned
courtly lover. None of the ironies visited upon Gatsby in the novel
is allowed to tarnish his first response to Daisy. The lack of self-

consciousness, the commitment to such pure feelings of sexual tenderness and compassion, distinguish Fitzgerald's romantic attitude toward women from any other modern novelist's.

The demands of feeling that Zelda Sayre brought to the courtship and marriage appear to have been as grand in their terms as Fitzgerald's. If we can trust his early descriptions of her in his fiction, she was above all ambitious, like the southern girl in "The Ice Palace" who was planning to live "where things happen on a big scale." And like the flappers in the early stories who baited their elders and showed in all their responses to life that they valued spontaneity and self-expression before those duller virtues that required self-control, Zelda Sayre was daring and had a local reputation for recklessness and unconventionality. She did what she wanted to, and her parents discovered that they belonged to that generation upon whom, as Fitzgerald once wrote in a story, "the great revolution in American family life was to be visited." Her youthful beauty gave her great confidence. The men in her life were expected on the one hand to make gallant gestures, and of these Fitzgerald was quite capable; on the other hand they were expected to promise her a solid and glittering background — here Fitzgerald's lack of expectations after he was discharged from the army in February 1919 sent them both into agonies of frustration.

For four months he struggled in New York to support himself by writing advertising copy by day and to make the fortune that would convince the girl by writing short stories at night. He sold just one story for $30, and by June he had lost the girl. Zelda broke the engagement. His response to her decision in the summer of 1919 was to chuck his New York job, return to St. Paul, and rewrite his novel. By early September he had finished *This Side of Paradise*, by the middle of the month Scribner's had accepted it, and by early November he had earned more than $500 from three recently written short stories. With the confidence of a real capitalist and the conviction that he had written a best-selling novel, Fitzgerald returned to Montgomery, and there Zelda promised to marry him in the spring when his novel was published.

F. Scott Fitzgerald

Fitzgerald did not hold Zelda Sayre morally responsible for the mercenary views she took of their engagement. They both felt poor, and they were both eager to participate in the moneyed society around them. In the United States in 1919, they agreed, the purpose of money was to realize the promises of life. When Gatsby says, in his famous remark, that Daisy's voice sounds like money, we should read him sympathetically enough to understand, as Arthur Mizener has pointed out, that he is not saying that he loves money or that he loves both Daisy and money, but that he loves what the possession of money has done for Daisy's charming voice. And yet after we have said this, we must also say that Daisy Buchanan, because of her money, is seen at last as a false woman and Gatsby as a simple boy from the provinces who has not been able to tell gilt from real gold. The circumstances of the Fitzgeralds' courtship and marriage seem fabulous — in the narrow sense of that word — because they often seem to suggest for us in outline the complex stories of women and marriage and money that Fitzgerald kept returning to in his fiction.

Fitzgerald was as fully aware of the power of women over men as D. H. Lawrence was, but in a different way. In his journal he once made a note that "Men get to be a mixture of the charming mannerisms of the women they have known." In Fitzgerald's fiction the villain has "animal magnetism" and masculinity but in the end he is stupid about women and treats them like whores. The Fitzgerald hero has softer qualities. "His mannerisms were all girls' mannerisms," he noted in plans for what sounds like a characteristic Fitzgerald hero, "rather gentle considerations got from [—] girls, or restrained and made masculine, a trait that, far from being effeminate, gave him a sort of Olympian stature that, in its all-kindness and consideration, was masculine and feminine alike." The men in his fiction are often, as he was, astonished by the fearlessness and recklessness of women. They are also finally made aware of the deceitfulness and moral complacency of many women. Jordan Baker in *The Great Gatsby* and Baby Warren in *Tender Is the Night*, for example, are studies of mercenary American women as dangerous to men as classical sorceresses.

Daisy Buchanan and Nicole Warren are fatally irresponsible human beings. All his critics have noticed Fitzgerald's ability to project himself into women's lives. Near the end of his life, when he had decided to see the story of *The Last Tycoon* through the eyes of Cecilia Brady, age twenty-five, he wrote to his editor, "Cecilia is the narrator because I think I know exactly how such a person would react to my story."

To understand Fitzgerald's life and his stories of love and marriage we must be prepared to accept the tragic love plot strongly implied in his biography: he so built himself into Zelda Fitzgerald's life that when in 1930 her life went down, her fall brought him down as well. From Rome during the winter of 1924–25 at the peak of his pleasure over having written *The Great Gatsby*, he wrote to John Peale Bishop: "The cheerfulest things in my life are first Zelda and second the hope that my book has something extraordinary about it. I want to be extravagantly admired again. Zelda and I sometimes indulge in terrible four day rows that always start with a drinking party but we're still enormously in love and about the only truly happily married people I know." This was the Fitzgerald marriage at the height of its turbulent career. In 1933 after Zelda's first severe illness and while they were living quietly and Scott Fitzgerald was making a valiant stand against alcoholism, he characterized their life together in far different terms. "We have a good way of living, basically, for us; we got through a lot and have some way to go; our united front is less a romance than a categorical imperative and when you criticize it in terms of a bum world . . . [it] seems to negate on purpose both past effort and future hope. . . ." The more knowledge we have of the Fitzgeralds' marriage, the less his choice of those strong words "categorical imperative" surprises us. Their married life was a continual source of both the "romance" and the moral education out of which his best fiction came.

The novel with which Fitzgerald won Zelda, *This Side of Paradise*, is usually praised for qualities that pin it closely to an exact moment in American life. Later readers are apt to come to it with the anticipation of an archaeologist approaching an interesting ruin. Its publication is always considered to be the event that ushered in the Jazz Age. Glenway Wescott, writing for his and Fitzgerald's generation, said that it had "haunted the decade like a song, popular but perfect." Social historians have pointed out that the college boys of the early twenties really read it. There have been public arguments as to whether or not the petting party first occurred when Fitzgerald's novel said it did or two years earlier. Anyone reading the novel with such interests will not be entirely disappointed. One of the responsibilities it assumes, especially in its first half, is to make the hero, Amory Blaine, report like a cultural spy from inside his generation. "None of the Victorian mothers — and most of the mothers were Victorian — had any idea how casually their daughters were accustomed to be kissed." "The 'belle' had become the 'flirt,' the 'flirt' had become the 'baby vamp.' " "Amory saw girls doing things that even in his memory would have been impossible: eating three-o'clock, after-dance suppers in impossible cafés, talking of every side of life with an air half of earnestness, half of mockery, yet with a furtive excitement that Amory considered stood for a real moral let-down." The "moral let-down" enjoyed by the postwar generation has given the work its reputation for scandal as well as for social realism.

Today, the novel's young libertines, both male and female, would not shock a schoolgirl. Amory Blaine turns out to be a conspicuous moralist who takes the responsibility of kissing very seriously and disapproves of affairs with chorus girls. (He has no scruples, it must be said, against going on a three-week drunk when his girl breaks off their engagement.) At the end of the story he is ennobled by an act of self-sacrifice in an Atlantic City hotel bedroom that no one would admire more than a Victorian mother. For modern readers it is probably better to take for granted the usefulness of *This Side of Paradise* for social historians and to admire from the distance of another age the obviously wholesome morality of the hero. Neither of these is the quality that saves the novel for a later time. What Fitzgerald is really showing is how a young American of his generation discovers what sort of figure he wants to cut, what modes of conduct, gotten out of books as well as out of a keen sense of his contemporaries, he wants to imitate. The flapper and her boy friend do not actually pet behind the closed doors of the smoking room. They talk, and each one says to the other, unconvincingly, "Tell me about yourself. What do you feel?" Meaning, "Tell me about myself. How do I feel?" The real story of *This Side of Paradise* is a report on a young man's emotional readiness for life.

The only interesting morality it presents is the implied morality that comes as a part of his feelings when the hero distinguishes, or fails to distinguish, between an honest and a dishonest emotion. The highly self-conscious purpose of telling Amory Blaine's story was, one suspects, to help Fitzgerald to discover who he really was by looking into the eyes of a girl — there are four girls — or into the mirror of himself that his college contemporaries made. And the wonder of it is that such a self-conscious piece of autobiography could be imagined, presented, and composed as a best-selling novel by a young man of twenty-three.

The novel is very uneven, and full of solemn attempts at abstract thought on literature, war, and socialism. It has vitality and freshness only in moments, and these are always moments of feeling. Fitzgerald said of this first novel many years later, "A lot of people thought it was a fake, and perhaps it was, and a lot of others thought it was a lie, which it was not." It offers the first evidence of Fitzgerald's possession of the gift necessary for a novelist who, like him, writes from so near his own bones, the talent that John Peale Bishop has described as "the rare faculty of being able to experience romantic and ingenuous emotions and a half hour later regard them with satiric detachment." The ingenuous emotions most necessary to the success of *This Side of Paradise* are vanity and all the self-regarding sentiments experienced during first love and the first trials of pride. The satire visited upon them is often as delicate and humorous as in this picture of Amory at a moment of triumphant egoism: "As he put in his studs he realized that he was enjoying life as he would probably never enjoy it again. Everything was hallowed by the haze of his own youth. He had arrived, abreast of the best of his generation at Princeton. He was in love and his love was returned. Turning on all the lights, he looked at himself in the mirror, trying to find in his own face the qualities that made him see more clearly than the great crowd of people, that made him decide firmly, and able to influence and follow his own will. There was little in his life now that he would have changed. . . . Oxford might have been a bigger field."

The ideas in the novel, unlike the tributes paid to a life of feeling, have the foreign country of origin and the importer's labels still on them. Edmund Wilson said *This Side of Paradise* was not really about anything. "Intellectually it amounts to little more than a gesture — a gesture of indefinite revolt." Toward the end of the novel Fitzgerald's normally graceful sentences begin to thicken and "sword-like pioneering personalities, Samuel Butler, Renan and Voltaire," are called in to add the weight of their names to Amory's reflections on the hypocrisy of his elders. The best pages of the novel come early, where Fitzgerald was remembering in marvelous detail the scenes at Newman School and Princeton. Later in his life he would always find it easy to return to those adolescent years, when feelings were all in all. Bishop once accused him of taking seventeen as his norm and believing that after that year life began to fall away from perfection. Fitzgerald replied, "If you make it fifteen I will agree with you."

The Fitzgerald novel, then, began in his acute awareness of a current American style of young life and in his complete willingness to use his own experience as if it were typical. The charm of his first stories and novels is simply the charm of shared vanity and enthusiasm for oneself as an exceptional person. Fitzgerald often persuades us that he was the one sensitive person there — on the country club porch or in a New York street — the first time something happened, or at the very height of the season. And when this ability to exploit his life began to succeed beyond his dreams, the only next step he could think of was to use it harder.

His success arrived almost overnight: 1920 was the *annus mira-*

bilis. In that year, the *Saturday Evening Post* published six of his stories, *Smart Set* five, and *Scribner's* two. In 1919 he had made $879 by writing; in 1920 he made $18,850 from his novel, from magazine stories and essays, and from the rights to two stories sold to the movies. His success with the *Saturday Evening Post* and the movies suggests how quickly he had discovered the formulas for popular fiction and the big money. Within fifteen years between 1919 and 1934 Fitzgerald earned, he estimated, $400,000, most of it writing for magazines and the movies. From the beginning of his success Fitzgerald was quite aware of the temptations of commercial writing and how well adapted he was to succumb to them. The question as to whether the conflict between the use and misuse of his talent opened the crack in Fitzgerald's self-respect that at last killed him as a novelist has been argued by many of his friends. Dos Passos spoke at his death for those who thought it did. Fitzgerald had invented for their generation, he said, the writing career based on the popular magazines and he was "tragically destroyed by his own invention."

Fitzgerald's struggle with his literary conscience is often apparent in his letters and journals. He wrote Maxwell E. Perkins, his editor at Scribner's, that he knew he had "a faculty for being cheap, if I want to indulge that." When in the winter of 1923–24 he needed money, concentrated on producing commercial stories for *Hearst's International*, and made $17,000, he wrote Edmund Wilson that "it was all trash, and it nearly broke my heart." But he also had another way of imagining himself: "I'm a workman of letters, a professional," he would say in this mood, "I know when to write and when to stop writing." He wanted to be both a good writer and a popular one. His high living, he knew, depended on magazine money and it is significant that he devoted most of his time to short fiction during those years between 1926 and 1931 when his life became most disordered and the completion of a new novel came hard. Yet he thought of himself most proudly as a novelist. His most poignant confession of a failure to be true to his talent he expressed to his daughter six months before he died: "Doubt and worry — you are as crippled by them as I am by my inability to handle money or my self-indulgences of the past. . . . What little I've accomplished has been by the most laborious and uphill work, and I wish now I'd *never* relaxed or looked back — but said at the end of *The Great Gatsby*: 'I've found my line — from now on this comes first. This is my immediate duty — without this I am nothing.' "

But the final record shows that he wrote four complete novels and more than a hundred and fifty short stories. Forty-six of them he chose to print in four separate collections. In an ambitious set of plans for future productions that he once projected, there were to be in his collected works seven novels and also seven volumes of short stories. He was quite aware of his achievements as a short story writer, and twentieth-century American writing would be much poorer if it lacked six, at least, of Fitzgerald stories which are brilliant, and perhaps thirty to forty more which are full of finely observed life.

The first collection of Fitzgerald's stories in 1921 was timed by Scribner's to profit from the vogue of *This Side of Paradise*. It was called *Flappers and Philosophers*. A second collection, *Tales of the Jazz Age*, was published a year later in the wake of his second novel, *The Beautiful and Damned*. The nineteen stories in the two collections represent with more variety and perhaps more immediacy than the two first novels the manners and morals that have come to compose, at least in the minds of later historians, the Jazz Age. In 1922 we catch a glimpse of Fitzgerald imagining his relation to his Jazz Age public when he writes his editor about the second book of stories: "It will be bought by *my own personal public*, that is by the countless flappers and college kids who think I am a sort of oracle." The various mysteries that the young oracle was making known to his followers may be observed in two slight, early stories, "The Jelly-Bean," and "Bernice Bobs Her Hair." They both follow conventional formulas of popular fiction, but the young people in the stories act out a new version of the American pastoral.

The man known as the Jelly-bean is a good-natured garage mechanic in a sleepy Georgia town, a son of one of the town's first families now fallen on evil days. He has been awakened to his true responsibilities in life by the kiss of a young flapper and Belle Dame sans Merci named Nancy Lamar. "With the awakening of his emotions, his first perception was a sense of futility, a dull ache at the utter grayness of his life." With this Keatsian strain life deepens for an American Jelly-bean. Nancy is the story's chief excitement. She drinks corn liquor, shoots craps with the men after a country club dance, and, in the story's best scene, wades through a pool of gasoline tapped from a car to remove a wad of chewing gum from the sole of her dancing slipper. Nancy lives with her dream of Lady Diana Manners. "Like to have boat. Like to sail out on a silver lake, say the Thames, for instance. Have champagne and caviare sandwiches along. Have about eight people." Bernice, who bobbed her hair on a dare, comes from another American Forest of Arden, Eau Claire, Wisconsin. She is an innocent who has to learn by rote a "line" for attracting boys — the same line that Fitzgerald taught his sister Annabel once when he despaired of her chances of becoming the Lady Diana Manners of St. Paul.

Fitzgerald had observed two provincial societies in Montgomery, Alabama, and St. Paul, and we can watch him exploiting like a veteran novelist details of types and manners in these two stories and in "The Ice Palace." Zelda Sayre posed as the model for a southern flapper in "The Ice Palace" and Fitzgerald used their own situation to imagine the shocks that might be in store for a lively southern girl among the likable Babbitts of Minnesota. All these stories, as well as that Hollywood natural "The Off-Shore Pirate," were imagined from a young girl's dreams of a glamorous life. "Dalyrimple Goes Wrong" examines from a young ex-soldier's point of view the deceits of the world of business and politics as it is being run by a hypocritical older generation. "The Lees of Happiness" and "The Cut-Glass Bowl" imagine American domestic tragedies, lives that go down in "the flight of time and the end of beauty and unfulfilled desire." There is more pathos in these Jazz Age stories than one might expect.

Two of the stories in the first collections are important, "May

Day" for what it attempts, and "The Diamond as Big as the Ritz" for what it achieves. "May Day" was probably a discarded beginning to a novel about New York. May Day 1919 was the exact day, Fitzgerald said later, when the Jazz Age began. The story is planned to carry more weight than the usual early Fitzgerald story. It uses three plots with intertwining action, like a Dos Passos chronicle novel, opens with an economic motif, the Manhattan crowds staring greedily at the glowing contents of shopwindows, and in other ways gives evidence of Fitzgerald's willingness to steal some pages from the American naturalists. The mob scenes and the two "primitives," the footloose soldiers looking for whiskey, may have come not from Fitzgerald's observation but from the novels of Norris and Dreiser. But if these are the story's weak spots they are also marks of its ambition. Fitzgerald wanted to use the whole loud and anarchic world of Manhattan as the background of his own forlorn state in the spring of 1919 when he was an ex-lieutenant writing advertising copy, broke, and heartsick at the loss of his girl. The portrait he draws of Gordon Sterrett, in the midst of the big money, desperately poor and depending on alcohol, shows how intensely he could project fears for his own failures — and perhaps how fascinated he would always be with the drama of failure. "I can't stand being poor," Gordon says. "You seem sort of bankrupt — morally as well as financially," says his rich Yale classmate. "Don't they usually go together?" Gordon asks. At the big dance at Delmonico's Gordon gets drunk and tells a girl how it feels to go to pieces, "Things have been snapping inside of me for four months like little hooks on a dress, and it's about to come off when a few more hooks go." Metaphors of bankruptcy and of coming unhooked are going to turn up later when Fitzgerald contemplates his own sense of failure.

"The Diamond as Big as the Ritz" is a satirical American fantasy that comes as squarely out of the bedazzled daydreams of the twenties as Hawthorne's wry fables came out of the 1840's when an earlier American generation had Utopian dreams of human nature. The young visitor to the diamond mountain kingdom, John T. Unger, from a little middle-western town named Hades, watches his host, Mr. Braddock Washington, the richest man in the world, turn at last into a madman who believes he can bribe God with his money. But young Unger has not learned much. After the diamond mountain has blown up he hates to return to his middle-class Hades with an heiress and no money: ". . . turn out your pocket and let's see what jewels you brought along. If you made a good selection we three ought to live comfortably all the rest of our lives." At the age of twenty-five Fitzgerald had written a highly imaginative folktale of modern American life.

The Beautiful and Damned was an attempt to write a dramatic novel about a promising American life that never got anywhere; "The Flight of the Rocket," it was once called. It was the first and least convincing of what were going to be three studies of American failures. As he started the novel in August 1920, Fitzgerald wrote to his publisher that his subject was ". . . the life of Anthony Patch between his 25th and 33rd years (1913–1921). He is one of those many with the tastes and weaknesses of an artist but with no actual creative inspiration. How he and his beautiful young wife are wrecked on the shoals of dissipation is told in the story." Anthony Patch, unlike Amory Blaine, was to be placed at some distance from Fitzgerald's life. He is an American aristocrat, the only heir of a multimillionaire grandfather, "Cross" Patch, whose money goes back to the Gilded Age but whose hypocritic puritanism is of the kind that Mencken was excoriating. Anthony's story opens as if he were going to be offered up on the smoking altars of American vulgarity and commercialism. After Harvard he spends an aesthetic year in Rome, then returns to a comfortable apartment on 52nd Street, to his small society of bachelor friends and an income of seven thousand a year left him by his mother. Anthony is not a spoiled rich boy. He is certainly not American Youth in revolt. He is simply a graceful outsider with no ambitions but to be a beleaguered gentleman, to despise his grandfather, and, he hopes, to stay unmarried.

It is hard to see where Fitzgerald is going to go with Anthony except into amiable eccentricity. He has no character except his vague cynicism, a smarting sensibility, and the seven thousand a year. But then he falls in love with Gloria Gilbert and Fitzgerald's novel begins to deepen. As a lover and a husband, and soon as a failure, inexplicable but pathetic, Anthony Patch becomes a genuine fictional character, if not a very clear one. His reality comes, as the reality of all Fitzgerald's unhappy heroes will come, out of the expression of a strong romantic will. All he has he invests in his life with Gloria. The final clue to their failure is never given us. It is not just the eternal enmity between their aspirations to beauty and the hungry generations that tread them down, though this is part of it. They live too high, waste their money, and burn themselves out. That they are simply lost from the start is almost assumed. The morning after one of their desperately drunken parties, they decide never again to give a damn, "Not to be sorry, not to loose one cry of regret, to live according to a clear code of honor toward each other, and to seek the moment's happiness as feverishly and persistently as possible." But Gloria is not enough of a Hemingway character, and Anthony is not at all one, and the code does not work. Gloria, whose conception owes something to Fitzgerald's admiration for Mencken's book on Nietzsche, begins to develop "her ancient abhorrence, a conscience."

The Beautiful and Damned is a novel of mood rather than a novel of character. The misfortunes of Anthony and Gloria are forced in the plot, but the mood in places is desperate. Fitzgerald does not know what to do with his hero and heroine in the end but make them suffer. The novel will place no blame, either on the nature of things or on the injustices of society. Anthony and Gloria are finally willing to accept all the unhappy consequences as if they had earned them, but the reader has stopped believing in the logic of consequences in this novel long before. The failure of *The Beautiful and Damned* suggests where the soft spots are going to occur in Fitzgerald's art of the novel, in the presentation of character and motivation. With Anthony Patch Fitzgerald assumes that if he has displayed a man's sensibility in some detail he has achieved the study of a tragic character. The "tragedies" suffered by Anthony and Gloria, Fitzgerald's members of the lost generation, lack a moral context as the characters in *The Sun*

Also Rises do not. Fitzgerald's fears of his own weaknesses and the excesses that, according to his troubled conscience, he and Zelda were learning to like too easily, endowed the parable of the Patches with moral weight and urgency for its author; but the reader has to invent the worth of the moral struggle for himself.

The Beautiful and Damned was a commercially successful novel, despite a mixed reception from reviewers. It sold 43,000 copies the first year after its serialization in the *Metropolitan Magazine*. Its success to some extent was owing to well-circulated rumors that it was autobiographical, as indeed it was in many places. Zelda Fitzgerald, in a review of the novel for the New York *Tribune*, confessed she recognized parts of her diary and some personal letters in the book. "In fact, Mr. Fitzgerald — I believe that is how he spells his name — seems to believe that plagiarism begins at home." Recognizable portraits of the Fitzgeralds appeared on the book's dust jacket. In June 1922 an essay on contemporary life in the New York *Times* recommended that remarkable book, *The Beautiful and Damned*, to anyone who wanted to understand what went on during a typical drunken party in prohibition America.

Most of Anthony and Gloria's parties occur in a cottage in Connecticut like the one the Fitzgeralds rented in Westport in May 1920 soon after their marriage. But they were too restless for suburban Connecticut and moved back to New York. In the summer of 1921 they were in England and France, and by August they had settled in St. Paul where their only child, a daughter, was born in October. They lived in St. Paul for a year after that and Fitzgerald wrote stories, began and discarded a novel with a Catholic and middle-western hero, and finished a first version of his comedy, *The Vegetable*. (It is a pretty bad play which failed on its tryout two years later.) St. Paul was too provincial for more than a short residence and by October 1922 they were living in their most memorable house, a large one in Great Neck, Long Island. One powerful image of their life on Long Island has entered American folk history through the pages in *The Great Gatsby* which describe Gatsby's parties and the people who came to them. In the Great Neck house the Fitzgeralds' life reached its expensive culmination. They spent $36,000 during their first year and then Fitzgerald wrote an essay for the *Saturday Evening Post* to show how they had done it. They entertained their literary set, which included Edmund Wilson, Ring Lardner, H. L. Mencken, and George Jean Nathan, and periodically Fitzgerald tried to stop drinking and get on with his new novel. In the spring of 1924 they decided that they must begin to save money and that the south of France was the place to do it. By June they were established in a villa at St. Raphaël on the Riviera, and in November Fitzgerald sent the manuscript of *The Great Gatsby* off to New York. It was published in April 1925.

The Great Gatsby has been discussed and admired as much as any twentieth-century American novel, probably to the disadvantage of Fitzgerald's other fiction. None of its admirers finds it easy to explain why Fitzgerald at this point in his career should have written a novel of such perfect art — though it is usually conceded that he never reached such heights again. His discovery of Conrad and James is sometimes given credit for teaching him a new sense of proportion and control over form. But *The Great Gatsby* does so many things well that "influences" will not explain them all. The real mystery of how the novel was conceived and written may have to do with how the undisciplined life of a Long Island and St. Raphaël playboy could yield such moments of detachment and impersonality as this novel required. If we can trust Fitzgerald's backward glance from 1934 when he was writing an introduction to the Modern Library edition of *Gatsby*, it was a matter of keeping his "artistic conscience" "pure." "I had just re-read Conrad's preface to *The Nigger*, and I had recently been kidded half haywire by critics who felt that my material was such as to preclude all dealing with mature persons in a mature world." Also in 1934 he wrote his friend Bishop that he thought of *Gatsby* as his *Henry Esmond* and *Tender Is the Night* as his *Vanity Fair*: "The dramatic novel has cannons [Fitzgerald's spelling was notoriously unreliable] quite different from the philosophical, now called the psychological novel. One is a kind of *tour de force* and the other a confession of faith. It would be like comparing a sonnet sequence with an epic." Fitzgerald's language of literary sources and literary analysis always has an innocent ring. It is probably best to remember the language he used when he wrote his editor his plans for a new novel. "I want to write something *new*, something extraordinary and beautiful and simple and intricately patterned."

The Great Gatsby is worthy of all these adjectives. It was new for Fitzgerald to succeed in placing a novel of contemporary manners at such a distance from himself. Telling the story through a Conradian narrator, who was half inside and half outside the action, prevented the errors of self-identification he had fallen into with Anthony Patch. And Gatsby is not allowed to be a character who invites questions about his credibility as Anthony did. He is a figure from a romance who has wandered into a novel, the archetypal young man from the provinces who wants to become Lord Mayor, and to wake the sleeping beauty with a kiss. "Also you are right about Gatsby being blurred and patchy. I never at any one time saw him clear myself," Fitzgerald wrote a friend. But in a tour de force it is the power behind the conception that matters, and Fitzgerald was himself so sure of Gatsby's essential and primitive springs of action that he has required us to share his belief in Gatsby or reject the whole affair. "That's the whole burden of this novel," he wrote in a letter, "— the loss of those illusions that give such color to the world so that you don't care whether things are true or false as long as they partake of the magical glory."

The short novel tells the story of how James Gatz, a poor farm boy from North Dakota, imitates the example of Benjamin Franklin and other proven American moralists and rises at last to be a rich and powerful criminal named Jay Gatsby. Along the way, when he is an anonymous young lieutenant in a Kentucky training camp, when American "society" is open to him for the first time, he meets and marries in his mind, in an act of absolute commitment, a lovely southern girl named Daisy Fay. But he has to leave Daisy behind when he goes to France; and he loses her to a rich American from Chicago, Yale, and Wall Street. The only course conceivable to him when he returns is to pursue Daisy and in the American way to convince her of her error, to show he is worthy of her by the only symbols available to them both, a large house with a swimming pool, dozens of silk shirts, and elaborate parties. But Daisy believes in the symbols themselves, and not in the purer reality which (for Jay Gatsby) they only faintly embody. She loses her nerve and sacrifices her lover to the world.

Gatsby's mingled dream of love and money, and the iron strength of his romantic will, make up the essence of the fable, but the art of its telling is full of astonishing tricks. To make the rise and fall of a gentleman gangster an image for the modern history of the Emersonian spirit of America was an audacious thing to attempt, but Fitzgerald got away with it. His own romantic spirit felt deeply what an Englishman has called the "myth-hunger" of Americans, our modern need to "create a manageable past out of an immense present." The poignant effect of the final, highly com‑ plex image of the novel, when Gatsby's dream and the American dream are identified, shows how deeply saturated with feeling Fitzgerald's historical imagination was. From his own American life he knew that with his generation the middle westerner had become the typical American and had returned from the old fron‑ tier to the East with a new set of dreams—about money. No reader needs to worry about Fitzgerald's complicated attraction to the glamorous rich in this novel if he puts his trust in the middle-western narrator, Nick Carraway. Nick guides us safely through all the moral confusions of the wealthy East and leads us in the end back to the provinces where the fundamental decencies de‑ pend upon a social order of families who have lived in the same house for three generations.

The success of Nick as a device for controlling the tone of the narrative is remarkable. It is the quality of his response to Gatsby that at crucial moments compels our suspension of disbelief. The tranquil tone of his recollected feelings gives the story its serenity and tempts some of its admirers to compare it to a pastoral poem. Nick is everywhere he is needed, but he never intrudes on a pre‑ sented scene. He is the butt of our ironies and his own. The range of the story's ironic intentions is very wide. They encompass the wonderfully comic vulgarity of Myrtle Wilson, Tom Buchanan's mistress, as well as Daisy's almost irresistible charm. Fitzgerald's imagination plays with wit and perfect taste over the suggestive details of the story's surface: cuff buttons, a supper of cold chicken and two bottles of ale, Gatsby's shirts, and the names of the people who came to his parties. The whole novel is an imaginative feat that managed to get down the sensational display of postwar America's big money, and to include moral instructions on how to count the cost of it all. *The Great Gatsby* has by this time entered into the national literary mind as only some seemingly effortless works of the imagination can. We can see better now than even some of Fitzgerald's appreciative first reviewers that he had seized upon an important set of symbols for showing that time had run out for one image of the American ego. Poor Gatsby had been, in the novel's terms, deceived into an ignorance of his real greatness by the American world that had for its great men Tom Buchanan and Meyer Wolfsheim, the Wall Street millionaire and his colleague the racketeer. The story does not pretend to know more than this, that Americans will all be the poorer for the profanation and the loss of Gatsby's deluded imagination.

The principal fact in Fitzgerald's life between his twenty-eighth and thirty-fourth year was his inability to write a new novel. He seems to have known all along the kind of novel he wanted to write: in his terms it was to be the "philosophical, now called the psychological novel." He began a novel called *The World's Fair*, and in 1929 when he abandoned it he had written over twenty thousand words in the history of a failed life quite different from Gatsby's. The new hero was to be a bright young movie-maker named Francis Melarky who comes to the Riviera on a vacation from Hollywood and there in a fit of anger murders his possessive mother. "In a certain sense my plot is not unlike Dreiser's in the American Tragedy," he told his editor Perkins. In 1929 he dropped the matricide plot, and changed his title to *The Drunkard's Holiday*. Then after Zelda became psychotic in 1930 he had a different kind of American tragedy to put at the center. The new novel, like *The Beautiful and Damned,* was to arise out of his own life. The pathos inherent in these years is that he seemed fated to create his own agony, and study it as if it wasn't his, before he could use it in the confessional novel he felt driven to write. Looking back on his life near the end of it, he saw what he had done and wrote to his daughter, then a freshman at Vassar, the coolest summation of the Fitzgerald legend ever made: "I am not a great man but sometimes I think the impersonal and objective quality of my talent and the sacrifices of it, in pieces, to preserve its essential value has some sort of epic grandeur. Anyhow after hours I nurse myself with delusions of that sort."

If we can accept Fitzgerald's self-analysis it only remains to be astonished at the terrible cost of preserving the "essential value" of his literary talent. Between the publication of *Gatsby* and the final return to America in 1931 the Fitzgeralds moved between Europe and America as if they could not find a home anywhere. In the south of France or in Paris Fitzgerald had even less control over his extravagance than he had in America. The sales of *Gatsby* were not up to the sales of his first two novels, but stage and screen rights brought him over $30,000. Despite yearly incomes that were always over $20,000 and often nearly $30,000, Fitzgerald came home in 1931 with hardly any money. These are the years of the steady production of magazine fiction and articles. Between 1925 and 1932 he published fifty-six stories, most of them in the *Saturday Evening Post.* But, as Malcolm Cowley has said, the critics did not read the *Post,* and Fitzgerald's reputation began the decline from which it never recovered in his lifetime.

The best stories of those years he selected for two collections, *All the Sad Young Men* (1926) and *Taps at Reveille* (1935). Two recently published collections, *The Stories of F. Scott Fitzgerald,* edited by Malcolm Cowley, and *Afternoon of an Author,* edited by Arthur Mizener, have assured the modern availability of all the good magazine fiction of Fitzgerald's last fifteen years. One of the best stories in *All the Sad Young Men* is "Winter Dreams," a Jay Gatsby-Daisy Buchanan story set in St. Paul and told as if this time Gatsby had wisely given up the enchantress and learned to settle for less. But Dexter Green's dreams, like Gatsby's, are more powerful than he knows. With their loss he has lost his capacity to love anything, or even to feel anything strongly again. "Absolution" is another early story which owes its strength to the conception of Gatsby. It is a provocative sketch of the boyhood days of James Gatz in the Red River Valley of North Dakota. Fitzgerald published it as a separate story after he decided to preserve the mystery of Gatsby's early years. "The Rich Boy," written in 1926, is by common consent one of the half-dozen best Fitzgerald stories. Anson Hunter's privileged New York world is solidly established because Fitzgerald seems so intent on understanding it. The concentration of good American material in this thirty-page story might have provided a lesser novelist – provided he could have understood Anson Hunter – with the substance of a full-length fiction. The story's success seems to justify Fitzgerald's interest in the lives of the rich. He once underlined for his Hollywood friend, Sheilah Graham, a sentence from an Arnold essay, "The question, *how to live*, is itself a moral idea," and in the margin he commented, "This is Arnold at his best, absolutely without preachment." It is entirely appropriate to associate Arnold's Victorian moral seriousness with the quality of Fitzgerald's mind when he wrote "The Rich Boy."

During three years beginning in 1928 he sent the *Saturday Evening Post* a series of fourteen stories out of his boyhood and young manhood. The first eight were based on a portrait of himself as Basil Duke Lee. The last six were built around Josephine, the portrait of the magnetic seventeen-year-old girl of his first love affair. It was characteristic of Fitzgerald to relive his youth during the frustrated and unhappy days of his early thirties. His characters always know how much of their most private emotional life depends upon what Anson Hunter calls the "brightest, freshest, rarest hours" which protect "that superiority he cherished in his heart." Fitzgerald was becoming acquainted with real despondency. His inability to write serious fiction sent him into desperate moods and touched off public acts of violence that ended in nights in jail. In 1928 he wrote Perkins from France, "If you see anyone

I know tell 'em I hate 'em all, him especially. Never want to see 'em again. Why shouldn't I go crazy? My father is a moron and my mother is a neurotic, half insane with pathological nervous worry. Between them they haven't and never have had the brains of Calvin Coolidge. If I knew anything I'd be the best writer in America."

What he knew was his own divided life, and after Zelda's breakdown he began to write the stories of self-appraisal and self-accusation that led up to *Tender Is the Night*. In the autumn of 1930 the *Post* published the first of them, "One Trip Abroad," a Jamesian fable of the deterioration of two American innocents in Europe. Fitzgerald once wrote in his notebook, "France was a land, England was a people, but America . . . was a willingness of the heart." Nelson and Nicole Kelly come to Europe with money, a pair of small talents, his for painting, hers for singing, and the naive hope that they will find somewhere the good life. But willingness of the heart is not enough. They are not serious and self-sufficient, their American vitality makes them restless, and they become dependent on people, parties, and alcohol. Their first sensitiveness to each other hardens into occasional violence, and they end up in the sanatoriums and rest hotels of Switzerland, "a country where very few things begin, but many things end." A better story, "Babylon Revisited" is a compassionate but morally strict portrait of a reformed American drunk who has to confront his complicity in his wife's death during a quarrel in Paris some years before. He wants desperately to get back his young daughter from her aunt and uncle's care, and he would give anything to "jump back a whole generation and trust in character again. . . ." But Charlie Wales cannot escape the furies from his past. He can only learn to face them with personal dignity.

Fitzgerald's big novel *Tender Is the Night* was written in its final form while Fitzgerald was living very close to his wife's illness. She was being treated by doctors in Baltimore — and writing her novel, *Save Me the Waltz*, to tell her version of their lives — and Fitzgerald and their daughter were making a home for her to return to in the countryside nearby. During 1932 and 1933 her health seemed to improve and he finished the manuscript. Then, early in 1934 when he was reading proofs of the novel, she had her most severe breakdown, and for the next six years, except for short periods of stability, she lived her life in hospitals. Their life together was over. It is astonishing that, written under such emotional pressures, *Tender Is the Night* is such a wise and objective novel as it is.

On the simplest level, it is the story of an American marriage. Dr. Richard Diver, a young American psychiatrist, practicing in Switzerland in 1919, falls in love with his patient, Nicole Warren of Chicago, knowing quite well that her transference to him is part of the pattern of her schizophrenia. By consecrating — to use Fitzgerald's word — himself to their marriage, she is finally cured but he is ruined. To imagine Nicole, Fitzgerald could start from Zelda in her illness and partial recovery. But his heroine is also depicted as a beautiful princess of a reigning American family, whose wealth is the source of a monstrous arrogance: Nicole's trauma was the result of her father's incestuous attack on her. Dick Diver is stigmatized with Fitzgerald's understanding of his own weaknesses. He suffers a kind of moral schizophrenia, for his precarious balance comes to depend on Nicole's need for him. After his morale has cracked he still tries to play the role of a confident man, and out of sheer emotional exhaustion he fades at last into the tender night, where he hopes nothing will ever be required of him again.

A weakness charged against the novel by some readers is that the causes of Dick Diver's deterioration are left unclear. Was it the careless, rich Nicole Warren who destroyed him, or his own bad judgment in choosing her? The only explanation the novel offers is Dick's willful self-sacrifice: he gave more generously of himself than any man could afford to. One of the reasons Dick is not coherent is that the quality of his devotion to Nicole — "a wild submergence of the soul, a dipping of all colors into an obscuring dye," it is called — is of the same degree of abandonment as Gatsby's devotion to Daisy. But Dick's romantic soul must be understood "psychologically" as Gatsby's did not need to be; the complexity of the task Fitzgerald set himself is one source of the novel's weakness. Another is Fitzgerald's use of the young movie star, Rosemary Hoyt, as the novel's Nick Carraway. Through her impressionable eyes we first see the Divers and their circle on the summer Riviera before we know the history of the marriage. To begin this long novel dramatically, as he had *Gatsby*, yields some exciting results, but Fitzgerald came to believe it was a mistake not to tell the events of the story chronologically. *Tender Is the Night* has had recent printings in both versions. Fitzgerald's readers can decide for themselves.

Notwithstanding these faults, *Tender Is the Night* is Fitzgerald's weightiest novel. It is full of scenes that stay alive with each rereading, the cast of characters is the largest he ever collected, and the awareness of human variety in the novel's middle distance gives it a place among those American novels which attempt the full narrative mode. Arnold's assumption that how to live is itself a moral idea provides the central substance of the novel. The society Dick has chosen is a lost one, but Dick must function as if he is not lost. To bring happiness to people, including his wife, is to help them fight back selfishness and egotism, to allow their human imaginations to function. To fill in the background of a leisured class with human dignity does not seem a futile mission to Dr. Diver until he fails. For Fitzgerald's hero "charm always had an independent existence"; he calls it "courageous grace." A life of vital response is the only version of the moral life Fitzgerald could imagine, and when Dr. Diver hears the "interior laughter" begin at the expense of his human decency he walks away. He returns to America and his life fades away in small towns in upstate New York as he tries unsuccessfully to practice medicine again.

Dick Diver is Fitzgerald's imagination of himself bereft of vitality, but also without his one strength of purpose, his devotion to literature. The poor reception of *Tender Is the Night* was a stiff blow to his confidence in himself as a writer when that confidence was about all he had left. Nearly all the influential critics discovered the same fault in the novel, that Fitzgerald was uncertain, and in the end unconvincing, about why Dick Diver fell to pieces.

Fitzgerald could only fight back in letters to his friends by asking for a closer reading of his complex story. The novel sold 13,000 copies. His short stories in *Taps at Reveille*, the next year, were greeted by even more hostile reviews and the volume sold only a few thousand. For a writer who in 1925 had received letters of congratulation from Edith Wharton, T. S. Eliot, and Willa Cather, it was depressing to realize that during 1932 and 1933, while he was writing *Tender Is the Night*, the royalties paid for all his previous writing had totaled only $50. His indebtedness to his agent and his publisher began to grow as the prices paid for his stories went down. And between 1934 and 1937 his daily life declined into the crippled state that is now known after his own description of it as "the crack-up." He first fell ill with tuberculosis, and then began to give in more frequently than ever before to alcohol and despondency. Twice before his fortieth birthday he attempted suicide. By 1937 at the age of forty-one he had recovered control sufficiently to accept a writing contract in Hollywood where he could begin to pay off his debts which by this time had grown to $40,000.

Fitzgerald's public analysis of his desperate condition, published in three essays in *Esquire* in the spring of 1936, will be read differently by different people. But some kind of public penance was probably a necessary part of the pattern of Fitzgerald's life. "You've got to sell your heart," he advised a young writer in 1938, and he had — from his first college writing to *Tender Is the Night*. "Forget your personal tragedy . . ." Hemingway wrote him in 1934 after reading *Tender Is the Night*. "You see, Bo, you're not a tragic character. Neither am I. All we are is writers and what we should do is write." Hemingway and Edmund Wilson both disapproved of Fitzgerald's confessions as bad strategy for a writer. The only explanation one can imagine Fitzgerald making to them is Gatsby's explanation, that it was only personal.

The crack-up essays have become classics, as well known as the best of Fitzgerald's short fiction. The spiritual lassitude they describe is attributed to the same "lesion of vitality" and "emotional bankruptcy" that Dick Diver and Anthony Patch and all Fitzgerald's sad young men suffer. Fitzgerald calls it becoming "identified with the objects of my horror and compassion." As Fitzgerald describes it here it closely resembles what in Coleridge's ode "Dejection" is called simply the loss of joy. The process of its withdrawal from Coleridge as a power which he had drawn on too often he describes as stealing "From my own nature all the natural man." Fitzgerald was conscious of his relation to the English Romantics in his confession. He calls up the examples of Wordsworth and Keats to represent good writers who fought their way through the horrors of their lives. The loss of his natural human pieties that Fitzgerald felt he associated with a memory of "the beady-eyed men I used to see on the commuting train from Great Neck fifteen years back – men who didn't care whether the world tumbled into chaos tomorrow if it spared their houses." Fitzgerald's style was never more gracefully colloquial or his metaphors more natural and easy than in these *Esquire* pieces. "I was impelled to think. God, was it difficult! The moving about of great secret trunks." The grace of the prose has made some readers suspect that Fitzgerald is withholding the real ugliness of the experience, that he is simply imitating the gracefully guilty man in order to avoid the deeper confrontation of horror. But his language often rises above sentiment and pathos to the pure candor of a generous man who decided "There was to be no more giving of myself" and then, in writing it down, tried to give once more.

Once settled in Hollywood and in love with Miss Graham Fitzgerald returned to the East only occasionally – and usually disastrously. He needed any strength he could muster to try to stay away from drinking and hold on to his contract as a movie writer. For a year and a half he commanded a salary of over $1000 a week, and, given the breaks, he said, he could double that within two years. One of his breaks was Miss Graham, who helped him to live a quiet productive life for almost a year after they met. But late in 1938 his contract was not renewed and in February 1939 he drank himself out of a movie job in Hanover, New Hampshire, a disaster that Budd Schulberg has turned into a novel and a play, *The Disenchanted.* For several months in 1939 he was in a New

York hospital but by July he was writing short stories again for *Esquire.* He wrote in all twenty-two stories in the eighteen months remaining to him, seventeen of them neat and comic little stories about a corrupt movie writer named Pat Hobby, and one little masterpiece, "The Lost Decade," a sardonic picture of a talented man who had been drunk for ten years.

During the last year of his life Fitzgerald wrote as hard as his depleted capacities allowed him on the novel he left half-finished at his death, *The Last Tycoon.* It is an impressive fragment. When it was published in 1941 many of Fitzgerald's literary contemporaries, including John Dos Passos and Edmund Wilson, called it the mature fulfillment of Fitzgerald's great talent, and a belated revaluation of Fitzgerald as a writer began.

The Last Tycoon had the mark of the thirties on it as surely as his early novels had the American boom as their principal theme. The subject was Hollywood as an industry and a society, but also as an American microcosm. Instead of drawing a deft impression of American society as he had in his earlier fiction, Fitzgerald now wanted to record it. The first hundred pages of the novel take us behind the doors of studios and executive offices in Hollywood with the authority of first-rate history. The history fastens on the last of the American barons, Hollywood's top producer, Monroe Stahr, and we watch him rule a complex industry and produce a powerful popular art form with such a dedication of intelligence and will that he becomes a symbol for a vanishing American grandeur of character and role. "Unlike *Tender Is the Night,*" Fitzgerald explained, "it is not the story of deterioration – it is not depressing and not morbid in spite of the tragic ending. If one book could ever be 'like' another, I should say it is more 'like' *The Great Gatsby* . . ." The plot was to show Stahr's fight for the cause of the powerful and responsible individual against Hollywood's labor gangsters and Communist writers. Violent action and melodrama were to carry the story, like a Dickens novel, to seats of power in Washington and New York. "Action is character," Fitzgerald reminded himself in one of his last notes on his novel's progress. The action is brilliantly conceived and economically executed. Fitzgerald's style is lean and clear. His power of letting his meanings emerge from incident was never more sharply displayed. At the center of his hero's last two years of life is an ill-starred love affair, like Fitzgerald's own, that comes too late and only reminds him of his lost first wife. But Fitzgerald kept his romantic ego in check in imagining Stahr. What obviously fascinated him was the creation of an American type upon whom responsibility and power had descended and who was committed to building something with his power, something that would last, even though it was only a brief scene in a movie.

It was an ironic and courageous image for Fitzgerald to cherish in the last days of his crippled life. He had not written order into his life, though he once noted wryly that he sometimes read his own books for advice. But his devotion to his writing up to the end shows how much his work flowed from his character as well as from his talent. It is hard in coming to terms with Fitzgerald to follow Lawrence's advice and learn to trust the tale, not the author. But if we succeed we shall learn that the aspects of himself that he continually made into the characters in his fiction are imaginatively re-created American lives. He often wrote that high order of self-revelation that reveals humanity.

William Faulkner

WILLIAM FAULKNER'S Yoknapatawpha County, Missis-
sippi, with Jefferson as the county seat, is both a mythical and an
actual region. Reality and myth are difficult to separate because
Faulkner has transcribed the geography, the history, and the people of northern Mississippi, and he has also transmuted them.
Clearly it is more sensible to see Yoknapatawpha County and its
people as a little self-contained world of the imagination than as
an accurate history, from the time of the Chickasaw Indians down
to the present, of northern Mississippi.

Yoknapatawpha County is an area of 2400 square miles, with
a population of 15,611 persons. There is the rich delta land of
the hunt; there is the sand and brush country; there is Jefferson,
with its jail, the town square, and the old houses emanating decay; there is Beat Four, and there is the Old Frenchman's Place;
there are dusty roads, swamps, cemeteries, a railroad, and there is
the great river, sometimes smooth and deep but when in flood
wild, turbulent, and destructive. More than several generations
inhabit Yoknapatawpha County: Indians, slaves, plantation own-
ers, Civil War soldiers, bushwackers, genteel old ladies, veterans,
first of the Civil War, then of World War I, and finally of World
War II, exploiters, servants, peddlers, preachers, lawyers, doctors,
farmers, college students, and many others. The pigeons in a
church belfry, the scent of honeysuckle, a sultry July afternoon,
the drugstore on Sunday afternoon, the rancid smells of a Negro
cabin, the clop-clop of a horse's hooves in the town square — these

and a hundred other scenes have, thanks to Faulkner's descriptive powers, become part of a timeless panorama.

And perhaps one should add that this mythical country, as a part of the South, is seen as being very different from the rest of the United States, the West, the East, and the North. The southerner, the resident of Yoknapatawpha County, carries his burden of guilt, his part in the troubled and painful heritage that began with slavery, and he responds to it in his individual way.

Northern Mississippi — especially the town of Oxford ("Jefferson") and Lafayette County ("Yoknapatawpha County") — was Faulkner's own territory. His family had lived there since before the Civil War. As a family they had moments of high achievement, and they saw days when the family and its future seemed menaced. Faulkner pondered the family history and his own personal history — and he used both in writing his stories.

William Faulkner was born in New Albany, Mississippi, in 1897. In 1902 his family moved to Oxford, the seat of the University of Mississippi, where his father, Murray C. Falkner, ran a livery stable and a hardware store, and later was business manager of the university. (The *u* was added to the family name by the printer who set up William's first book, *The Marble Faun*.) Faulkner's mother was Maud Butler. There were four children: William, Murray, John, and Dean.

William C. Falkner, William's great-grandfather, was born in 1825. He has been a legendary figure in northern Mississippi. The details in his life, many of which turn up in his great-grandson's books, read like episodes in a picaresque novel. Twice he was acquitted of murder charges. He was a severe disciplinarian and a dashing soldier as the colonel of a group of raiders in the Civil War. He had begun as a poor youngster trying to earn enough money to help his widowed mother, but he ended his career as the owner of a railroad and a member of the state legislature. He was killed by his former railroad partner shortly after he had defeated the latter for a seat in the legislature. Appropriately, there is a statue of William C. Falkner facing his railroad.

William C. Falkner's son, J. W. T. Falkner, the novelist's grandfather, was a lawyer, a banker, and an assistant United States attorney. He was active in the "rise of the 'rednecks,'" the political movement that gave greater suffrage to tenant farmers. Those residents of Oxford who can remember him say he was a man of stiff dignity, deaf, and with a testy, explosive temper.

The great-grandfather and the grandfather are obviously the originals for Colonel Sartoris and Bayard Sartoris in *Sartoris, The Unvanquished*, and many other stories. They are a part of the legend of the Old South, and they play an important part in Faulkner's Yoknapatawpha saga. Faulkner's immediate family seem, in a more indirect fashion, to be the originals for the Compson family. They are central in *The Sound and the Fury*, but they appear also in other stories.

William Faulkner was a poor student, and left high school after the tenth grade for a job in his grandfather's bank. He read widely, and wrote poetry. He also tried his hand at painting. He was a moody young man and a puzzle to the townspeople of Oxford. In 1914 he began a friendship with Phil Stone, a young lawyer, which gave him a chance for literary discussions and helped acquaint him with such rising reputations as Conrad Aiken, Robert Frost, Ezra Pound, and Sherwood Anderson.

Because he was underweight and only five feet five in height, Faulkner was turned down by the United States Army. He succeeded, however, in joining the Royal Flying Corps in Toronto, Canada, as a cadet. On December 22, 1918, the date of demobilization, he became an honorary second lieutenant. Like most other writers of his age, Faulkner has often been preoccupied with both the events and the implications of World War I. His early books deal with it, and one of his later, *A Fable*.

As a veteran he was allowed to enroll at the University of Mississippi, where he studied English, Spanish, and French, but he was in residence for only one full academic year. Some of his contributions to student publications suggest that he was a witty and sardonic young man who was having difficulty in finding himself either as an artist or professionally. He took a job in a bookstore in New York City, but this did not last long and he was soon back in Oxford. For two years he did odd jobs, as a carpenter and house painter, then became postmaster at the university. He soon resigned, saying in his letter of resignation, "I will be damned if I propose to be at the beck and call of every itinerant scoundrel who has two cents to invest in a postage stamp." This same year, 1924, saw the publication of *The Marble Faun*, an imitative book of poems. Stone had subsidized its publication.

Faulkner decided to go to Europe, by way of New Orleans. Once in New Orleans, however, he stayed for six months. He wrote a few sketches for the *Times-Picayune* entitled "Mirrors of Chartres Street," contributed to the *Double-Dealer*, an important "little magazine," and became friends with Sherwood Anderson, at that time one of the most admired of American writers. He also wrote his first novel, *Soldiers' Pay*, which Anderson helped him get published. He and Anderson remained friends despite differences in temperament which occasioned quarrels and despite Faulkner's having written a parody of Anderson's style in *Sherwood Anderson and Other Creoles*, a volume of drawings by William Spratling, one of his New Orleans friends. In this book there is a drawing by Spratling of Faulkner and himself sitting at a table painting, writing, and drinking. On the wall there is a sign reading "Viva Art." Beneath Faulkner's chair are three gallons of corn liquor. In June 1925, Faulkner and Spratling shipped on a freighter for Italy and a walking trip through France and Germany.

Faulkner was back in New York for the publication, in March 1926, of *Soldiers' Pay*, a self-consciously elegant novel about the "lost generation." Its style is indebted to Swinburne and Beardsley, or, more generally, to the *fin de siècle* tradition. This is an example: "They had another drink. The music beat on among youthful leaves, into the darkness, beneath the gold and mute cacophony of stars. The light from the veranda was lost, the house loomed huge against the sky: a rock against which waves of trees broke, and breaking were forever arrested: and stars were golden unicorns neighing unheard through blue meadows, spurning them with hooves sharp and scintillant as ice. The sky, so remote, so sad, spurned by the unicorns of gold, that, neighing soundlessly from dusk to dawn had seen them, had seen her — her taut body prone and naked as a narrow pool . . . " The *fin de siècle* tradition never matured in the United States, unless it can be said to have matured in the poetry of Wallace Stevens, but in the young Faulkner America had a writer greatly attracted to it. Thematically the novel comes to very little, but clearly the young man who wrote it had talent. *Soldiers' Pay* received favorable reviews, and its publisher signed a contract for a second novel. Faulkner went off to Pascagoula, Mississippi, to write it.

Mosquitoes, published in 1927, used New Orleans as a setting. Insofar as it has a theme *Mosquitoes* says that actions are more important than words and doers more important than talkers. It is a satirical novel, but most of the satire is heavy-handed. One of the characters, Dawson Fairchild, is based on Anderson, and one of the more interesting parts of the book is a series of "tall tales" which Faulkner later said he and Anderson had worked up together. *Mosquitoes* was less well received than *Soldiers' Pay*.

Sartoris (1929) helped Faulkner find himself as a writer. Doing it, he "discovered that writing is a mighty fine thing; it enabled you to make men stand on their hind legs and cast a long shadow." *Sartoris* is an uncritical account of the Sartoris (or Falkner) family legend, brought down to Faulkner's own generation, and centered in young Bayard, a war veteran. He is one of the young men Gertrude Stein called the "lost generation," but he is also preoccupied with his southern heritage. *Sartoris* is a source book for many later stories, and in writing it Faulkner began to see and feel the dignity and pathos of what was to become his most persistent subject matter.

While writing *Sartoris* Faulkner had also been working on *The Sound and the Fury*. They were published within a few months of each other. *Sartoris* marks the end of an apprenticeship. *The Sound and the Fury* is the work of a major writer.

In June 1929 Faulkner married Estelle Oldham and settled down to a career as a writer. Within a ten-year span he wrote and published most of what has come to be regarded as his major work. There were trips to Hollywood, where he worked on movie scripts, and trips to New York City, but mostly he remained in Oxford. *Sanctuary* brought him notoriety. Critical acclaim came more slowly. Oddly, the French recognized Faulkner's power more quickly and more widely than Americans did. André Malraux wrote a preface for *Sanctuary*, and Jean-Paul Sartre wrote a long critical essay on Faulkner's work. In 1946, when Malcolm Cowley published his influential *Portable Faulkner*, all of Faulkner's books were out of print, and there had been very little serious criticism devoted to Faulkner. But valuable studies began in 1946, and now there is hardly a critical or scholarly journal that has failed to devote article after article to Faulkner. The Nobel Prize was awarded to him in 1950. Faulkner, accompanied by his daughter, went to Sweden, and delivered an address that has been widely acclaimed. Many other awards followed, including Pulitzer prizes for *The Town* and, posthumously, *The Reivers*. Faulkner visited European countries, especially France, spent some weeks in Japan in 1955, and made occasional public appearances in the United States. In 1957 he was a writer in residence at the University of Virginia. Three weeks after being thrown from a horse, he died, from a heart attack, in Oxford, Mississippi, July 6, 1962.

Many editions of Faulkner's books continue to appear, especially in inexpensive reprints; versions of some of them are done for television and the movies; and *Requiem for a Nun* had a run as a Broadway play, was performed in many European countries, and in France was adapted by Albert Camus. Faulkner has been accepted as a great American writer, despite occasional cries of dissent from readers and sometimes from critics who feel he is overvalued, is wildly rhetorical or merely obscure and difficult to read. The admirers of Faulkner sometimes claim that his detractors disparage him because they fail to understand the nature of his genius, and his detractors sometimes say Faulkner's admirers are bemused by his rhetoric. The truth lies in between.

Robert Penn Warren, in an article first published in 1946, says this: "William Faulkner has written nineteen books which for range of effect, philosophical weight, originality of style, variety of characterization, humor, and tragic intensity, are without equal in our time and country. Let us grant, even so, that there are grave defects in Faulkner's work. Sometimes the tragic intensity becomes mere emotionalism, the technical virtuosity mere complication, the philosophical weight mere confusion of mind. Let us grant that much, for Faulkner is a very uneven writer. The unevenness is, in a way, an index to his vitality, his willingness to take risks, to try for new effects, to make new explorations of material and method." Mr. Warren implies that Faulkner's admirers do him no service when they refuse to recognize that his limitations are sometimes inextricably intertwined with his great achievements.

A few of Faulkner's critics have also tried to schematize his themes, saying, for example, that he favors the antebellum "aristocrats" and their descendants over other groups in southern society, or that he is anti-modern and sees only evils in twentieth-century industrialization and mechanization. Anyone who takes Faulkner's novels in chronological order, summarizing their plots and analyzing their themes, as is done here, can see that no such schematic account really works.

The critic of, say, Robert Frost, Wallace Stevens, or Ernest Hemingway can write a long essay tracing persistent themes. In each of these writers there is a homogeneity of subject and point of view from the first book to the last. This is not the case with Faulkner. Nor is there a large "philosophical" subject, as there is in Henry James or Robert Penn Warren, that is being investigated and enlarged in each succeeding book. One can say that Faulkner lived in a section of the country where nineteenth-century pieties are more alive than they are in other regions of the United States and that these pieties sometimes conflicted with the assumptions that Faulkner as a product of the twentieth century tended to hold. But again this conflict is not the controlling or central theme in any particular novel. Perhaps the best way of generalizing about Faulkner's themes is to say that he accepts the elementary Christian virtues, providing one adds at once that certain of the forms of conduct Faulkner seems to advocate in certain novels would be seen as perverse or as evil by most orthodox Christians. A fair and just method in writing about his career — the method attempted in this essay — is to take the major works one at a time, summarizing the action, sorting out the themes, and describing, since Faulkner is an important innovator, the method of narration.

Faulkner once said he had "written his guts" into *The Sound and the Fury*. Many of his admirers believe it is his best novel, and one of the greatest novels written in the twentieth century. Without doubt it is a work of great virtuosity, even genius, but there is some critical disagreement about what Faulkner was trying to say in it.

The Sound and the Fury is clearly a "modern" novel. It is in the impressionistic tradition of James, Conrad, Crane, Ford Madox Ford, and Joyce — the tradition that said "Life does not narrate but makes impressions on our brains." And that said the novelist allows, or seems to allow, the story to tell itself; he does not intrude. (To Joyce in particular Faulkner owes the interior monologue, the stream of consciousness, and portmanteau words.) Occasionally, however, Faulkner does intrude, but in a special sense: he lends his own rhetorical voice, a kind of chorus, to a character. For example, Quentin Compson, who ordinarily is shown thinking in a disordered, disturbed, even mad fashion, suddenly remembers in a quite different sort of language a train trip during which he had seen, from the window, an old Negro astride a small mule. This is the passage:

Then the train began to move. I leaned out the window, into the cold air, looking back. He stood there beside the gaunt rabbit of a mule, the two of them shabby and motionless and unimpatient. The train swung around the curve, the engine puffing with short, heavy blasts, and they passed smoothly from sight that way, with that quality about them of shabby and timeless patience, of static serenity: that blending of childlike and ready incompetence and paradoxical reliability that tends and protects them it loves out of all reason and robs them steadily and evades responsibility and obligations by means too barefaced to be called subterfuge even and is taken in theft or evasion with only that

frank and spontaneous admiration for the victor which a gentleman feels for anyone who beats him in a fair contest, and withal
a fond and unflagging tolerance for whitefolks' vagaries like that
of a grandparent for unpredictable and troublesome children
which I had forgotten.

The passage is very similar to *Sartoris* in which Faulkner himself is doing the narrating. Faulkner's rhetorical voice intrudes in
this fashion in all the books subsequent to *The Sound and the
Fury*. But primarily the characters think and speak in their own
peculiar fashion. Thus Benjy, the idiot, watching a golfing match:
"Through the fence, between the curling flower spaces, I could
see them hitting. They were coming toward where the flag was
and I went along the fence. Luster was hunting in the grass by
the flower tree. They took the flag out, and they were hitting."
All of Benjy's thoughts have to do with sensations, with smells,
eating, going to bed, or tones of voice. Time past and time present
merge and interflow in his mind. He never speculates or plans
— he feels. Jason Compson's thoughts and speech are invariably
ironic, expressing his bitter humor and frustration: "I told Mother
goodnight and went on to my room and got the box out and
counted it again. I could hear the Great American Gelding snor-
ing away like a planing mill. I read somewhere they'd fix men that
way to give them women's voices. But maybe he didn't know what
they'd done to him. I dont reckon he even knew what he had been
trying to do, or why Mr. Burgess knocked him out with the fence
picket." Everywhere in *The Sound and the Fury* the reader sees,
hears, and experiences, whether it is the young Compson children
getting ready for bed, the tone of the genteel and whining Mrs.
Compson, the decency and patience of Dilsey, the magnificently
rendered Negro sermon, or the sound of Queenie's hooves in the
town square.

The primary story being told in *The Sound and the Fury* is
the decline of a family. The family has had generals, a governor,
and wealthy planters. They had owned the Compson Mile. In a
chronology of the Compsons, done for Malcolm Cowley's *Portable Faulkner*, Faulkner traces the family history from 1699 to

1945. But the novel proper is limited from June 2, 1910, to April 8, 1928, and it tells what happens to the last generation of Compsons. Mr. Compson is a witty but alcoholic lawyer, and Mrs. Compson is preoccupied with her honor, faded glories, and present indignities, such as her idiot son and ineffectual brother Maury. Candace, Quentin, Jason, and Benjy are seen as children and as adults.

Quentin is seen in Cambridge, Massachusetts, readying himself for suicide: he contemplates his family but particularly Candace's fornication with Dalton Ames and her marriage to Sydney Herbert Head. His experiences during that day (June 2, 1910) impinge in a shadowy way on his memories, more especially his frustrated desire to free himself and Candace from time's meaningless roar. Behind his desire to commit incest with Candace was the hope that this would cause Jehovah to cast them into hell for eternity. But his father had told him that virginity was an ideal invented by men, and that his talk of incest was merely a way of giving himself a significance neither he nor anyone else can have. Except for Candace, Quentin also feels unloved. Once he says, *"I have no mother."*

As an adult, Jason IV, Quentin's brother, works in a hardware store, plays the stock market, and systematically steals the money Candace sends for the board and room of her illegitimate daughter, named Quentin. The girl, to whom Jason is always mean and sometimes cruel, steals the money from him and runs off with a fellow employed by a carnival. Jason is unable either to find them or to recover the money — and his frustrations are nearly unbearable. Jason is scornful of tradition, of principle and honor.

It is Dilsey, the old Negress, decent, sympathetic, and responsible, who provides the coherence and moral principles against which the Compsons are, by implication, judged. She is one of Faulkner's most memorable characters.

Faulkner has said *The Sound and the Fury* is a story of "lost innocence." It is also the history of an inward-turning family living for the most part in the past. As such, it is reminiscent of Hawthorne's *The House of the Seven Gables.* It is also reminiscent of Dostoevski's *The Brothers Karamazov*. One critic has said that Quentin has some kinship with Raskolnikov in *Crime and Punishment*. If *The Sound and the Fury* is seen as essentially Quentin's story (certainly a partial and lopsided emphasis) it becomes the search of the modern protagonist, usually a sensitive aesthete, for a sense of radical significance. It can also be read as a failure of love within a family, an absence of self-respect and of mutual respect. It is a southern story. It is a twentieth-century story. And as the fall of a house it is akin to some of the most ancient stories in Western literature.

As I Lay Dying (1930) is both a simple and a puzzling book. Structurally and stylistically it exhibits Faulkner's amazing virtuosity. Concentrating on a character at a time, fifteen of them in all, the action breaks into sixty sections. Each character, simultaneously refracting and participating in the forward movement of the story, cuts into the substance and suggests meanings to the degree possible to his consciousness and perception. The technique makes for what Henry James called the "highest possible degree of saturation." But it also makes for some confusion. Is it Addie's story? Or Darl's or Cash's, or the story of all of them and that of the other participants as well? A further complication is that *As I Lay Dying* exists on two levels, as a ritualistic and symbolic journey and as a naturalistic and psychological story. For, although it is set in Mississippi and is about a "redneck" family, *As I Lay Dying* evokes memories of ancient times and places far away. Neither *As I Lay Dying* nor any other Faulkner novel should be read as having a one-to-one relationship with northern Mississippi. They are highly stylized stories — and their geography is more of the soul than of Mississippi.

The funeral journey could suggest the Mosaic trek out of Egypt, the crossing of the river Jordan, the difficult journey of the dead across the river Styx, the long caravans on sacred journeys to Mecca or to some sanctuary within Mongolia or Tibet. Addie Bundren's funeral journey has an epic tone. It is a ritual, the fulfilling of a promise. Each member of the family is given an opportunity to ponder his relationship to the others, especially to Addie. But Addie herself is not a simple or absolute symbol of virtue and wisdom, although she is an amazingly vital and in some ways an admirable person. *As I Lay Dying* does not minimize selfishness, aggrandizement, obsessions, or plain human stupidity. In tone it can be quiet, grim, wild, bizarre, or sublime. Faulkner does not pretend that at the journey's end each character has had his opportunity to drink from the cup of wisdom and go home fully renewed. Darl goes mad, little Vardaman is as bemused as ever, Dewey Dell is simply frustrated, and Anse has used the burial journey as a way of getting a new wife.

Essentially this is the action: Addie Bundren is dying. Cash, the eldest son, is building a coffin for her. Anse, her husband, allows others to carry his burdens and is given to easy self-justification. Darl, the second son, rejected by Addie, has what is sometimes called "second sight." Jewel is Addie's illegitimate son, fathered by Whitfield, a self-justifying preacher. Dewey Dell, the fourth child, is pregnant by Lafe, a neighbor boy. Darl knows, without being told, that Jewel is Addie's illegitimate, as well as best loved, son, and he knows Dewey Dell wants to get to Jefferson to buy abortion pills. The youngest child Vardaman, who sometimes seems moronic, thinks Dr. Peabody has killed his mother, and confuses a dead fish with his dead mother. (Dr. Peabody, entering the action from outside the family, provides a way of evaluating them.) Addie wants to be buried in Jefferson, where her family are buried. Exacting a promise from Anse, she feels, will involve him, and possibly allow her life to enter his in a way it never had before. After her death, the family set out for Jefferson. The journey is a nightmare. The coffin is upset in a stream. Cash's leg is broken and Anse, to save money, coats it with cement. Darl sets fire to a barn to destroy Addie's corpse, but she is saved by Jewel. Buzzards follow them. A druggist refuses to sell pills to Dewey Dell, and a soda clerk seduces her. Anse borrows a spade and shovel to dig Addie's grave. Darl is taken off to the asylum in Jackson, and Anse, having taken Dewey Dell's money, buys new teeth and gets himself a new wife.

Addie's belief is that one should violate one's aloneness, should not allow words like *sin* or *love* to serve in lieu of violation and involvement. And she has tried to live this way — getting ready to be dead. This doctrine is sometimes said to be the theme of the novel. But Addie also has curious rationalizations: Cash is her true son, she says, because while carrying him she had not yet realized that Anse's life did not violate hers nor her life violate his. Her second child Darl seemed a betrayal, and she rejects him. Then she had Jewel — but Whitfield is like Anse, so she feels Jewel is solely hers. She had Dewey Dell and Vardaman to make up for her having had Jewel. The two sons she accepts, Cash and Jewel, make great sacrifices to get her to Jefferson. Darl hates Jewel because Addie loved him, and he tries to prevent her getting there. He says: "I have no mother." Dewey Dell is indifferent to her mother and Vardaman is incapable of a moral decision.

There are several themes. According to Addie, one has an obligation to be involved, and to accept the accompanying and inevitable violence and suffering. Cash and Jewel apparently accept her doctrine, and live by it. Anse and the remaining children, for various reasons, do not. The three children are also victims of the lack of love between Anse and Addie. Addie, while faithful to her belief in the need for violation, is not faithful to Darl, Dewey Dell, or Vardaman, the children of her flesh though not of her doctrine. She rejects them. And in Darl, as a poetic, speculative type ("sicklied o'er with the pale cast of thought"), there is a third theme. He is not unlike Quentin Compson (both see themselves as motherless) in his preoccupation with man as a lost creature in the universe. He gives himself to speculations and searches into the dark corners of other people's minds. Cash holds fast to the physical world, and so does Jewel. But Darl, like Quentin Compson, loses his hold and goes mad.

These, then, are the major themes — Addie's doctrine of involvement, the consequences that follow the breakdown of family love, and the dangers in turning away from action and giving oneself to endless speculation. And if one wanted to concentrate attention on Anse, or certain other characters, undoubtedly still further themes could be pointed up. The fifteen characters in their relationships with each other, especially with Addie, and in the way they illuminate the several themes seem a part of the world's mystery and irreducible complexity.

Sanctuary (1931) made Faulkner famous. In the preface to the Modern Library edition, he says he once asked himself what would sell at least 10,000 copies. He hit upon the horrific story of the rape of a coed by a perverted gangster, wrote it in three weeks, and sent it off. His publisher, Harrison Smith, answered almost at once, "Good God, I can't publish this. We'd both be in jail." This was before Faulkner had written either *The Sound and the Fury* or *As I Lay Dying*. He says he had forgotten about it when the galleys arrived. Harrison Smith had obviously changed his mind. At the cost of several hundred dollars to himself Faulkner made extensive revisions.

Sanctuary is a "thriller," or, in its own way, what another writer, Graham Greene, calls an "entertainment." It is not Faulkner's fiction at its serious best. At least one of the themes — the attack on modernism — is stated too insistently and without qualification. And the image of the world as a "cooling ball in space," borrowed from *fin de siècle* writers, is self-consciously "literary." But *Sanctuary* is obviously the work of a skillful and highly inventive novelist.

The sexual evils in *Sanctuary* are identified with the oldness and the decay of the world, with the grape and honeysuckle, and the changing seasons; there is "a conspiracy of female flesh and female season." Sex "writhes like cold smoke." Throughout the book descriptions and characterizations are made in terms of nature and flower imagery. There are also descriptions and characterizations made in terms of metallic and mechanical images. Both serve to suggest a society for whom sex is only lust and human relationships merely amoral engagement.

Sanctuary opens as a Gothic story, then moves toward and merges into a double vision, as though in montage, of amoral modernism and the world as ripe and overripe. The Gothic beginnings include the remote Old Frenchman's Place, a decayed plantation house, surrounded by a foreboding woods. The sky is dark, there are dimly perceived movements, and strange sounds. There is a blind man whose "cataracted eyes looked like two clots of phlegm." The maiden-heroine is Temple Drake, the hero is the ineffectual and alcoholic Gowan Stevens; they are parodies of the usual Gothic heroine and hero. Temple flees from Lee Goodwin, who plans to seduce her, and escapes, with the aid of the moron Tommy, to a rat-infested corncrib. She is discovered there by Popeye, who shoots Tommy and rapes her with a corncob, a scene that outdoes any of the sexual crimes found in Gothic fiction. Popeye sets her up in a Memphis whorehouse. He arranges for a young man named Red to be her lover, and he, Popeye, is present during their lovemaking. Temple becomes thoroughly depraved, a fact upon which much of the subsequent action depends.

Popeye is sometimes said to represent amoral modernism. He is impotent, but with the aid of Natural Lust (Red), he corrupts Southern Womanhood (Temple), and she becomes his ally. Formalized Tradition (Horace Benbow, the lawyer) tries to defend Goodwin, who is accused of the murder of Tommy, but the Amoral Modernists (the politicians, the townspeople, and Eustace Graham, the district attorney) see to it that Goodwin is lynched. Faulkner himself said that Popeye was "all allegory." Oddly, near the end of the story, Faulkner attempts to account for him psychologically and naturalistically, by recounting Popeye's childhood, thereby destroying some of his effectiveness as a symbol of amoral modernism.

Much of the humor of *Sanctuary* — the scenes with the three madams, Miss Reba's sense of propriety, Uncle Bud's getting drunk, and the escapades of Virgil and Fonzo Snopes — is folk humor. Some of the satire on the townspeople of Jefferson is in the realistic tradition. And there are the characters carried over from *Sartoris*. That the humor, satire, and predefined characterizations (Narcissa's character is different in the two books) do not destroy but rather merge into the nightmarish quality of the book is a tribute to Faulkner's ability to control his materials. But their complexity may also suggest that Faulkner was more concerned with telling a sensational, grim, and sometimes funny story than he was with investigating its significances.

Light in August (1932) is a novel about the spirit of righteousness. Possibly it is in this book that Faulkner is closest to Hawthorne. A source of the spirit of persecution, as developed by both writers, is puritanical righteousness, the inability or refusal to forgive human frailty, the placing of duty above charity. Protestantism, as treated in *Light in August*, is grim, demanding, "stern and implacable." Gail Hightower, the old minister, says that this spirit is behind the lynching of Joe Christmas, the culmination of the novel's action. Of the community he says: "Pleasure, ecstasy they cannot seem to bear. Their escape from it is in violence, in drinking and fighting and praying; catastrophe too, the violence identical and apparently inescapable. *And so why should not their religion drive them to crucifixion of themselves and one another?* And they will do it gladly, gladly. . . . Since to pity him would be to admit self-doubt and to hope for and need pity themselves. They will do it gladly, gladly. That's what is so terrible, terrible."

Faulkner chose to make the community of Jefferson Presbyterian or Calvinist. The United States Census figures show that the Baptists are by far the largest Protestant group in Mississippi, the Methodists the second largest, and the Presbyterians a small minority. Faulkner's reasons for doing this presumably were literary or dramatic. It allowed him to introduce the doctrines of predestination and of man's terrible depravity. (He also attributes such doctrines to the family of Calvin Burden, from New England, even though he says they were Unitarian.) A second reason possibly is that he wanted to stress the Scotch-Irish origins of the majority of the townspeople. (In one of the interviews in *Faulkner at Nagano*, Faulkner is quoted as saying his townspeople are of "Scottish descent." He should have said that many of them are also of Scotch-Irish descent.) Eupheus Hines, the mad grandfather of Joe Christmas, is forever talking about predestination and depravity; Joanna Burden, Joe's guilt-ridden lover, believes that God did not intend that the Negro's plight be ameliorated; and Simon McEachern, Joe's foster father, is a stern Presbyterian elder and on one occasion "the representative of a wrathful and retributive Throne."

But *Light in August* is not wholly an attack on Protestant excesses. Percy Grimm, the town's instrument in killing Joe, does not act in the name of Deity. He sees himself as the agent of patriotism— and Faulkner seems to be saying, through Grimm, whom he once called a Nazi, that patriotism can also generate the sort of righteousness that leads to persecution. Lena Grove and Byron Bunch believe in that peace which, as Hightower describes it, results from sinning and being forgiven. Both of them are fallible, and both are capable of guile. But they are also kindly and sympathetic, and they are able to accept as well as extend charity.

Light in August can also be read in more strictly psychological terms. The child, Joe, is the illegitimate son of Eupheus Hines' daughter. Joe's father is never seen, but he may (only *may*) have been a Negro. Hines refuses to call a doctor for his daughter and she dies in childbirth. On Christmas day (thus the name, Joe Christmas) Hines puts the child into an orphanage, where he is treated impersonally and coldly. On one occasion, while eating stolen toothpaste, he uncomprehendingly witnesses the love-making of the dietician and an intern. He expects to be punished, but the dietician tries to buy his silence. His mad grandfather hovers at the edge of his life, something after the manner of Chillingworth in *The Scarlet Letter*. Later, McEachern, on whose farm he lives and works, disciplines him severely. There is no affection in their relationship. Mrs. McEachern tries to scheme with Joe to outwit McEachern, but the boy refuses her help, her sympathy and affection. Thus Joe is denied a system of rules and sanctions administered with love. For the rest of his life he refuses to give affection or to receive it. Even though he could pass as a white man, Joe chooses to present himself as a Negro; he wants to be rejected. On the other hand, he refuses to accept Negro status in a white society — and in the end this, in part, causes his break with Joanna, which leads to his killing her and to his being lynched.

Hightower also is the product of a too strict upbringing. And his weak constitution is the result of his father's refusal of charity for his wife and child. The young Hightower escapes, by fantasy, into the life his grandfather had lived as a Confederate raider. Hightower enters the church for two reasons, as a shelter from the world and as a means of joining his grandfather's ghost in Jefferson. He meets and marries a girl, the daughter of one of the seminary teachers, who wants desperately to escape from the seminary. He fails her as a husband, and after several affairs she kills herself. His parishioners reject him, and even try to make him leave Jefferson, but he stays on in the town. Only Byron Bunch befriends him. Late in his life Hightower realizes the nature of his own failures, as well as the failure of the church. He makes a futile effort to save Christmas, and he befriends Lena and her child.

Light in August can be interpreted religiously or psychologically — the interpretations come to the same point, that men should treat each other charitably and be tolerant of human weaknesses. If they fail to do so they invite the persecutions, the perversions, and the violence of which the novel is largely composed.

Light in August is very skillfully done. There are three story strands, and each is narrated in a way that illuminates the theme and creates a sense of great variety and multiplicity of life. Although *Light in August* seems to have come out of Faulkner's visceral life, and to exist as a breathing, throbbing, tormented community of human beings, it exhibits a greater intellectual play and resonance than any of his other novels. It may be his highest achievement as a novelist.

Pylon (1935) is a failure, at least when seen in relation to the several books published immediately before it and to *Absalom, Absalom!*, published the year following it. The setting is New Valois, or New Orleans, and the central characters are a reporter, his editor, and a "family" of stunt fliers. Faulkner is not writing about Yoknapatawpha, but he did know New Orleans well, and he knew the newspaper world and stunt flying. The failure does not derive from a limited knowledge of his subject; it derives from a failure in conception.

Faulkner apparently set out to explain the curious "family" — Laverne and her two bed companions, Jack Holmes, a parachute jumper, and Roger Shumann, who races the planes. Laverne does not know which man is the father of her six-year-old boy. The reporter gets involved with the "family" during their stay in New Valois. Early in the novel, he says to his editor, Hagood: "Because they ain't human like us; they couldn't turn those pylons like they do if they had had human blood and senses and they wouldn't want to or dare to if they just had human brains. Burn them like this one tonight and they don't even holler in the fire; crash and it ain't even blood when you haul him out: It's cylinder oil the same as in the crankcase." These people, as Faulkner saw them, belonged to the then new world of machines and speed, which was totally different from anything man had previously known. But when he tries to explain them, to show how and why they are a different breed of human beings, his imagination fails him.

There are no interior monologues, and one never learns what goes on in Roger Shumann's head as he races a plane, finally crashing to his death, or what Jack or Laverne feels during a race or when jumping. Nor is there any attempt to explain their intense sexuality in relation to speed and to jumping, although such a relationship is clearly implied. The explanations for the conduct of Laverne, Roger, Jack, and the mechanic Jiggs are sociological, accounts of their childhoods. None of this illuminates their being a different breed.

In *Faulkner at Nagano*, Faulkner says, "My characters, luckily for me, name themselves. I never have to hunt for their names. Suddenly they tell me who they are. In the conception, quite often, but never very long after I have conceived that character, does he name himself. When he doesn't name himself, I never do. I have written about characters whose names I never did know. Because they didn't tell me. There was one in *Pylon*, for instance, he was the central character in the book, he never did tell me who he was." This is a very revealing comment — and if one considers the names of characters in *Light in August*, for example, one realizes that a character's name in Faulkner's fiction is usually an important part of the characterization itself. The reporter in *Pylon* did not reveal his name because he does not wholly exist. He is borrowed from the dramatis personae of T. S. Eliot. In one chapter his lament is called "Lovesong of J. Alfred Prufrock." Hagood, his editor, is borrowed from Hollywood's conception of newspaper editors, loud, tough, but with hearts of gold.

The whole background of the book, New Orleans, the population, the newspaper office, and the airport, is described as a wasteland. This is a not untypical passage:

She looked at him now: the pale stare without curiosity, perfectly grave, perfectly blank, as he rose, moved, dry loose weightless and sudden and longer than a lath, the disreputable suit ballooning even in this windless conditioned air as he went toward the candy counter. Above the shuffle and murmur of feet in the lobby and above the clash and clatter of crockery in the restaurant the amplified voice still spoke, profound and effortless, as though it were the voice of the steel-and-chromium mausoleum itself, talking of creatures imbued with motion though not with life. . . .

It is as though Faulkner had borrowed, from Eliot, the backdrop of the wasteland and put in front of it his strange "family." The background is painted skillfully enough, but it does not really help to explain the fliers. As always in Faulkner's fiction, there are excellent scenes and striking characters (Jiggs is an example), but the failure of *Pylon* is a failure of its inner life. Faulkner had the *idée*, or germ, for a novel, but it did not develop or mature. The characterization of the reporter wavers because Faulkner does not understand him, the fliers are seen only from the outside, and finally the reader is left with a suspicion or the conviction that the *idée* for *Pylon* was not a good one, or if it was that Faulkner did not know how to make it expand and reveal itself. Interesting too is the fact that *Pylon*, almost alone among

Faulkner's novels, shows no advance in or interest in developing the techniques of fiction.

Absalom, Absalom! (1936) is a pivotal story in Yoknapatawpha stories, and for it Faulkner drew his now famous map with this legend: "Jefferson Co., Mississippi, Area, 2400 Square Miles — Population, Whites, 6298; Negroes, 9313, William Faulkner, Sole Owner and Proprietor." Quentin Compson, soon to go to Harvard, is asked by Miss Rosa Coldfield to tell the story of Thomas Sutpen, her brother-in-law, whom she sees as a "demon," a man so possessed by an ambition to build an impressive plantation and to found a line that he destroys everyone close to him. At Harvard, Quentin is asked by Shreve McCannon to tell him about the South: "Tell me about the South. What's it like there. What do they do there. Why do they live there. . . ." In response Quentin tells the story of Thomas Sutpen and Sutpen's family, aided by letters from his father, and with Shreve's shrewd guesses and inferences thrown in. And at the end, Shreve says, " 'Now I want you to tell me just one thing more. Why do you hate the South?' 'I dont hate it,' Quentin said, quickly, at once, immediately; 'I dont hate it,' he said. *I dont hate it* he thought, panting in the cold air, the iron New England dark; *I dont. I dont! I dont hate it! I dont hate it.*" Sutpen's story, told in a series of anecdotes, guesses, and inferences, represents the South to Quentin. His investigation of Sutpen's rise and fall and the family's subsequent destruction is also an investigation of his own heritage.

Thomas Sutpen's ambition had first been kindled when as a child of a very poor family he had been turned away from the front door of a plantation house, turned away by a liveried Negro. In his early teens he had run away to the West Indies, where he later married Eulalia Bon, and fathered a child, Charles. Learning his wife had a small amount of Negro blood, he had left her and the child. In Mississippi, he bought land from the Indians, built a plantation house, Sutpen's Hundred, married Ellen Coldfield, the daughter of a poor but highly respectable shopkeeper, and fathered two children, Henry and Judith. At the university, Henry met Charles Bon, who was there at his mother's instigation. Thomas Sutpen soon learned the identity of Charles. Sutpen's wife, Ellen, not knowing who Charles was, wanted to see Judith marry him. Thomas Sutpen refused his permission, and Henry quarreled with his father and went off to New Orleans with Charles. Soon they were all caught up in the Civil War, but Thomas Sutpen continued to refuse any sign of recognition or affection toward Charles. Henry learned that Charles was his brother, but, despite this, was willing to condone Charles' marriage with Judith, believing that this perverse relationship would be an appropriate badge of the family's and the South's defeat. It was only when he learned that Charles had Negro blood that he refused to allow it. Charles persisted and Henry killed him. Sutpen himself was finally killed by Wash Jones, the father of Milly Jones, upon whom Sutpen had begot a child. Sutpen had repudiated her because the child was a girl. Sutpen's flaw — he is forever asking what went wrong in his "design" — was not merely his flaw, it was Henry's flaw, and the South's flaw: the inability to accept the Negro as human equal. It was over this that the war was fought and because of this that the Sutpen family was ruined. For example, Charles Etienne St. Valery Bon, the son of Charles Bon, flailed out at the white world much in the way Joe Christmas did. In Thomas Sutpen's case there is a terrifying innocence or literalness in his pursuit of his ambition to found a family. His adherence to his region's attitude toward the Negro is a part of this innocence.

The above is a sketchy account of a story that is heavy with mythic overtones and told in a baroque and frequently tortured prose. Occasionally a character speaks in his or her own voice, but usually the narration is in Faulkner's rhetorical "voice." This passage is Quentin's account of Henry and Charles riding up to the old house:

(It seemed to Quentin that he could actually see them, facing one another at the gate. Inside the gate what was once a park now spread, unkempt, in shaggy desolation, with an air dreamy, remote and aghast like the unshaven face of a man just waking from ether, up to a huge house where a young girl waited in a wedding dress made from stolen scraps, the house partaking too of that air of scaling desolation, not having suffered from invasion but a shell marooned and forgotten in a backwater of catastrophe — a skeleton giving of itself in slow driblets of furniture and carpet, linen and silver, to help to die torn and anguished men who knew, even while dying, that for months now the sacrifice and the anguish were in vain. They faced one another on the two gaunt horses, two men, young, not yet in the world, not yet breathed over long enough, to be old but with old eyes, with unkempt hair and faces gaunt and weathered as if cast by some spartan and even niggard hand from bronze, in worn and patched gray weathered now to the color of dead leaves, the one with the tarnished braid of an officer, the other plain of cuff, the pistol lying yet across the saddle bow unaimed, the two faces calm, the voices not even raised: *Dont you pass the shadow of this post, this branch, Charles;* and *I am going to pass it Henry*) "— and then Wash Jones sitting that saddleless mule before Miss Rosa's gate, shouting her name into the sunny and peaceful quiet of the street, saying 'Air you Rosie Coldfield? Then you better come on out yon. Henry has done shot that durn French feller. Kilt him dead as beef.' "

Frequently the sentences, sometimes a page long, are impressions, seemingly collected piecemeal — inside parentheses or dashes, or in series of phrases and clauses — until a whole scene is dramatically rendered. The elements described within the sentence exist as in a continuum, in living relationships. The total action of the novel also has that quality of seeming to be always in motion, moving forward and backward in time, and constantly adding meanings. Something said in the first chapter is more fully understood chapters later when a relevant detail is added, but is not wholly understood until even a later chapter. *Absalom, Absalom!* is a kind of vortex, with characters and events ever in motion, but finally the reader is able to see that there is a still point at the bottom of the cone, the point in relation to which the characters and events have meaning.

The Unvanquished (1938) is composed of five fairly long stories, each involving Bayard Sartoris' experiences of the Civil War. He and Ringo, his Negro companion, have a number of Tom Sawyerish adventures. In the earlier stories they are boys, in the final story Bayard is a law student at the university, and the war is over. Some of the critics, such as George Marion O'Donnell, who see Faulkner as an apologist for the "aristocrat" of the Old South say this is a novel about the conflict between the Sartorises, who act "traditionally," and the Snopeses, who have no ethical code and employ low cunning. This interpretation of *The Unvanquished* is surely wrong. Some of the stories were published in "slick" magazines and have a minimum of inner life. One sees the boys firing on a troop of Yankees, then scooting for the house and being hid under the wide skirts of Bayard's grandmother, Rosa Millard, while the Yankees search for them, or sees John Sartoris outwitting a Yankee patrol. In one of the stories, "Skirmish at Sartoris," Aunt Louisa insists that Drusilla marry John Sartoris because Drusilla, dressed as a man, has ridden with his raiders. The marriage ceremony is interrupted long enough for John Sartoris to ride to town and shoot two men, thus disenfranchising the Negroes. Then the ceremony is performed. There is almost no attempt to explore the meaning of John Sartoris' action. The only story with thematic force is "Odor of Verbena," in which Bayard, now grown, refuses to engage in a duel with Redlaw, who has shot John Sartoris. Bayard has come to see that John Sartoris' loyalty to a former way of life invited not merely heroics but wanton killing. He sees Drusilla as "voracious," wholly indifferent to killing if done in the name of "honor." And he sees that George Wyatt and other gentlemen who want Redlaw killed are playing parts in a theatrical game.

Insofar as *The Unvanquished* is about the "southern code" it is a criticism of that code. But for the most part, the actions in *The Unvanquished* are romantic episodes, the adventures of the two boys and the dashing exploits of John Sartoris. There are many Yoknapatawpha characters brought into the stories, but none of them lives intensely or very meaningfully.

During his stay in New Orleans, Faulkner undoubtedly heard Sherwood Anderson talk about Hemingway. Anderson and Hemingway had known each other since the winter of 1920–21. In 1923 the *Little Review* carried several of Hemingway's stories. That same year the Contact Publishing Company in Dijon published his *Three Stories and Ten Poems*. Other stories appeared in the *Transatlantic*. *In Our Time* appeared in 1925. One may assume that Faulkner knew the Hemingway stance and the Hemingway dramatis personae. *Soldiers' Pay*, in large part, reads like a pastiche of *The Sun Also Rises*. Joe Gilligan and Margaret Powers are ineffective variations on Jake Barnes and Lady Brett. Bayard Sartoris is a kind of Hemingway "initiate," except that he does not really understand the Hemingway code; he feels empty, bleak, hopeless — and seeks his own death.

When he came to write *The Wild Palms* (1939), Faulkner was fully aware of the differences between his vision of the world and Hemingway's vision. Yet there are many parallels with Hemingway's *A Farewell to Arms* in the part of Faulkner's book called "The Wild Palms," which is a love story; "Old Man," the second story in the book, is about a convict and his experiences during a great Mississippi flood.

In "The Wild Palms" Henry Wilbourne, a young intern, falls in love with Charlotte, married and the mother of two children. Charlotte, the more dedicated of the two, urges their absolute commitment to love. She believes that society destroys love. They live in Chicago, on a lake in northern Wisconsin, at a mine in Utah. They know cold and poverty, but nothing is allowed to interfere with their love. Charlotte becomes pregnant and urges Wilbourne to perform an abortion. For a time he refuses but then does as she asks. They return to the Gulf Coast. Charlotte hemorrhages and dies. Wilbourne is arrested, tried, and sent to prison.

In *A Farewell to Arms* Lt. Frederic Henry and Catherine Barkley also resign from society. Like Faulkner's couple, Henry and Catherine feel the world is blind to the needs of lovers. The idyll enjoyed by Hemingway's characters is more peaceful than the "idyll" of Faulkner's lovers, but both women die, one from abortion, the other after childbirth. In both stories the men say that if society catches you "but off step once" (Wilbourne) or "off base" (Henry) it destroys you. When near death both women are on fire from pain, and say "Don't touch me!" In both stories the men are reluctantly allowed to see the corpses of their lovers. In

"The Wild Palms" defeat is symbolized by palms jeering and risible in the wind. In *A Farewell to Arms* it is the rain.

During the Chicago interlude Faulkner's lovers meet a character named McCord, who says, "Yah . . . Set, ye armourous sons, in a sea of hemingwaves." McCord is a bluff newspaperman, and sounds like a Hemingway character or like Hemingway himself. Outdoorsy, he belongs to the country associated with Nick Adams' fishing and hunting and adventures in Michigan. At one point Wilbourne says he has learned something about love from McCord and asks his blessing. " 'Take my curse,' McCord said."

Most commentaries on *The Wild Palms* and *A Farewell to Arms* say that Hemingway's love story is more poignant and touching than Faulkner's — and it is. But Faulkner's all-for-love is not "loaded" to the extent Hemingway's is. Charlotte's love is at the expense of her husband, her children, her own life, and Wilbourne's career and peace of mind. She is not in love with Wilbourne, she is in love with love. Like Hemingway initiates she finds the *meaning* in sex and love. In a sense, Wilbourne is her victim. Faulkner is not saying he accepts the doctrine that society destroys love. On the contrary, he is saying that an excessive commitment to love is itself destructive.

In commenting about the two story lines in *The Wild Palms* Faulkner said that when he finished the first chapter of the love story he felt something was missing. "So I wrote on the Old Man story until *The Wild Palms* rose back to pitch." On yet another occasion, he said he put the two stories together because neither story alone was long enough for book publication. The former explanation makes better sense.

"Old Man" is a criticism of the love story. The Tall Convict, the principal character, accepts his obligations, and goes to almost ridiculous lengths to satisfy his sense of duty. He fights the river in flood, subdues snakes and alligators, avoids bullets intended for him, and voluntarily returns to prison after anguishing adventures. In his bunk, he enjoys watching the smoke from his cigar curl upward in the twilight. He asks only "permission to endure to buy air, to feel sun," and to feel the earth under his feet. Like Dilsey and Byron Bunch, the Tall Convict is one of Faulkner's accepters. Like the character in *As I Lay Dying*, he does not believe "life is supposed to be easy on folks." He knows, although he would not know how to say it, "that love no more exists just at one spot and in one moment and in one body out of all the earth and all time . . . than sunlight does."

The convict does little or no theorizing about his lot. He is courageous and dedicated because he feels compelled to be. He accepts the lot fate has cast him for, and he is happy in it. He is truly free. The lovers refuse to let their love confront limitations or restraints — and in the struggle they are completely, or almost completely, destroyed.

The dramatis personae of *The Hamlet* (1940) are "rednecks," poor farmers. Faulkner describes them as being descendants of nonslaveholders. They have Welsh, Scotch, and English names. "They supported their own churches and schools, they married and committed infrequent adulteries and more frequent homicides among themselves. . . . They were Protestants and Democrats and prolific." Faulkner treats most of them with respect, and there is no indication that he is contemptuous or entertains feelings of superiority about them because of their nonaristocratic heritage.

Essentially *The Hamlet* is the story of the Snopes family, especially Flem, moving into Frenchman's Bend, twenty miles from Jefferson, and systematically defrauding the community. Neither Flem's face nor voice ever indicates emotion and he doesn't even entertain the possibility of acting decently or respecting the rules of fair play. He takes advantage of every gesture of good will made toward him. This is a description of an early encounter between him and Jody Varner, who has heard that Ab Snopes, Flem's father, is a barn burner, and is rightfully fearful:

"Howdy," he said. "You're Flem, aint you? I'm Varner."

"That so?" The other said. He spat. He had a broad flat face. His eyes were the color of stagnant water. He was soft in appearance like Varner himself, though a head shorter, in a soiled white shirt and cheap gray trousers.

"I was hoping to see you," Varner said. "I hear your father has had a little trouble once or twice with landlords. Trouble that might have been serious." The other chewed. "Maybe they never treated him right; I dont know about that and I dont care. What I'm talking about is a mistake, any mistake can be straightened out so that a man can still stay friends with the fellow he aint satisfied with. Dont you agree to that?" The other chewed steadily. His face was as blank as a pan of uncooked dough. "So he wont have to feel that the only thing that can prove his rights is something that will make him have to pick up and leave the country the next day," Varner said. "So there wont come a time some day when he will look around and find out he has run out of new country to move to." Varner ceased. He waited so long this time that the other finally spoke, though Varner was never certain whether this was the reason or not:

"There's a right smart of country."

Flem victimizes the Varners, who are the largest landowners in Frenchman's Bend, marries Eula Varner, a symbol of fertility, of the pagan ripening of spring and summer, dupes most of the townspeople, outwitting even the wily Ratliff, and at the book's end is headed for Jefferson.

The Hamlet is episodic, part of it incorporating earlier short stories. And although the parts dealing with Flem are told mostly in a folk idiom, there are many highly rhetorical and lyrical passages, some of them running for many pages. These passages are mostly devoted to descriptions of Eula and to the idiot Ike Snopes's grotesque love for a cow. There are four story strands dealing with love — there is the marriage of Houston, a farmer, Mink Snopes's marriage, the amours of Eula and her loveless marriage to Flem, and Ike's love for the cow. Ironically Ike's love is a purer form of affirmation and of respect than any of the seemingly "normal" loves. Whether or not the courtly and romantic language in which it is described is an effective device is another question. The writing itself is both dazzling and beautiful. It contrasts sharply with the folk language of the other sections.

Discussions of "native American prose" are usually related to the "tall tale" tradition of the frontier, especially the Southwest. Among the best known of the tall tales are A. B. Longstreet's

Georgia Scenes (1835) and George W. Harris' *Sut Lovingood's Yarns* (1867). It was Mark Twain who first elevated or transformed this sort of humor into literature. In idiom the tall tale is invariably folksy and ungrammatical, and the manner of narration includes both understatement and wild exaggeration. With *The Hamlet*, Faulkner made a major contribution to this "native" strain in American writing. (Ratliff, the sewing machine agent, who is both a participant in and an interpreter of much of the action, belongs to a similar tradition, the Yankee peddler of nineteenth-century literature. Like Ratliff, the peddler was practical, shrewd, witty, and sometimes caustic.) At least three major scenes in *The Hamlet* — the story of horse swapping, Flem Snopes's outwitting the devil, and the wild charging of a horse through a house — are borrowed from the tall-tale tradition.

The Hamlet is a comic novel. It participates in the ancient tradition of man satirizing his own weaknesses. Flem is personal aggrandizement incarnate, and Ratliff is his shrewd, witty, but fallible opponent. The humor of *The Hamlet* is grim, but even so it is humor of a more solacing sort than is to be found in any of the earlier books.

Go Down, Moses (1942) resembles *The Unvanquished* to the extent that both books are composed of interrelated stories. The comparison ends there, however, because *Go Down, Moses* is a serious and moving examination of the shame and pathos of white and black relationships. Undoubtedly the best of the seven stories is the frequently anthologized "The Bear." Properly enough, it is to "The Bear" that many critics turn when trying to explain Faulkner's social and moral doctrines — for in it Faulkner says that a right attitude toward nature should lead one to the right attitude toward human beings, white and black.

Old Ben, the bear, is more than a bear to be hunted — it is a symbol of the wilderness, of freedom, courage, and of the fruitful earth. Sam Fathers, son of a Chickasaw chief and a Negro slave, understands the wilderness and teaches its lessons to Isaac (Ike) McCaslin. From Sam Fathers Ike learns endurance, humility, and courage. No one owns or should own nature — and no one should exploit it. In the first version, published as a short story, Faulkner presents a sacramental view of the world, not unlike that of Coleridge's Ancient Mariner. In the second, revised, version which appears in *Go Down, Moses*, other elements are introduced: the exploitations of civilization and the evils of slavery.

There are two story strands in *Go Down, Moses*, the history of Ike and the history of mulatto "heirs" of old Carothers McCaslin, Ike's grandfather. Ike learns that these heirs usually suffered greatly, mostly from the humiliation of being treated as chattel, as objects, rather than as persons. A partial exception to this is Lucas Beauchamp, who was to become a central figure in *Intruder in the Dust* and who refused to accept the role of inferior being. The antecedents to *Intruder in the Dust* are in "The Fire and the Hearth," the second section of *Go Down, Moses*. Roughly half of the stories in *Go Down, Moses* are about Ike and the wilderness, and half are about the Negroes.

The two story lines meet in the revised "The Bear." Old Ben turns on those who exploit the wilderness, and he is destroyed. And in the long fourth section, Ike and his cousin McCaslin Edmonds discuss the heritage of Carothers McCaslin's Negro heirs. Faulkner's point is that a proper attitude toward the wilderness would, or should, lead to a proper attitude toward the Negro. The point is repeated in "Delta Autumn," in which Ike is an old man of seventy.

Much of the writing in *Go Down, Moses*, especially in "The Bear," has an hallucinatory beauty, especially those scenes describing Old Ben and the virgin fields and forests. Possibly the second best story is "Pantaloon in Black," a marvelous rendering of the actions of a young grief-crazed Negro. However, not all the stories are so successful, nor do all of them fall easily into place in the intended over-all pattern. "Was" is a humorous account of Uncle Bud and Uncle Buck, and of the latter's being trapped into a marriage he was far from desiring. The three chapters entitled "The Fire and the Hearth" have the appearance of incidents that Faulkner intended to work up into a novel. "The Old People" seems largely a preparation for "The Bear," and "Go Down,

Moses," interesting in some of its characterizations, a tacked-on story that adds little or nothing to the themes developed in "The Bear." At its best, however, *Go Down, Moses* provides images of piety, justice, and decency more moving than any similar passages in American literature.

All the novels published after *Go Down, Moses* exhibit Faulkner's characteristic virtues, especially his willingness to try new forms, and his wit, but they also suggest a weakening of his powers. Much of the former hypnotic quality in the rhetoric is diminished, and Faulkner seems less concerned to dramatize his stories. Also he became self-consciously didactic. Social problems invite solutions, and as an eminent writer, and a Nobel Prize winner, he was expected to provide them. Whether he assumed this new role willingly, or out of a sense of duty, does not matter. It was not a role suited to his peculiar genius.

Intruder in the Dust (1948), the first of the late novels, is a moving account of the relationships between young Charles Mallison and Lucas Beauchamp — the slow process of the boy's learning to accept the old Negro as human equal. It is reminiscent of Huck Finn and Nigger Jim. And the rather bizarre incidents — the boy and an elderly lady digging up a corpse, one body being substituted for another, a burial in quicksand, and the actions of the tough Gowrie family from Beat Four — are also reminiscent of the melodrama of *Huckleberry Finn*. On this level *Intruder in the Dust* is a fine story, but Faulkner was not satisfied to let well enough alone. He introduced Gavin Stevens, Charles's uncle, and Lucas' lawyer, and put into Stevens' mouth garrulous and often extraneous speeches about the South versus the North, and the methods that should be followed to bring about better race relations. Unfortunately Stevens' theories are not always convincing, and they seriously interfere with the pace of what would otherwise be a simple and possibly a graceful story.

Knight's Gambit (1949) is a series of detective stories, but Faulkner was unwilling to stay within the conventions of that genre. He employs the usual detective story gimmicks, but adds to them the sort of psychological probing and characterizations that are

peculiar to the short story or the novel. The contrasting conven
tions almost cancel each other out.

In 1950 Faulkner published *Collected Stories*, a drawing together of *These Thirteen* (1931) and *Dr. Martino* (1934), plus
additional stories. There are a few rather run-of-the-mill stories as
there would be in any such collection, but there are enough good
ones to make it clear that Faulkner is among the masters. None
of his contemporaries who are acclaimed as short-story writers has
either his intensity or range. Possibly the best of the stories are
"Red Leaves," about the death of the old Indian chief, Issetibbe-
ha, "Wash," the basis for *Absalom, Absalom!*, "That Evening
Sun," "Dry September," "A Rose for Emily," and "Barn Burning."
The world of Faulkner's short fiction is Shakespearean in its
multiplicity of characters and its variety of nuance, gesture, time,
and place.

Requiem for a Nun (1951), a sequel to *Sanctuary*, is a strange
morality play involving Temple Drake and Gowan Stevens, as
well as Nancy Manigoe and Gavin Stevens. The acts of the play,
reminiscent of Jacobean drama, are interlarded with long historical chapters on Jefferson and the state of Mississippi. Temple and
Gowan, young students in *Sanctuary*, are here a good deal older,
and the parents of a young child. Both of them are restless and
unhappy. The action, which includes the murder of the child by
Nancy Manigoe, carries them to a point where they believe in
purification by suffering and are ready to accept their burdens.
The chapters, involving Temple and Gowan in history, are more
convincingly done, but they do not keep *Requiem for a Nun*
from being a poor performance for a writer of William Faulkner's
stature.

A Fable (1954), set in France, is also a strange book, not so
much a novel as an allegory about man's search for peace. Unfortunately the message or doctrine Faulkner put into it is either
confused and badly worked out or is expressed in such a vague
manner that it is extremely difficult to comprehend. There are
occasional descriptive passages of great brilliance, but few if any
entire scenes are so rendered that they come alive in the reader's

imagination. *A Fable* seems to have been conceived as a speech, or an extended piece of rhetoric, rather than as a novel.

The Town (1957), the second of a promised series on the Snopes clan, is an improvement on *A Fable* but a lesser work than *The Hamlet*. Many of the old characters are in it, but Faulkner, having telescoped time, has also included Charles Mallison and Gavin Stevens. Eula and Flem are not as vividly realized as they are in *The Hamlet*, and the action as a whole is less sharply rendered. But with *The Mansion* (1959), a novel devoted mostly to Mink Snopes, Faulkner shows much of his former power.

The Reivers (1962), published shortly before his death, is Faulkner's most autobiographical novel, a nostalgic reliving of his boyhood in Oxford, when the automobile was new, and wet roads could be all but impassable quagmires. Characters include Boon Hogganbeck, from "The Bear," and Miss Reba, her husband, and the Memphis cathouse, earlier described in *Sanctuary*. The humor has little of the grimness of Faulkner's earlier comedy, but many of the episodes are amusing, and the world of his own childhood is skillfully evoked.

The themes in Faulkner's novels and short stories have to do with the elementary Christian virtues of self-respect and mutual respect, forgiveness of others as well as oneself, fortitude, a proper balance between humility and pride, and charity. Although he disavows any particular orthodoxy, Faulkner obviously accepts the Christian moral code. He is not, however, wholly admiring of practicing Christians. Some of his bitterest satire is at the expense of self-assured piousness. He despises stiff-necked and literal-minded righteousness, whether it is in the service of the southern mores or of Christian doctrines. Since so many of his stories have southern settings, these virtues and vices are frequently presented in a context of white and black relationships. And sometimes his concern with them leads him to study the southern heritage and the "southern code."

Faulkner is a great writer, possibly the finest American novelist, but an essential simplicity of mind is a part of his genius. He is not a sophisticated writer in the sense that Henry James or Joseph Conrad or James Joyce is sophisticated. When he undertakes subjects of a certain magnitude and order, as he did with *Pylon* and *A Fable*, he flounders badly. But when he is treating subjects and themes that he feels in his bones — the frustration of the Negro in "Dry September," the decency of Dilsey in *The Sound and the Fury*, the self-preoccupation of Anse Bundren in *As I Lay Dying*, or the anguish of young Sarty Snopes in "Barn Burning" — Faulkner is magnificent. Faulkner's themes are as simple and as complicated, and persistent, as those in the Bible.

Fortunately, his powers of inventiveness were very great, and he contributed to the theory of the novel as an art form. No other American novelist has created so many memorable characters, and possibly none of them has been his equal as a creator of multiple and varied sorts and levels of life within a novel, as in, say, *Light in August* or *The Hamlet*. Faulkner did not suffer from a lack of imagination.

He was also a master of style, of a "high rhetoric" and of a "folk rhetoric." One of his critics has said, "Faulkner's prose has an archaic sound, like a hunter's horn." This is a good characterization. Faulkner's language and his fictional world evoke the past, or, better, relate the past to the present. Reading Faulkner one feels involved in a long history, of torment, suffering, and anguish but also of endurance, dedication, and love.

When Faulkner was writing and publishing the works of his middle and greatest period, most of his contemporaries, for example Theodore Dreiser, Sinclair Lewis, and John Dos Passos, were writing a more "realistic" fiction. It was more realistic in the sense that they were less likely to create allegorical characters, to invent highly symbolic actions, or to write a poetic or richly rhetorical prose. Their kind of realism was an effort to reflect everyday experience or "ordinary reality." It was a period when many Americans were suspicious of rhetoric, elegance, style, even literary conventions. They would have denied that the "realism" of Dreiser or Lewis or Dos Passos was itself a literary convention. Fiction was held to have documentary value in the sense that

Lewis' Main Street was precisely Main Street, Sauk Centre, Minnesota, where the author had grown up. There was some bewilderment therefore when readers confronted *Sanctuary* or *As I Lay Dying* or *The Hamlet*. Either Faulkner was showing Mississippi as it actually was, or he was exaggerating, and in the latter case he was not telling the truth. More recent criticism has helped to clarify the fact that the literary conventions employed by Faulkner were not those, at least not exclusively those, of the "new realism."

In retrospect we can see that Faulkner's fiction in some ways is closer to earlier literary conventions than it is to the "new realism." The sensational and eerie imaginings of Charles Brockden Brown, Edgar Allan Poe, and even Ambrose Bierce, those specialists in the *frisson*, are clearly a part of Faulkner's heritage. Present too are Hawthorne's allegory and Gothic romance, both employed in a detached explication of a people of grim righteousness. Cooper's protagonists of innocence are there, and so too is the tall tale. And in at least one respect, Faulkner is reminiscent of Melville: both writers, out of an inherited tradition of hope and expectation, can create a vision of pure innocence, and they can create, out of a personal skepticism of profound depths, a vision of nightmarish horror. Faulkner was also aware of the Elizabethan and Jacobean drama, the Russian novel, and the "modern" novel as it was created by James, Conrad, and Joyce. Faulkner's dual heritage, American and European, is not uncomplicated — and he was conscious of its variety.

Ernest Hemingway

During his lifetime Ernest Hemingway was very probably America's most famous writer. His style, his "hero" (that is to say the protagonists of many of his works, who so resemble each other that we have come to speak of them in the singular), his manner and attitudes have been very widely recognized — not just in the English-speaking world but wherever books are widely read. It may be that no other novelist has had an equivalent influence on the prose of modern fiction, for where his work is known it has been used: imitated, reworked, or assimilated. In addition he had an extraordinary reputation as a colorful human being, and for over thirty years his every escapade was duly reported in the press. But for a long time neither he nor his work was well understood, and despite a considerable growth in understanding during the last decade, neither is yet understood as well as it might be.

There is never a simple key to any writer worth much attention, but in the case of Hemingway there is something that looks so like a key — even conceivably a master key — that it cannot escape any informed and thoughtful reader's notice. It lies waiting, curiously (a few might say fatefully), in the very first story in his first book of short stories, which was his first significant book of any kind.

The book appeared in 1925, and is called *In Our Time*. Very probably the author intended his title as a sardonic allusion to a well-known phrase from the Church of England's Book of Common Prayer: "Give peace in our time, O Lord." At any rate the most striking thing about the volume is that there is no peace at

153

all in the stories. The next most striking thing about them (long unremarked, since it was not clear to readers that he was the central figure in the stories in which he appears) is that half of the stories are devoted to the spotty but careful development of a crucial but long-ignored character — a boy, then a young man — named Nick Adams. These stories are arranged in the chronological order of Nick's boyhood and early manhood, and are intimately related, one to another. Indeed in this aspect the book is almost a "novel," for some of the stories are incomprehensible if one does not see the point, and it is often subtle, of some earlier piece.

The most significant and interesting of these stories, however, is that first one. It is called "Indian Camp," and it reveals a great deal about what its author was up to for some thirty-five years of his writing career. It tells about a doctor, Nick's father, who delivers an Indian woman of a baby by Caesarean section, with a jackknife and without anesthesia. The woman's invalid husband lies in a bunk above his screaming wife; Nick, a young boy, holds a basin for his father; four men hold the mother down until the child is born. When it is over the doctor looks in the bunk above and discovers that the husband, who has listened to the screaming for two days, has cut his head nearly off with a razor.

A careful reading of this story will show that Hemingway is not primarily interested, here, in these shocking events: he is interested in their effect on the little boy who witnessed them. For the moment the events do not seem to *have* any great effect on the boy. But it is very important that he is later on a badly scarred and nervous young man, and here Hemingway is relating to us the first reason he gives why that is so.

The story has already provided, then, a striking insight into the nature of his work. But it has, in addition, a notable conclusion, as Nick and his father discuss death — and death specifically by one's own hand:

"Why did he kill himself, Daddy?"
"I don't know, Nick. He couldn't stand things, I guess."
"Do many men kill themselves, Daddy?"
"Not very many, Nick." . . .

They were seated in the boat, Nick in the stern, his father rowing. . . . In the early morning on the lake sitting in the stern of the boat with his father rowing, he felt quite sure that he would never die.

Now from a purely aesthetic point of view it is perfectly irrele·vant, but from a human and biographical point of view perfectly unavoidable, to remark the uncanny fact that the originals of both these characters, making their first appearances here as doctor and son, were destined to destroy themselves. Clarence Edmonds Hemingway, M.D., the prototype for Dr. Adams, while in ill-health committed suicide with a pistol (a relic of the Civil War which the writer's mother later sent him) in 1928; the son, the prototype for Nick Adams, Ernest (Miller) Hemingway, blew most of his head off, with a favorite shotgun, in 1961. "He couldn't stand things, I guess."

As closely as this are many of the key events in the life of the hero tied to the life of the writer. Nearly as simple as this was his preoccupation with violence, and above all the fact of violent death. And seldom in the whole history of literature can there have been a more unlikely focusing on things-to-come as in this first little story.

The six following stories from *In Our Time* concerning Nick Adams are not so violent as "Indian Camp," but each of them is unpleasant or upsetting in some way or other. In one, "The Doctor and the Doctor's Wife," Nick discovers that he is unsure about his father's courage and is completely dissatisfied with his mother's way of looking at things. Two others, "The End of Something" and "The Three-Day Blow," detail among other matters the disturbing end of an adolescent love affair. In "The Battler" Nick is knocked off a moving freight train by a brakeman, and encounters a crazy ex-prizefighter who nearly beats him up, along with an extremely polite Negro hobo who in his own way is even more sinister. One should suspect that Nick is being exposed to more than may be entirely good for him.

Immediately following "The Battler" comes a little sketch, less than a page long, which serves to confirm this suspicion. It tells us that Nick is in World War I, that he has been wounded, and that he has made a "separate peace" with the enemy — is not fighting for his country, or any other, any more. It would be quite impossible to exaggerate the importance of this short scene in any understanding of Hemingway and his work. It will be duplicated at more length by another protagonist, named Frederic Henry, in *A Farewell to Arms*, and it will serve as a climax in the lives of all of Hemingway's heroes, in one way or another, for at least the next quarter-century.

The fact that Nick is seriously injured is significant in two important ways. First, the wound intensifies and epitomizes the wounds he has been getting as a boy growing up in the American Middle West. From here on the Hemingway hero will appear to us as a wounded man — wounded not only physically but, as soon becomes clear, psychologically as well. Second, the fact that Nick and his friend, also wounded, have made a "separate peace," are "Not patriots," marks the beginning of the long break with organized society as a whole that stays with Hemingway and his hero through several books to come, and into the late 1930's. Indeed the last story in this first volume, called "Big Two-Hearted River," is a kind of forecast of these things. It is obscure until one sees the point, and almost completely so; its author complained in 1950 that the tale was twenty-five years old and still had not been understood by anyone. But it is really a very simple "story." It is a study of a young man who has been hurt in the war, who is all by himself on a fishing trip, escaping everyone. He is suffering from what used to be called "shell shock"; he is trying desperately to keep from going out of his mind.

In his next two collections of short stories, *Men without Women* (1927) and *Winner Take Nothing* (1933), Hemingway included several more stories about Nick Adams. They do not change anything, but they fill in some of the gaps in his sketchy career. In one, an eternally reprinted tale called "The Killers," he is exposed to a sickening situation in which a man refuses to run any more from some gangsters who are clearly going to murder him. In another, "The Light of the World," he is somewhat prematurely introduced into the seamy realms of prostitution and homosexuality. In a third, "Fathers and Sons," he is deeply troubled by thoughts of his father's death. (At the time we cannot know exactly why, and do not know until many years later when the hero, now under the name of Robert Jordan, in *For Whom the Bell Tolls,* returns to this situation and explains; *his* father committed suicide.) And in a fourth, "A Way You'll Never Be," Nick meets the fate he was trying desperately to avoid in "Big Two-Hearted River" and, as a direct result of his war experiences, goes entirely out of his mind.

Further gaps in the picture we should have of Nick are filled by several stories Hemingway wrote in the first person. It is abundantly clear that the narrator of them is Nick, and in one of the tales, a war story called "Now I Lay Me," he is called by that name. This one is a story about insomnia, which Nick suffered for a long time following his wounding; he cannot sleep "for thinking," and several things that occupy his mind while he lies awake relate closely to scenes and events in stories already mentioned. "In Another Country" extends the range of Hemingway's essential interest from Nick to another individual casualty of the war, and thus points toward *The Sun Also Rises,* where a whole "lost generation" has been damaged in the same disaster. A further development occurs in "An Alpine Idyll," which returns us to a postwar skiing trip Nick took in a tale called "Cross Country Snow"; here the interest focuses on the responses of Nick and others to a particularly shocking situation, as it did in the more famous "Killers." But whereas in the earlier story Nick was so upset by the thought of the man who was passively waiting to be murdered that he wanted to get clean out of the town where the violence impended, healthy tissue is now growing over his wounds, and the point of the story lies in the development of his defenses.

By now it is perfectly clear what kind of boy, then man, this Adams is. He is certainly not the simple primitive he is often mistaken for. He is honest, virile, but — clearest of all — very sensitive. He is an outdoor male, and he has a lot of nerve, but he is also very nervous. It is important to understand this Nick, for soon, under other names in other books, he is going to be known half the world over as the "Hemingway hero": every single one of these men has had, or has had the exact equivalent of, Nick's childhood, adolescence, and young manhood. This man will die a thousand times before his death, and although he would learn how to live with some of his troubles, and how to overcome others, he would never completely recover from his wounds as long as Hemingway lived and recorded his adventures.

Now it is also clear that something was needed to bind these wounds, and there is in Hemingway a consistent character who performs that function. This figure is not Hemingway himself in disguise (which to some hard-to-measure extent the Hemingway hero was). Indeed he is to be sharply distinguished from the hero, for he comes to balance the hero's deficiencies, to correct his stance. We generally, though unfelicitously, call this man the "code hero" — this because he represents a code according to which the hero, if he could attain it, would be able to live properly in the world of violence, disorder, and misery to which he has been introduced and which he inhabits. The code hero, then, offers up and exemplifies certain principles of honor, courage, and endurance which in a life of tension and pain make a man a man, as we say, and enable him to conduct himself well in the losing battle that is life. He shows, in the author's famous phrase for it, "grace under pressure."

This man also makes his first appearance in the short stories. He is Jack, the prizefighter of "Fifty Grand," who through a superhuman effort manages to lose the fight he has promised to lose. He is Manuel, "The Undefeated" bullfighter who, old and wounded, simply will not give up when he is beaten. He is Wilson, the British hunting guide of "The Short Happy Life of Francis Macomber," who teaches his employer the shooting standards that make him, for a brief period preceding his death, a happy man. And, to distinguish him most clearly from the Hemingway hero, he is Cayetano, the gambler of "The Gambler, the Nun and the Radio," who with two bullets in his stomach will not show a sin-

gle sign of suffering, while the generic Nick, here called Mr. Fra-
zer, is shamed to suffer less but visibly. The finest and best known
of these code heroes appears, however, in Hemingway's most re
cent novel. He is old Santiago of *The Old Man and the Sea*. The
chief point about him is that he behaves perfectly — honorably
with great courage and endurance — while losing to the sharks the
giant fish he has caught. This, to epitomize the message the code
hero always brings, is life: you lose, of course; what counts is how
you conduct yourself while you are being destroyed.

The three matters already introduced — the wound, the break
from society, the code (and a working adjustment of these things)
— are the subjects of all of Hemingway's significant work outside
as well as inside the short stories. This work comes to ten book-
length pieces: six novels, a burlesque, a book on big-game hunting,
one on bullfighting, and a play. The pattern already set up will, it
is hoped, help to place these works and to clarify their meanings.

It will not help much with the first of them, however, for this
is an anomaly: the burlesque, a "satirical novel," *The Torrents of
Spring*. It appeared in 1926, and is a parody of Sherwood Anderson's novels in general, and of his *Dark Laughter* (1925) in particular. It is a moderately amusing performance, especially if one
will first take the trouble to read or reread the specific object of
attack; there were ridiculous elements even in Anderson's "better" novels, and Hemingway goes unerringly to them. But this
book, dashed off in a great hurry, has never had as many readers
as Hemingway's other books, and it has no relation to anything
else he has written — except that in it he was declaring himself
free of certain egregious weaknesses in a man who had at one
time influenced him. It is said that he was also breaking his contract with his publishers, Boni and Liveright, who would feel that
they must reject this satire on one of their leading writers; thus
Hemingway would be free to take his work to Scribner's, whom he
much preferred.

It is very doubtful that Hemingway intended his book primarily as a means whereby he might change publishers. But

Liveright did reject it, Scribner's did bring it out, and thus Scribner's have been able to publish the rest of his work. Nor did they have to wait long to prove the wisdom of their acceptance of Hemingway, for his first true novel, *The Sun Also Rises*, came into their hands the same year. This book in time became a best seller and made its author's reputation. *The Sun Also Rises* reintroduces us to the hero, here called Jake Barnes. His wound, again with both literal and symbolic meanings, is transferred from the spine (where Nick was hit) to the genitals: Jake was, to speak loosely, emasculated in the war. His wound, then, has undergone a significant transformation, but he is still the hero, still the man who cannot sleep when his head starts to work, and who cries in the night. He has also parted with society and the usual middle-class ways; he lives in Paris with an international group of expatriates, a dissolute collection of amusing but aimless people — all of them, in one way or another, blown out of the paths of ordinary life by the war. This was, as Gertrude Stein had remarked to Hemingway, the "lost generation," and in this book Hemingway made it famous.

Although it is not highly developed yet, Jake and the few people he likes have a code. There are certain things that are "done," and many that are "not done," and one of the characters distinguishes people as belonging or not belonging according to whether they understand or not. The whole trouble with Robert Cohn, a writer, for instance, is that he does not understand, and he is sharply juxtaposed to a young bullfighter named Romero (an early code hero) who, in the way he conducts himself both personally and professionally, does understand.

The action of the novel is taken up with drinking, fishing, and going to the bullfights, as well as with the promiscuous affairs of a young lady named Brett Ashley. Brett is in love with Jake, and he with her, but since he is wounded as he is there is not much they can do about it. Brett, although engaged to a man who like herself and Jake is a casualty of the war, passes from Cohn to Romero and then — because she has principles too — she leaves him and in the end is back, hopelessly, with Jake. Nothing leads anywhere in the book, and that is perhaps the real point of it. The action comes full circle — imitates, that is, the sun of the title, which also rises, only to hasten to the place where it arose (the title is, of course, a quotation from Ecclesiastes). For the most part the novel is a delightful one. The style is fresh and sparkling, the dialogue is fun to read, and the book is beautifully and meaningfully constructed. But its message is that for these people at least (and one gets the distinct impression that other people do not matter very much), life is futile.

It happens that this is not precisely the message Hemingway intended to give. He once said that he regarded the line "you are all a lost generation," which he used as an epigraph, as a piece of "splendid bombast," and that he included the passage from Ecclesiastes, also quoted as an epigraph, to correct the remark attributed to Miss Stein. As far as he was concerned, he wrote his editor Maxwell Perkins, the point of his novel is, as the Biblical lines say in part, that "the earth abideth forever."

To be sure, some support for these contentions can be found in the novel itself. Not quite all the characters are "lost" — Romero is not — and the beauty of the eternal earth is now and again richly invoked. But most of the characters do seem lost indeed, a great deal of the time, and few readers have taken the passage from Ecclesiastes as Hemingway did. The strongest feeling in it is not that the earth abides forever, but that all motion is endless, circular, and unavailing; and for all who know what the Preacher said, the echo of "Vanity of vanities; all is vanity" is nearly as strong. For once Hemingway's purpose and accomplishment are here two things, but the result is nonetheless impressive, and *The Sun Also Rises* remains one of the two best novels he wrote.

The other is his next book, *A Farewell to Arms* (1929), and one thing it does is to explain how the characters of *The Sun Also Rises*, and the hero particularly, got the way they are. In the course of the novel Lt. Frederic Henry is wounded in the war as was Nick Adams (although now the most serious of his injuries is to his knee, which is where Hemingway himself was hardest hit). Henry shows clearly the results of this misfortune; again he cannot sleep at night unless he stops thinking; again, when he does sleep he has nightmares. While recuperating in Milan, he falls in love with an English nurse, but when he is returned to the front he is forced to desert the army in which he has been fighting in order to save his life. He escapes to Switzerland with the nurse, a compliant young woman named Catherine Barkley who is now pregnant with his child, and there she dies in childbirth. Henry is left, at the end, with nothing. A man is trapped, Hemingway seems to be saying. He is trapped biologically and he is trapped socially; either way it can only end badly, and there are no other ways.

Once again this is a beautifully written book. The prose is hard and clean, the people come to life instantly and ring true. The novel is built with scrupulous care. A short introductory scene at the very start presents an ominous conjunction of images — of rain, pregnancy, and death — which set the mood for, and prefigure, all that is to follow. Then the action is tied into a perfect and permanent knot by the skill with which the two themes are brought together. As the intentionally ambiguous title suggests, the two themes are of course love and war. (They are developments, incidentally, from two early fragments: the sketch, "Chapter VI," in which Nick was wounded, and the "love story," called "A Very Short Story," that immediately followed it in *In Our Time*.)

Despite the frequency of their appearance in the same books, love and war are — to judge from the frequency with which writers fail to wed them — an unlikely mixture. But in this novel their courses run exactly, though subtly, parallel, so that in the end we feel we have read one story, not two. In his affair with the war Henry goes through six phases: from desultory participation to serious action and a wound, and then through his recuperation in Milan to a retreat which leads to his desertion. Carefully interwoven with all this is his relationship with Catherine, which undergoes six precisely corresponding stages: from a trifling sexual affair to actual love and her conception, and then through her confinement in the Alps to a trip to the hospital which leads to her death. By the time the last farewell is taken, the stories are as one in the point, lest there be any sentimental doubt about it, that life, both personal and social, is a struggle in which the Loser Takes Nothing, either.

But like all of Hemingway's better books this one is bigger than any short account of it can indicate. For one thing there is the stature of Frederic Henry, and it is never more clear than here that he is the Hemingway "hero" in more senses than are suggested by the term "protagonist." Henry stands for many men; he stands for the experience of his country: in his evolution from complicity in the war to bitterness to escape, the whole of America could read its recent history in a crucial period, Wilson to Harding. When he expressed his disillusionment with the ideals the war claimed to promote, and jumped in a river and deserted, Henry's action epitomized the contemporary feeling of a whole nation. Not that the book is without positive values, however — as is often alleged, and as Robert Penn Warren, for one, has disproved. Henry progresses from the messiness represented by the brothel to the order that is love; he distinguishes sharply between the disciplined and competent people he has to do with and the disorderly and incompetent ones: the moral value of these virtues is not incidental to the action but a foundation on which the book is built. Despite such foundations, however, the final effect of this mixture of pessimism and ideals is one of tragedy and despair.

The connection between Hemingway and his hero was always intimate, and in view of the pessimism of these last two books it is perhaps not suprising that his next two books, which were works of nonfiction, find the hero — Hemingway himself, now, without disguise — pretty much at the end of his rope, and in complete escape from the society he had renounced in *A Farewell to Arms*. The books are *Death in the Afternoon* (1932) and *Green Hills of Africa* (1935). Neither of them is of primary importance. The first is a book about bullfighting, one of a surprising number of subjects in which the author was learned; the second is a book on big-game hunting, about which he also knew a great deal. But the books are really about death — the death of bulls, bullfighters, horses, and big game; death is a subject which by his own admission obsessed Hemingway for a long time. Both books are also a little hysterical, as if written under great nervous tension. To be sure the bullfighter is a good example of the man with the code. As he acts out his role as high priest of a ceremonial in which men pit themselves against violent death, and, with a behavior that formalizes the code, administers what men seek to avoid, he is the very personification of "grace under pressure." And both volumes contain long passages — on writing, Spain, Africa, and other subjects — that are well worth reading. But more clearly than anything else the books present the picture of a man who had, since that separate peace, cut himself so completely off from the roots that nourish that he was starving. The feeling is strong that he would have to find new roots, or re-establish old ones, if he were going to write any more good novels.

This process was not a painless one, and Hemingway's next book, *To Have and Have Not* (1937), amply betrays that fact. This is a novel, though not a good one — at least not for this novelist. But it is one in which its author clearly showed that he had learned something that would become very important to him before he was done writing. As often before, and later too, it is the code hero, piratically named Harry Morgan, who teaches the lesson. The novel tells the story of this man who is forced, since he cannot support his wife and children through honest work, to go his own way: he becomes an outlaw who smuggles rum and people into the United States from Cuba. In the end he is killed, but before he dies he has learned the lesson that Hemingway himself must recently have learned: alone, a man has no chance.

It is regrettable that this pronouncement, articulating a deathbed conversion, does not grow with any sense of inevitability out of the action of the book. A contrast between the Haves and the Have Nots of the story is meant to be structure and support for the novel and its message, but the whole affair is unconvincing. The superiority of the Nots is apparently based on the superiority of the sex life of the Morgans, on some savage disgust aimed at a successful writer in the book, and on some callow explanations of how the Haves got their money. Just how all these things lead to Harry's final pronouncement was Hemingway's business, and it was not skillfully transacted.

But the novel itself is of minor significance. What it represents in Hemingway is important. Here is the end of the long exile that began with Nick Adams' separate peace, the end of Hemingway's ideological separation from the world: a man has no chance alone. As a matter of fact, by 1937, the year of this novel, Hemingway had come close to embracing the society he had deserted some twenty years before, and was back in another "war for democracy."

More than any other single thing, it seems to have been the civil war in Spain that returned Hemingway to the world of other people. He was informally involved in that war, on the Loyalist side, and his next full-length work was a play, called *The Fifth Column* (1938), which praises the fighters with whom he was associated and declares his faith in their cause. The play is distinguished by some excellent talk, and marred by a kind of cops-and-robbers action. The Hemingway hero, now called simply Philip, is immediately recognizable. He is still afflicted with his memories, and with insomnia and horrors in the night. A kind of Scarlet Pimpernel dressed as an American reporter, Philip appears to be a charming but dissolute wastrel, a newsman who never files any stories. But actually, and unknown to his mistress, Dorothy, he is up to his neck in the Loyalist fight. The most striking thing about him, however, is the distance he has come from the hero, so like him in every other way, who decided in *A Farewell to Arms* that such faiths and causes were "obscene."

But it is almost no distance at all from the notion that a man has no chance alone to the thought that "No man is an *Iland*, intire of itself. . . ." These words, from a devotion by John Donne, are part of an epigraph to Hemingway's next novel, whose title, *For Whom the Bell Tolls* (1940), comes from the same source. The bell referred to is a funeral bell: "And therefore never send to know for whom the *bell* tolls; It tolls for *thee*."

This time the novel is true to its controlling concept. It deals with three days in the life of the Hemingway hero, now named Robert Jordan, who is fighting as an American volunteer in the

Spanish civil war. He is sent to join a guerrilla band in the mountains near Segovia to blow up a strategic bridge, thus facilitating a Loyalist advance. He spends three days and nights in the guerrillas' cave, while he awaits what he expects will be his own destruction, and he falls in love with Maria, the daughter of a Republican mayor who has been murdered — as she herself has been raped — by the Falangists. Jordan believes the attack will fail, but the generals will not cancel it until it is too late. He successfully destroys the bridge, is wounded in the retreat, and is left to die. But he has come to see the wisdom of such a sacrifice, and the book ends without bitterness.

This is not a flawless novel. For one thing the love story, if not sentimental, is at any rate idealized and very romantic; for another, there are a good many passages in which Jordan appears more to be struggling for the faith on which he acts than to have achieved it. The hero is still the wounded man, and new incidents from his past are supplied to explain why this is so; two of the characters remark pointedly that he was too young to experience the things he tells them of having experienced. But Jordan has learned a lot, since the old days, about how to live and function with his wounds, and he behaves well. He dies, but he has done his job, and the manner of his dying convinced many readers of what his thinking had failed to do: that life is worth living and that there are causes worth dying for.

The skill with which this novel was for the most part written demonstrated that Hemingway's talent was once again intact and formidable. None of his books had evoked more richly the life of the senses, had shown a surer sense of plotting, or provided more fully living secondary characters, or livelier dialogue. But following this success (this was the most successful of all his books so far as sales are concerned), he lapsed into a silence that lasted a whole decade — chiefly because of nonliterary activities in connection with World War II. And when he broke this silence in 1950 with his next book, a novel called *Across the River and into the Trees*, the death of his once-great gifts was very widely advertised by the critics and reviewers.

To be sure, this is a poor performance. It is the story of a peace-time army colonel (but almost an exact self-portrait) who comes on leave to Venice to go duck-shooting, to see his very young girl friend, and to die, all of which he does. The colonel is the hero again, this time called Richard Cantwell, and he has all the old scars, particularly the specific ones he received as Frederic Henry in *A Farewell to Arms*. Again there is the "Hemingway heroine," a title that designates the British nurse, Catherine, of that novel, and the Spanish girl Maria of *For Whom the Bell Tolls*, and now the young Italian countess Renata of this novel. (They are all pretty much the same girl, though for some reason their nationality keeps changing, as the hero's never does, and they grow younger as the hero ages.) There are also many signs of the "code." But the code in this book has become a sort of joke; the hero has become a good deal of a bore, and the heroine has become a wispy dream. The distance that Hemingway once maintained between himself and his protagonist has disappeared, to leave us with a self-indulgent chronicling of the author's every opinion; he acts as though he were being interviewed. The novel reads like a parody of the earlier works.

But there is one interesting thing about it. Exactly one hundred years before the appearance of this novel Nathaniel Hawthorne published *The Scarlet Letter*, in which he wrote: "There is a fatality, a feeling so irresistible and inevitable that it has the force of doom, which almost invariably compels human beings to linger around and haunt, ghostlike, the spot where some great and marked event has given the color to their lifetime; and still the more irresistibly, the darker the tinge that saddens it." From Hawthorne himself and Poe, from Hawthorne's Hester Prynne and Melville's Ahab right down to J. D. Salinger's "Zooey," who is unwilling to leave New York ("I've been *run over* here — twice, and on the same damn *street*") — no one in the history of American letters has demonstrated Hawthorne's insight with as much force and clarity as have Hemingway and his hero. And nowhere in Hemingway is the demonstration more clear than in *Across the River and into the Trees*, for it is here that Colonel Cantwell

167

makes a sort of pilgrimage to the place where he — and where Nick Adams, and Frederic Henry (and Hemingway himself) — was first wounded. He takes instruments, and locates by survey the exact place on the ground where he had been struck. Then, in an act of piercing, dazzling identification, he builds a very personal if ironic sort of monument to the spot, acknowledges and confronts the great, marked event that colored his lifetime — and Hemingway's writing-time — and comes to the end of his journey (or the end so far), not at the place where he first lived, but where first he died.

The critics who professed to see in this book the death of Hemingway's talent, as well as of his hero, happily proved to be mistaken, for they were forced almost unanimously to accept his next book, called *The Old Man and the Sea*, as a triumph. This very short novel, which some insist on calling rather a long short story (and it was for some time rumored to be part of a longer work-in-progress), concerns an old Cuban fisherman. After eighty-four days without a fish Santiago ventures far out to sea alone, and hooks a giant marlin in the Gulf Stream. For two days and two nights the old man holds on while he is towed farther out to sea; finally he brings the fish alongside, harpoons it, and lashes it to his skiff. Almost at once the sharks begin to take his prize away from him. He kills them until he has only his broken tiller to fight with. Then they eat all but the skeleton, and he tows that home, half-dead with exhaustion, and makes his way to bed to sleep and dream of other days.

The thing that chiefly keeps *The Old Man and the Sea* from greatness is the sense one has that the author was imitating instead of creating the style that made him famous. But this reservation is almost made up for by the book's abundance of meaning. As always the code hero, here Santiago, comes with a message, and it is essentially that while a man may grow old, and be wholly down on his luck, he can still dare, stick to the rules, persist when he is licked, and thus by the manner of his losing win his victory. On another level the story can be read as an allegory entirely personal to its author, as an account of his own struggle, his determination, and his literary vicissitudes. Like Hemingway, Santiago is a master who sets out his lines with more care and precision than his competitors, but he has not had any luck in a long time. Once he was very strong, the champion, yet his whole reputation is imperiled now, and he is growing old. Still he feels that he has strength enough; he knows the tricks of his trade; he is resolute, and he is still out for the really big success. It means nothing that he has proved his strength before; he has got to prove it again, and he does. After he has caught his prize the sharks come and take it all away from him, as they will always try to do. But he caught it, he fought it well, he did all he could and it was a lot, and at the end he is happy.

To take the broadest view, however, the novel is a representation of life as a struggle against unconquerable natural forces in which a kind of victory is possible. It is an epic metaphor for life, a contest in which even the problem of right and wrong seems paltry before the great thing that is the struggle. It is also something like Greek tragedy, in that as the hero falls and fails, the audience may get a memorable glimpse of what stature a man may have. And it is Christian tragedy as well, especially in the several marked allusions to Christian symbolism, particularly of the crucifixion — a development in Hemingway's novels that begins, apparently without much importance, in the early ones, gathers strength in *Across the River and into the Trees*, and comes to a kind of climax in this book.

Although the view of life in this novel had a long evolution from the days of total despair, it represents nonetheless an extraordinary change in its author. A reverence for life's struggle, and for mankind, seems to have descended on Hemingway like the gift of grace on the religious. The knowledge that a simple man is capable of the decency, dignity, and even heroism that Santiago possesses, and that his battle can be seen in heroic terms, is itself, technical considerations for the moment aside, perhaps the greatest victory that Hemingway won. Very likely this is the sort of thing he had in mind when he remarked to someone, shortly after finishing the book, that he had got, finally, what he had been working for all of his life.

Although he is known to have left a good deal of unpublished writing behind him — fiction, biography, and poetry, and at least some of it reputedly ready for the printer — Hemingway brought out nothing of real significance after *The Old Man and the Sea.* Nor, with the exception of a selection by Gene Z. Hanrahan of interesting and lively articles produced in the early 1920's for the Toronto *Star* and called, a little unfortunately, *The Wild Years* (1962), has anything appeared posthumously. But one may still have considerable hope for more, as well as for an authorized biography being written by Carlos Baker.

One reason for this silence late in Hemingway's lifetime appears to have been ill health. Incessant physical damage took its eventual toll, and the author seems never to have entirely recovered from grievous injuries suffered during his last trip to Africa. Another reason was probably even simpler: taxes, for he was in that not altogether unenviable position where a substantial part of the profit from new work went to the government. If, however, he left, say, a couple of novels and some stories behind him (the profits from a single short story, "The Snows of Kilimanjaro," must by this time be approaching $200,000), then his last wife, his three sons, and his grandchildren should eventually be fairly well off.

Hemingway the man is of considerable interest, and his life was colorful. He was born Ernest Miller Hemingway in an intensely middle-class suburb of Chicago called Oak Park, Illinois, on July 21, 1899. His father was a doctor, devoted to hunting and fishing; his mother was a religious and musical woman, and a struggle over which direction the boy should take appears to have been won by the former. The parts of his childhood that seem to have stayed most deeply with Hemingway were spent up in Michigan on vacations, and are reflected in several of the stories about young Nick Adams.

As a boy Hemingway learned to box (permanently damaging

an eye in the process) and he played high school football. He was not much pleased with the latter activity, however, partly because he was already more interested in writing. Working for his English classes and the school paper, he composed light verse, wrote a good many columns in imitation of Ring Lardner (a practice at which he became very adept), and tried his hand at some short stories. Although it looked for many years as though he was cut out to be a humorist, he also turned his hand to more serious fiction, and this is really the most impressive part of his juvenilia; already he was choosing to write about northern Michigan, and many of the features of his later style — especially some of the earmarks of his famous dialogue — are discernible in this early prose.

About half-seriously, doubtless, Hemingway remarked a few years ago that the best training for a writer is an unhappy boyhood. He himself, however, appears to have been reasonably happy a good part of the time. But he seems also to have been on occasion deeply dissatisfied with his homelife and with Oak Park. Twice he was a runaway, and no sooner did he graduate from high school than he was off for Kansas City, never really to return home. If it had not been for parental objections that he was too young (seventeen), and if not for his bad eye, he would have gone much farther away, for he was desperately eager to get into the war. Repeatedly rejected by the army, he went instead to the Kansas City *Star*, then one of the country's best newspapers, lied about his age (which accounts for the fact that his birth date was long given as 1898), and partly on the strength of his high school newspaper experience landed a job as a reporter. Here he was known for his energy and eagerness, and for the fact that, in the line of duty, he always wanted to ride the ambulances. Finally able to get into the war as an honorary lieutenant in the Red Cross, he went overseas, in a state of very great excitement, as an ambulance driver. He was severely wounded, while passing out chocolate to the troops in Italy, at Fossalta di Piave, on July 8, 1918, and was decorated by the Italians for subsequent heroism. A dozen operations were performed on his knee, and after his recuperation in Milan he was with the Italian infantry until the Armistice.

After the war, "literally shot to pieces," according to a friend, he returned to the United States, his riddled uniform with him. Heading for northern Michigan again, he spent a time reading, writing, and fishing. Then he worked for a while in Canada for the Toronto *Star*, moved temporarily to Chicago, found himself unhappy with America, married, and took off for Paris as a foreign correspondent, employed again by the Toronto *Star*. He served in this role for some time, and then settled down in Paris to become once and for all, under the guidance of Gertrude Stein and others, a writer. Though it brought little in the way of money, his work soon began to attract attention, and *The Sun Also Rises* made him famous while he was still in his twenties. After that time he had no serious extended financial troubles, and with both critics and the general public commanded a very wide following.

From other standpoints, Hemingway's story was one of mixed success and failure. His first three marriages — to Hadley Richardson, the mother of his first son, to Pauline Pfeiffer, the mother of his second two boys, and to Martha Gellhorn, the novelist — all ended in divorce. (His fourth wife was the former Mary Welsh of Minnesota — all the other wives came from St. Louis — whom he met in England in 1944.) For a long time, the whole span of the thirties during which he lived mostly in Key West, Florida, his work did more to advance his reputation as sportsman and athlete than as a writer of memorable fiction. During the forties his non-literary activities were even more spectacular, and though he published only one book in this period he was very much alive. There is subject matter for several romantic novels in his World War II adventures alone.

In 1942 he volunteered himself and his fishing boat, the *Pilar*, for various projects to the United States Navy, was accepted, and for two years cruised off the coast of Cuba with a somewhat suicidal plan for the destruction of U-boats in the area. In 1944 he was in England, and as an accredited correspondent went on several missions with the RAF. Shortly before the invasion of

France he was in an auto wreck which necessitated the taking of fifty-seven stitches in his head. But he pulled the stitches out on D Day, and after the breakthrough in Normandy attached himself to the division of his choice, the Fourth of the First Army, with which he saw considerable action at Schnee Eifel, in Luxembourg, and in the disaster at Hürtgen Forest. At one point in a battle, according to the commanding officer of the division ("I always keep a pin in the map for old Ernie Hemingway"), he was sixty miles in front of anything else in the First Army. Ostensibly a correspondent he was by now running his own small, informal, but effective army — motorized, equipped with "every imaginable" German and American weapon, and nearly weighed down with bottles and explosives. The history books have it that the French liberated their own capital from the Germans, and so they did, but the fact remains that Hemingway and his company of irregulars were engaged in a skirmish at the Arc de Triomphe when Leclerc's army was at the south bank of the Seine. The writer and his troops were soon billeted at the Ritz, which they had exclusively liberated.

The Heroic Hemingway and the Public Hemingway produced somehow a Legendary Hemingway, an imaginary person who departed from the actual one at some point that is next to impossible to define. There was something about him that excited strange enthusiasms and even stranger antipathies. A good deal of what we think we know about him carries an air of having been gone over by a press agent. But some facts can be verified. In addition to the ones already given, it can be stated that Hemingway lived most of his last years on a "farm" called Finca Vigia on a hilltop at San Francisco de Paula, nine miles outside Havana; that he was generous, extremely perceptive about people, deeply and widely read as a student of literature, a bit of a linguist, and an expert in navigation, military history, and tactics. It is perhaps also relevant to note that he was in some private, unorthodox way a convert to Roman Catholicism. In view of the personal difficulties following his wounding in World War I, it is certainly relevant to record the fact that through a rigorous exercise of an impressive will, he overcame his fears; professional soldiers in World War II have testified that he seemed to them the bravest man they had ever seen.

He was a gifted, strong personality, and at times eccentric. In *Across the River and into the Trees* Cantwell's driver speculates that some of the colonel's eccentricities are the result of his having been so often injured. Although this diagnosis may seem both offhand and indirect, one of the consequences of Hemingway's physical adventures was that he, like Cantwell, physically long retained the record of about as many blows as a man may take and live. Understandably he did not wish to go down in history for this fact. But there seems little or no danger of that, and a list of his major injuries is certainly impressive and possibly significant. His skull was fractured at least once; he sustained at least a dozen brain concussions, several of them serious ones; he was in three bad automobile accidents; and a few years ago in the African jungle he was in two airplane accidents in the space of two days, during which time he suffered severe internal injuries, "jammed" his spine, and received a concussion so violent that his eyesight was impaired for some time. (It was on this occasion that quite a few newspapers printed obituaries, which he read, after his recovery, with great pleasure; the notices were favorable.) In warfare alone he was shot through nine parts of the body, and sustained six head wounds. When he was blown up in Italy at the age of eighteen, and was left, for a time, for dead, the doctors removed all of the 237 steel fragments which had penetrated him that they could get at.

Some amount of such gossip is relevant to any discussion of Hemingway's work if only because it confirms and informs the picture of him which the work has given us. Our view of that work is in turn informed and confirmed by modern psychology, which offers an account of how many of the things to be found in Hemingway come to be there. This is no place to go into the niceties and vagaries of contemporary psychoanalytic theory, much of it post-Freudian, but it is perhaps not out of place to remark that such theory does give an explanation of the pre-

occupations Hemingway's books and life reflect. His hero's nightmares and insomnia (attendant on his first serious wounding), his
preoccupation with death, and with the scene of what was nearly
his own premature end, his devotion to hunting and fishing, his
intellectual limitations — all these things and several others may
be accounted for in psychoanalytic terms. They used to be called
symptoms of "shell shock"; now it is called "traumatic neurosis."
The name matters very little. The point is that our understanding
of Hemingway has medical backing, if such is desired. The point
is further that his work so faithfully and accurately documented
how this kind of illness conducts itself that it in turn lends considerable credence to the medical theory.

And his end, his own death, reconfirms the view. Retreating
very quietly from Castro's Cuba, as no longer the place for him,
to Franco's Spain, where he was not bothered, despite *For Whom
the Bell Tolls*, and where he could follow the bullfights again, he
did produce "The Dangerous Summer," a somewhat abortive —
or at any rate intentionally journalistic — account of these fights.
Then he returned to the States, and settled near Sun Valley, Idaho.
He was not at all well. In addition to damages already noted he
was suffering from high blood pressure and skin cancer — perhaps
from hepatitis, diabetes mellitus, and (most serious) hemochroma-
tosis as well. Even more significant was the fact that visitors
reported him shockingly frail, withdrawn, and in a state of acute
anxiety and deep depression (for which last he had undergone a
total of twenty-five electroshock treatments while twice hospital-
ized at the Mayo Clinic). He was more querulous about the critics
in general (this one among them) than ever. Soon the world,
which knew little or nothing of the seriousness of his condition,
was to be stunned on July 2, 1961, by the violent end that his
first really important story had, by hindsight, so unwittingly and
obscurely pointed toward.

There should be no inference here that psychological hypothesis
or ill-health in any way detracts from or qualifies Hemingway's
accomplishment. Emphatically the contrary. "The world breaks
everyone and afterward many are strong at the broken places,"

as he remarked in *A Farewell to Arms*. His own life and career were for a very long time an extraordinary illustration of that notion. He developed his strength, personal and aesthetic, into a truly formidable thing, and the experience of a great many people could be called upon to show that the more one knew of the man and what he accomplished, the more admiration one was likely to have for him.

But primary attention should go of course to Hemingway the writer, not the man — and still less the case history — and there is little doubt that his technical achievement has been great. Indeed in the view of many people it is his simple, fresh, and clean prose style that is his true claim to renown and permanence. Those responsible for bestowing the Nobel Prize for Literature seemed to reflect this view, for in 1954 when he was awarded it they cited "his powerful style-forming mastery of the art of modern narration. . . ."

It is of course not true, as has been alleged, that this style sprang from nowhere. Actually it had a long evolution, which may be said to have begun when Mark Twain wrote the first paragraph of his *Adventures of Huckleberry Finn* (1884). What Twain was trying to do in this novel is very clear. He was trying to write as an American boy might speak — write, that is, not a "literary" English style, but a natural spoken English. Or rather a natural spoken American, for Twain was the first man to "write American," at least to do it really well. He found a freshness and a poetry in that speech which have not diminished one particle with the passing of the years. It is far too much to say, as Hemingway himself once said, that "all modern American literature" comes from that one book, but the book does indeed represent the true beginning of a widespread contemporary American style.

Other writers came between Twain and Hemingway in this evolution. It would be possible to draw up an extraordinary list of parallels between the lives and personalities of Hemingway and an intervening writer: Stephen Crane. Both men began their careers very young as reporters, then foreign correspondents. Both journeyed widely to wars. Each was profoundly shocked by the death of his father; each childhood was marred by the experience of violence; each man found in warfare an absorbing formalization of violence and an essential metaphor for life. Each tested himself against violence and in the end was cited for courage — and so on and on. Perhaps all this helps to account for the fact that a great many of the characteristics of Hemingway's prose — its intensity, its terse, unliterary tone, and many of the features of the dialogue, for instances — can be found first, when he is at his best, in Crane. (This is a debt which Hemingway also, obliquely, acknowledged.)

Any effort to write a simple, spare, concise, and yet repetitive prose — clean, free of cliché and "artful" synonyms and all but the smallest and simplest of words — could and did benefit as well from the efforts of Gertrude Stein. In addition, Hemingway's early stories show a debt to Sherwood Anderson, and a good many other writers seem also to have had at least a small hand in the forming of him. The names F. Scott Fitzgerald, Ezra Pound, Ring Lardner, Joseph Conrad, Ford Madox Ford, and Ivan Turgenev should appear, among others, on any list that pretended to be complete.

Almost all writers show their chief debts in their earliest work. In Hemingway's case, however, the situation is complicated by the fact that eighteen of his earliest stories, and the first draft of a first novel — the better part of his production for four years — were in a suitcase that was stolen from his first wife on a train to Lausanne. Thus the material that almost certainly recorded the most imitative and faltering steps of a person learning a new skill is missing, and almost certainly for good. Not missing, however, are a few copies of a pamphlet called *Three Stories and Ten Poems* which he published at Dijon in 1923, and we must settle for this. As the title suggests, Hemingway made his debut, a sort of a false start, as a poet. Most of the verse in this volume brings to mind the poetry either of Stephen Crane or of Vachel Lindsay, and is without other real interest. The three stories — "Up in Michigan," "Out of Season," and "My Old Man" — are on the other hand already accomplished performances, and as such were reprinted in *In Our Time*. But they still reveal something of the influences of other writers on this one, and include as well Hemingway's first attempt to work at what became his major theme.

The clearest direct obligation is to Sherwood Anderson, for "My Old Man" seems transparently Hemingway's version of Anderson's widely reprinted "I Want to Know Why," which had appeared two years earlier. Both stories are about horse racing, told by boys in their own vernacular; in each case the boy has to confront mature problems while undergoing a painful disillusionment with an older man he had been strongly attached to. (Hemingway claimed that he had not read any Anderson when he wrote "My Old Man," but if this is so the coincidences are very remarkable indeed.) "Out of Season," a tale of lovers under the spell of disenchantment, is reminiscent of Scott Fitzgerald's *The Beautiful and Damned* (1922). But "Up in Michigan" is much the most important of the *Three Stories*; it is a tale of initiation, precisely parallel to the stories of Nick Adams soon to be written. It takes place in the locale of "Indian Camp," and just as Nick in that episode was first exposed to violence, brutality, and pain, so in this story a girl named Liz learns a similar lesson, but for girls. The dogged simplicity of "Up in Michigan" suggests both Anderson and Gertrude Stein, but it is too hardheaded for the former, and cut off by its subject matter from the latter. All Hemingway had to do, once he had written it, was to take up a protagonist in whom he could see himself more directly, and he would have the adventures of Nick Adams.

The influence of other writers on even so distinctive a writer as Hemingway is sometimes perceptible even in work that is completely mature. Good cases in point are two of his best and best known stories, "The Snows of Kilimanjaro" and "The Short Happy Life of Francis Macomber." Both are unmistakably Hemingway, and both are substantially dependent on, or allied to, earlier fiction. "The Short Happy Life" is among other things a detailed description of the process of learning the code, and its value. Macomber, a coward, learns the code from Wilson, his professional hunting guide, and becomes in the process, for a short happy lifetime, a man. He confronts danger at first with a terrible fear, and when it comes he bolts and flies in a panic. But on the next occasion he is wakened from a kind of fighting trance to discover that his fear is gone, his manhood attained, and his life (for a moment) begun.

The story is authentic, vintage Hemingway. But insofar as it deals with Macomber's warlike relations with his wife Margot, it is a very close development and intensification of some notions about the relationship of the sexes in America as put down by D. H. Lawrence in an essay he once wrote on Hawthorne's *Scarlet Letter*. And to the much larger extent that it deals with fear and manhood, it is an almost exact reworking of the story Stephen Crane told in *The Red Badge of Courage*, a novel for which Hemingway long ago expressed his great — possibly excessive — admiration.

Similarly "The Snows of Kilimanjaro" is a story whose technique has been, deservedly, much praised; again few could mistake it for the work of another writer. But several of its basic ingredients are strongly reminiscent of other writers, and its most unusual structure has an exact precedent in an experimental tale published in 1891 by Ambrose Bierce and called "An Occurrence at Owl Creek Bridge," a story Hemingway was also known to admire. Both stories deal with a man at the point of death who imaginatively experiences his escape in such a realistic fashion that the reader is fooled into believing that it has been made. Both stories open with the situation of impending death, then flash back to explain how the situation came about, and then flash "forward" with the imaginary escape, only to conclude with the objective information that the death has indeed occurred.

Some of Hemingway's longer pieces have similar affiliations. If for instance *To Have and Have Not* does not owe a good deal to such an unlikely combination of books as James Joyce's *Ulysses* and Frank Norris' *Moran of the Lady Letty* (and Jack London's *Sea Wolf*) then we have on our hands a set of impossible coincidences. It is not at all, however, that Hemingway's work seems derived. Gertrude Stein thought it did: "he looks like a modern and he smells of the museums," she said. Edmund Wilson disagreed: "Hemingway should perhaps more than anyone else be allowed to escape the common literary fate of being derived from other people." And Alfred Kazin concurred, writing that he "had no basic relation to any prewar culture."

It seems entirely possible that all of these judgments are wrong. Hemingway took a good deal from other writers, but if he smells of the museums Miss Stein's nose was one of the few to detect the odor. Like most writers, he went to those who preceded him for what his experience and taste made meaningful and attractive to him. With the force of his personality and the skill of his craft he made what he borrowed distinctly and undeniably his own.

More striking, however, is the extent to which, once Hemingway got started, other writers began to make it all theirs. There is probably no country in which American books are read whose literature has been entirely unaffected by Hemingway's work; in his own country we are so conditioned to his influence that we hardly ever notice it any more. On the positive side he taught the values of objectivity and honesty, helped to purify our writing of sentimentality, literary embellishment, padding, and a superficial artfulness. Almost singlehanded he revitalized the writing of dialogue. His influence has extended even more pervasively, however, to the realms of the subliterary, and here the results, through no direct fault of his, have been much less appealing. Many writers, of the "tough-detective school" in particular, demonstrate what happens when the attitudes and mannerisms which have meaning in one novelist are taken over by others, for whom they have rather different meanings, or none. Violence is the meaningful core of Hemingway, but the host of novelists and short-story and script writers who have come to trade on him have seized a bag of tricks — usually a mixture of toughness and sex, with protagonists based on crude misunderstandings of one or the other — or both — of the heroes. In their hands the meanings either are cheap and sordid, or have departed altogether.

It is Hemingway's prose style, however, that has been most imitated, and it is as a stylist that he commands the most respect.

His prose is easily recognized. For the most part it is colloquial, characterized chiefly by a conscientious simplicity of diction and sentence structure. The words are normally short and common ones and there is a severe economy, and also a curious freshness, in their use. As Ford Madox Ford remarked some time ago, in a line that is often (and justifiably) quoted, the words "strike you, each one, as if they were pebbles fetched fresh from a brook." The typical sentence is a simple declarative one, or a couple of these joined by a conjunction. The effect is of crispness, cleanness, clarity, and a scrupulous care. (And a scrupulous care went into the composition; Hemingway worked very slowly and revised extensively. He claimed to have rewritten the last page of *A Farewell to Arms* thirty-nine times, and to have read through the manuscript of *The Old Man and the Sea* some two hundred times before he was finished with it.)

It is a remarkably unintellectual style. Events are described strictly in the sequence in which they occurred; no mind reorders or analyzes them, and perceptions come to the reader unmixed with comment from the author. The impression, therefore, is of intense objectivity; the writer provides nothing but stimuli. Since violence and pain are so often the subject matter, it follows that a characteristic effect is one of irony or understatement. The vision is narrow, and sharply focused.

The dialogue is equally striking, for Hemingway had an ear like a trap for the accents and mannerisms of human speech; this is chiefly why he was able to bring a character swiftly to life. The conversation is far from a simple transcription, however, of the way people talk. Instead the dialogue strips speech to an essential pattern of mannerisms and responses characteristic of the speaker, and gives an illusion of reality that reality itself would not give.

Nothing in this brief account of the "Hemingway style" should seem very surprising, but the purposes, implications, and ultimate meanings of this manner of writing are less well recognized. A style has its own content, and the manner of a distinctive prose style has its own meanings. The things that Hemingway's style most conveys are the very things he says outright. His style is as communicative of the content as the content itself, and is a large and inextricable part of the content. The strictly disciplined controls exerted over the hero and his nervous system are precise parallels to the strictly disciplined sentences. The "mindlessness" of the style is a reflection and expression of the need to "stop thinking" when thought means remembering the things that upset. The intense simplicity of the prose is a means of saying that things must be *made* simple, or the hero is lost, and in "a way you'll never be." The economy and narrow focus of the prose controls the little that can be absolutely mastered. The prose is tense because the atmosphere in which the struggle for control takes place is tense, and the tension in the style expresses that fact.

These notions are scarcely weakened by the reminder that the style was developed and perfected in the same period when the author was reorganizing his personality after the scattering of his forces in Italy. These efforts were two sides of one effort. Hemingway once said, in a story called "Fathers and Sons," that if he wrote some things he could get rid of them; it is equally to the point that he wrote them in the style that would get rid of them. The discipline that made the new personality made the prose style that bespoke the personality. The style is the clear voice of the content. It was the end, or aim, of the man, and a goal marvelously won. It was the means of being the man. An old commonplace never had more force than here: the style *is* the man.

One of the most common criticisms of Hemingway used to be that he had wandered too far from his roots, his traditions, and had got lost. People who made this criticism usually said that the author should find a way home to some such tradition as is to be found in a novel like Mark Twain's *Huckleberry Finn* — this one, presumably, because it seems to be by almost unanimous consent the most American of all novels. This is of course the book that Hemingway said all modern American writing comes from; the suspicion is forced on us that someone is confused.

It was the critics who were confused, partly because they missed some of the depths and subtleties in both writers. The curious truth is that if the pattern in Hemingway's work discussed here — the pattern of violence, psychological wounding, escape, and death — has any validity, then Hemingway never got very far from *Huckleberry Finn*. A careful reading of that novel will show precisely that pattern. The adventures of Huckleberry Finn and of Nick Adams are remarkably of a piece. "It made me so sick I most fell out of the tree," says Huck of his exposure to the Grangerford-Shepherdson feud. "I ain't a-going to tell *all* that happened. . . . I wished I hadn't ever come ashore that night to see such things — lots of times I dream about them."

There is so much either hilarious or idyllic in the novel about this boy that we are easily but mistakenly diverted from the spill of blood that gives the book a large part of its meaning and deeply affects Huck. Life on the Mississippi around 1845 could be gory, and Twain based his novel largely on experiences he himself had undergone as a boy, or had known intimately of, and had never quite got over. (We know, for instance, that he witnessed four murders.) A lot of this experience found its way into the book, and it is impossible to understand the novel completely without seeing what all this violence results in. But the results are clear: Huck's overexposure to violence finally wounds him. Each episode makes a mark, and each mark leaves a scar. Every major episode in the novel, with the exceptions only of the rather irrelevant Tom Sawyer scenes at the beginning and conclusion, ends in violence, in physical brutality, and usually in death. All along the way are bloodshed and pain, and there are thirteen separate corpses. The effect of all this, and the only effect that is relevant to the main plot, is that it serves to wound Huck Finn. Either tortured with nightmares or unable to sleep at all ("I couldn't, somehow, for thinking"), he is "made sick" by — among other things — the thought of a man left alone to drown, by the sale of some colored servants, and by the departure of the Duke and the King, tarred, feathered, and astraddle a rail. In addition he is becoming disgusted with mankind in general. Exposed to more bloodshed, drowning, and sudden death than he can handle, he is himself their casualty. And from his own experience Mark Twain could make the prediction: Huck isn't ever going to get over them.

Here, transparently, is the pattern of violence and psychological wounding we have been reading in Hemingway. The rest of it, the elements of escape and death, though in part submerged in symbolism, are also demonstrable in the same book. Huck's whole journey is of course made up of a series of escapes — escapes for the most part down a mighty and deeply mysterious river. His strange journey down the glamorous Mississippi, blurred, mythic, and wondrously suggestive, becomes in the end a supremely effortless flight into a dark and silent unknown. Symbolically Huck escapes more than he is aware of, and into something which — if this were literal and not metaphorical — he could not return from. Over and over again his silent, effortless, nighttime departures down the black and mighty stream compel us. In the end they transport us from a noisy, painful, and difficult life to the safety of the last escape of all. In the end as well, Twain is forced to drop Huck and to turn the story over to Tom Sawyer. The reason is not hard to find: Huck had grown too hot to handle. A damaged boy, tortured by the terror he has witnessed and been through, afflicted with insomnia and bad dreams, and voluntarily divorced from the society in which he had grown up, Huck could no longer be managed by a man who had not solved his own complications, many of which he had invested in the boy. What the author did not realize was that in his journey by water he had been hinting at a solution all along: an excessive exposure to violence and death produced first a compulsive fascination with dying, and finally an ideal symbol for it.

The parallel is complete. In both Huck and Nick, Hemingway's generic hero, we have a sensitive, rather passive but courageous and masculine boy, solitary and out of doors, who is dissatisfied with respectability, chiefly as represented by a Bible-quoting woman of the house. Each runs away from home. "Home" in both cases — St. Petersburg or northern Michigan — was a place of violence and pain, but though it was easy to flee the respectability, off on their own both boys came up against brutality harder than ever. Both were hurt by it and both ended by rebelling utterly against a society that sponsored, or permitted, such horror. Nick decides that he is not a patriot, and makes his own peace with the enemy; Huck decides that he will take up wickedness, and go to hell. He lights out for the territory, the hero for foreign lands. Huck and Nick are very nearly twins. Two of our most prominent heroes, Huck and the Hemingway hero, are casualties whom the "knowledge of evil," which Americans are commonly said to lack, has made sick.

This theme of the boy shattered by the world he grows up in is a variation on one of the most ancient of all stories, and one of the greatest of all American stories, which relates the meeting of innocence and experience. It was a primary theme of our first professional man of letters, Charles Brockden Brown, and it has run through our literature ever since. In the latter half of the nineteenth century it was related at what might be called the very poles of our national experience — on the frontier and in Europe — and with the steady flow of travelers abroad it was primarily in Europe that the drama of the meeting of youth and age was enacted. Here developments of the theme ranged all the way from comic and crude accounts of innocents abroad to the subtleties of Hawthorne and James, with their pictures of American visitors under the impact of the European social order.

The story is a great American story not only because it is based on the experience of every man as he grows up, but also on the particular and peculiar history of the country. Once we were fully discovered, established, and unified we began to rediscover the world, and this adventure resulted in our defining ourselves in the light of people who did not seem, to us or to them, quite like us.

The stories of Huck Finn and the Hemingway hero share this general theme, for they tell again what happens when innocence, or a spontaneous virtue, meets with something not at all itself. But they are variations on the theme. The traveling comedians in Europe made spectacles of their ignorance, but usually had the last laugh. The more serious pilgrims were usually enriched at their pain, but showed up well in the process, often displaying a kind of power that comes from purity. But there is nothing subtle about the force that confronts the natural goodness of Huck and Nick. It is violence, an essential experience of the frontier, and also in our time — which is a wartime — of the American in Europe. And there is nothing triumphant about the beating which innocence takes, or about what happens to it after it is beaten.

The repetition of Twain's story by Hemingway establishes a continuity of American experience from one century to another, and reinforces the meaning of either story taken separately. The narrative begins to take on overtones that are larger than the facts themselves would seem to warrant. Indeed we might, conscious that we employ an abused term loosely, call it a "myth." At any rate it is a highly suggestive tale that falls, not surprisingly, within the Christian system and relates once more the fall of man, the loss of paradise. But it is an American myth, and it reveals us in a way that no historical, social, or philosophical treatise can do. It speaks to the people of the country from which it springs, and to the world, if it cares to hear, in such a way as to say: We start out smiling and well disposed to the world and our fellowmen. We see ourselves in the image of a naturally good, innocent, and simple boy, eager and expectant. But in the process of our going out into the world we get struck down, somehow, and after that it is hard for us to put ourselves all the way back together again.

This myth seems to bespeak in Americans an innocent desire for a decent life on the one hand and a sense of betrayal on the other. It says that we would do justly and be kind, that we wished no evil to anyone. But it also says that as we grew up evil was everywhere, and our expectations were sold out. The myth is one attempt to explain us, to ourselves and to the world. It also tries to explain why it is that despite all our other, opposing myths — of success, progress, the certain beneficence of technical advance, and the like — we are neither completely happy nor whole. It says, rather wistfully, we would have been, we could have been, but we were wounded before we were grown by the world we were given to grow in. The original beauty of a new country, the anticipation of the possibilities of life in what seemed the most promising world since Eden, were part of a seduction that went bad and should have ended at the doctor's. This is not a story that we believe literally, of course. No myth is to be taken literally or we would not, nowadays, call it a myth. But in a figurative way, on a metaphorical level, one suspects that we believe something of this sort about our experience in the world.

It remains to say something about Hemingway's world — the world his experience caused his imagination to create in books. It is, of course, a very limited world that we are exposed to through him. It is, ultimately, a world at war — war either literally as armed and calculated conflict, or figuratively as marked everywhere with violence, potential or present, and a general hostility. The people of this world operate under such conditions — of apprehension, emergency, stiff-lipped fear, and pleasure seized in haste — as are imposed by war. Restricted grimly by the urgencies of war, their pleasures are limited pretty much to those the senses can communicate, and their morality is a harshly pragmatic affair; what's moral is what you feel good after. Related to this is the code, summarizing the virtues of the soldier, the ethic of wartime. The activities of escape go according to the rules of sport, which make up the code of the armistice, the temporary, peacetime modification of the rules of war.

Hemingway's world is one in which things do not grow and bear fruit, but explode, break, decompose, or are eaten away. It is saved from total misery by visions of endurance, competence, and courage, by what happiness the body can give when it is not in pain, by interludes of love that cannot outlast the furlough, by a pleasure in the countries one can visit, or fish and hunt in, and the cafés one can sit in, and by very little else. Hemingway's characters do not "mature" in the ordinary sense, do not become "adult." It is impossible to picture them in a family circle, going to the polls to vote, or making out their income tax returns. It is a very narrow world. It is a world seen through a crack in the wall by a man pinned down by gunfire. The vision is obsessed by violence, and insists that we honor a stubborn preoccupation with the profound significance of violence in our time.

187

We may argue the utter inadequacy of the world Hemingway refracted and re-created; indeed we should protest against it. It is not the world we wish to live in, and we usually believe that actually we do not live in it. But if we choose to look back over our time, what essential facts can we stack against the facts of violence, evil, and death? We remember countless "minor" wars, and two tremendous ones, and prepare for the day when we may be engaged in a holocaust beyond which we cannot see anything. We may argue against Hemingway's world, but we should not find it easy to prove that it is not the world we have been living in.

It is still too early to know which of all the worlds our writers offer will be the one we shall turn out to have lived in. It all depends on what happens and you never know at the time. "Peace in our time," however, was Hemingway's obscure and ironic prophecy, stated at the start and stuck to. From the beginning his eyes were focused on what may turn out decades hence to have been the main show. With all his obvious limitations, it is possible that he said many of the truest things of our age truly, and this is such stuff as immortalities are made on.

C. HUGH HOLMAN

Thomas Wolfe

Thomas Wolfe grappled in frustrated and demonic fury with what he called "the strange and bitter miracle of life," a miracle which he saw in patterns of opposites. The elements of life and of art seem to have existed for him as a congeries of contradictions, and he could not understand a thing until its negation had been brought forth. The setting down of these opposites is the most obvious single characteristic of his work, the significant parts of which are four vast novels, seven short novels, two collections of short stories, and an essay in criticism — all fragments of an incomplete whole, only the most shadowy outlines of which are discernible.

Even the titles of his books — *Look Homeward, Angel*, with its suggestion of near and far; *Of Time and the River*; *From Death to Morning*; *The Web and the Rock*; *You Can't Go Home Again*, with its idea of home and exile; *The Hills Beyond*, with its suggestion of movement, of extension — reflect this view of experience. So do his geographical oppositions — South and North, country and city, plain and "enfabled rock," America and Europe — and the contrasting pairs into which he regularly grouped his characters — father and mother, Jew and Gentile, South and North Carolinian, poor and rich, true artist and aesthete. Wolfe's vision of himself carried the same pattern of oppositions; in *The Web and the Rock* Esther Jack sums up the autobiographical hero with these words: "He has the face of a demented angel . . . and there is madness and darkness and evil in his brain. He is more cruel than death, and more lovely than a flower. His heart was made for love, and it is full of hate and darkness."

There is also a basic conflict of themes in Wolfe's work. He declared, "I have at last discovered my own America. . . . And I shall wreak out my vision of this life, this way, this world and this America, to the top of my bent, to the height of my ability, but with an unswerving devotion, integrity and purity of purpose." He saw himself as one with Walt Whitman, Mark Twain, and Sherwood Anderson, whom he called "men who have seen America with a poet's vision." The "epic impulse," the desire to define in fiction the American character and to typify the American experience, was obsessively present in his work. Yet another theme, contradictory but equally persistent in his work, was loneliness and the isolation of the incommunicable self. In a major sense, his subject matter was himself, his self-discovery and his groping toward self-knowledge; his forte was the lyrical expression of personal emotion and the rhetorical expression of personal attitudes. Aside from Whitman, no other major American writer ever celebrated himself at such length, with such intensity, or with so great a sense of his own importance as Wolfe did. The private self and the public seer were roles that he was never quite able to harmonize, and yet he persisted in playing them both.

This fundamental concern with opposites is reflected in Wolfe's literary style itself — in the balanced antitheses that abound in his writing, in his shocking juxtaposition of images, in his use of contradictory phrases, such as "changeless change," "splendid and fierce and weak and strong and foolish," "of wandering forever and the earth again," and "the web and the rock." In fact, Wolfe was a writer with two distinctive and contrasting styles. On one level he wrought with lyrical intensity a web of sensuous images capable of evoking from his readers a response almost as intense as that resulting from direct experience. Of American writers in this century, Ernest Hemingway is Wolfe's only equal at the evocative representation of the physical world through images so startlingly direct that they seem to rub against the reader's raw nerve ends. Wolfe said, "The quality of my memory is characterized, I believe, in a more than ordinary degree by the intensity of its sense impressions, its power to evoke and bring back the odors, sounds, colors, shapes, and feel of things with concrete vividness." At its best his style was superbly suited for transferring this concrete vividness to the reader.

Yet Wolfe was seldom content to let the scene or the senses speak for themselves; rather, he felt an obligation to define the emotion which he associated with the scene and to suggest a meaning, a universality, a significance through rhetorical exhortation. The resulting passages are marked by extravagant verbal pyrotechnics — by apostrophe, by incantation, by exhortation, by rhapsodic assertion, and, all too often, by rant and bombast. The lyric style evokes in the reader the ineffable emotion called forth in Wolfe by the scene; then the rhetorical assertion attempts to utter the ineffable and to articulate the transcendent aspects of the scene which Wolfe fears that the reader otherwise may miss. While passages in this second style often succeed magnificently in lifting the reader with their cadenced chants to glimpse Wolfe's ultimate visions, it is also true that such passages sometimes degenerate into dithyrambic incantations that become strident, false, and meaningless. Few writers have been so clearly at the same time both the masters and the slaves of language.

The same contrasts are apparent in the structural qualities of Wolfe's fiction. On the level of dramatic scene, fully realized and impacted with immediacy, Wolfe could construct magnificently. Single episodes of his work, published separately as short stories, are powerful narrative units. "The Child by Tiger," first a short story in the *Saturday Evening Post* and later an episode in *The Web and the Rock,* is a clear example; so are "Only the Dead Know Brooklyn," "The Lost Boy," and "An Angel on the Porch." In the middle length of the short novel he worked with perhaps his greatest effectiveness. He produced seven pieces in this middle length, all of them originally published in magazines as independent entities, although five were later fragmented and distributed through the full-length novels. They include *The Web of Earth,* in a structural sense his most completely successful work; *A Por-*

trait of Bascom Hawke, which was later fragmented and distributed through *Of Time and the River* as a portrait of Bascom Pentland; *No Door*, whose thematic organization was a microcosm which he later expanded into *Of Time and the River*; and *The Party at Jack's*, which, in an expanded form, was incorporated into *You Can't Go Home Again*. These short novels represent strong dramatic and narrative writing, rich in subject matter, firm in control, often objective in point of view.

Furthermore, Wolfe projected ambitious plans for his books. Out of the experiences which were to be the material of his fiction he wished to weave a myth of his native land, an embodiment of its nature and its spirit. At a time when the American critic was just beginning to be concerned with the newer concepts of myth, Wolfe wrote, in the manuscript later published as the title piece of *The Hills Beyond*: "The Myth is founded on *extorted* fact; wrenched from the context of ten thousand days. . . . For it is not a question of having faith, or lack of it. It is a simple fact of seeing." In order to contain and define this mythic aspect of human experience, Wolfe sought in old myths and in fable, as well as in the structure of his own experience, the enclosing form for his utterance. *Of Time and the River* in one of its earlier projections was to be called *Antaeus*, and its characters were to symbolize Heracles, Poseidon, Gaea, Helen, Demeter, Kronos, Rhea, Orestes, Faustus, Telemachus, Jason. After outlining the proposed plot in a letter to Maxwell E. Perkins, his editor, he wrote: "Now, don't get alarmed at all this and think I'm writing a Greek myth. All of this is never mentioned once the story gets under way, but . . . it gives the most magnificent plot and unity to my book." Such projects are one of the staples of Wolfe's correspondence with the editors at Scribner's and at Harper's and with his agent.

Yet, in sharp contrast to the dramatic power in individual scenes and the magnificent and mythic scope in plan, the realized larger units of his work show a formlessness and plotlessness that have baffled and perplexed the critic of Wolfe since he first published a novel. The structure of his works, at least on the surface, seems to be the simple chronological pattern of his own life, their incidents those participated in or witnessed. Scholars and critics have explored the close relationship of Wolfe's work to his life, and they have found that, despite his frequent disclaimers that his work is no more autobiographical than that of other novelists, the use of direct experience and the representation of actual persons and events are very great in his novels. Floyd C. Watkins, who examined Wolfe's use of materials drawn from his home town, Asheville, concluded, "there are many more than 300 characters and places mentioned by name or described in *Look Homeward, Angel,* and probably there is not an entirely fictitious person, place, or incident in the whole novel." Wolfe's disarming statement, "Dr. Johnson remarked that a man would turn over half a library to make a single book: in the same way, a novelist may turn over half the people in a town to make a single figure in his novel," is no defense at all when the people of the town are merely represented under the thinnest and most transparent disguises, and when the changes in name are as slight as "Chapel Hill" to "Pulpit Hill," "Raleigh" to "Sydney," "Woodfin Street" to "Woodson Street," or "Reuben Rawls" to "Ralph Rolls." His father's name is changed from "W. O. Wolfe" to "W. O. Gant," his mother's from "Eliza Westall Wolfe" to "Eliza Pentland Gant," his brother's from "Ben Wolfe" to "Ben Gant."

Wolfe's artistic method was a combination of realistic representation and romantic declaration; and it seems to have reflected accurately a contradictory — or perhaps double — view of the nature of art. On one hand, he was committed to the detailed, exact, accurate picturing of the actual world — committed to such an extent that he found it hard to represent anything that he had not personally experienced. On the other hand, his view of the nature and function of art was essentially that of the nineteenth-century Romantic poets and critics.

In one sense this aesthetic view was a natural outgrowth of his education. Six teachers had major influences on Wolfe, and five of them were clear-cut romantics. Margaret Roberts, who taught him for four years in a boys' preparatory school, made an indelible impression upon him with her love for the English poets; Mrs.

Roberts, represented in *Look Homeward, Angel* as Margaret Leonard, filled the boy with a corresponding love of Wordsworth, Burns, Coleridge, Herrick, Carew, Jonson, Shakespeare, Poe, Hawthorne, Melville, and Scott. At the University of North Carolina he studied under Horace Williams, a philosophy professor whom he represented as Vergil Weldon and whom he called "Hegel in the Cotton Belt." Williams, who was a mystic, taught him a rather loose form of the Hegelian dialectic, in which a concept, or thesis, inevitably generates its opposite, or antithesis, and the interaction of the two produces a new concept, or synthesis. He also studied under Frederick Koch, who was beginning his work with the Carolina Playmakers and was encouraging his students to write folk plays, finding and underscoring the strange in the commonplace. Wolfe's first successful literary efforts were one-act plays written for Koch and produced by the Playmakers with Wolfe acting in them. At Chapel Hill he was also greatly influenced by the teaching of the Spenserian scholar Edwin A. Greenlaw and by his theories of the inseparable relationship of "literature and life." At Harvard an important influence was John Livingston Lowes, who was writing *The Road to Xanadu* while Wolfe was a graduate student in his classes and whose view of the nature of Coleridge's imagination remained for Wolfe until his death a truthful picture of the workings of the artist's mind. At Harvard, too, he was influenced by George Pierce Baker, famous as the director of the "47 Workshop" in drama, although he later broke with Baker, at least partially as a result of dissatisfaction with the brittle and essentially anti-romantic views of students whom Baker applauded.

The marked romanticism of his aesthetic theory, with its pronounced distrust of almost all forms of intellectualism and its emphasis on the expression of the artist's feelings as the highest objective of a work of art, was at a polar extreme from the view Wolfe later developed of the novelist as national prophet obligated to represent the social scene; and his own novels are caught between the tug of the representation of the nation and the expression of the self.

Wolfe's tendency to see and to express things in terms of oppositions may have been learned at the feet of Horace Williams; it is possible that, as some critics have asserted, it represented a failure of his mind adequately to grapple with the problems before it; certainly it was, to some extent, an expression of his southern qualities, for the typical native of the southern states is fascinated by paradox, enamored of ambiguity, devoted to the particular and the concrete, and, although a dreamer of grandiose dreams, seldom the articulator of effective larger structures. The men of Wolfe's region were, like Wolfe himself, caught between the romantic view of their own past and the realistic fact of their present poverty. And over the years they have proved themselves capable of living with unresolved contradictions. Yet Thomas Wolfe was marked almost from his birth by certain unique paradoxes, which formed a peculiar aspect of his life, and therefore an inevitable aspect of his autobiographic art.

Thomas Wolfe was born in Asheville, North Carolina, which he was to call Altamont and Libya Hill in his novels, on October 3, 1900. He was, therefore, a southerner, yet his native state in 1900 was in the midst of its espousal of the Populist movement that has left a heritage of liberalism in educational, social, and economic matters quite different from that in most of the rest of the South. Furthermore, Wolfe came from a mountain town far removed from even the dream of a South of tall white columns and banjo-strumming darkies, a town which was soon to be caught in a real estate fever and go on a middle-class speculative binge, keyed, as Wolfe lamented, to Yankee materialism and dollar greed. In *You Can't Go Home Again* he described that binge and its painful aftermath in coruscating detail. It would have been hard to find a southern town more thoroughly middle class than Asheville in the years of Wolfe's childhood; yet it was a town still of its region, tasting on its tongue the bitterness of defeat, the sharp sting of southern poverty, and the acrid flavor of racial injustice. This middle-class world was his particular subject throughout his career, although he qualified its customary "booster" optimism by the more pessimistic approach natural to a poverty-stricken region still conscious — as no other part of America is — of defeat.

His mother was Julia Elizabeth Westall Wolfe, a member of a mountain clan memorialized by her son as the "time-devouring" Joyners and Pentlands, and she symbolized for him the protean texture of the South, which was always feminine in his view, "the dark, ruined Helen of his blood." The Westalls were people of some prominence in their region, men and women of medium standing in Asheville and its encircling hills. His mother had been a schoolteacher and a book saleswoman before she became the third wife of William Oliver Wolfe, a native of Pennsylvania. W. O. Wolfe was a stonecutter by profession, owning his own business, and he was a powerful man of great gusto, vast appetites, and a torturing need to assert himself vividly against his drab world. Wolfe's representations of his parents as Eliza and W. O. Gant are among his greatest portraits, and their chance meeting and marriage in a southern hill town were central to his view of the "bitter mystery" of his life. He opens his first novel, *Look Homeward, Angel*, with a speculation on "that dark miracle of chance which makes new magic in a dusty world" and symbolizes it through "A destiny that leads . . . from Epsom into Pennsylvania, and thence into the hills that shut in Altamont." He saw Eugene Gant, the hero of that novel, as "the fusion of two strong egotisms, Eliza's inbrooding and Gant's expanding outward."

Thomas was the youngest of the Wolfes' eight children, of whom two died in infancy. During his childhood his mother bought a boardinghouse and moved into it, taking Thomas and his brother Ben with her and leaving W. O. Wolfe and their daughter Mabel in the old house. (The other two sons and a daughter were no longer living at home.) Wolfe's childhood was spent in a family divided between two home establishments, with itinerate boarders as his closest companions, except for his brother Ben, whom he idolized and whose death left upon Thomas' spirit a scar that never healed. Wolfe regarded himself in later life as "God's Lonely Man," and he attributed that loneliness to the experiences of his childhood. In 1933 he wrote his sister, "I think I learned about being alone when I was a child about eight years old and I think that I have known about it ever since."

He attended public school until he was eleven; then he entered a small private school operated by Mr. and Mrs. J. M. Roberts. Wolfe was a bright and perceptive boy, and during the four years he spent at the Roberts' school he was almost totally absorbed in learning. At the age of fifteen — three years ahead of his contemporaries — he entered the University of North Carolina at Chapel Hill, the only one of his family to reach that educational level.

At the time he entered it, the university was undergoing the changes that converted it from a leisurely undergraduate liberal arts college into a university engaged in research and graduate instruction and that made it the focal point of the New South movement, the center of southern liberalism. Once more the southern boy was caught up in the fabric of change, confronted by the oppositions of the old and the new. In the university Wolfe proved to be a good student and a "big man on the campus," being active in debate, publications, and fraternities, as well as working with the Playmakers. He was graduated at the age of twenty, with an urge to study further and the desire to become a playwright.

Borrowing from his mother against his anticipated share in his father's estate, Wolfe went to Harvard, where he studied for three years, and earned the Master of Arts degree in English literature. But the central interest of his Harvard years was in the "47 Workshop" in drama and the furtherance of his projected career as a playwright. The picture he paints of the Workshop in *Of Time and the River* is a satiric attack on pretension and lifeless aestheticism, although his portrait of Professor Baker as "Professor Hatcher" (in the original notes for the novel he had called him "Butcher"), while tainted with malice, is still drawn with respect.

Although teachers as eminent as John Livingston Lowes praised Wolfe's "very distinct ability" as a scholar, he had chosen playwriting for his career, and he vainly tried his fortunes peddling his plays in New York City in the fall of 1923 before he accepted appointment as instructor in English at New York University in January 1924. Wolfe taught at the university, satirically represented as the School of Utility Cultures in *Of Time and the River*, intermittently until the spring of 1930. During this period he made several European tours, met and had a violent love affair with Mrs. Aline Bernstein, a scene and costume designer seventeen years his senior and a married woman with two children. She is the "Esther Jack" of his later novels.

It was in London in the autumn of 1926 that Wolfe began committing to paper in the form of a huge novel the steadily accelerating flood of his childhood memories. The mounting manuscript bore the stamp of the immersion in literature and poetry which had been a major element of Wolfe's life up to that point, but above all it bore, by his own testimony, the mark of Joyce's *Ulysses*. Discernible in it too were traces of H. G. Wells and Sinclair Lewis. When he returned to New York, he continued the writing of the book, while his love affair with Mrs. Bernstein waxed and waned and waxed again. Both have left records of the affair, Mrs. Bernstein in *The Journey Down*, an autobiographical novel, and Wolfe in *The Web and the Rock*. The exact measure of Mrs. Bernstein's influence in disciplining Wolfe's monumental flow of memory, energy, and words into the form which *Look Homeward, Angel* had taken by its completion in first draft in March 1928 is a matter of debate but it was certainly great. The manuscript of the book was complete, in any case, when, after a violent quarrel with Mrs. Bernstein, Wolfe went again to Europe in July, leaving it with an agent. When he returned to New York in January 1929 it was to find a letter from Maxwell E. Perkins, editor of Charles Scribner's Sons, publishers, expressing an interest in the novel, if it could "be worked into a form publishable by us."

Wolfe renewed the affair with Mrs. Bernstein, to whom *Look Homeward, Angel* is dedicated, and worked desperately to cut and arrange the material of his manuscript into a publishable book. In its original form, *Look Homeward, Angel* was the detailed and intense record of the ancestry, birth, childhood, adolescence, and youth of Eugene Gant. It began with a ninety-page sequence on Eugene's father's life, and it concluded when, after Eugene's graduation from college, he discovers, in an imaginary conversation with the ghost of his brother, that "*You* are your world," and, leaving home, "turns his eyes upon the distant soaring ranges." Perkins insisted on the deletion of the historical opening, on the removal of some extraneous material, and on minor rearrangements, but the novel when it was published on October 18, 1929, probably had undergone little more editorial supervision than long manuscripts by exuberant but talented first novelists generally undergo. As it was to work out, *Look Homeward, Angel* was more unqualifiedly Wolfe's in conception, writing, arrangement, and execution than any other work of long fiction that was ever to be published under his name.

Its lyric intensity and its dramatic power were immediately recognized and hailed; even before Sinclair Lewis, in accepting the Nobel Prize in 1930, praised him highly, Wolfe was recognized as a figure to be reckoned with in the literary world. His native Asheville paid him the tribute of being collectively indignant at the portrait of itself in the novel. A novelistic career of great promise was launched, and Wolfe, who had hungered for fame, suddenly found that he didn't want it. Not only were the members of his family hurt and the people of Asheville angry, but he also felt the obligation of producing a second work that represented an advance over the first. This proved to be one of the major struggles of his life.

He resigned from New York University, ended the affair with Mrs. Bernstein, and went to Europe for a year on a Guggenheim fellowship. When he returned to America, he established himself in an apartment in Brooklyn and took up the lonely vigil with himself and his writing which he describes in *The Story of a Novel* and portrays in *You Can't Go Home Again*. Before *Look Homeward, Angel* was published, he had begun planning the new novel and writing parts of it. During the lonely years in Brooklyn, he struggled in growing desperation to produce the second book. The short novel *A Portrait of Bascom Hawke* in 1932 shared a short novel contest prize of $5000 offered by *Scribner's Magazine*. Another short novel, *The Web of Earth,* was written and published in *Scribner's Magazine* during the early Brooklyn years. A reminiscence of her life by Eliza Gant, *The Web of Earth* is one of his most successful pieces of work. Nowhere else does the Joycean influence on Wolfe find as direct and as satisfying an expression as it does here.

The success of these two short novels encouraged Wolfe to continue to work in this form, and between 1932 and 1934 he produced *Death the Proud Brother,* which was reprinted in *From Death to Morning; Boom Town,* which appears in greatly modified form in *You Can't Go Home Again;* and *No Door.* Scribner's planned at one time in 1934 to issue *No Door* as a separate volume, but the short novel was finally broken into two parts and published in *Scribner's Magazine* as "No Door" and "The House of the Far and Lost." The work was first published in its complete short novel form in 1960 in *The Short Novels of Thomas Wolfe.* However, Wolfe's accomplishment in this work was by no means lost, for the thematic structure which he evolved in *No Door* became the model which he followed in organizing *Of Time and the River.*

Despite the fact that Wolfe was living almost entirely on the rather slender proceeds from the sale to magazines of his short stories and his short novels, when he was approached by a representative of Metro-Goldwyn-Mayer about the possibility of his doing motion picture writing at $1000 to $1500 a week, he declined it on the grounds that he had "a lot of books to write."

He was struggling with a vast novel, to be entitled "The October Fair," which would be in at least four volumes and would have a time span from the Civil War to the present, with hundreds of characters and a new protagonist, David Hawke, replacing Eugene Gant. Maxwell Perkins was working with him every night and on weekends in an attempt to give the new work an acceptable structure and symmetry. It is difficult to separate in Wolfe's letters what is defensible judgment based on fact and what is the frenzied product of his febrile imagination; yet, if his versions are to be trusted even in minor part, Maxwell Perkins had a truly major role to play in the formulation of his second novel. It was Perkins, Wolfe said, who suggested what Wolfe took to be the theme of the new novel, "the search for a father." Seemingly it was Perkins who turned him back to Eugene Gant and away from David Hawke; it was Perkins who discouraged his attempts at formulations of his vision of America in other terms than those of the autobiographical "apprenticeship novel," for Wolfe had worked out a number of elaborate schemes for his new novel. And it was Perkins who insisted that *Of Time and the River* was ready to be published and in 1935 sent it to the printers despite Wolfe's protest.

Of Time and the River was a mammoth book, continuing the chronicle of Eugene Gant's sensibility. It opens as he leaves Altamont for Harvard, follows him there, to New York City where he teaches in the School of Utility Cultures, to Europe, where he begins the writing of a novel and has a frustrating love affair with a girl named Ann, and concludes as he meets Esther on the boat back to America. *Look Homeward, Angel,* although it had lacked the traditional novelistic structure, had a certain unity through its concentration on a family, a mountain town, and a way of life. In reading it one was caught up in the sharp impressions of youth and somehow rushed along to that moment of self-realization with which it ended. *Of Time and the River* had less plot, more introspection, less structural cohesion, more rhetoric. Large segments of the book exist without thematic or plot relevance; some of the best scenes and most effective portraits seem to be dramatic intrusions, and it is only when one knows the rest of the story as it is revealed in *The Web and the Rock* that one is able to appreciate the climactic significance of the meeting with Esther with which the book closes.

That these events have meaning for Wolfe beyond their merely personal expression — indeed, that Eugene Gant is in an undefined way the generic Everyman of Whitman's poems or the racial hero of the national epic — one senses from the amount of rhetorical extrapolation by which the hero becomes one with the world, his experiences one with the national experience. Sometimes the rhetoric is wonderfully handled. Indeed, *Of Time and the River* is unusually rich in Wolfe's "poetic passages," but the organization of the materials of the story so that they speak a national myth through self-sufficient action is not attempted with any consistency in the book.

It was greeted with mixed reactions. Many hailed it as a fulfillment of the earnest given by *Look Homeward, Angel*; but its formlessness, its lack of story, and its rhapsodic extravagance were also inescapable, and the really serious critical questions which have been debated about Wolfe's work ever since were first clearly expressed about this novel. These questions are whether it is legitimate in fiction to substitute autobiography and reporting for creation; whether rhetorical assertion, however poetic, can be an acceptable substitute for dramatic representation; whether immediacy can ever be properly bought at the expense of aesthetic distance; and, inevitably, what constitutes form.

In the fall of 1935 a group of stories and sketches originally written as parts of the novel but published in periodicals and excluded from the completed work was assembled and published under the title *From Death to Morning*. This volume, which was attacked by the critics when it appeared and which sold poorly, has never received the attention it deserves. The stories reprinted in it are extremely uneven in quality, but they show Wolfe as a serious experimenter in fiction. His mastery of the short and middle forms of fiction is demonstrated here in such works as *Death the Proud Brother*, "Only the Dead Know Brooklyn," "In the Park," and *The Web of Earth*. That the book would take a critical pounding Wolfe knew, but he said, "I believe that as good writing as I have ever done is in this book." The judgment is startlingly accurate.

Yet if this volume demonstrated a technical virtuosity with which Wolfe is seldom credited, it also showed through its characters and incidents the essential unity and hence the basic autobiographical tendency in his total work. When, in 1936, Wolfe published a little essay in criticism, *The Story of a Novel*, originally a lecture given at a writers' conference at Boulder, Colorado, this record of how he wrote *Of Time and the River*, told with humility and straightforward honesty, seemed to many critics to prove that he simply was not a novelist: in two long novels and a volume of short stories, Wolfe had written out of his direct experience, seemingly without a sense of form, and under the direction of the editors at Scribner's. More than one critic found this situation less than admirable. Robert Penn Warren summed up the case: ". . . despite his admirable energies and his powerful literary endowments, his work illustrates once more the limitations, perhaps the necessary limitations, of an attempt to exploit directly and naïvely the personal experience and the self-defined personality in art." And Bernard De Voto, in a savage attack, declared Wolfe to possess great narrative and dramatic talents but to be unable to realize them in novelistic form; he was guilty of leaving coexisting with true fictional materials too much "placental" matter "which nature and most novelists discard." De Voto also charged that Wolfe's novels were put together by "Mr. Perkins and the assembly-line at Scribner's." That Wolfe was a genius he conceded, but he added that "genius is not enough."

The De Voto article hurt Wolfe deeply. In 1936 a desire to prove De Voto wrong (perhaps heightened by an unconscious awareness that in certain respects at least he was right) joined with many other factors to make Wolfe wish to change his publisher. Among the reasons were a dispute with Perkins about Wolfe's representation of Scribner's people in a story, a disagreement over the cost of corrections in *Of Time and the River*, a group of libel suits which Scribner's wanted to settle out of court, and, most important of all, Wolfe's awareness that his attitudes were incompatible with those of Perkins and that he wanted to go in directions in which Perkins did not wish him to travel. The long and agonizing break with Scribner's, begun in mid-1936, was finally effected in 1937, when Wolfe formed a publishing arrangement with Harper and Brothers, with Edward C. Aswell to act as his editor.

He spent the summer of 1937 working in a cabin in the North Carolina mountains and was happy to find that he was received by his people with pride and pleasure, that they had forgiven him; but he also learned from the experience that "you can't go home again," an idea that loomed large in his thinking and which symbolized for him the fact that we move onward not backward. He was working hard, with the frenzied expenditure of energy of which he was capable, getting material ready to show Aswell as the beginning of a book. At that time he was again projecting a story of great magnitude in at least four volumes, and he was seeking forms and structures through which it could be made into a mythic record of "an innocent man's discovery of life and the world." At one time the book was to be called "The Vision of Spangler's Paul," with the subtitle "The Story of His Birth, His Life, His Going To and Fro in the Earth, His Walking Up and Down in It: His Vision Also of the Lost, the Never-Found, the Ever-Here America." At another time he changed his protagonist's name to Doaks, in an effort to symbolize his typical nature, and wrote "The Doaksology," a history of his family. Finally, he selected George Webber as his protagonist — a character physically very much like the David Hawke whom he had wished to make the hero of *Of Time and the River* — and wrote of him: "The protagonist becomes significant not as the tragic victim of circumstances, the romantic hero in conflict and revolt against his environment, but as a kind of polar instrument round which the events of life are grouped, by means of which they are touched, explained, and apprehended, by means of which they are seen and ordered."

In May 1938 he delivered a great mass of manuscript, perhaps a million words, to Aswell. It represented an ordering of the materials on which he was working, but not a book ready for the press. He himself estimated that more than a year's work remained to be done before the first volume of the new work would be ready. Then he left on a tour of the West which ended with his serious illness from pneumonia in Vancouver, followed by a worsening of his condition in Seattle, and the discovery, after he had been moved to the Johns Hopkins hospital in Baltimore, that the pneumonia had released old sealed-off tuberculosis bacteria in his lungs and that these bacteria had gone to his brain. On September 15, 1938, eighteen days before his thirty-eighth birthday, he died.

Edward Aswell extracted the materials for three books from the mountain of manuscript which Wolfe left. The first, *The Web and the Rock* (1939), is apparently in a form not too different from that which Wolfe had planned, although the last 400 pages of it are still in the earlier and more extravagant style of *Of Time and the River*, rather than the sparser and more controlled style of the opening sections. The new protagonist, George Webber, is surprisingly like Eugene Gant, although his physical characteristics and his family life have changed. The early sections of the book take him through childhood, to college, and then to New York City. There he meets Esther Jack and the novel becomes the record of a tempestuous love affair. Then Webber goes to Germany, is badly beaten in a riot at a festival, the *Oktoberfest*, in Munich, and, through a monologue between his body and his soul, Webber understands that he must turn from his immersion in himself and his past. "He knew and accepted now its limitations" and ". . . looked calmly and sanely forth upon the earth for the first time in ten years." *The Web and the Rock* is a flawed and very imperfect book, seeming to be the forced union of two inharmonious parts. Yet it is much more nearly a novel than *Of Time and the River*, and in the early parts, prepared for publication during the last year of Wolfe's life, it shows a groping toward the control of material and a desire to represent dramatically rather than to assert rhetorically. Wolfe was still grappling with the problem of novelistic form and language, and grappling with at least limited success.

The second of the books which Aswell assembled is much less a novel than *The Web and the Rock*. *You Can't Go Home Again* (1940) is a bringing together in a narrative frame of large units of material which Wolfe had completed but only partially arranged at the time of his death. It continues the story of George Webber, but in it what Wolfe meant when he said that the protagonist was to be a "kind of polar instrument, round which the events of life are grouped," becomes clearer. The book — it is hardly a novel at all — has the very loose narrative structure of George Webber's life: he returns from Europe, writes his book, goes to Libya Hill (Asheville) for his aunt's funeral, travels in Europe, sees the emptiness of fame in the person of Lloyd McHarg (Sinclair Lewis), travels in Germany and comprehends the horror of the Nazi regime, and writes a long letter setting forth his credo. Yet what gives the book vitality is not George and his experiences — although those dealing with the publication and reception of his novel *Look to the Mountains* are extremely interesting to the Wolfe student — but the view of life which is seen through George. Mr. Katamoto, Mr. Jack and the party at his house, Judge Bland and the satiric picture of the moral and material collapse of Libya Hill, Daisy Purvis, Lloyd McHarg, Foxhall Edwards and his family, Mr. C. Green, who jumps from the twelfth story of the Admiral Francis Drake Hotel, the frightened little Jew on the train out of Germany — it is in such materials as these that the dramatic strength of the book resides.

You Can't Go Home Again is freer than his other books of the rhapsodic assertion that so often replaces dramatic statement. Those who have found Wolfe's strength in his ability to depict character and to invest scenes with life and movement are likely to find in *You Can't Go Home Again* both his best writing and a discernible promise of greater work and greater control to come. On the other hand, those who see Wolfe's strength to be peculiarly his power with words are likely to feel that the dramatic and narrative success of *You Can't Go Home Again* was bought at the price of his most distinctive qualities. As a novel it is the least satisfactory of his works, yet in its pages are to be seen, dimly and afar off it is true, the faint outline of what he was striving for in his vast and unrealized plans for the "big book."

The third volume that Aswell mined from the manuscript was *The Hills Beyond* (1941), a collection of fragments and sketches. A few of the stories were published in magazines after 1935, but most of them were previously unpublished units of the manuscript. Two distinguished short stories are here, "The Lost Boy" and "Chickamauga," together with a 150-page fragment, "The Hills

Beyond," which is a narrative of the Joyners and would have been the early introductory material to the big book. "The Hills Beyond" parallels, in subject matter, material which Wolfe tried to introduce at the beginning of each of his major stories. In this fragment Wolfe's efforts at being an objective novelist have more immediately apparent success than they do elsewhere, and he seems to be moving much more toward the realism of the southern frontier and away from the romanticism of his early career. Valuable though it is to have as many of the self-contained fragments of the Wolfe manuscripts as we can get, *The Hills Beyond* adds very little to Wolfe's stature as a novelist.

In 1948 *Mannerhouse*, one of the plays which Wolfe had tried very hard to peddle to professional producers but without success, was published from the manuscript. An abbreviated version of his ten-scene play *Welcome to Our City* was published in *Esquire Magazine* in 1957. Both are documents purely of historical importance. With the publication of *The Hills Beyond* most of Wolfe's significant work was in print, and, incomplete though it is as a record of his vast and ambitious project, it is all that remains of his efforts to formulate in fiction a vision of himself and his world. The manuscripts out of which Aswell quarried the last three books are now in the William B. Wisdom Collection at Harvard. They contain many scenes, characters, and sections that have never been published, but the unpublished materials will probably have to await a completely new editing of the total manuscripts before they will find an audience.

Wolfe's career, like his works, became a matter of debate before his death; and his untimely demise, when seemingly the world was all before him and his prodigious talent was still groping toward an adequate mode of expression, increased the debate without giving appreciable weight to any of the answers. He remains, despite his thirty-seven years, a "golden boy" cut off in the moment of the flowering of his talent, and the issue of whether he had already done all that he was capable of and was, therefore, saved by death from tasting the fruits of a certain diminution of power or whether a major talent went unrealized through the cruel accident of time will remain as unresolved with him as it has been with all the other "golden boys" who tasted too early "the bitter briefness of our days."

The remark of William Faulkner, "I rated Wolfe first [among modern American writers] because we had all failed but Wolfe had made the best failure because he had tried hardest to say the most," is a peculiarly unsatisfying and unrewarding comment which merely restates the question; although his added remark, "He may have had the best talent of us, he may have been 'the greatest American writer' if he had lived longer, though I have never held much with the 'mute inglorious Milton' theory," helps a little.

One of the principal facts of Wolfe's career is summed up in his statement to Edward Aswell: "I began life as a lyrical writer . . . I began to write with an intense and passionate concern with the designs and purposes of my own youth; and like many other men, that preoccupation has now changed to an intense and passionate concern with the designs and purposes of life." This extension of interest to the surrounding world, to "life," was obsessively present with Wolfe from the time of the publication of *Look Homeward, Angel* to his death. In 1929, when the new book was to be "The October Fair," he described it to the Guggenheim Foundation: "It tries to find out why Americans are a nomad race (as this writer believes); why they are touched with a powerful and obscure homesickness wherever they go, both at home and abroad." In 1930 he wrote Perkins: "I believe I am at last beginning to have a proper use of a writer's material: for it seems to me he ought to see in what has happened to him the elements of the universal experience." He wrote John Hall Wheelock, another editor at Scribner's, enthusiastically about a section of "The October Fair" which he had just completed: "In *Antaeus*, in a dozen short scenes, told in their own language, we see people of all sorts *constantly in movement*, going somewhere." But in the same letter he also says, "God knows what Maxwell Perkins will say when he sees it." He was always toying with ideas like his largely unwritten "The Hound of Darkness," of which he said, "It will be a great tone-symphony of night — railway yards, engines, freights, deserts, a clopping hoof, etc. — seen *not by a definite personality,* but haunted throughout by a *consciousness* of personality."

After *Look Homeward, Angel,* he wanted to abandon Eugene Gant for a less autobiographical protagonist, David Hawke, and to write his next novel in the first person — apparently realizing that a first-person narrator is less in the forefront of a story and is more a transmitting vehicle than the third-person protagonist. But during the years of agonized labor by himself and with Perkins most of these plans went by the wayside. Maxwell Perkins believed that Wolfe's second novel should continue the story of Eugene Gant and should center itself exclusively in Gant's consciousness. Perkins wrote, "The principle that I was working on was that this book, too [as *Look Homeward, Angel* had], got its form through the senses of Eugene," and he told how he objected to scenes in the novel that were not recorded through Eugene's perceptions; he tried, for example, to exclude the episodes about Gant's death — one of the most memorable sequences that Wolfe ever wrote. The struggle by which *Of Time and the River* achieved publication over Wolfe's protest is well known; but the depth of Wolfe's dissatisfaction with the book became clear only with the publication of the *Letters* in 1956. When *Of Time and the River* appeared, he wrote Perkins, ". . . as I told you many times, I did not care whether the final length of the book was 300, 500, 1000 pages, so long as I had realized completely and finally my full intention — and that was not realized. I still sweat with anguish — with a sense of irremediable loss — at the thought of what another six months would have done to that book — how much more whole and perfect it would have been. Then there would have been no criticism of its episodic character — for, by God, in purpose and in spirit, that book was not episodic, but a living whole and I could have made it so."

There is certainly the possibility that Wolfe was too completely lost in the deluge of his own memories and words to form them into an intelligent large whole in the years between 1930 and

1935 — although his most distinguished short and middle-length fiction was done in this period — and the sometimes violent midwifery of Perkins may have been essential to getting anything publishable from the laboring author. On the other hand, when one examines the first 300 pages of *The Web and the Rock* and recalls that it is Wolfe's own work done without editorial assistance or thinks of the power and directness of the first two books of *You Can't Go Home Again*, it is difficult not to wish that Wolfe had been free to try.

To the imponderable *if's* which haunt the mind in the case of an artist too youthfully dead must be added in Wolfe's case this one: what might his career have been if he had struggled through toward the realization of form without the assistance of Perkins? Certainly if Wolfe had written *Of Time and the River* without Perkins' aid, it would have been a radically different book and possibly a much better one. But he did not, and so the fact remains that only as the lyric recorder of his youth was Wolfe truly successful in the longer fictional forms. His great vision of being the critic of his society and the definer of his nation can be seen in fragments but its large outline is shadowy and incomplete.

It is for this reason that the central problems concerning Wolfe as a writer are as intimately tied up in his personality and his career as they are in his work. Louis D. Rubin, Jr., in an excellent critical study of Wolfe, has asked that the autobiographical quality of the novels be accepted as clear fact and they then be examined as novels, as works of art. When this is done — and Mr. Rubin does it with great skill — *Look Homeward, Angel* emerges as Wolfe's only satisfactory full-length novel, and in his other book-length works one almost has the feeling of an expense of talent in a waste of formlessness. Perhaps such a conclusion is proper — certainly it is the one reached by many of the best and most rigorous of American critics — but it leaves untouched the question of Wolfe's power and the continuing and mounting success which he has with readers.

Wolfe's failure to write his own books as he wanted them written cannot ultimately be laid at any door other than his own.

The causes of this failure are complex: they include his own lack of security (his extreme sensitivity to reviews shows that such a lack was there), his desire to achieve publication at whatever cost (there is evidence of this quality in his letters), and a deep-seated affection for Perkins and gratitude to him. As William Faulkner once declared, "The writer's only responsibility is to his art. He will be completely ruthless if he is a good one . . . If a writer has to rob his mother, he will not hesitate." Paradoxically, Thomas Wolfe devoted his life and his energies to the creation of art with a single-mindedness not surpassed in this century — he is almost archetypally the "dedicated writer" — and yet he lacked that ultimate ruthlessness of which Faulkner speaks. For a writer whose talent is of the magnitude of Wolfe's and whose plans have the scope and importance that his do, such a failing cannot be easily brushed aside. On this point he was highly culpable — he did not make the longer forms of fiction, at whatever cost, the adequate vehicles of his vision and his talent; he did not subject his ego to the discipline of his own creative imagination — and the price he has paid for the failure has been very great indeed. It is the price of being a writer of inspired fragments and of only one satisfying larger work and that an imperfect one.

Here the oppositions in Wolfe reach a crucial test. He seemed always to feel that when the contrasting opposites were defined the synthesis would result automatically; he was always stating a thing and its opposite and allowing the "miracle" of their coexistence to stand. Here in his own work the fact of his great talent and the fact of his ambitious projects were never submitted to the discipline which would have made a synthesis of them; they were allowed to coexist without serious efforts at fusion.

This aspect of Wolfe's work points to its essential romanticism, to the extent to which it is imbedded in the doctrine of self-expression and self-realization. Whitman once wrote: " 'Leaves of Grass' . . . has mainly been the outcropping of my own emotional and other personal nature — an attempt, from first to last, to put a *Person* . . . freely, fully and truly on record." This is basically

Wolfe's accomplishment, although he was clearly striving toward something else in the last seven years of his life.

Wolfe's work is not, therefore, of primary value as a group of novels, or even in terms of his shadowy larger plan. His total work stands, as do so many other monuments of romantic art, as a group of fragments imperfectly bodying forth a seemingly ineffable cosmic vision in terms of the self of the artist. Although it contains large areas of poor and even bad writing, scenes that do not come off or that bear no relevance to what has gone before, and rhapsodies that fail utterly to communicate, it also contains some of the best writing done by an American this century, and it merits our thoughtful examination.

The most obvious of Wolfe's strengths is his ability with language. The word has for him unique powers; he was fascinated by language, enchanted with rhythms and cadences, enamored of rhetorical devices. Language was the key he sought to unlock mysteries and to unloose vast forces; he approached it almost in the spirit of primitive magic. This aspect of language he expressed in the paragraph printed as a prologue to *The Web and the Rock*: "Could I make tongue say more than tongue could utter! Could I make brain grasp more than brain could think! Could I weave into immortal denseness some small brede of words, pluck out of sunken depths the roots of living, some hundred thousand magic words that were as great as all my hunger, and hurl the sum of all my living out upon three hundred pages — then death could take my life, for I had lived it ere he took it: I had slain hunger, beaten death!"

Another aspect of his effective use of language is his accurate and vivid dialogue. Wolfe had a remarkable ear for folk speech, and his people speak personal dialects set down with great verisimilitude. His characters sometimes seem to talk forever, but their speech is always marked by distinctiveness in diction, syntax, and cadence. Accuracy, however, is a less obvious quality of their speech than gusto and vigor are. There is a feeling of great energy in the speech of most of them. The clearest example of Wolfe's mastery of the spoken language is to be seen in *The Web of Earth* but it is apparent in almost everything that he wrote.

He declared that he sought a language, an articulation: "I believe with all my heart, also, that each man for himself and in his own way, each man who ever hopes to make a living thing out of the substances of his one life, must find that way, that language, and that door — must find it for himself." He sought this language, this tool of communication, not only in the rolling periods of rhetoric but also in the sensuous image drawn from the "world's body," which is a distinctive aspect of the language of lyric and dramatic writing. And here, in the concrete and particularized representation of the sensory world, he was triumphantly the master. It is Wolfe's ability to evoke the world's body which is responsible for the sense of total reality which his work produces in the young and impressionable, and it is this seeming immersion in the sensuous which makes him sometimes appear to be more the poet of the senses than of sense.

This concern with language, one so great that he might have said of his total work, as Whitman did of *Leaves of Grass*, that it was "only a language experiment," is the logical expression of one of Wolfe's major themes, the loneliness at the core of all human experience. He saw each individual in the world as living in a compartment in isolation from his fellows and unable to communicate adequately with them. It is this tragedy of loneliness that is at the heart of Eugene Gant's experience and makes *Look Homeward, Angel* a book which can appropriately bear the subtitle "A Story of the Buried Life." The desire to break down the walls keeping him from communion with others is at least a part of "man's hunger in his youth," in *Of Time and the River*. The need Wolfe's characters have for a language with which to breach the isolating walls is very great. In a scene in *Of Time and the River*, Helen, Eugene Gant's sister, is lying awake in the darkness: "And suddenly, with a feeling of terrible revelation, she saw the strangeness and mystery of man's life; she felt about her in the darkness the presence of ten thousand people, each lying in his bed, naked and alone, united at the heart of night and darkness, and listening, as she, to the sounds of silence and of sleep. . . . And it seemed to her that if men would only listen in the darkness, and send the language of their naked lonely spirits across the silence of the night, all of the error, falseness and confusion of their lives would vanish, they would no longer be strangers, and each would find the life he sought and never yet had found." There are few lonelier people in fiction than W. O. and Eliza Gant. Each is lost in an envelope of private experience and each tries vainly to express himself — W. O. through rhetoric, invective, alcohol, and lust; Eliza through garrulity, money, and real estate. The terrible incompatibility in which they live reaches its almost shocking climax when, in the last moments of Gant's life, they finally speak across the void to each other, and Gant's expression of kindness dissolves Eliza into tears.

Wolfe described the controlling theme of all his books as "the search for a father" — the theme he said he consciously made central in *Of Time and the River* at Perkins' suggestion. Perkins had intended merely to suggest a type of plot, but Wolfe took the suggestion as a statement of philosophical theme, and he defined that search as a search for certainty, an "image of strength and wisdom external to his [man's] need and superior to his hunger." In one sense, this search is the seeking for an individual with whom communication can be established and maintained. The search grows out of Eugene's loneliness in his childhood and the sense of isolation which he has in his world. It is intensified by his inability to communicate his love to his brother Ben. In his later life, whether for Gant or for George Webber, it finds expression in the relationships established and broken with Francis Starwick, Esther Jack, and Foxhall Edwards, to name only the major figures. About all these relationships there is a recurrent pattern: the new person is approached with eagerness; an intense relationship is established; then a failure of communication and understanding occurs; and Gant-Webber rejects the friendship. The affair with Esther Jack is, perhaps, the clearest example of this pattern. It is debatable whether the idea of the search for the father, with its suggestion of myth and of fable, defines as well as does the representation of loneliness the fundamental theme of Thomas Wolfe, whether that loneliness be described as the search for "a stone, a leaf, an unfound door," as the urge to wandering and the counter tug of home (so well articulated in *The Web of Earth* and parts of *Of Time and the River*), or as the desire vicariously to be one with and to understand "ten thousand men" in the cities, the towns, and the hamlets of America.

Here Wolfe's concern with oppositions takes on its tragic overtone. The essentially contradictory aspect of life creates barriers of race, of place, of heritage, of language, and as he portrays these barriers, he tries to lead us to say at the end of the Gant-Webber chronicle, as he says at its beginning: "Naked and alone we came into exile. In her dark womb we did not know our mother's face: from the prison of her flesh have we come into the unspeakable and incommunicable prison of this earth." Thus, as Wolfe sees it, all human experience seeks the "great forgotten language, the lost lane-end into heaven." Certainly, as several critics have pointed out, there are Wordsworthian suggestions here. Out of some transcendent glory of childhood, we gradually are hemmed in by the growing prison house of the world, the luster and glory of life are gradually tarnished, and we are forced further away from communion. But there are also suggestions of a book which Wolfe knew and praised and whose formlessness he defended, Laurence Sterne's *Tristram Shandy*. Sterne's novel is concerned with the education of the young through the impact of the world outside upon the young mind. It is told through the memories in maturity of Tristram, and it is the associational pattern of those memories which determines the form of the book. At the core of *Tristram Shandy* is the tragedy of isolation. W. O. Gant has in one sense a recognizable ancestor in "My Father" Walter Shandy, who sought in vain for a word to communicate with wife and brother. Loneliness, memory, and time are intertwined in the sad comedy of the Shandean world. And so they are in Wolfe's.

For while the Wolfean character cannot find a language through which to speak, cannot break through "the incommunicable prison of this earth," he is the victim of more than silence and the lack of a language — he is also the victim of time. And the entity time is for Wolfe the great factor in life and in his books and the only really serious philosophical concept which he uses in his fiction. One of the structural problems with which he grappled seriously throughout his novelistic career was the finding of a means by which to represent adequately his views of time, which he saw as threefold.

The first and most obvious element of time, he believed, is that of simple chronology, the element that carries a narrative forward; this may be called "clock time." The second element is past time, the "accumulated impact of man's experience so that each moment of their lives was conditioned not only by what they experienced in that moment, but by all that they had experienced up to that moment." This past time exists in the present principally through the action of the memory, being triggered by a concrete sensory impression which in some way recalls the past. However, as Margaret Church has pointed out, memory in Wolfe merely recalls this past; it does not re-create it or actually assert its continued existence, as Bergson's and Proust's theories of time tend to do. All this action — the present and the recollections of the past in the present — takes place against what Wolfe calls "time immutable, the time of rivers, mountains, oceans, and the earth; a kind of eternal and unchanging universe of time against which would be projected the transience of man's life, the bitter briefness of his day." It is this inexorable forward flow of time, pictured as a river or more often as a train, which constantly carries man away from his golden youth, which is "lost and far" and can exist again only in memory. It is Wolfe's repeated representation of his protagonist as a narrator reporting his present emotions as he remembers the past in sensuous detail which, at least in part, creates the nostalgic quality of his writing.

Wolfe's problem was the picturing of scenes so that an awareness of these three elements of time was created. In a given situation a man caught in his particular instant in time has it enriched and rendered more meaningful as the past impinges upon him through memory, and he gets thereby a sense of the abso-

lute time within which his days are painfully brief. Wolfe gives
this concept fictional expression in his four-part story "The Lost
Boy." In the first part, a boy, Grover, passes an initiation point
in life, as his father intercedes for him with a candy store keeper.
" 'This is Time,' thought Grover. 'Here is the Square, here is my
father's shop, and here am I.' " The second part is the mother's
reminiscence years later about Grover on a train trip to the St.
Louis Fair. Her monologue ends, "It was so long ago, but when
I think of it, it all comes back . . . I can still see Grover just the
way he was, the way he looked that morning when we went down
through Indiana, by the river, to the Fair." The third part is a
monologue by the sister, recounting Grover's death. It ends, "It
all comes back as if it happened yesterday. And then it goes away
again, and seems farther off and stranger than if it happened in
a dream." In the fourth part, the brother, who was a very small
boy when Grover died, goes to the house in St. Louis where it
happened and tries by the use of memory to bring back the "lost
boy." This section ends: "And out of the enchanted wood, that
thicket of man's memory, Eugene knew that the dark eye and the
quiet face of his friend and brother — poor child, life's stranger,
and life's exile, lost like all of us, a cipher in blind mazes, long
ago — the lost boy was gone forever, and would not return." The
ultimate meaning of the statement "You can't go home again,"
which Wolfe used over and over in the last year of his life, is to
be found here. "Home" is a symbol of the past, of what has been
lost; for the holder of a romantic view of childhood, it is a peculiarly effective and revealing symbol. None of us, it says, can
return to the lost childhood, the lost community, the fading glory;
for time carries us inexorably away. We can't go home again.

In Wolfe's work this vision of time is always associated with
the sense of being alone, of being isolated. In *Of Time and the
River* he tries to enumerate the concrete memories which taken
together make up the remembered past for America, and then he
says: "But this was the reason why these things could never be forgotten — because we are so lost, so naked and so lonely in America.
Immense and cruel skies bend over us, and all of us are driven

on forever and we have no home. Therefore, it is not the slow, the punctual sanded drip of the unnumbered days that we remember best, the ash of time; nor is it the huge monotone of the lost years, the unswerving schedules of the lost life and the well-known faces, that we remember best. It is a face seen once and lost forever in a crowd, an eye that looked, a face that smiled and vanished on a passing train." And a little later, he describes the way in which the past almost forcefully entered the present for him: ". . . always when that lost world would come back, it came at once, like a sword thrust through the entrails, in all its panoply of past time, living, whole, and magic as it had always been." It is like a sword because it cuts sharply and deeply and hurts very much. Perhaps the one emotion which Wolfe describes most effectively is this pain from which comes the sudden hunger for a lost and almost forgotten aspect of life, for "the apple tree, the singing, and the gold." Wolfe succeeds in giving us this sense of the onward rush of time and the death of the morning's gold, an awareness of the price that is paid before the "years of philosophic calm" can come. Since this feeling is very much a part of youth and its pain and *Weltschmerz*, its inarticulate melancholy, he speaks with peculiar authority to the very young and to those older chiefly through their memories of having been very young.

Wolfe did not theorize about these concepts of time, or, except in passing, discuss them. He probably did not know the works of Proust at all well, despite the degree to which the sense impressions in the present restored the lost past for both of them. Karin Pfister has suggested that Wolfe's time theories may owe something to those of Bergson, to whom Proust was also a debtor. As a novelist Wolfe seemingly was fascinated by the mystery rather than the metaphysics of time. In *The Web and the Rock* he wrote: "Time is a fable and a mystery . . . it broods over all the images of earth . . . Time is collected in great clocks and hung in towers . . . and each man has his own, a different time."

The river and the ocean he used as large symbols for "time immutable," yet his clearest figure for the ceaseless motion and the inexorable passage of time is the train. No American in the past fifty years has been more the poet of trains. Their rushing across the face of the earth, the glimpses of life to be seen flashing past their speeding windows, the nostalgic and lonely wail of their whistles in the night, even their sounds echoing in depots, which in *Of Time and the River* he imagines to be the very sounds of time itself — all these characteristics Wolfe associates with loneliness and movement and the sad passage of time.

Yet in one sense Wolfe's characters transcend his themes. The paradox here is a very great one: Wolfe, who asserted that no man could know his brother, described his fellowmen with deep understanding; Wolfe, whose subject seemed always to be himself, whose characters are drawn in large measure from real life rather than imagined, and who presented his world chiefly through the consciousness of an autobiographical hero, created a group of characters so fully realized that they live with great vigor in the reader's mind. *Look Homeward, Angel* is perhaps the most autobiographical novel ever written by an American, yet the protagonist, Eugene Gant, is a much less vivid person than the members of his family. It is W. O. Gant, Eliza, Helen, and brother Ben who glow with life and absorb our imaginations. Eugene himself is more a "web of sensibility" and a communicating vehicle than a person, or perhaps it is that he seems to us more nearly ourselves and less someone whom we are observing. In *Of Time and the River* the Gant family, Bascom Pentland, Francis Starwick, Abraham Jones, and Ann are more convincingly persons than the hero is. In *The Web and the Rock*, there is less centering in the consciousness of the protagonist and George Webber exists more as an individual than Eugene does. The result is that the other characters of this novel and *You Can't Go Home Again* are seen in relation to the protagonist rather than through him. Yet in these books too Wolfe's gift for creating believable people of unbelievable gusto is very impressive. Certainly among all his memorable creations Esther Jack, Dick Prosser, Nebraska Crane, Judge Rumford Bland, and Foxhall Edwards would stand high.

Wolfe's concentration upon people of excessive vigor may be the result of his vitalism, his worship of life as a pervasive force and a supreme value in itself. Certainly, whether as the result of philosophical attitude or of mere artistic excess, the characters in Wolfe's work loom larger than life and are possessed of an awesome and sometimes awful dynamism. They are large in body, appetite, feeling, disease, and suffering. They crowd the canvas to the exclusion of the background and even of the context of action. Possibly this lack of aesthetic distance, which is one of the most obvious qualities of Wolfe's work, results from his extreme subjectivity, but it is also attributable in part to his view of life. Bella Kussy thinks that the example of vitalism run rampant which Wolfe saw in Nazi Germany cured him, and that the German experience caused his concern in his last years with social rather than personal consequences. The tendency toward social criticism, however, was present in his work some time before he was made shockingly aware of the direction that Nazi Germany was taking.

Among the important influences on the social aspect of Wolfe's work was that of Sinclair Lewis, whose satiric condemnation of a materialistic society dedicated to bulk, glitter, and the conscious disregard of beauty made a powerful impact on the young writer. As early as 1923 Wolfe wrote his mother contemptuously of "those people who shout 'Progress, Progress, Progress' — when what they mean is more Ford automobiles, more Rotary Clubs, more Baptist Ladies Social unions." This attitude is just about the extent of the social criticism in *Look Homeward, Angel*, although it is often expressed in that novel. Wolfe's tendency toward satire is clearly present in the book, but it is satire aimed at Main Street and Booster's Club targets; in the name of beauty it is attacking blatant commercialism and its attendant ugliness.

The years that Wolfe spent in Brooklyn during the depths of the depression were filled with social lessons for him. "Everywhere around me," he wrote later, "during these years, I saw the evidence of an incalculable ruin and suffering. . . . universal calamity had somehow struck the life of almost every one I knew." He became convinced that something was basically wrong with such a social order. His letters show that he had wanted to make what he and Perkins regarded as a "Marxist" interpretation of the social scene in *Of Time and the River*, although Perkins dissuaded him from doing it. The egalitarianism and the essentially middle-class economic radicalism of his native region reasserted themselves in his thinking during this period, and in *You Can't Go Home Again* they find expression. A sense of primary social injustice in the world is an operative force in Book II, "The World That Jack Built," which was originally published as the short novel *The Party at Jack's* and which contrasts the world of the very wealthy with that of the laboring classes that serve it; in the section "The Hollow Men," dealing with the suicide of C. Green and asserting the primary worth of the individual in a society that would reduce him to a mere statistic; in Book IV, " 'I Have a Thing to Tell You,' " also originally a short novel, with its angry picture of Nazi Germany; and in the revised segments from the short novel "Boom Town," with its satiric pictures of Libya Hill in the grip of the real estate boom and in the disaster of the crash, where ignoble motives of little men play destructively upon the common greed of their fellow citizens.

One of the repeated charges that Wolfe made against Perkins was that he was a "conservative," whereas Wolfe had become what he called a "revolutionary." Yet his social thinking is lacking in depth and significance. Pamela Hansford Johnson is probably too harsh when she says, "His is a young man's socialism, based on the generous rage, the infuriated baffled pity; like the majority of young, middle-class intellectuals, he looked for 'the people' in the dosshouse and upon the benches of the midnight parks." But, as E. B. Burgum has noted, ". . . he was so constituted that he must fight alone." In that aloneness he was unable to act as a part of any coordinated social scheme. The future of America which he asserts at the conclusion of *You Can't Go Home Again* is really an act of faith — and of a faith still based on the spiritual as opposed to the material, on the reawakening of "our own democracy" within us. Here, as a social critic, he again reminds us most of Whitman. For Whitman in *Democratic Vistas* saw with mounting alarm the pattern that his nation was following and opposed it to the expanding realization of the self, of "Personalism," which it was the poet's program to advance. This is a defensible and even an admirable position, but the work of those who hold it can seldom bear the logical scrutiny of those who espouse specific social programs. As contrasted with Maxwell Perkins, Wolfe properly regarded himself as a "revolutionary," yet he remained the most persuasive advocate of an enlightened middle-class democracy that America has produced this century.

It was inevitable that the centrality of loneliness and separateness in Wolfe's experience and his writing, coupled with the social problems and the human suffering of the years of his active career, should have fostered in him a sense of evil in the world and have given a tragic quality to his writing. His very method of oppositions would lead him to a Manichaean cosmic view. Furthermore, he was a product of a region steeped in defeat, suffering, and the acceptance of an unthinkable inevitability. As C. Vann Woodward has stated it, "Nothing about [its] history is conducive to the theory that the South was the darling of divine providence." Something of this attitude — which, in Wolfe, E. B. Burgum inaccurately called "reconciliation with despair" — is a part of the heritage of all southerners, even in the liberal areas of the South such as the one in which Wolfe grew up.

Wolfe wrote of the shock he experienced in Brooklyn during the depression at the "black picture of man's inhumanity to his fellow man . . . of suffering, violence, oppression, hunger, cold, and filth and poverty," and added, "And from it all, there has come the final deposit, a burning memory, a certain evidence of the fortitude of man, his ability to suffer and somehow to survive." Loneliness and suffering and pain and death — these are the things which man — frail, weak, hauntingly mortal — can expect. Yet man, for Wolfe, is also a noble creature. The despair of the literary naturalist, so common in America in the twentieth century, is not a part of his thinking. In a too obvious extension of speeches by Hamlet and Jaques, in the twenty-seventh chapter of *You Can't Go Home Again*, Wolfe attempts to answer the question "What is man?" and in his answer states as clearly as he was ever to do the basic contradiction and the tragic magnitude of the earthly experience. Man is "a foul, wretched, abominable creature . . . it is impossible to say the worst of him . . . this travesty of waste and sterile breath." Yet his accomplishments are magnificent. The individual, viewed as physical animal, is a "frail and petty thing who lives his days and dies like all the other animals and is forgotten. And yet, he is immortal, too, for both the good and the evil that he does live after him." In the teeming, uneven pages of Wolfe's work this vision of man possessed of tragic grandeur — essentially the vision of the nineteenth-century Romantic — is presented with great intensity.

Wolfe believed that the American experience demanded a new art form and a new language for the expression of this view, however. Like Whitman, he invited the Muse to "migrate from Greece and Ionia," and

> Making directly for this rendezvous, vigorously clearing
> a path for herself, striding through the confusion,
> By thud of machinery and shrill steam-whistle
> undismay'd,
> Bluff'd not a bit by drain-pipe, gasometers, artificial
> fertilizers,
> Smiling and pleas'd with palpable intent to stay,
> She's here, install'd amid the kitchen ware!

Wolfe wrote: ". . . in the cultures of Europe and of the Orient the American artist can find no antecedent scheme, no structural plan, no body of tradition that can give his own work the validity and truth that it must have. It is not merely that he must make somehow a new tradition for himself, derived from his own life and from the enormous space and energy of American life . . . it is even more than this, that the labor of a complete and whole articulation, the discovery of an entire universe and of a complete language, is the task that lies before him."

In his attempt to accomplish that task Wolfe strove with unceasing diligence. That he failed to realize the full structural plan of his work in the years in which he lived is obvious; that he made no whole articulation of the space and energy of American life is obvious; that he failed to formulate a completely adequate language for the singer of America in fiction is also obvious. What he might have done and even why he did not accomplish more of it become finally unanswerable questions; they tease the mind without enlightening it. We must ultimately accept or reject what he did accomplish.

Wolfe's kind of imagination and his artistic attitudes and methods equipped him well for the depiction of character and the portrayal of action in self-contained but isolated sequences. He seems to have functioned most naturally and best when he was depicting his recollections of individual people and specific actions, when he was making the effort which F. Scott Fitzgerald praised in him and called "the attempt . . . to recapture the exact feel of a moment in time and space, exemplified by people rather than by things . . . an attempt at a mature memory of a deep experience."

Hence he showed a control and an objectivity in his short stories and his short novels that effectively belies the charge of formlessness. Yet his desire to find a new "structural plan" and as a kind of national epic-maker to create the "complete and whole articulation" of America led him to fragment these effective short fictions and use them as portions of the record of the total experience by which his Whitmanesque narrator knows and expresses his native land. He never succeeded completely in this effort, and the result is that the parts of his books are often better than the wholes which they go together to create. Despite his bardic effort and his epic intention, his total work — however flawed, imperfect, fragmentary — is ultimately the record of a self and only very partially that of a nation. Wolfe himself described its strength and suggested its great weakness when he called it "a giant web in which I was caught, the product of my huge inheritance — the torrential recollectiveness, derived out of my mother's stock, which became a living, million-fibered integument that bound me to the past, not only of my own life, but of the very earth from which I came, so that nothing in the end escaped from its inrooted and all-feeling explorativeness." To the end Thomas Wolfe retained a childlike, pristine delight in the manifold shapes, colors, odors, sounds, and textures of experience and his work communicates this delight — shadowed with a nostalgia for things past — with almost total authority.

The measure of this accomplishment is not small. *Look Homeward, Angel* is a richly evocative account of the pains and joys of childhood and youth, peopled with a host of living characters. With all its flaws, it is a fine novel, and one that gives promise of enduring. In Wolfe's total work a personality is set down with a thoroughness and an honesty, with an intensity and a beauty of language unsurpassed by any other American prose writer, even though, aside from *Look Homeward, Angel*, it is only in the short novels that we find really sure artistic control, and sprinkled through the other books are passages of very bad writing and of irrelevant action.

Wolfe began obsessed with paradox and contradiction; the shape of his whole career reflects startling contrast. He who would have written the definition of his nation left primarily the definition of a self; he who would have asserted that though we "are lost here in America . . . we shall be found" was from birth to death a lonely man, vainly seeking communion. He survives — and probably will continue to survive — as the chronicler of a lost childhood, a vanished glory, the portrayer of an individual American outlined, stark and lonely, beneath a cruel sky.

Nathanael West

NATHANAEL WEST was born Nathan Weinstein in New York City on October 17, 1903, the child of Jewish immigrants from Russia. His mother, Anna Wallenstein Weinstein, came of a cultivated family, and had been a beautiful girl, courted in Europe by the painter Maurice Stern. As a housewife she turned stout and bossy. West's father, Max Weinstein, a building contractor, was slight, kind, and shy. Of West's two sisters, the elder, Hinda, somewhat resembled the mother, and the younger, Lorraine (called Laura), was more like the father. West was particularly devoted to his father, and so close to his younger sister that in later life he repeatedly said he could never marry less fine a woman than his sister Laura.

The boy West attended P.S. 81 and P.S. 10, both in Manhattan, where he showed no academic distinction. He was a thin, awkward, and ungainly child. Summers he went to Camp Paradox in the Adirondacks, and a former counselor remembers him as "a quiet chap and not much of a mixer." Baseball was his passion, although he tended to daydream in the outfield. When a fly ball hit him on the head and bounced off for a home run, he got the nickname, "Pep," that stayed with him all his life.

Otherwise West seems to have spent most of his time reading. If his sisters' recollection can be trusted, he read Tolstoi at ten, and by thirteen he was familiar with Dostoevski and other Russian literature, Flaubert, and Henry James. He trained his bull terrier to bite anyone who came into his room when he was reading. After his graduation from P.S. 10, West enrolled at De Witt Clinton High School, where he soon distinguished himself as one of the weakest students in the school. He took no part in any extracurricular activity. In June 1920, West left Clinton without graduating.

In September 1921, West was admitted to Tufts University, on the strength of what now seems to have been a forged transcript from De Witt Clinton. Two months later, as a result of academic difficulties, he withdrew. In February 1922, he was admitted to Brown University as a transfer student from Tufts, this time on the basis of the transcript of the record of another Nathan Weinstein at Tufts. Once enrolled at Brown, West got serious, and managed not only to pass his courses but to graduate in two and a half years.

At Brown, West developed another personality, or showed another side of his personality than the solitary dreamer. He became an Ivy League fashion plate, wearing Brooks Brothers suits and shirts, and a homburg. A college friend, Jeremiah Mahoney, recalls that West looked like a "well-heeled mortuary assistant." Although his manner was reserved, he was friendly and gregarious, generous with his large allowance from his father, and a fairly good banjo player. With girls, he tended to be either too shy or too brash. One summer, West and another college friend, Quentin Reynolds, worked as hod carriers for West's father, and West not only built muscles on his thin frame but got on surprisingly well with the workmen.

West received little or no education in the Jewish religion, and although he was probably ritually circumcised, he was never confirmed in a Bar Mitzvah ceremony. During his years at Brown, West threw off what he could of his Jewishness, and suffered from the rest. "More than anyone I ever knew," his friend John Sanford later reported, "Pep writhed under the accidental curse of his religion." West had nothing to do with any organized Jewish activity on campus, hung around the snobbish Gentile fraternities, and was intensely anxious to be pledged and intensely bitter that he never was. "Nobody ever thought of Pep as being Jewish," a college friend has said, but apparently the Brown fraternities did.

West's great success at Brown was as an aesthete. He dabbled in mysticism, ritual magic, and medieval Catholicism, quoted from obscure saints, discovered Joyce, and for a while was a Nietzschean. S. J. Perelman, a college friend who later married West's sister Laura, recalled that West was the first man on campus to read *Jurgen*. He was equally devoted to Baudelaire, Verlaine, and Rimbaud, Huysmans and Arthur Machen. His personal library was the largest any Brown man had at the time, and he loaned books liberally. Relying on the other Nathan Weinstein's credits in science and economics, West was able to confine himself almost entirely to courses in literature, philosophy, and history. His principal extracurricular activity was working as an editor of *Casements*, the Brown literary magazine. He drew its first cover design, naturally of casements, and contributed a poem, "Death," and an article, "Euripides — a Playwright." The 1924 *Liber Brunensis*, the yearbook, identified West as a genius with an unpredictable future.

After his graduation in 1924, West persuaded his father to send him to Paris, where he spent two happy years and grew a red beard. He returned to New York early in 1926, worked for his father for a while, and then in 1927, through a family connection, got a job as assistant manager at the Kenmore Hotel on East 23rd Street. Put on night duty, he was able to spend the nights reading. He gave rooms to his Brown friends and *their* homeless friends, among them Dashiell Hammett, who finished *The Maltese Falcon* as West's bootleg guest at the Kenmore. In 1928 he progressed to the same job at a fancier hotel, the Sutton on East 56th Street, where he put up other indigent writers, at reduced rates or no charge at all, among them Erskine Caldwell and James T. Farrell. After the stock market crash, which ruined West's father, the Sutton's sun deck became a favored spot for suicides, and West took to calling it "Suicide Leap."

West's first novel, *The Dream Life of Balso Snell*, seems to have been first written in college, but he rewrote it at the Sutton, and in 1931 he managed to get it privately printed in a limited edition of 500 copies. One review appeared, in *Contempo*, but otherwise *Balso Snell* caused no stir whatsoever. The book listed "Nathanael West" as author and thus marked West's official change of name. He had spent much of his class time at Brown doodling "Nathan von Wallenstein Weinstein," which was the name signed to his *Casements* contributions, but even that had turned out to be not Gentile enough. West explained to William Carlos Williams how he got the name: "Horace Greeley said, 'Go West, young man.' So I did." West's anti-Semitism was now considerable. He referred to Jewish girls as "bagels," and avoided them.

In 1931, West took a leave from the Sutton and he and Sanford, another aspiring novelist, rented a shack in the Adirondacks near Warrensburg, New York. Here they wrote in the mornings and fished and hunted in the afternoons. West was working on *Miss Lonelyhearts*, reading each sentence back aloud, producing about a hundred words a day. He rewrote the manuscript five or six times, in the Adirondacks, then back at the Sutton; finally, having quit the Sutton, in a hotel in Frenchtown, New Jersey.

Late in 1932 West and the Perelmans bought a farmhouse in Bucks County, Pennsylvania, and Mrs. Weinstein soon moved in to take over the cooking and try to persuade West to return to the hotel business. In 1933 *Miss Lonelyhearts* was published, and it was reviewed enthusiastically. Unfortunately, the publisher, Horace Liveright, chose that moment to go bankrupt, the printer refused to deliver most of the edition, and by the time West got another publisher to take it over, the reviews were forgotten. Altogether *Miss Lonelyhearts* sold fewer than 800 copies, and West's total income from his first two books and three years of writing came to $780.

In 1932 West had become co-editor with Dr. Williams of a little magazine, *Contact*, and he published articles and chapters of *Miss Lonelyhearts* in it and in *Contempo* in 1933. In August 1933, he became associate editor of a magazine, *Americana*, edited by Alexander King. Before *Americana* expired in November, West managed to publish a Hollywood story, "Business Deal," and some excerpts from *Balso Snell* in it. West then wrote some stories for the slick magazines, but did not succeed in selling any. He applied for a Guggenheim fellowship, with F. Scott Fitzgerald as one of his sponsors, but failed to get it.

West next wrote *A Cool Million* in a hurry, hoping to profit from the reviews of *Miss Lonelyhearts* and make some money. It appeared in 1934, was unfavorably reviewed, sold poorly, and was soon remaindered.

West's personal life in the East was no more successful than his literary career. *Balso Snell* was dedicated to Alice Shepard, a Roman Catholic girl who had gone to Pembroke College with West's sister Laura. He was secretly engaged to her from 1929 to 1932, then publicly engaged, but they never married, although West had bought a marriage license and carried it around with him for several years. His poverty was the explanation given out, but in Sanford's opinion the engagement foundered on the religious difference.

West had been to Hollywood for a few months in 1933, when *Miss Lonelyhearts* was sold to Twentieth Century-Fox and West received a writing contract at $350 a week. He was given little to do, saw his novel made into a Lee Tracy murder thriller, and came back to New York in July disillusioned and bitter. Nevertheless, in 1935, when every other possibility seemed closed to him, West returned to Hollywood and went to work for Republic Studios as a script writer. He switched to RKO Radio in 1938, and also worked for Universal-International Pictures. In the remaining few years of his life, West turned out a number of trivial screenplays, alone or in collaboration, among them *Five Came Back, I Stole a Million,* and *Spirit of Culver.* As a result of his facility as a script writer, West was able to live in comfort and security for the first time since the 1929 crash. He worked a few hours a week dictating to a secretary, and spent most of his weekends on hunting trips, following the season down from Oregon through California into Mexico each year. He acquired two hunting dogs, which slept on his bed, and he explained to people that he needed a house and servants for the dogs.

West made it clear that he despised the "pants pressers" of Hollywood, and he tried to escape in a number of fashions. He collaborated on two plays for Broadway, but the first never got there and the second only lasted two performances, winning from Brooks Atkinson the accolade "nitwit theatre." He became a fellow traveler of the Communist party, signing the call for the American Writers Congress in 1935, joining the Screen Writers Guild, and working strenuously on behalf of Loyalist Spain and other causes. (Earlier, in 1933, he had published a Marxist poem in *Contempo*. Before leaving for California in 1935 he had picketed Orbach's with other Communist sympathizers and was jailed for a few hours "for obstructing traffic.") He was, luckily, unable to get his political orientation explicitly into his fiction.

West published *The Day of the Locust* in 1939, hoping its success would get him out of Hollywood, but despite some good reviews it was a commercial failure, selling fewer than 1500 copies. (West's publisher, Bennett Cerf, explained to him that it failed because women readers didn't like it.)

West's isolation ended suddenly and surprisingly in 1940, when he fell in love with Eileen McKenney, the protagonist of Ruth McKenney's *My Sister Eileen*. They were married in April, and spent a three-month honeymoon in Oregon, hunting and fishing. On West's return he got a higher paid job at Columbia Pictures; later Columbia bought *A Cool Million* and a screen treatment of it on which West had collaborated. The great happy period of West's life, begun in the spring, did not last out the year. On December 22, the Wests were returning from a hunting trip in Mexico, when West, a poor driver, went through a stop sign near El Centro, California. Their station wagon crashed into an automobile. Eileen died instantly, West an hour later on the way to the hospital. He was thirty-seven. His body was shipped to New York and buried in a Jewish cemetery.

Since his death West's reputation has risen continuously. *Miss Lonelyhearts* has sold 190,000 copies in paperback, and *The Day of the Locust* 250,000. Scholarly articles about West, here and abroad, multiply cancerously. *Miss Lonelyhearts* has been made into a play, a more faithful film than the Lee Tracy one, and an opera. In 1946 it was translated into French by Marcelle Sibon as *Mademoiselle Cœur-Brisé*, with an introduction by Philippe Soupault, and it has had a visible effect on later French fiction. Since 1949, all West's books but the first have been published in England. When the four novels were reissued in this country in one volume in 1957, all the reviews were favorable, and there was general agreement that West was one of the most important writers of the thirties, as American as apple pie. West's picture appeared on the cover of the *Saturday Review*, looking very Jewish.

The Dream Life of Balso Snell (1931) is almost impossible to synopsize. A poet named Balso Snell finds the wooden Trojan Horse and has a picaresque journey up its alimentary canal. In the course of his travels he encounters: a Jewish guide; Maloney the Areopagite, a Catholic mystic; John Gilson, a precocious schoolboy; and Miss McGeeney, John's eighth-grade teacher. Each has a story, sometimes several stories, to tell, and their stories merge with their dreams and with Balso's dreams in a thoroughly confusing, and deliberately confusing, fashion. The book ends with Balso's orgasm, still in the bowels of the horse, during a dream of rapturous sexual intercourse with Miss McGeeney. Balso is dreaming the schoolboy's dream, and may have become the schoolboy.

The overwhelming impression the reader gets is of the corruption and repulsiveness of the flesh. In one of John Gilson's fantasies of beating a mistress, he explains his action: "I have a sty on my eye, a cold sore on my lip, a pimple where the edge of my collar touches my neck, another pimple in the corner of my mouth, and a drop of salt snot on the end of my nose." Furthermore, "It seems to me as though all the materials of life — wood, glass, wool, skin — are rubbing against my sty, my cold sore and my pimples." When Balso encounters Miss McGeeney, a middle-aged tweedy woman disguised for the moment as a beautiful naked young girl, she offers him her poetic vision: "Houses that are protuberances on the skin of streets — warts, tumors, pimples, corns, nipples, sebaceous cysts, hard and soft chancres."

In a dream within his dream, Balso is attracted to girl cripples: "He likened their disarranged hips, their short legs, their humps, their splay feet, their wall-eyes, to ornament." He cries tenderly to one of them, Janey the hunchback: "For me, your sores are like flowers: the new, pink, budlike sores, the full, rose-ripe sores, the sweet, seed-bearing sores. I shall cherish them all." One of Balso's beautiful memories in the book is of a girl he once loved who did nothing all day but put bits of meat and gravy, butter and cheese, on the petals of roses so that they would attract flies instead of butterflies and bees.

As the human body is seen as a running sore, Christianity is seen entirely in terms of Christ's wounded and bleeding body. Maloney the Areopagite is writing a hagiography of Saint Puce, a flea who was born, lived, and died in the armpit of Jesus Christ. Maloney's blasphemous idea that Saint Puce was born of the Holy Ghost enables West to mock the mysteries of Incarnation, as the flea's feasting on the divine flesh and blood enables West to mock Eucharist. The Passion is burlesqued by Maloney, who is encountered naked except for a derby stuck full of thorns, trying to crucify himself with thumbtacks, and by Beagle Darwin, a fictional invention of Miss McGeeney's, who does a juggling act, keeping in the air "the Nails, the Scourge, the Thorns, and a piece of the True Cross."

Nor is West's bitterness in the book reserved for Christianity. Judaism comes in for its share. The song in praise of obscene roundness that Balso makes when he starts his journey concludes:

> Round and Ringing Full
> As the Mouth of a Brimming Goblet
> The Rust-Laden Holes
> In Our Lord's Feet
> Entertain the Jew-Driven Nails.

The guide turns out to be not only a Jew, but a Jew who at the mention of such melodious Jewish names as Hernia Hornstein and Paresis Pearlberg finds it necessary to affirm: "I am a Jew.

I'm a Jew! A Jew!" Balso answers politely that some of his best friends are Jews, and adds Doughty's epigram: "The semites are like to a man sitting in a cloaca to the eyes, and whose brows touch heaven."

The strength of *Balso Snell* lies in its garish comic imagination. Maloney's crucifixion with thumbtacks is not only a serious theme that West's later work develops, it is also funny and, as a parody of the stance of Roman Catholic mysticism, devastating. The account in John Gilson's journal of his Gidean and Dostoevskian murder of an idiot dishwasher is repulsive but genuinely imagined, and its unconscious sexual motivation is boldly dramatized: stripping for the crime, John notices his genitals tight and hard; afterwards he feels like a happy young girl, "kittenish, cuney-cutey, darlingey, springtimey"; when he sees sailors on the street, he flirts and camps and feels "as though I were melting — all silk and perfumed, pink lace." The hunchback Janey is a nightmarish vision of the female body as terrifying, transformed into comedy: she has a hundred and forty-four exquisite teeth, and is pregnant in the hump.

Some of West's language in the book foreshadows his later triumphs. Janey imagines death to be "like putting on a wet [bathing] suit — shivery." John describes his dual nature to his fantasy-mistress, Saniette: "Think of two men — myself and the chauffeur within me. This chauffeur is very large and dressed in ugly ready-made clothing. His shoes, soiled from walking about the streets of a great city, are covered with animal ordure and chewing gum. His hands are covered with coarse woollen gloves. On his head is a derby hat." Sometimes John speaks in a voice we can hear as the youthful West's. He tells Balso: "I need women and because I can't buy or force them, I have to make poems for them. God knows how tired I am of using the insanity of Van Gogh and the adventures of Gauguin as can-openers." John explains his position in a pamphlet, which he sells to Balso for a dollar. In it he confesses: "If it had been possible for me to attract by exhibiting a series of physical charms, my hatred would have been less. But I found it necessary to substitute strange conceits, wise and witty sayings, peculiar conduct, Art, for the muscles, teeth, hair, of my rivals."

The weaknesses of *Balso Snell* are all characteristically juvenile. The principal one is the obsessive scatology, which soon becomes boring. "O Anus Mirabilis!" Balso cries of his rectal entrance to the Trojan Horse, and his roundness song takes off from that anal image. "Art is a sublime excrement," he is told by the Jewish guide (who seems to justify only the first half of Doughty's aphorism). John sees journal-keepers in excremental imagery: "They come to the paper with a constipation of ideas — eager, impatient. The white paper acts as a laxative. A diarrhoea of words is the result." When the idiot dishwasher swallows, John compares it to "a miniature toilet being flushed." As John beats Saniette, he cries: "O constipation of desire! O diarrhoea of love!" He has visions of writing a play that will conclude when "the ceiling of the theatre will be made to open and cover the occupants with tons of loose excrement." Balso speaks "with lips torn angry in laying duck's eggs from a chicken's rectum." James F. Light reports that West was fond of quoting Odo of Cluny's reference to the female as *"saccus stercoris,"* but the book's scatological obsession is clearly not restricted to the female. It is no less than a vision of the whole world as one vast dungheap.

Balso Snell is complex and stratified, so much so that at one point we get Janey's thinking as Beagle imagines it in a letter actually written by Miss McGeeney and read by Balso in his dream within a dream. But the book has no form, and consists merely of a series of encounters and complications, terminated rather than resolved by the orgasm. We can sense West's dissatisfaction with it as not fully realized in his re-use of some of its material in later works. Some of *Balso Snell* is extremely schoolboyish, like the guide's aphorism, "A hand in the Bush is worth two in the pocket," or Balso's comment on Maloney's story of the martyrdom and death of Saint Puce: "I think you're morbid. . . . Take cold showers."

When *Miss Lonelyhearts* was published two years later, in 1933, West told A. J. Liebling that it was entirely unlike *Balso Snell*, "of quite a different make, wholesome, clean, holy, slightly mystic and inane." He describes it in "Some Notes on Miss Lonelyhearts" as a "portrait of a priest of our time who has had a religious experience." In it, West explains, "violent images are used to illustrate commonplace events. Violent acts are left almost bald." He credits William James's *Varieties of Religious Experience* for its psychology. Some or all of this may be Westian leg-pull.

The plot of *Miss Lonelyhearts* is Sophoclean irony, as simple and inevitable as the plot of *Balso Snell* is random and whimsical. A young newspaperman who writes the agony column of his paper as "Miss Lonelyhearts" has reached the point where the joke has gone sour. He becomes obsessed with the real misery of his correspondents, illuminated for him by the cynicism of William Shrike, the feature editor. Miss Lonelyhearts pursues Shrike's wife Mary, unsuccessfully, and cannot content himself with the love and radiant goodness of Betty, his fiancée. Eventually he finds his fate in two of his correspondents, the crippled Peter Doyle and his wife Fay. Miss Lonelyhearts is not punished for his tumble with Fay, but when on his next encounter he fights her off, it leads to his being shot by Doyle.

The characters are allegorical figures who are at the same time convincing as people. Miss Lonelyhearts is a New England puritan, the son of a Baptist minister. He has a true religious vocation or calling, but no institutional church to embody it. When Betty suggests that he quit the column, he tells her: "I can't quit. And even if I were to quit, it wouldn't make any difference. I wouldn't be able to forget the letters, no matter what I did."

In one of the most brilliant strokes in the book, he is never named, always identified only by his role. (In an earlier draft, West had named him Thomas Matlock, which we could translate "Doubter Wrestler," but no name at all is infinitely more effective.) Even when he telephones Fay Doyle for an assignation, he identifies himself only as "Miss Lonelyhearts, the man who does the column." In his namelessness, in his vocation without a church, Miss Lonelyhearts is clearly the prophet in the reluctance stage, when he denies the call and tells God that he stammers, but Miss Lonelyhearts, the prophet of *our* time, is stuck there until death.

Miss Lonelyhearts identifies Betty as the principle of order: "She had often made him feel that when she straightened his tie, she straightened much more." The order that she represents is the innocent order of Nature, as opposed to the disorder of sinful Man. When Miss Lonelyhearts is sick, Betty comes to nourish him with hot soup, impose order on his room, and redeem him with a pastoral vision: "She told him about her childhood on a farm and of her love for animals, about country sounds and country smells and of how fresh and clean everything in the country is. She said that he ought to live there and that if he did, he would find that all his troubles were city troubles." When Miss Lonelyhearts is back on his feet, Betty takes him for a walk in the zoo, and he is "amused by her evident belief in the curative power of animals." Then she takes him to live in the country for a few days, in the book's great idyllic scene. Miss Lonelyhearts is beyond such help, but it is Betty's patient innocence — she is as soft and helpless as a kitten — that makes the book so heartbreaking. She is an innocent Eve to his fallen Adam, and he alone is driven out of Eden.

The book's four other principal characters are savage caricatures, in the root sense of "caricature" as the overloading of one attribute. Shrike is a dissociated half of Miss Lonelyhearts, his cynical intelligence, and it is interesting to learn that Shrike's rhetorical masterpiece, the great speech on the varieties of escape, was spoken by Miss Lonelyhearts in an earlier draft. Shrike's name is marvelously apt. The shrike or butcherbird impales its prey on thorns, and the name is a form of the word "shriek." Shrike is of course the mocker who hands Miss Lonelyhearts his crown of thorns, and throughout the book he is a shrieking bird of prey; when not a butcherbird, "a screaming, clumsy gull."

Shrike's wife Mary is one vast teasing mammary image. As Miss Lonelyhearts decides to telephone Mary in Delehanty's speakeasy, he sees a White Rock poster and observes that "the artist had taken a great deal of care in drawing her breasts and their nipples stuck out like tiny red hats." He then thinks of "the play Mary made with her breasts. She used them as the coquettes of long ago had used their fans. One of her tricks was to wear a medal low down on her chest. Whenever he asked to see it, instead of drawing it out she leaned over for him to look. Although he had often asked to see the medal, he had not yet found out what it represented." Miss Lonelyhearts and Mary go out for a gay evening, and Mary flaunts her breasts while talking of her mother's terrible death from cancer of the breast. He finally gets to see the medal, which reads "Awarded by the Boston Latin School for first place in the 100 yd. dash." When he takes her home he kisses her breasts, for the first time briefly slowing down her dash.

The Doyles are presented in inhuman or subhuman imagery. When, in answer to Fay's letter of sexual invitation, Miss Lonelyhearts decides to telephone her, he pictures her as "a tent, hair-covered and veined," and himself as a skeleton: "When he made the skeleton enter the flesh tent, it flowered at every joint." Fay appears and is a giant: "legs like Indian clubs, breasts like balloons and a brow like a pigeon." When he takes her arm, "It felt like a thigh." Following her up the stairs to his apartment, "he watched the action of her massive hams; they were like two enormous grindstones." Undressing, "she made sea sounds; something flapped like a sail; there was the creak of ropes; then he heard the wave-against-a-wharf smack of rubber on flesh. Her call for him to hurry was a sea-moan, and when he lay beside her, she heaved, tidal, moon-driven." Eventually Miss Lonelyhearts "crawled out of bed like an exhausted swimmer leaving the surf," and she soon drags him back.

If Fay is an oceanic monster, Peter Doyle is only a sinister puppy. In bringing Miss Lonelyhearts back to the apartment at Fay's order, he half-jokes, "Ain't I the pimp, to bring home a guy for my wife?" Fay reacts by hitting him in the mouth with a rolled-up newspaper, and his comic response is to growl like a dog and catch the paper with his teeth. When she lets go of her end, he drops to his hands and knees and continues to imitate a dog on the floor. As Miss Lonelyhearts leans over to help him up,

"Doyle tore open Miss Lonelyhearts' fly, then rolled over on his back, laughing wildly." Fay, more properly, accepts him as a dog and kicks him.

The obsessive theme of *Miss Lonelyhearts* is human pain and suffering, but it is represented almost entirely as female suffering. This is first spelled out in the letters addressed to Miss Lonely-hearts: Sick-of-it-all is a Roman Catholic wife who has had seven children in twelve years, is pregnant again, and has kidney pains so excruciating that she cries all the time. Desperate is a sixteen-year-old born with a hole in her face instead of a nose, who wants to have dates like other girls. Harold S. writes about his thirteen-year-old deaf-and-dumb sister Gracie, who was raped by a man when she was playing on the roof, and who will be brutally punished if her parents find out about it. Broad Shoulders was hit by a car when she was first pregnant, and is alternately persecuted and deserted by an unbalanced husband, in five pages of ghastly detail. Miss Lonelyhearts gets only two letters about male suffering, one from a paralyzed boy who wants to play the violin, the other from Peter Doyle, who complains of the pain from his crippled leg and the general meaninglessness of life.

The theme of indignities committed on women comes up in another form in the stories Miss Lonelyhearts' friends tell in Delehanty's. They seem to be exclusively anecdotes of group rape, of one woman gang-raped by eight neighbors, of another kept in the back room of a speakeasy for three days, until "on the last day they sold tickets to niggers." Miss Lonelyhearts identifies himself with "wife-torturers, rapers of small children." At one point he tries giving his readers the traditional Christian justification for suffering, that it is Christ's gift to mankind to bring them to Him, but he tears up the column.

Ultimately the novel cannot justify or even explain suffering, only proclaim its omnipresence. Lying sick in bed, Miss Lonely-hearts gets a vision of human life: "He found himself in the window of a pawnshop full of fur coats, diamond rings, watches, shotguns, fishing tackle, mandolins. All these things were the paraphernalia of suffering. A tortured high light twisted on the blade of a gift knife, a battered horn grunted with pain." Finally his mind forms everything into a gigantic cross, and he falls asleep exhausted.

The book's desperate cry of pain and suffering comes to a focus in what Miss Lonelyhearts calls his "Christ complex." He recognizes that Christ is the only answer to his readers' letters, but that "if he did not want to get sick, he had to stay away from the Christ business. Besides, Christ was Shrike's particular joke." As Miss Lonelyhearts leaves the office and walks through a little park, the shadow of a lamppost pierces his side like a spear. Since nothing grows in the park's battered earth, he decides to ask his correspondents to come and water the soil with their tears. He imagines Shrike telling him to teach them to pray each morning, "Give us this day our daily stone," and thinks: "He had given his reader many stones; so many, in fact, that he had only one left — the stone that had formed in his gut."

Jesus Christ, Shrike says, is "the Miss Lonelyhearts of Miss Lonelyhearts." Miss Lonelyhearts has nailed an ivory Christ to the wall of his room with great spikes, but it disappoints him: "Instead of writhing, the Christ remained calmly decorative." Miss Lonelyhearts recalls: "As a boy in his father's church, he had discovered that something stirred in him when he shouted the name of Christ, something secret and enormously powerful." Unfortunately, he recognizes, it is not faith but hysteria: "For him, Christ was the most natural of excitements."

Miss Lonelyhearts tells Betty he is "a humanity lover," but Shrike more aptly identifies him a "leper licker." "If he could only believe in Christ," Miss Lonelyhearts thinks, "then everything would be simple and the letters extremely easy to answer." Later he recognizes that "Shrike had accelerated his sickness by teaching him to handle his one escape, Christ, with a thick glove of words." He decides that he has had a part in the general betrayal of suffering mankind: "The thing that made his share in it particularly bad was that he was capable of dreaming the Christ dream. He felt that he had failed at it, not so much because of Shrike's jokes or his own self-doubt, but because of his lack of humility." Miss Lonelyhearts concludes that "with him, even the word Christ was a vanity." When he gets drunk with Doyle, he calls on Christ joyously, and goes home with Doyle to bring the glad tidings to both Doyles, to heal their marriage. He preaches "love" to them and realizes that he is only writing another column, switches to preaching Christ Jesus, "the black fruit that hangs on the crosstree . . . the bidden fruit," and realizes that he is only echoing Shrike's poisoned rhetoric.

What Miss Lonelyhearts eventually achieves, since he cannot believe in the real Christ, and refuses to become a spurious Christ, is Peter's condition. He becomes the rock on which the new church will be founded, but it is the church of catatonic withdrawal. After three days in bed Miss Lonelyhearts attains a state of perfect calm, and the stone in his gut expands until he becomes "an ancient rock, smooth with experience." The Shrikes come to take him to a party at their apartment, and against this rock the waves of Shrike dash in vain. When Mary wriggles on Miss Lonelyhearts' lap in the cab, "the rock remained perfect." At the party he withstands Shrike's newest mockery, the Miss Lonelyhearts Game, with indifference: "What goes on in the sea is of no interest to the rock." Miss Lonelyhearts leaves the party with Betty: "She too should see the rock he had become." He shamelessly promises her marriage and domesticity: "The rock was a solidification of his feeling, his conscience, his sense of reality, his self-knowledge." He then goes back to his sickbed content: "The rock had been thoroughly tested and had been found perfect."

The next day Miss Lonelyhearts is burning with fever, and "the rock became a furnace." The room fills with grace, the illusory grace of madness, and as Doyle comes up the stairs with a pistol Miss Lonelyhearts rushes downstairs to embrace him and heal his crippled leg, a miracle that will embody his succoring all suffering mankind with love. Unable to escape Miss Lonelyhearts' mad embrace, terrified by Betty coming up the stairs, Doyle tries to toss away the gun, and Miss Lonelyhearts is accidentally shot. He falls dragging Doyle down the stairs in his arms.

It is of course a homosexual tableau — the men locked in embrace while the woman stands helplessly by — and behind his other miseries Miss Lonelyhearts has a powerful latent homosexuality. It is this that is ultimately the joke of his name and the book's title. It explains his acceptance of teasing dates with Mary and his coldness with Mary; he thinks of her excitement and notes: "No similar change ever took place in his own body, however. Like a dead man, only friction could make him warm or violence make him mobile." It explains his discontent with Betty. Most of all it explains his joy at being seduced by Fay — "He had always been the pursuer, but now found a strange pleasure in having the roles reversed" — and how quickly the pleasure turns to disgust.

The communion Miss Lonelyhearts achieves with Doyle in Delehanty's consists in their sitting silently holding hands, Miss Lonelyhearts pressing "with all the love he could manage" to overcome the revulsion he feels at Doyle's touch. Back at the Doyles', after Doyle has ripped open Miss Lonelyhearts' fly and been kicked by his wife, they hold hands again, and when Fay comes back in the room she says "What a sweet pair of fairies you guys are." It is West's ultimate irony that the symbolic embrace they manage at the end is one penetrating the body of the other with a bullet.

We could, if we so chose, write Miss Lonelyhearts' case history before the novel begins. Terrified of his stern religious father, identifying with his soft loving mother, the boy renounces his phallicism out of castration anxiety — a classic Oedipus complex. In these terms the Shrikes are Miss Lonelyhearts' Oedipal parents, abstracted as the father's loud voice and the mother's tantalizing breast. The scene at the end of Miss Lonelyhearts' date with Mary Shrike is horrifying and superb. Standing outside her apartment door, suddenly overcome with passion, he strips her naked under her fur coat while she keeps talking mindlessly of her mother's death, mumbling and repeating herself, so that Shrike will not hear their sudden silence and come out. Finally Mary agrees to let Miss Lonelyhearts in if Shrike is not home, goes inside, and soon Shrike peers out the door, wearing only the top of his pajamas. It is the child's Oedipal vision perfectly dramatized: he can clutch at his mother's body but loses her each time to his more potent rival.

It should be noted that if this is the pattern of Miss Lonelyhearts' Oedipus complex, it is not that of West, nor are the Shrikes the pattern of West's parents. How conscious was West of all or any of this? I would guess, from the book's title, that he was entirely conscious of at least Miss Lonelyhearts' latent homosexuality. As for the Oedipus complex, all one can do is note West's remarks in "Some Notes on Miss Lonelyhearts": "Psychology has nothing to do with reality nor should it be used as motivation. The novelist is no longer a psychologist. Psychology can become much more important. The great body of case histories can be used in the way the ancient writers use their myths. Freud is your Bulfinch; you can not learn from him."

The techniques West uses to express his themes are perfectly suited to them. The most important is a pervasive desperate and savage tone, not only in the imagery of violence and suffering, but everywhere. It is the tone of a world where unreason is triumphant. Telling Miss Lonelyhearts that he is awaiting a girl "of great intelligence," Shrike "illustrated the word *intelligence* by carving two enormous breasts in the air with his hands." When Miss Lonelyhearts is in the country with Betty, a gas station attendant tells him amiably that "it wasn't the hunters who drove out the deer, but the yids." When Miss Lonelyhearts accidentally collides with a man in Delehanty's and turns to apologize, he is punched in the mouth.

The flowering cactus that blooms in this wasteland is Shrike's rhetoric. The book begins with a mock prayer he has composed for Miss Lonelyhearts, and every time Shrike appears he makes a masterly speech: on religion, on escapes, on the gospel of Miss Lonelyhearts according to Shrike. He composes a mock letter to God, in which Miss Lonelyhearts confesses shyly: "I read your column and like it very much." He is a cruel and relentless punster and wit. In his sadistic game at the party, Shrike reads aloud letters to Miss Lonelyhearts. He reads one from a pathetic old woman who sells pencils for a living, and concludes: "She has rheum in her eyes. Have you room in your heart for her?" He reads another, from the paralyzed boy who wants to play the violin, and concludes: "How pathetic! However, one can learn much from this parable. Label the boy Labor, the violin Capital, and so on . . ." Shrike's masterpiece, the brilliant evocation of the ultimate inadequacy of such escapes as the soil, the South Seas, Hedonism, and art, is a classic of modern rhetoric, as is his shorter speech on religion. Here are a few sentences from the latter: "Under the skin of man is a wondrous jungle where veins like lush tropical growths hang along overripe organs and weed-like entrails writhe in squirming tangles of red and yellow. In this jungle, flitting from rock-gray lungs to golden intestines, from liver to lights and back to liver again, lives a bird called the soul. The Catholic hunts this bird with bread and wine, the Hebrew with a golden ruler, the Protestant on leaden feet with leaden words, the Buddhist with gestures, the Negro with blood."

The other cactus that flowers in the wasteland is sadistic violence. The book's most harrowing chapter, "Miss Lonelyhearts and the lamb," is a dream or recollection of a college escapade, in which Miss Lonelyhearts and two other boys, after drinking all night, buy a lamb to barbecue in the woods. Miss Lonelyhearts persuades his companions to sacrifice it to God before barbecuing it. They lay the lamb on a flower-covered altar and Miss Lonelyhearts tries to cut its throat, but succeeds only in maiming it and breaking the knife. The lamb escapes and crawls off into the underbrush, and the boys flee. Later Miss Lonelyhearts goes back and crushes the lamb's head with a stone. This nightmarish scene, with its unholy suggestions of the sacrifices of Isaac and Christ, embodies the book's bitter paradox: that sadism is the perversion of love.

Visiting Betty early in the novel, aware "that only violence could make him supple," Miss Lonelyhearts reaches inside her robe and tugs at her nipple unpleasantly. "Let me pluck this rose," he says, "I want to wear it in my buttonhole." In "Miss Lonelyhearts and the clean old man," he and a drunken friend find an old gentleman in a washroom, drag him to a speakeasy, and torment him with questions about his "homosexualistic tendencies." As they get nastier and nastier, Miss Lonelyheart feels "as he had felt years before, when he had accidentally stepped on a small frog. Its spilled guts had filled with him pity, but when its suffering had become real to his senses, his pity had turned to rage and he had beaten it frantically until it was dead." He ends by twisting the old man's arm until the old man screams and someone hits Miss Lonelyhearts with a chair.

The book's only interval of decency, beauty, and peace is the pastoral idyll of the few days Miss Lonelyhearts spends with Betty in the country. They drive in a borrowed car to the deserted farmhouse in Connecticut where she was born. It is spring, and Miss Lonelyhearts "had to admit, even to himself, that the pale new leaves, shaped and colored like candle flames, were beautiful and that the air smelt clean and alive." They work at cleaning up the place, Betty cooks simple meals, and they go down to the pond to watch the deer. After they eat an apple that has ominous Biblical overtones, Betty reveals that she is a virgin and they go fraternally to bed. The next day they go for a naked swim; then, with "no wind to disturb the pull of the earth," Betty is ceremonially deflowered on the new grass. The reader is repeatedly warned that natural innocence cannot save Miss Lonelyhearts: the noise of birds and crickets is "a horrible racket" in his ears; in the woods, "in the deep shade there was nothing but death — rotten leaves, gray and white fungi, and over everything a funereal hush." When they get back to New York, "Miss Lonelyhearts knew that Betty had failed to cure him and that he had been right when he had said that he could never forget the letters." Later, when Miss Lonelyhearts is a rock and leaves Shrike's party with Betty, he tries to create a miniature idyll of innocence by taking her out for a strawberry soda, but it fails. Pregnant by him and intending to have an abortion, Betty remains nevertheless in Edenic innocence; Miss Lonelyhearts is irretrievably fallen, and there is no savior who can redeem.

The book's pace is frantic and its imagery is garish, ugly, and compelling. The letters to Miss Lonelyhearts are "stamped from the dough of suffering with a heart-shaped cookie knife." The sky looks "as if it had been rubbed with a soiled eraser." A bloodshot eye in the peephole of Delehanty's glows "like a ruby in an antique iron ring." Finishing his sermon to the "intelligent" girl, Shrike "buried his triangular face like the blade of a hatchet in her neck." Miss Lonelyhearts' tongue is "a fat thumb," his heart "a congealed lump of icy fat," and his only feeling "icy fatness." Goldsmith, a colleague at the paper, has cheeks "like twin rolls of smooth pink toilet paper." Only the imagery of the Connecticut interlude temporarily thaws the iciness and erases the unpleasant associations with fatness and thumb. As Miss Lonelyhearts watches Betty naked, "She looked a little fat, but when she lifted something to the line, all the fat disappeared. Her raised arms pulled her breasts up until they were like pink-tipped thumbs."

The unique greatness of *Miss Lonelyhearts* seems to have come into the world with hardly a predecessor, but it has itself influenced a great many American novelists since. *Miss Lonelyhearts* seems to me one of the three finest American novels of our century. The other two are F. Scott Fitzgerald's *The Great Gatsby* and Ernest Hemingway's *The Sun Also Rises*. It shares with them a lost and victimized hero, a bitter sense of our civilization's falsity, a pervasive melancholy atmosphere of failure and defeat. If the tone of *Miss Lonelyhearts* is more strident, its images more garish, its pace more rapid and hysterical, it is as fitting an epitome of the thirties as they are of the twenties. If nothing in the forties and fifties has similarly gone beyond *Miss Lonelyhearts* in violence and shock, it may be because it stands at the end of the line.

A Cool Million, subtitled "The Dismantling of Lemuel Pitkin," is a comic, even a parody, novel, to some extent a reversion to the world of *Balso Snell.* It tells the story of Lemuel Pitkin, a poor but honest Vermont boy, as he attempts to make his way in the world. As he confronts each experience with the old-fashioned virtues of honesty, sobriety, good sportsmanship, thrift, bravery, chivalry, and kindness, he is robbed, beaten up, mutilated, cheated, and victimized. In an interwoven subplot, Elizabeth Prail, a neighbor who similarly represents decent American girlhood, is sexually mistreated: raped, beaten by a sadist, kidnapped by white slavers and sold into prostitution, turned out to walk the streets, and so forth. Meanwhile their town banker, "Shagpoke" Whipple, a former President of the United States, creates an American fascist movement and takes over the country.

The total effect is that of a prolonged, perhaps overprolonged, jape. The stages of the action are the stages of Lem's dismantling: thrown into jail in a frame-up, he loses all his teeth because the warden believes teeth to be the source of moral infection; rescuing a banker and his daughter from a runaway horse, Lem loses an eye; kidnapped by agents of the Communist International, he is involved in an automobile collision and loses a thumb; trying to save Betty from rape, he is caught in a bear trap that the villain has planted, which costs him a leg, and while unconscious in the trap he is scalped by a Harvard-educated Indian. He is eventually hired as stooge for a vaudeville act and demolished during each performance; when he is hit with a mallet, "His toupee flew off, his eye and teeth popped out, and his wooden leg was knocked into the audience." Eventually Lem is shot down onstage while making a speech for American fascism. As a result of his martyrdom Whipple's Leather Shirts triumph, and Pitkin's Birthday becomes a national holiday, on which the youth of America parade singing "The Lemuel Pitkin Song."

What form the book has comes from these ritual stages of dismemberment, but in a truer sense *A Cool Million* is formless, an inorganic stringing together of comic set-pieces, with the preposterous incidents serving merely to raise the various topics West chooses to satirize. Thus Betty's residence in Wu Fong's brothel sets off pages of comic description, first of the brothel as a House of All Nations, then, when Wu Fong is converted by the "Buy American" campaign of the Hearst newspapers, into an all-American establishment. West joyously describes the regional costumes and decor of each girl at considerable length, concluding with the cuisine:

When a client visited Lena Haubengrauber, it was possible for him to eat roast groundhog and drink Sam Thompson rye. While with Alice Sweethorne, he was served sow belly with grits and bourbon. In Mary Judkins' room he received, if he so desired, fried squirrel and corn liquor. In the suite occupied by Patricia Van Riis, lobster and champagne wine were the rule. The patrons of Powder River Rose usually ordered mountain oysters and washed them down with forty-rod. And so on down the list: while with Dolores O'Riely, tortillas and prune brandy from the Imperial Valley; while with Princess Roan Fawn, baked dog and firewater; while with Betty Prail, fish chowder and Jamaica rum. Finally, those who sought the favors of the "Modern Girl," Miss Cobina Wiggs, were regaled with tomato and lettuce sandwiches and gin.

The introduction of a Pike County "ring-tail squealer" and "rip-tail roarer" gives West an opportunity to improvise tall talk and anecdotes concluding: "His bones are bleachin' in the canyon where he fell." The Indian chief who scalps Lem is a Spenglerian philosopher and critic of our gadget civilization, and his speech to the tribe to rouse them for the warpath is a long comic diatribe, culminating in: "But now all the secret places of the earth are full. Now even the Grand Canyon will no longer hold razor blades." Later Lem and Whipple join up with a traveling show exhibiting a Chamber of American Horrors, and West gives himself a chance to describe some of the horrors of American life. In one exhibit, all the materials are disguised: "Paper had been made to look like wood, wood like rubber, rubber like steel, steel like cheese, cheese like glass, and, finally, glass like paper." In another, function is disguised: "The visitor saw flower pots that were really victrolas, revolvers that held candy, candy that held collar buttons and so forth." West here is entirely indiscriminate. The accompanying pageant of American history consists of sketches "in which Quakers were shown being branded, Indians brutalized and cheated, Negroes sold, children sweated to death," as though these acts were on the order of disguising paper to look like wood.

It is at once comic and depressing, the fitting work of a man Robert M. Coates has called "the most thoroughly pessimistic person I have ever known." If its indictment of American material civilization does not go very deep, its awareness of the precariousness of American freedom does, and the book is perhaps strongest as a political warning. Writing just after the accession of Hitler, West felt the vulnerability of America to totalitarianism disguised as superpatriotism, and he makes it disturbingly convincing. Whipple's bands of the mindless and disaffected, got up in fringed deerskin shirts, coonskin caps, and squirrel rifles, are the same joke as Lena Haubengrauber's clients washing down roast groundhog with Sam Thompson rye, but here it images our nightmare. Recruiting on street corners, Whipple alternates appeals to destroy the Jewish international bankers and the Bolshevik labor unions with shouts of "Remember the Alamo! Remember the Maine!" and "Back to the principles of Andy Jackson and Abe Lincoln!"

In his final tribute to the martyred Lemuel Pitkin at the end of the book, as his storm troops parade down Fifth Avenue, Whipple makes it clear that the true enemy from which his National Revolutionary party has delivered the country is "sophistication." Lem's life represented the expectations of American innocence, frustrated by "sophisticated aliens," and the revolution has been made by those who share Lem's expectations. As such it is the revolt of the frustrated and tormented lower middle class, a fantasy foreshadowing of the riot at the end of *The Day of the Locust*. To become the Horst Wessel of American fascism, in West's ugliest joke, Lem has stepped out of a Norman Rockwell cover for the *Saturday Evening Post*.

What makes this cautionary tale convincing in *A Cool Million* is West's sense of the pervasiveness of American violence. It is like the savagery of Russian life in Leskov or Gorki. We see Betty Prail at twelve, the night her family's house burns down and her parents are killed in the fire. When the firemen finally arrive, drunk, they do nothing to put out the fire. Instead they loot the house while the chief rapes Betty, leaving her naked and unconscious on the ground. She is then sent to an orphan asylum, and put out at fourteen to be a maid in the household of Deacon Slemp, where in addition to her other duties she is enthusiastically beaten twice a week on the bare behind by the Deacon, who gives her a quarter after each beating.

In this world where firemen are looters and rapists and church elders perverts and hypocrites, policemen appear only to beat up the victims of crimes. When Lem is first seized by the police, on his way to the big city to make his fortune, a patrolman clubs him on the head, one detective kicks him in the stomach, and a second kicks him behind the ear; all three actions unrelated to any of the remarks they make to Lem, but rather, natural reflexes. When Lem faints from the wound he received from stopping the runaway horse, he is found by a policeman, who establishes communication by kicking him in the groin. The brutal image of the police in the book is always the raised truncheon, the doubled fist, the foot drawn back.

The weaknesses of the book are perhaps the inevitable weaknesses of the form, jokes that do not come off and failures of tone. Sometimes the book is almost unbelievably corny and heavy-handed. When he is in this mood, West will even have someone address a Chinese in pidgin and be answered in flawless English.

The uncertainty of tone is mainly in regard to sex. When West is openly vulgar, he is fine, but on occasion he seems to smirk, and then he is less fine. A scene between Lem, captured by Wu Fong's men, dressed in a tight-fitting sailor suit, and set up as a homosexual prostitute in the brothel, and his client, a lisping Indian maharajah, is perhaps the most extreme failure. The first rape of Betty by the drunken fire chief is disturbing and effective, but her thousandth rape is boring and meaningless, as comedy, social comment, or even titillation. Betty is almost invariably unconscious when raped, an oddly necrophiliac touch, and sometimes the details lead us to expect a salacious illustration on the next page.

West's last book, *The Day of the Locust* (1939), is a novel about a young painter named Tod Hackett, working at a Hollywood movie studio as a set and costume designer, and some people he encounters. These are principally Faye Greener, a beautiful young girl whom he loves; her father Harry, an old vaudeville comic; Earle Shoop, Faye's cowboy beau; Miguel, Earle's Mexican friend who breeds fighting cocks; Abe Kusich, a dwarf racetrack tout; and Homer Simpson, an innocent from the Middle West also in love with Faye. In the course of the novel Harry dies, and Faye and her friends go to live with Homer. The action is climaxed by a wild party at Homer's, after which Faye and Miguel end up in bed. This results, the next day, in Homer's demented murder of a boy, which in turn precipitates a riot in the streets, on which the book ends. The title comes from the plague of locusts visited on Pharaoh in the Book of Exodus.

Like the characters in *Miss Lonelyhearts*, the characters in *The Day of the Locust* tend to be symbolic abstractions, but here with some loss of human reality. Tod, who never quite comes to life (mainly, I think, because of West's efforts to keep him from being autobiographical), represents The Painter's Eye. All through the book he is planning a great canvas, "The Burning of Los Angeles," which will sum up the whole violent and demented civilization. It is to show the city burning at high noon, set on fire by a gay holiday crowd, who appear carrying baseball bats and torches: "No longer bored, they sang and danced joyously in the red light of the flames." In the foreground, Tod and his friends flee the mob in various characteristic postures: Faye naked and running rather proudly, throwing her knees high; Homer half-asleep; Tod stopping to throw a stone at the crowd. Meanwhile the flames lick avidly "at a corinthian column that held up the palmleaf roof of a nutburger stand."

Faye is nothing like the Fay of *Miss Lonelyhearts* (as the Betty of *A Cool Million* is nothing like the Betty of *Miss Lonelyhearts* — West was overeconomical of names). Faye is seventeen, "a tall girl with wide, straight shoulders and long, swordlike legs." She has "a moon face, wide at the cheek bones and narrow at chin and brow," her hair is platinum-blonde, her breasts are "placed wide apart and their thrust" is "upward and outward," her buttocks look "like a heart upside down." She dresses like a child of twelve, eats an apple with her little finger curled, and has a brain the size of a walnut.

Like Betty in *Miss Lonelyhearts*, Faye represents Nature, but now Nature's appearance of innocence is seen as deceptive, and Faye is as far as can be from Betty. Tod looks at an inviting photograph of her, lying "with her arms and legs spread, as though welcoming a lover," and thinks: "Her invitation wasn't to pleasure, but to struggle, hard and sharp, closer to murder than to love. If you threw yourself on her, it would be like throwing yourself from the parapet of a skyscraper. You would do it with a scream. You couldn't expect to rise again. Your teeth would be driven into your skull like nails into a pine board and your back would be broken. You wouldn't even have time to sweat or close your eyes." What then is Tod's conclusion? "If she would only let him, he would be glad to throw himself, no matter what the cost." Luckily, she never lets him.

All experience rolls off Faye. She smells to Tod like "buckwheat in flower"; when she leans toward him, drooping slightly, "he had seen young birches droop like that at midday when they are over-heavy with sun." When she announces her intention of becoming a call girl, Tod decides that "her beauty was structural like a tree's, not a quality of her mind or heart. Perhaps even whoring wouldn't damage it for that reason." A spell of whoring does not in fact damage it, and when Tod sees her later: "She looked just born, everything moist and fresh, volatile and perfumed." In her natural acceptance of the world of sexuality, she is, as Homer tells Tod proudly, "a fine, wholesome child."

This vision of Nature emphasizes its infuriating invulnerability, and Tod not only wants to smash himself on it, but in other moods, to smash Faye. He thinks: "If he only had the courage to throw himself on her. Nothing less violent than rape would do. The sensation he felt was like that he got when holding an egg in his hand. Not that she was fragile or even seemed fragile. It wasn't that. It was her completeness, her egglike self-sufficiency, that made him want to crush her." Seeing her again, Tod feels: "Her self-sufficiency made him squirm and the desire to break its smooth surface with a blow, or at least a sudden obscene gesture, became irresistible." When Faye disappears at the end of the book, Tod cannot decide whether she has gone off with Miguel or gone back to being a call girl. "But either way she would come out all right," he thinks. "Nothing could hurt her. She was like a cork. No matter how rough the sea got, she would go dancing over the same waves that sank iron ships and tore away piers of reinforced concrete." Tod then produces an elaborate fantasy of waiting in a parking lot to knock Faye unconscious and rape her, and he steps from that into the riot of the book's last scene.

The men around Faye are in their different fashions as mindless as she. Her father, Harry Greener, after forty years in vaudeville and burlesque, no longer has any personality apart from his clowning role. "It was his sole method of defense," West explains. "Most people, he had discovered, won't go out of their way to punish a clown." West invents a superb clown act for him, presented in the form of an old clipping from the Sunday *Times*, but the clowning we see in the book is of a more poignant sort, his comic act peddling home-made silver polish.

Faye's cowboy, Earle Shoop, is an image of virile idiocy. "He had a two-dimensional face that a talented child might have drawn with a ruler and a compass. His chin was perfectly round and his eyes, which were wide apart, were also round. His thin mouth ran at right angles to his straight, perpendicular nose. His reddish tan complexion was the same color from hairline to throat, as though washed in by an expert, and it completed his resemblance to a mechanical drawing." His conversation consists of "Lo, thar," "Nope," and "I was only funning."

The Mexican, Miguel, is an image of pure sensuality: "He was toffee-colored with large Armenian eyes and pouting black lips. His head was a mass of tight, ordered curls." When Faye responds to him, "his skin glowed and the oil in his black curls sparkled." Early in the book we see him rhumba with Faye, until jealousy drives Earle to smash him over the head with a stick. Later he tangos with her, a tango that ends in bed. "Mexicans are very good with women," Tod decides, as the moral of the episode.

Homer is the most completely abstracted character in the book. As Mary Shrike in *Miss Lonelyhearts* is entirely reduced to Breasts, so Homer is entirely reduced to an image of Hands, enormous hands independent of his body. We see him waking in the morning: "Every part was awake but his hands. They still slept. He was not surprised. They demanded special attention, had always demanded it. When he had been a child, he used to stick pins into them and once had even thrust them into a fire. Now he used only cold water." We see him plunge his hands into the washbasin: "They lay quietly on the bottom like a pair of strange aquatic animals. When they were thoroughly chilled and began to crawl about, he lifted them out and hid them in a towel." In the bath: "He kept his enormous hands folded quietly on his belly. Although absolutely still, they seemed curbed rather than resting." When Homer cuts his hand opening a can, "The wounded hand writhed about on the kitchen table until it was carried to the sink by its mate and bathed tenderly in hot water."

When Faye cries at their first meeting, Homer makes "his big hands dance at the end of his arms," and "several times his hands moved forward to comfort her, but he succeeded in curbing them." As he and Faye sit and eat: "His hands began to bother him. He rubbed them against the edge of the table to relieve their itch, but it only stimulated them. When he clasped them behind his back, the strain became intolerable. They were hot and swollen. Using the dishes as an excuse, he held them under the cold water tap of the sink." When Faye leaves, Homer is too bashful to say anything affectionate, but: "His hands were braver. When Faye shook good-bye, they clutched and refused to let go." After she leaves, "His hands kept his thoughts busy. They trembled and jerked, as though troubled by dreams. To hold them still, he clasped them together. Their fingers twined like a tangle of thighs in miniature. He snatched them apart and sat on them."

During the final party, when Tod sits outside talking to Homer, he watches Homer's hands doing "the most complicated tic" Tod had ever seen, "manual ballet": "His big hands left his lap, where they had been playing 'here's the church and here the steeple,' and hid in his armpits. They remained there for a moment, then slid under his thighs. A moment later they were back in his lap. The right hand cracked the joints of the left, one by one, then the left did the same service for the right. They seemed easier for a moment, but not for long." Each time the hands start the routine, Homer tries to trap them between his knees, but each time they struggle to get free, and eventually they crawl out again, since Homer must compulsively perform the ritual three times.

This garish and remarkable image is built up throughout the book to embody all of Homer's repressed violence; the hands are strangler's hands, rapist's hands. For reasons impossible to imagine or justify, West let it all go to waste. When Homer's violence finally does break out, when Faye's leaving has driven him out of his mind, he kills a boy who has hit him in the face with a stone by stomping him to death, never touching him with his hands.

The most grotesque character in this gallery of grotesques is the dwarf, Abe Kusich. When Tod first meets him, he is wearing perfect dwarf headgear, a high green Tyrolean hat. Unfortunately, "the rest of his outfit didn't go well with the hat. Instead of shoes with long points and a leather apron, he wore a blue, double-breasted suit and a black shirt with a yellow tie. Instead of a crooked thorn stick, he carried a rolled copy of the *Daily Running Horse*." His tiny size is made pathetic in an image of his catching Tod's attention by tugging at the bottom of his jacket, but it is accompanied by an unbelievable pugnacity, verbal and physical. He is a small murderous animal like Homer's hands, and he too finally erupts into violence, responding to a kick in the stomach from Earle by squeezing Earle's testicles until he collapses.

West's earlier title for *The Day of the Locust* was *The Cheated*, and the latent violence of the cheated, the mob that fires Los Angeles in Tod's picture, and riots in the flesh at the end of the book, is its major theme. The cheated are recognizable by sight in Hollywood: "Their clothing was somber and badly cut, bought from mail-order houses." They stand on the streets staring at passers-by, and "when their stare was returned, their eyes filled with hatred." They are the people who have "come to California to die." At one point Tod wonders "if he weren't exaggerating the importance of the people who come to California to die. Maybe they weren't really desperate enough to set a single city on fire, let alone the whole country." His ultimate discovery is that they are.

Some of the cheated come to Harry's funeral, "hoping for a dramatic incident of some sort, hoping at least for one of the mourners to be led weeping hysterically from the chapel." As he stares at them, "it seemed to Tod that they stared back at him with an expression of vicious, acrid boredom that trembled on the edge of violence." In the book's last scene, the cheated line up by the thousands outside Kahn's Persian Palace Theatre for the première of a new picture. The mob terrifies Tod, and he now recognizes it as a demonic collective entity, unstoppable once aroused except by machine guns. In one of West's rare Marxist slantings, the mob includes no workingmen, but is entirely "made up of the lower middle classes." Tod concludes:

It was a mistake to think them harmless curiosity seekers. They were savage and bitter, especially the middle-aged and the old, and had been made so by boredom and disappointment.

All their lives they had slaved at some kind of dull, heavy labor, behind desks and counters, in the fields and at tedious machines of all sorts, saving their pennies and dreaming of the leisure that would be theirs when they had enough. Finally that day came. They could draw a weekly income of ten or fifteen dollars. Where else should they go but California, the land of sunshine and oranges?

Once there, they discovered that sunshine isn't enough. They get tired of oranges, even of avocado pears and passion fruit. Nothing happens. They don't know what to do with their time. They haven't the mental equipment for leisure, the money nor the physical equipment for pleasure. Did they slave so long just to go on an occasional Iowa picnic? What else is there? They watch the waves come in at Venice. There wasn't any ocean where most of them came from, but after you've seen one wave you've seen them all. The same is true of the airplanes at Glendale. If only a plane would crash once in a while so that they could watch the passengers being consumed in a "holocaust of flame," as the newspapers put it. But the planes never crash.

Their boredom becomes more and more terrible. They realize that they've been tricked and burn with resentment. Every day of their lives they read the newspapers and went to the movies. Both fed them on lynchings, murder, sex crimes, explosions, wrecks, love nests, fires, miracles, revolutions, wars. This daily diet made sophisticates of them. The sun is a joke. Oranges can't titillate their jaded palates. Nothing can ever be violent enough to make taut their slack minds and bodies. They have been cheated and betrayed. They have slaved and saved for nothing.

As the marching Leather Shirts were West's fantasy of American fascism, this vicious mob of the cheated lower middle class is his fantasy of American democracy, and it is overpowering and terrifying. The rest of Hollywood, the cheaters, have no more cultural identity than the "cheated," but their plight is comic or pathetic rather than menacing. They inhabit the Chamber of American Horrors, come to life. They live in "Mexican ranch houses, Samoan huts, Mediterranean villas, Egyptian and Japanese temples, Swiss chalets, Tudor cottages, and every possible combination of these styles." Tod sees "a miniature Rhine castle with tarpaper turrets pierced for archers. Next to it was a little highly colored shack with domes and minarets out of the *Arabian Nights*." The house Homer rents is Irish peasant style: "It had an enormous and very crooked stone chimney, little dormer windows with big hoods and a thatched roof that came down very low on both sides of the front door. This door was of gumwood painted like fumed oak and it hung on enormous hinges. Although made by machine, the hinges had been carefully stamped to appear hand-forged. The same kind of care and skill had been used to make the roof thatching, which was not really straw but heavy fireproof paper colored and ribbed to look like straw." The living room is "Spanish," with red and gold silk armorial banners and a plaster galleon; the bedrooms "New England," with spool beds made of iron grained like wood.

The people are as spurious as the houses and things. An old Hollywood Indian called Chief Kiss-My-Towkus speaks a language of "Vas you dere, Sharley?" Human communication is impossible anywhere in Hollywood. At a party of movie people, the men go off to talk shop and at least one woman assumes that they are telling dirty jokes. Harry and Faye are unable to quarrel in words, but have bitter wordless battles in which he laughs insanely, she sings and dances. Even Faye's sensual gesture of wetting her lips with her tongue as she smiles is meaningless. At first Tod takes it to be an invitation, and dreams: "Her lips must taste of blood and salt." Eventually he discovers the truth: "It was one of her most characteristic gestures and very effective. It seemed to promise all sorts of undefined intimacies, yet it was really as simple and automatic as the word thanks. She used it to reward anyone for anything, no matter how unimportant."

One of the clues West gives to his conception of the nature and destiny of his characters is subtly dropped in a comic scene. Tod and Homer meet a neighbor of Homer's, Maybelle Loomis, and her eight-year-old son, Adore, whom she has trained as a performer. He is dressed as an adult, his eyebrows are plucked, and he sings a salacious song with a mechanical counterfeit of sexuality: "When he came to the final chorus, his buttocks writhed and his voice carried a top-heavy load of sexual pain." In a more personal display, Adore makes horrible faces at Homer, and Mrs. Loomis apologizes: "He thinks he's the Frankenstein monster." Adore *is* the Frankenstein monster, and it is he who is killed by Homer in the book's last scene. But Homer too is the Frankenstein monster, getting out of bed "in sections, like a poorly made automaton," and his hands are progeny monsters. Earle is a lesser monster, a wound-up cowboy toy, and Miguel is a phallic Jack-in-the-box. More than any of them, Faye is a Frankenstein monster, a mechanical woman self-created from bits of vanished film heroines, and her invulnerability is the invulnerability of the already dead. Here is the novel's deepest indictment of the American civilization it symbolizes in Hollywood: if the rubes are cheated by the image of an artificially colored orange, Tod is more deeply cheated by a zombie love; our dreams are fantasies of death.

In his article "Some Notes on Violence," published in *Contact* in 1932, West writes: "What is melodramatic in European writing is not necessarily so in American writing. For a European writer to make violence real, he has to do a great deal of careful psychology and sociology. He often needs three hundred pages to motivate one little murder. But not so the American writer. His audience has been prepared and is neither surprised nor shocked if he omits artistic excuses for familiar events." The action of *The Day of the Locust* is the releasing of springs of violence that have been wound too tight: Abe's sexual maiming of Earle, Miguel smashing Abe against the wall in retaliation, Homer's brutal murder of Adore, the riot of the cheated. All of these are directly or indirectly inspired by Faye: Earle and Abe and Miguel are competing for Faye, Faye has made Homer insane, Homer's act triggers the mob's insanity.

The party scene consists of a progressive stripping of Faye. She receives her five male guests wearing a pair of green silk lounging pajamas with the top three buttons open. By the time she dances with Miguel all the buttons are open. In the succeeding fight her pajamas are badly torn, and she takes off the trousers, revealing tight black lace drawers. When Homer finds her in bed with Miguel, she is naked. It beautifully represents a metaphoric stripping of Faye in the course of the book. Darwin writes that we observe the face of Nature "bright with gladness," and forget the war to the death behind its innocent appearance. Faye is that bright glad face of Nature, and the stripping gradually reveals the violence and death her beauty conceals. The novel is a great unmasking of a death's head.

West's literary techniques in *The Day of the Locust* develop organically out of his themes. The imagery for Hollywood is wild and surrealist. Tod's friend Claude Estee, a successful screen writer, has a lifesize rubber dead horse, bloated and putrefying, in his swimming pool. The supermarket plays colored spotlights on the food: "The oranges were bathed in red, the lemons in yellow, the fish in pale green, the steaks in rose and the eggs in ivory." As Tod walks through the movie lot looking for Faye, it becomes the nightmare of history: stepping through the swinging door of a Western saloon, he finds himself in a Paris street; crossing a bridge marked "To Kamp Komfit," he finds himself in a Greek temple; he walks on, "skirting the skeleton of a Zeppelin, a bamboo stockade, an adobe fort, the wooden horse of Troy, a flight of baroque palace stairs that started in a bed of weeds and ended against the branches of an oak, part of the Fourteenth Street elevated station, a Dutch windmill, the bones of a dinosaur, the upper half of the Merrimac, a corner of a Mayan temple." "A dream dump," he concludes. "A Sargasso of the imagination!"

"Having known something of the Hollywood West saw at the time he was seeing it," Allan Seager has written, "I am of the opinion that *Locust* was not fantasy imagined but fantasy seen." Although West probably invented the specific details of the dead horse and the pale green supermarket fish, the fireproof paper thatch and his old favorite the Trojan Horse, there is a sense in which Seager's remark is true: these things are no more garish than what West actually did see in Hollywood. West's technique in the book is often, as Seager suggests, what the artists call *objets trouvés*: he finds in reality the symbol he needs, rather than creating it. When *The Day of the Locust* appeared, I recall thinking how masterfully West had invented the bloody sex-drenched details of the cockfight that leads up to the book's final party. Having since been to cockfights, I now know that every symbolic detail was realistically observed, and the object of my admiration in connection with the scene is no longer West's brilliance of invention but his brilliance of selection.

The humor of the book arises out of its themes, the incongruities of Hollywood and its lack of a cultural identity. Standing on the porch of his plantation mansion, Claude Estee cries, "Here, you black rascal! A mint julep," and a Chinese servant promptly brings a Scotch and soda. What do the Gingos, an Eskimo family brought to Hollywood to make retakes of an Arctic film, eat? Naturally, smoked salmon, white fish, and marinated

herring, bought at Jewish delicatessens. The spoken language in
the book is a tribute to the delicacy of West's ear. It includes
Harry Greener's vaudeville jargon: "Joe was laying up with a
whisker in the old Fifth Avenue when the stove exploded. It was
the broad's husband who blew the whistle." Along with it there
is the very different belligerent idiom of Abe Kusich, shouting
"No quiff can give Abe Kusich the fingeroo and get away with
it," calling Earle a "pee-hole bandit," or boasting after he has
incapacitated him, "I fixed that buckeroo." At the same time
there is the witty and epigrammatic conversation of Claude and
Tod. Typically, Claude describes Mrs. Jenning's brothel as "a
triumph of industrial design," Tod answers that he nevertheless
finds it depressing, "like all places for deposit, banks, mail boxes,
tombs, vending machines," and Claude then improvises on that
set theme. Claude is clearly West's ideal vision of himself: "He
was master of an involved comic rhetoric that permitted him to
express his moral indignation and still keep his reputation for
worldliness and wit."

Some of the images in the book are as powerful as any in *Miss
Lonelyhearts*. One is bird blood. We see it first as Earle plucks
some quail: "Their feathers fell to the ground, point first, weighed
down by the tiny drop of blood that trembled on the tips of their
quills." It reappears magnified and horrible as the losing cock's
beak breaks: "A large bubble of blood rose where the beak had
been." Another powerful image is of Homer crying, at first making a sound "like that of a dog lapping gruel," then in his madness
sobbing "like an ax chopping pine, a heavy, hollow, chunking
noise." A third image is the scene of male communion between
Tod and Homer, resembling that between Miss Lonelyhearts and
Doyle, and like it a prelude to violence. Tod and Homer leave
the party to sit out on the curb, and Homer sits inarticulate, with
a "sweet grin on his face," then takes Tod's hand and makes "trem-
bling signals of affection."

The book's most vivid sustained image, perhaps more powerful
than anything in *Miss Lonelyhearts*, is the riot, which is night-
marishly sexual as well as threatening. Swept along by the mob,

Tod is thrown against a young girl whose clothes have been half torn off. With her thigh between his legs, she clings to him, and he discovers that she is being attacked from behind by an old man who has a hand inside her dress and is biting her neck. When Tod frees her from the old man, she is seized by another man, as Tod is swept impotently by. In another part of the crowd, they are talking with delight of a pervert who ripped up a girl with a pair of scissors, as they hug and pinch one another. Tod finally kicks off a woman trying to hang on to him, and escapes with no more than his leg broken, and a vision of the mob for his painting as "a great united front of screwballs and screwboxes."

Despite this and other very powerful scenes, I think that *The Day of the Locust* ultimately fails as a novel. Shifting from Tod to Homer and back to Tod, it has no dramatic unity, and in comparison with *Miss Lonelyhearts*, it has no moral core. Where Miss Lonelyhearts' inability to stay in Betty's Eden is heartbreaking, Tod's disillusion with Faye is only sobering, and where the end of the former is tragic, the end of this, Tod in the police car screaming along with the siren, is merely hysteric.

There is humor but little joy in West's novels, obsessive sexuality but few consummations (except for that sit-up-and-lie-down doll Betty Prail). The world West shows us is for the most part repulsive and terrifying. It is his genius to have found objective correlatives for our sickness and fears: our maimed and ambivalent sexuality, our terror of the idiot mass, our helpless empathy with suffering, our love perverted into sadism and masochism. West did this in convincing present-day forms of the great myths: the Quest, the Scapegoat, the Holy Fool, the Dance of Death. His strength lay in his vulgarity and bad taste, his pessimism, his nastiness. West could never have been the affirmative political writer he sometimes imagined, or written the novels that he told his publisher, just before his death, he had planned: "simple, warm and kindly books." We must assume that if West had lived, he would have continued to write the sort of novels he had written before, perhaps even finer ones.

In his short tormented life, West achieved one authentically great novel, *Miss Lonelyhearts*, and three others less successful as wholes but full of brilliant and wonderful things. He was a true pioneer and culture hero, making it possible for the younger symbolists and fantasists who came after him, and who include our best writers, to do with relative ease what he did in defiance of the temper of his time, for so little reward, in isolation and in pain.

SELECTED BIBLIOGRAPHIES

Selected Bibliographies

EDITH WHARTON
Works

NOVELS AND COLLECTIONS OF SHORT STORIES

The Greater Inclination. New York: Scribner's, 1899.
The Touchstone. New York: Scribner's, 1900.
Crucial Instances. New York: Scribner's, 1901.
The Valley of Decision. New York: Scribner's, 1902.
Sanctuary. New York: Scribner's, 1903.
The Descent of Man and Other Stories. New York: Scribner's, 1904.
The House of Mirth. New York: Scribner's, 1905.
Madame de Treymes. New York: Scribner's, 1907.
The Fruit of the Tree. New York: Scribner's, 1907.
The Hermit and the Wild Woman and Other Stories. New York: Scribner's, 1908.
Tales of Men and Ghosts. New York: Scribner's, 1910.
Ethan Frome. New York: Scribner's, 1911.
The Reef. New York: Appleton, 1912.
The Custom of the Country. New York: Scribner's, 1913.
Xingu and Other Stories. New York: Scribner's, 1916.
Summer. New York: Appleton, 1917.
The Marne. New York: Appleton, 1918.
The Age of Innocence. New York: Appleton, 1920.
The Glimpses of the Moon. New York: Appleton, 1922.
A Son at the Front. New York: Scribner's, 1923.
Old New York: False Dawn (The 'Forties); The Old Maid (The 'Fifties); The Spark (The 'Sixties); New Year's Day (The 'Seventies). New York: Appleton, 1924.
The Mother's Recompense. New York: Appleton, 1925.
Here and Beyond. New York: Appleton, 1926.
Twilight Sleep. New York: Appleton, 1927.
The Children. New York: Appleton, 1928.
Hudson River Bracketed. New York: Appleton, 1929.
Certain People. New York: Appleton, 1930.
The Gods Arrive. New York: Appleton, 1932.
Human Nature. New York: Appleton, 1933.

The World Over. New York: Appleton-Century, 1936.
Ghosts. New York: Appleton-Century, 1937.
The Buccaneers. New York: Appleton-Century, 1938.

POETRY

Verses. Newport, R.I.: C. E. Hammett, Jr., 1878.
Artemis to Actaeon and Other Verse. New York: Scribner's, 1909.
Twelve Poems. London: The Medici Society, 1926.

NONFICTION

The Decoration of Houses (with Ogden Codman, Jr.). New York: Scribner's, 1897.
Italian Villas and Their Gardens. New York: Century, 1904.
Italian Backgrounds. New York: Scribner's, 1905.
A Motor-Flight through France. New York: Scribner's, 1908.
Fighting France, from Dunkerque to Belfort. New York: Scribner's, 1915.
French Ways and Their Meaning. New York: Appleton, 1919.
In Morocco. New York: Scribner's, 1920.
The Writing of Fiction. New York: Scribner's, 1925.
A Backward Glance. New York: Appleton-Century, 1934.

TRANSLATIONS

The Joy of Living, by Hermann Sudermann. New York: Scribner's, 1902.

COMPILATIONS

The Book of the Homeless. New York: Scribner's, 1916.
Eternal Passion in English Poetry (with Robert Norton and Gaillard Lapsley). New York: Appleton-Century, 1939.

Critical and Biographical Studies

Andrews, Wayne. Introduction to *The Best Short Stories of Edith Wharton.* New York: Scribner's, 1958. (Includes fragments from Mrs. Wharton's diary.)
Brooks, Van Wyck. *The Confident Years.* New York: Dutton, 1952.
Browne, E. K. *Edith Wharton, Étude Critique.* Paris: Librairie E. Droz, 1935.
Edel, Leon. "Edith Wharton," in *The Dictionary of American Biography,* Volume 22. New York: Scribner's, 1958.
James, Henry. *Letters to Walter Berry.* Paris: Black Sun Press, 1928.
Kazin, Alfred. *On Native Grounds.* New York: Reynal and Hitchcock, 1942.
Lubbock, Percy. *Portrait of Edith Wharton.* New York: Appleton-Century-Crofts, 1947.
Nevius, Blake. *Edith Wharton, A Study of Her Fiction.* Berkeley and Los Angeles: University of California Press, 1953.
Origo, Iris. "The Homecoming," *New Statesman and Nation,* February 16, 1957.
Wilson, Edmund. *The Wound and the Bow.* Boston: Houghton Mifflin, 1941.
———. *Classics and Commercials.* New York: Farrar, Straus, 1950.

SINCLAIR LEWIS

Works

Our Mr. Wrenn: The Romantic Adventures of a Gentle Man. New York: Harper, 1914.

SELECTED BIBLIOGRAPHIES

The Trail of the Hawk: A Comedy of the Seriousness of Life. New York: Harper, 1915.

The Job: An American Novel. New York: Harper, 1917.

The Innocents: A Story for Lovers. New York: Harper, 1917.

Free Air. New York: Harcourt, Brace, and Howe, 1919.

Main Street: The Story of Carol Kennicott. New York: Harcourt, Brace, 1920.

Babbitt. New York: Harcourt, Brace, 1922.

Arrowsmith. New York: Harcourt, Brace, 1925.

Mantrap. New York: Harcourt, Brace, 1926.

Elmer Gantry. New York: Harcourt, Brace, 1927.

The Man Who Knew Coolidge: Being the Soul of Lowell Schmaltz, Constructive and Nordic Citizen. New York: Harcourt, Brace, 1928.

Dodsworth. New York: Harcourt, Brace, 1929.

Ann Vickers. New York: Doubleday, Doran, 1933.

Work of Art. New York: Doubleday, Doran, 1934.

Selected Short Stories. New York: Doubleday, Doran, 1935.

Jayhawker: A Play in Three Acts (written with Lloyd Lewis). New York: Doubleday, Doran, 1935.

It Can't Happen Here. New York: Doubleday, Doran, 1935.

The Prodigal Parents. New York: Doubleday, Doran, 1938.

Bethel Merriday. New York: Doubleday, Doran, 1940.

Gideon Planish. New York: Doubleday, Doran, 1943.

Cass Timberlane: A Novel of Husbands and Wives. New York: Random House, 1945.

Kingsblood Royal. New York: Random House, 1947.

The God-Seeker. New York: Random House, 1949.

World So Wide. New York: Random House, 1951.

From Main Street to Stockholm: Letters of Sinclair Lewis, 1919–1930, edited by Harrison Smith. New York: Harcourt, Brace, 1952.

The Man from Main Street: Selected Essays and Other Writings, 1904–1950, edited by Harry E. Maule and Melville H. Cane. New York: Random House, 1953.

Critical and Biographical Studies

Grebstein, Sheldon Norman. *Sinclair Lewis.* New York: Twayne, 1962.

Guthrie, Ramon. "Sinclair Lewis and the 'Labor Novel,' " *Proceedings* (Second Series, Number 2), American Academy of Arts and Letters. New York, 1952. (An interesting account of Lewis' attempt to write his labor novel.)

———. "The 'Labor Novel' That Sinclair Lewis Never Wrote," *New York Herald Tribune Books,* February 10, 1952. (A shorter version of the preceding.)

"Harrison, Oliver" (Harrison Smith). *Sinclair Lewis.* New York: Harcourt, Brace, 1925. (A promotion piece commissioned by Lewis' publisher.)

Hoffman, Frederick J. *The Twenties: American Writing in the Postwar Decade.* New York: Viking, 1955.

Lewis, Grace Hegger. *Half a Loaf.* New York: Liveright, 1931. (This novel by Lewis' first wife is a bizarre *roman à clef.*)

———. *With Love from Gracie.* New York: Harcourt, Brace, 1955. (A biographical memoir following closely *Half a Loaf.*)

Manson, Alexander (as told to Helen Camp). "The Last Days of Sinclair Lewis," *Saturday Evening Post,* 223:27, 110–12 (March 31, 1951). (An account by Lewis' last secretary, much less effective than Perry Miller's.)

269

Miller, Perry. "The Incorruptible Sinclair Lewis," *Atlantic*, 187:30–34 (April 1951). (A persuasively written impression of Lewis' last days in Florence.)

Schorer, Mark. *Sinclair Lewis: An American Life.* New York: McGraw-Hill, 1961. (Contains a reliable check list of Lewis' publications.)

——, ed. *Sinclair Lewis: A Collection of Critical Essays.* Englewood Cliffs, N.J.: Prentice-Hall (Spectrum Books), 1962. (The best critical writing about Lewis is contained in this collection.)

Sherman, Stuart Pratt. *The Significance of Sinclair Lewis.* New York: Harcourt, Brace, 1922. (A promotion piece commissioned by Lewis' publishers.)

Thompson, Dorothy. "Boy and Man from Sauk Centre," *Atlantic*, 206:39–48 (November 1960). (A touching piece of reminiscent speculation.)

Van Doren, Carl. *Sinclair Lewis: A Biographical Sketch.* With a Bibliography by Harvey Taylor. New York: Doubleday, Doran, 1933. (A promotion piece commissioned by Lewis' publisher; the bibliography is highly unreliable.)

F. SCOTT FITZGERALD

Works

This Side of Paradise. New York: Scribner's, 1920.

Flappers and Philosophers. New York: Scribner's, 1921. (Contains "The Offshore Pirate," "The Ice Palace," "Head and Shoulders," "The Cut-Glass Bowl," "Bernice Bobs Her Hair," "Benediction," "Dalyrimple Goes Wrong," and "The Four Fists.")

The Beautiful and Damned. New York: Scribner's, 1922.

Tales of the Jazz Age. New York: Scribner's, 1922. (Contains "The Jelly-Bean," "The Camel's Back," "May Day," "Porcelain and Pink," "The Diamond as Big as the Ritz," "The Curious Case of Benjamin Button," "Tarquin of Cheapside," "O Russet Witch!" "The Lees of Happiness," "Mr. Icky," and "Jemina.")

The Vegetable, or From President to Postman. New York: Scribner's, 1923.

The Great Gatsby. New York: Scribner's, 1925.

All the Sad Young Men. New York: Scribner's, 1926. (Contains "The Rich Boy," "Winter Dreams," "The Baby Party," "Absolution," "Rags Martin-Jones and the Pr–nce of W–les," "The Adjuster," "Hot and Cold Blood," "The Sensible Thing," and "Gretchen's Forty Winks.")

Tender Is the Night. New York: Scribner's, 1934.

Taps at Reveille. New York: Scribner's, 1935. (Contains Basil: 1. "The Scandal Detectives," 2. "The Freshest Boy," 3. "He Thinks He's Wonderful," 4. "The Captured Shadow," 5. "The Perfect Life"; Josephine: 1. "First Blood," 2. "A Nice Quiet Place," 3. "A Woman with a Past"; and "Crazy Sunday," "Two Wrongs," "The Night of Chancellorsville," "The Last of the Belles," "Majesty," "Family in the Wind," "A Short Trip Home," "One Interne," "The Fiend," and "Babylon Revisited.")

The Last Tycoon, edited by Edmund Wilson. New York: Scribner's, 1941.

The Crack-Up, edited by Edmund Wilson. New York: New Directions, 1945. (Contains "Echoes of the Jazz Age," "My Lost City," "Ring," " 'Show Mr. and Mrs. F. to Number——,'" "Auction—Model 1934," "Sleeping and Waking," "The Crack-Up," "Handle with Care," "Pasting It Together," "Early Success," "The Note-Books," Letters.)

The Stories of F. Scott Fitzgerald, a Selection of 28 stories with an Introduction by Malcolm Cowley. New York: Scribner's, 1951. (Contains eighteen stories from the four earlier volumes and "Magnetism," "The Rough Crossing,"

"The Bridal Party," "An Alcoholic Case," "The Long Way Out," "Financing Finnegan," "Pat Hobby Himself: A Patriotic Short, Two Old Timers," "Three Hours between Planes," and "The Lost Decade," all previously uncollected.)

Afternoon of an Author; A Selection of Uncollected Stories and Essays, with an Introduction and Notes by Arthur Mizener. New York: Scribner's, 1958. (Contains twelve stories and eight essays: "A Night at the Fair," "Forging Ahead," "Basil and Cleopatra," "Outside the Cabinet-Maker's," "One Trip Abroad," "I Didn't Get Over," "Afternoon of an Author," "Design in Plaster," Pat Hobby: 1. "Boil Some Water — Lots of It," 2. "Teamed with Genius," 3. "No Harm Trying," "News of Paris — Fifteen Years Ago," "Princeton," "Who's Who — and Why," "How to Live on $36,000 a Year," "How to Live on Practically Nothing a Year," "How to Waste Material: A Note on My Generation," "Ten Years in the Advertising Business," "One Hundred False Starts," and "Author's House.")

The Pat Hobby Stories, with an Introduction by Arnold Gingrich. New York: Scribner's, 1962. (Contains "Pat Hobby's Christmas Wish," "A Man in the Way," "Boil Some Water — Lots of It," "Teamed with Genius," "Pat Hobby and Orson Welles," "Pat Hobby's Secret," "Pat Hobby, Putative Father," "The Homes of the Stars," "Pat Hobby Does His Bit," "Pat Hobby's Preview," "No Harm Trying," "A Patriotic Short," "On the Trail of Pat Hobby," "Fun in an Artist's Studio," "Two Old-Timers," "Mightier Than the Sword," "Pat Hobby's College Days.")

The Letters of F. Scott Fitzgerald, edited by Andrew Turnbull. New York: Scribner's, 1963.

Bibliographies

Beebe, Maurice, and Jackson R. Bryer. "Criticism of F. Scott Fitzgerald: A Selected Checklist," *Modern Fiction Studies,* 7:82–94 (Spring 1961).

Bryer, Jackson R. "F. Scott Fitzgerald and His Critics: A Bibliographical Record," *Bulletin of Bibliography,* 23:155–58, 180–83, 201–7 (January–September 1962).

Mizener, Arthur. "Fitzgerald's Published Work," *The Far Side of Paradise.* Boston: Houghton Mifflin, 1951.

Critical and Biographical Studies

Barrett, William. "Fitzgerald and America," *Partisan Review,* 18:345–53 (May–June 1951).

Bewley, Marius. "Scott Fitzgerald and the Collapse of the American Dream," in *The Eccentric Design: Form in the Classic American Novel.* New York: Columbia University Press, 1959.

Bishop, John Peale. "The Missing All," *Virginia Quarterly Review,* 13:107–21 (Winter 1937).

Bruccoli, Matthew J. *The Composition of Tender Is the Night.* Pittsburgh: University of Pittsburgh Press, 1963.

———, ed. *Fitzgerald Newsletter.* Number 1 (Spring 1958) to date.

Callaghan, Morley E. *That Summer in Paris; Memories of Tangled Friendships with Hemingway, Fitzgerald, and Some Others.* New York: Coward-McCann, 1963.

Chase, Richard. *The American Novel and Its Tradition.* Garden City, N.Y.: Doubleday (Anchor Books), 1957. Pp. 162–67.

Eble, Kenneth E. *F. Scott Fitzgerald.* New York: Twayne, 1963.

Geismar, Maxwell. "F. Scott Fitzgerald: Orestes at the Ritz," in *The Last of the Provincials: The Americal Novel, 1915–1925.* Boston: Houghton Mifflin, 1943.

Goldhurst, William. *F. Scott Fitzgerald and His Contemporaries.* Cleveland: World, 1963.

Graham, Sheilah, and Gerold Frank. *Beloved Infidel.* New York: Holt, 1958. Pp. 173–338.

Harding, D. W. "Scott Fitzgerald," *Scrutiny,* 18:166–74 (Winter 1951–52).

Hoffman, Frederick J. "Points of Moral Reference: A Comparative Study of Edith Wharton and F. Scott Fitzgerald," in *English Institute Essays* 1949, edited by Alan Downer. New York: Columbia University Press, 1950.

——, ed. *The Great Gatsby: A Study.* New York: Scribner's, 1962.

Kazin, Alfred, ed. *F. Scott Fitzgerald: The Man and His Work.* Cleveland: World, 1951.

Kuehl, John. "Scott Fitzgerald's Reading," *Princeton University Library Chronicle,* 22:58–89 (Winter 1961).

Leighton, Lawrence. "An Autopsy and a Prescription," *Hound and Horn,* 5:519–39 (July 1932).

Miller, James E., Jr. *The Fictional Technique of Scott Fitzgerald.* International Scholars Forum, vol. 9. The Hague: Martinus Nijhoff, 1957.

Mizener, Arthur. *The Far Side of Paradise.* Boston: Houghton Mifflin, 1951.

——. "Scott Fitzgerald and the 1920's," *Minnesota Review,* 1:161–74 (January 1961).

——. "Scott Fitzgerald and the Top Girl," *Atlantic Monthly,* 207:55–60 (March 1961).

——, ed. *F. Scott Fitzgerald: A Collection of Critical Essays.* Englewood Cliffs, N.J.: Prentice-Hall (Spectrum Books), 1963.

Modern Fiction Studies, vol. 7 (Spring 1961). (Essays on Fitzgerald by A. E. Dyson, Eugene White, Donald A. Yates, Matthew J. Bruccoli, Kent and Gretchen Kreuter, Robert F. McDonnell, John E. Hart, and John Kuehl.)

Moers, E. F. "F. Scott Fitzgerald: Reveille at Taps," *Commentary,* 34:526–30 (December 1962).

Morris, Wright. "The Function of Nostalgia — F. Scott Fitzgerald," in *The Territory Ahead.* New York: Harcourt, Brace, 1958.

Perosa, Sergio. *L'arte di F. Scott Fitzgerald.* Rome: Edizioni di Storia e Letteratura, 1961.

Piper, Henry Dan. "Frank Norris and Scott Fitzgerald," *Huntington Library Quarterly,* 19:393–400 (August 1956).

Schulberg, Budd. "Old Scott: The Mask, the Myth, and the Man," *Esquire,* 55:96–101 (January 1961).

Tompkins, C. "Living Well Is the Best Revenge," *New Yorker,* 38:31–69 (July 28, 1962).

Turnbull, Andrew. *Scott Fitzgerald.* New York: Scribner's, 1962.

WILLIAM FAULKNER

Works

The Marble Faun, with a Preface by Phil Stone. Boston: The Four Seas Company, 1924.

Soldiers' Pay. New York: Boni and Liveright, 1926.

Mosquitoes. New York: Boni and Liveright, 1927.

Sartoris. New York: Harcourt, Brace, 1929.

The Sound and the Fury. New York: Jonathan Cape and Harrison Smith, 1929.

As I Lay Dying. New York: Jonathan Cape and Harrison Smith, 1930.

Sanctuary. New York: Jonathan Cape and Harrison Smith, 1931.

These Thirteen. New York: Jonathan Cape and Harrison Smith, 1931. (Contains "Victory," "All the Dead Pilots," "Crevasse," "A Justice," "Mistral," "Ad Astra," "Red Leaves," "Divorce in Naples," "Carcassone," "A Rose for Emily," "Hair," "That Evening Sun," and "Dry September.")

Idyll in the Desert. New York: Random House, 1931. (A limited edition of 400 copies; never reprinted.)

Miss Zilphia Gant. The Book Club of Texas, 1932. (A limited edition of 300 copies; never reprinted.)

Light in August. New York: Harrison Smith and Robert Haas, 1932.

Salmagundi. Milwaukee: The Casanova Press, 1932. (Contains early essays and poems, mostly from the *Double-Dealer*.)

A Green Bough. New York: Harrison Smith and Robert Haas, 1933.

Doctor Martino and Other Stories. New York: Harrison Smith and Robert Haas, 1934. (Contains "Black Music," "Leg," "Doctor Martino," "Fox Hunt," "Death Drag," "There Was a Queen," "Smoke," "Turn About," "Beyond," "Wash," "Elly," "Mountain Victory," "Honor.")

Pylon. New York: Harrison Smith and Robert Haas, 1935.

Absalom, Absalom! New York: Random House, 1936.

The Unvanquished. New York: Random House, 1938.

The Wild Palms. New York: Random House, 1939.

The Hamlet. New York: Random House, 1940.

Go Down, Moses and Other Stories. New York: Random House, 1942. (In subsequent printings and other editions, "and Other Stories" was omitted from the title, thus emphasizing the unity of the collection.)

Intruder in the Dust. New York: Random House, 1948.

Knight's Gambit. New York: Random House, 1949. (Contains "Smoke," reprinted from *Doctor Martino*, "Monk," "Hand upon the Waters," "Tomorrow," "An Error in Chemistry," and "Knight's Gambit.")

Collected Stories of William Faulkner. New York: Random House, 1950. (Reprints all the stories from *These Thirteen* and *Doctor Martino* as well as "Artist at Home," "The Brooch," "Centaur in Brass," "A Courtship," "Golden Land," "Lo!" "Mule in the Yard," "My Grandmother Millard and General Bedford Forrest and the Battle of Harrykin Creek," "Pennsylvania Station," "Shall Not Perish," "Shingles for the Lord," "The Tall Men," "That Will Be Fine," "Two Soldiers," and "Uncle Willy.")

Notes on a Horsethief. Greenville, Miss.: The Levee Press, 1951.

Requiem for a Nun. New York: Random House, 1951.

A Fable. New York: Random House, 1954.

Big Woods. New York: Random House, 1955. (A collection of earlier stories plus "Race at Morning.")

New Orleans Sketches by William Faulkner. Tokyo, Japan: The Hokuseido Press, 1955. (Contains the "Mirrors of Chartres Street" sketches which appeared originally in the *Times-Picayune*.)

Faulkner at Nagano. Tokyo, Japan: The Kenkyusha Press, 1956. (Contains interviews Faulkner gave during his visit to Japan, plus statements and speeches.)

Faulkner in the University, edited by Frederick L. Gwynn and Joseph Blot-

ner. Charlottesville, Va.: University Press of Virginia, 1959. (Contains questions put to Faulkner by students and faculty and his replies.)
The Town. New York: Random House, 1957.
The Mansion. New York: Random House, 1959.
The Reivers. New York: Random House, 1962.
William Faulkner: Early Prose and Poetry, edited by Carvel Collins. Boston: Little, Brown, 1962.

Bibliographies

Beebe, Maurice. "Criticism of William Faulkner: A Selected Checklist with an Index to Studies of Separate Works," *Modern Fiction Studies,* 2:150–64 (Autumn 1956). (Published at Purdue University, Lafayette, Indiana.)
Daniel, Robert W. *A Catalogue of the Writings of William Faulkner.* New Haven, Conn.: Yale University Library, 1942.
Meriwether, James B. "William Faulkner: A Checklist," *Princeton Library Chronicle,* 18:136–58 (Spring 1957).

Critical and Biographical Studies

Beck, Warren. *Man in Motion.* Madison: University of Wisconsin Press, 1961.
Brooks, Cleanth. *William Faulkner: The Yoknapatawpha Country.* New Haven, Conn.: Yale University Press, 1963.
Campbell, Harry M., and Ruel E. Foster. *William Faulkner: A Critical Appraisal.* Norman: University of Oklahoma Press, 1951.
Cullen, John B. *Old Times in the Faulkner Country.* Chapel Hill: University of North Carolina Press, 1961.
Hoffman, Frederick J. *William Faulkner.* New York: Twayne, 1961.
—— and Olga Vickery, eds. *William Faulkner: Three Decades of Criticism.* East Lansing: Michigan State University Press, 1960.
Howe, Irving. *William Faulkner: A Critical Study.* New York: Random House, 1952; revised 1962.
Miner, Ward L. *The World of William Faulkner.* Durham, N.C.: Duke University Press, 1952.
O'Connor, William Van. *The Tangled Fire of William Faulkner.* Minneapolis: University of Minnesota Press, 1954.
Thompson, Lawrance. *William Faulkner.* New York: Barnes and Noble, 1963.

ERNEST HEMINGWAY
Principal Works

Three Stories and Ten Poems. Paris and Dijon: Contact Publishing Co., 1923.
In Our Time. New York: Boni and Liveright, 1925.
The Torrents of Spring. New York: Scribner's, 1926.
The Sun Also Rises. New York: Scribner's, 1926.
Men without Women. New York: Scribner's, 1927.
A Farewell to Arms. New York: Scribner's, 1929.
Death in the Afternoon. New York: Scribner's, 1932.
Winner Take Nothing. New York: Scribner's, 1933.
Green Hills of Africa. New York: Scribner's, 1935.
To Have and Have Not. New York: Scribner's, 1937.
The Fifth Column and the First Forty-Nine Stories. New York: Scribner's, 1938.
For Whom the Bell Tolls. New York: Scribner's, 1940.

Across the River and into the Trees. New York: Scribner's, 1950.
The Old Man and the Sea. New York: Scribner's, 1952.

Bibliographies

Baker, Carlos. "A Working Checklist of Hemingway's Prose, Poetry, and Journalism — with Notes," in *Hemingway: The Writer as Artist.* Princeton, N.J.: Princeton University Press, 1952; third edition, enlarged, 1963.
————. "A Checklist of Hemingway Criticism," in *Hemingway and His Critics: An International Anthology.* New York: Hill and Wang, 1961.
Beebe, Maurice. "Criticism of Ernest Hemingway: A Selected Checklist with an Index to Studies of Separate Works," *Modern Fiction Studies,* 1:36–45 (August 1955).
Samuels, Lee. *A Hemingway Check List.* New York: Scribner's, 1951.

Biographies

Hemingway, Leicester. *My Brother, Ernest Hemingway.* Cleveland: World, 1962.
Ross, Lillian. *Portrait of Hemingway.* New York: Simon and Schuster, 1961.
Sanford, Marcelline Hemingway. *At the Hemingways: A Family Portrait.* Boston: Little, Brown, 1962.

Critical Studies

Baker, Carlos. *Hemingway: The Writer as Artist.* Princeton, N.J.: Princeton University Press, 1952; third edition, enlarged, 1963.
————, ed. *Hemingway and His Critics: An International Anthology.* New York: Hill and Wang, 1961. (Essays by George Plimpton, André Maurois, Edmund Wilson, Lionel Trilling, H. E. Bates, Mark Spilka, Harry Levin, Mario Praz, Pier Francesco Paolini, Deming Brown, Ivan Kashkeen, Michael F. Moloney, Frederic I. Carpenter, Arturo Barea, Horst Oppel, Joseph Warren Beach, Melvin Backman, Clinton S. Burhans, Jr., and Keiichi Harada.)
Fenton, Charles A. *The Apprenticeship of Ernest Hemingway.* New York: Farrar, Straus, and Young, 1954.
Killinger, John. *Hemingway and the Dead Gods: A Study in Existentialism.* Lexington: University of Kentucky Press, 1961.
McCaffery, John K. M., ed. *Ernest Hemingway: The Man and His Work.* Cleveland: World, 1950. (Essays by John Groth, Gertrude Stein, Malcolm Cowley, Lincoln Kirstein, Max Eastman, J. Kashkeen, Elliot Paul, Delmore Schwartz, Edgar Johnson, Maxwell Geismar, Alfred Kazin, Edward Fenimore, James T. Farrell, James Gray, Edmund Wilson, Leo Gurko, W. M. Frohock, John Peale Bishop, Edwin Berry Burghum, George Hemphill, and Theodore Bardacke.)
Modern Fiction Studies, Volume 1 (August 1955). (Essays by Melvin Backman, Tom Burnam, C. Hugh Holman, Bernard S. Oldsey, H. K. Russell, and Green D. Wyrick.)
Rovit, Earl. *Ernest Hemingway.* New York: Twayne, 1963.
Sanderson, S. F. *Ernest Hemingway.* New York: Grove, 1961.
Weeks, Robert P., ed. *Hemingway: A Collection of Critical Essays.* Englewood Cliffs, N.J.: Prentice-Hall, 1962. (Essays by Lillian Ross, Malcolm Cowley, E. M. Halliday, Harry Levin, Leslie Fiedler, D. H. Lawrence, Philip Young,

Sean O'Faolain, Cleanth Brooks and Robert Penn Warren, Carlos Baker, Mark Spilka, Ray B. West, Jr., Nemi D'Agostino, Joseph Waldmeir, and Leon Edel.)
Young, Philip. *Ernest Hemingway.* New York: Rinehart, 1952.

THOMAS WOLFE
Principal Works

Look Homeward, Angel. New York: Scribner's, 1929.
Of Time and the River. New York: Scribner's, 1935.
From Death to Morning. New York: Scribner's, 1935.
The Story of a Novel. New York: Scribner's, 1936.
The Web and the Rock. New York: Harper, 1939.
You Can't Go Home Again. New York: Harper, 1940.
The Hills Beyond. New York: Harper, 1941.
Thomas Wolfe's Letters to His Mother Julia Elizabeth Wolfe, edited with an Introduction by John Skally Terry. New York: Scribner's, 1943.
Mannerhouse: A Play in a Prologue and Three Acts. New York: Harper, 1948.
A Western Journal. Pittsburgh: University of Pittsburgh Press, 1951.
The Correspondence of Thomas Wolfe and Homer Andrew Watt, edited by Oscar Cargill and Thomas Clark Pollock. New York: New York University Press, 1954.
The Letters of Thomas Wolfe, collected and edited by Elizabeth Nowell. New York: Scribner's, 1956.
Welcome to Our City: A 10-Scene Play, Esquire Magazine, 48:58–83 (October 1957).
The Short Novels of Thomas Wolfe, edited with an Introduction and Notes by C. Hugh Holman. New York: Scribner's, 1961. (Contains the original versions of *A Portrait of Bascom Hawke, The Web of Earth, No Door, "I Have a Thing to Tell You,"* and *The Party at Jack's.*)
Thomas Wolfe's Purdue Speech, edited by William Braswell and Leslie A. Field. Lafayette, Ind.: Purdue University Studies, 1964.

Books of Selections

The Face of a Nation: Poetical Passages from the Writings of Thomas Wolfe [selected by John Hall Wheelock]. New York: Scribner's, 1939.
A Stone, a Leaf, a Door: Poems by Thomas Wolfe, selected and arranged in verse by John S. Barnes. New York: Scribner's, 1945.
The Portable Thomas Wolfe, edited by Maxwell Geismar. New York: Viking, 1946. (Contains *The Story of a Novel,* episodes from each of the novels, and six short stories.)
The Thomas Wolfe Reader, edited with an Introduction and Notes by C. Hugh Holman. New York: Scribner's, 1962. (Contains *The Story of a Novel* and selections from all of Wolfe's other books.)

Bibliographies

Holman, C. Hugh. "Thomas Wolfe: A Bibliographical Study," *Texas Studies in Literature and Language,* 1:427–45 (Autumn 1959).
Johnson, Elmer D. *Of Time and Thomas Wolfe: A Bibliography with a Character Index of His Works.* New York: Scarecrow Press, 1959. (See, however,

Alexander D. Wainwright's review in *Papers of the Bibliographical Society of America*, 55:258–63 (July–September 1961), for corrections.)

Kauffman, Bernice. "Bibliography of Periodical Articles on Thomas Wolfe," *Bulletin of Bibliography*, 17:162–65, 172–90 (May, August 1942).

Preston, George R., Jr. *Thomas Wolfe: A Bibliography*. New York: Charles S. Boesen, 1943.

Critical and Biographical Studies

Most of the good critical and biographical essays of less than book length are reprinted in Holman, *The World of Thomas Wolfe*, and Walser, *The Enigma of Thomas Wolfe*. The following list includes some additional articles as well as books that may profitably be consulted.

Adams, Agatha Boyd. *Thomas Wolfe: Carolina Student*. Chapel Hill: University of North Carolina Library, 1950.

Angoff, Charles. "Thomas Wolfe and the Opulent Manner," *Southwest Review*, 48:vi–vii, 81–84 (Winter 1963).

Baker, Carlos. "Thomas Wolfe's Apprenticeship," *Delphian Quarterly*, 23:20–25 (January 1940).

Beach, Joseph Warren. *American Fiction: 1920–1940*. New York: Macmillan, 1941. Pp. 173–215.

Budd, Louis J. "The Grotesques of Anderson and Wolfe," *Modern Fiction Studies*, 5:304–10 (Winter 1959–60).

Daniels, Jonathan. *Thomas Wolfe: October Recollections*. Columbia, S.C.: Bostick and Thornley, 1961.

Delakas, Daniel L. *Thomas Wolfe, la France, et les romanciers français*. Paris: Jouve & Cie., 1950.

Eaton, Clement. "Student Days with Thomas Wolfe," *Georgia Review*, 17:146–55 (Summer 1963).

Field, Leslie A. "Wolfe's Use of Folklore," *New York Folklore Quarterly*, 16:203–15 (Autumn 1960).

Geismar, Maxwell. *Writers in Crisis*. Boston: Houghton Mifflin, 1942. Pp. 185–236.

Holman, C. Hugh. " 'The Dark Ruined Helen of His Blood': Thomas Wolfe and the South," in *South: Modern Southern Literature in Its Cultural Setting*, edited by Louis D. Rubin, Jr., and Robert D. Jacobs. Garden City, N.Y.: Doubleday, 1961. Pp. 177–97.

——, ed. *The World of Thomas Wolfe*. New York: Scribner's, 1962. (Contains *The Story of a Novel* and selected critical essays.)

Johnson, Pamela Hansford. *The Art of Thomas Wolfe*. New York: Scribner's, 1963. (A reprint of *Hungry Gulliver* (New York: Scribner's, 1948), which was an American edition of *Thomas Wolfe: A Critical Study* (London: William Heinemann, 1947).)

Kearns, Frank, ed. "Tom Wolfe on the Drama," *Carolina Quarterly*, 11:5–10 (Spring 1960). (An autobiographical sketch by Wolfe.)

Kennedy, Richard S. *The Window of Memory: The Literary Career of Thomas Wolfe*. Chapel Hill: University of North Carolina Press, 1962.

Ledig-Rowohlt, H. M. "Thomas Wolfe in Berlin," *American Scholar*, 22:185–201 (Spring 1953).

Little, Thomas. "The Thomas Wolfe Collection of William B. Wisdom," *Harvard Library Bulletin*, 1:280–87 (Autumn 1947).

McElderry, B. R., Jr. "The Autobiographical Problem in Thomas Wolfe's Earlier Novels," *Arizona Quarterly*, 4:315–24 (Winter 1948).

———. "The Durable Humor of *Look Homeward, Angel*," *Arizona Quarterly*, 11:123–28 (Summer 1955).

———. "Thomas Wolfe: Dramatist," *Modern Drama*, 6:1–11 (May 1963).

———. *Thomas Wolfe*. New York: Twayne, 1964.

Muller, Herbert J. *Thomas Wolfe*. Norfolk, Conn.: New Directions, 1947.

Norwood, Hayden. *The Marble Man's Wife: Thomas Wolfe's Mother*. New York: Scribner's, 1947.

Nowell, Elizabeth. *Thomas Wolfe: A Biography*. Garden City, N.Y.: Doubleday, 1960.

Pfister, Karin. *Zeit und Wirklichkeit bei Thomas Wolfe*. Heidelberg: Carl Winter, 1954.

Pollock, Thomas Clark, and Oscar Cargill. *Thomas Wolfe at Washington Square*. New York: New York University Press, 1954.

Reaver, J. Russell, and Robert I. Strozier. "Thomas Wolfe and Death," *Georgia Review*, 16:330–50 (Fall 1962).

Reeves, George M., Jr. *Thomas Wolfe et Europe*. Paris: Librairie Marcel Didier, 1955.

Reeves, Paschal. "The Humor of Thomas Wolfe," *Southern Folklore Quarterly*, 24:109–20 (June 1960).

Ribalow, Harold U. "Of Jews and Thomas Wolfe," *Chicago Jewish Forum*, 13:89–99 (1954).

Rubin, Louis D., Jr. *Thomas Wolfe: The Weather of His Youth*. Baton Rouge: Louisiana State University Press, 1955.

———. *The Faraway Country*. Seattle: University of Washington Press, 1963. Pp. 72–104.

———. "The Self Recaptured," *Kenyon Review*, 25:393–415 (Summer 1963).

Skipp, Francis E. "The Editing of *Look Homeward, Angel*," *Papers of the Bibliographical Society of America*, 57:1–13 (First quarter 1963).

Thornton, Mary L., ed. " 'Dear Mabel': Letters of Thomas Wolfe to His Sister, Mabel Wolfe Wheaton," *South Atlantic Quarterly*, 60:469–83 (Autumn 1961).

Walser, Richard. *Thomas Wolfe: An Introduction and Interpretation*. New York: Barnes and Noble, 1961.

———, ed. *The Enigma of Thomas Wolfe: Biographical and Critical Selections*. Cambridge, Mass.: Harvard University Press, 1953.

Watkins, Floyd C. "Thomas Wolfe and the Southern Mountaineer," *South Atlantic Quarterly*, 50:58–71 (January 1951).

———. "Thomas Wolfe and the Nashville Agrarians," *Georgia Review*, 7:410–23 (Winter 1953).

———. *Thomas Wolfe's Characters: Portraits from Life*. Norman: University of Oklahoma Press, 1957.

Wheaton, Mabel Wolfe, and LeGette Blythe. *Thomas Wolfe and His Family*. Garden City, N.Y.: Doubleday, 1961.

NATHANAEL WEST

The only book so far published on West is James F. Light's *Nathanael West: An Interpretative Study*, to which Mr. Hyman expresses his indebtedness for nearly all of the biographical information included here. All four of West's novels are available in the one-volume *The Complete Works of Nathanael West*. A West library thus consists essentially of two books.

SELECTED BIBLIOGRAPHIES
Works

The Dream Life of Balso Snell. Paris and New York: Contact Editions, 1931.
Miss Lonelyhearts. New York: Liveright, 1933.
A Cool Million. New York: Covici-Friede, 1934.
The Day of the Locust. New York: Random House, 1939.
"Some Notes on Violence," *Contact*, 1:132–33 (October 1932).
"Some Notes on Miss Lonelyhearts," *Contempo*, 3:1–2 (May 15, 1933).
"Business Deal," *Americana*, 1:14–15 (October 1933).
"Soft Soap for the Barber," *New Republic*, 81:23 (November 1934).
The Complete Works of Nathanael West. New York: Farrar, Straus, and Cudahy, 1957.

Bibliography

White, William. "Nathanael West: A Bibliography," *Studies in Bibliography*, 11:207–24 (1958). (Papers of the Bibliographical Society of the University of Virginia, Charlottesville, Virginia.)

Critical and Biographical Studies

Aaron, Daniel. "The Truly Monstrous: A Note on Nathanael West," *Partisan Review*, 14:98–106 (February 1947).
———. "Writing for Apocalypse," *Hudson Review*, 3:634–36 (Winter 1951).
Coates, Robert M. "Messiah of the Lonely Hearts," *New Yorker*, 9:59 (April 15, 1933).
———. Introduction to *Miss Lonelyhearts*. New York: New Directions, 1946, 1950.
Cohen, Arthur. "Nathanael West's Holy Fool," *Commonweal*, 64:276–78 (June 15, 1956).
Gehman, Richard B. Introduction to *The Day of the Locust*. New York: New Directions, 1950.
Liebling, A. J. "Shed a Tear for Mr. West," *New York World Telegram*, June 24, 1933, p. 14.
Light, James F. *Nathanael West: An Interpretative Study*. Evanston, Ill.: Northwestern University Press, 1961.
McKenney, Ruth. *Love Story*. New York: Harcourt, Brace, 1950. Pp. 175–76, 195–97.
Podhoretz, Norman. "A Particular Kind of Joking," *New Yorker*, 33:156–65 (May 18, 1957).
Rosenfeld, Isaac. "Faulkner and Contemporaries," *Partisan Review*, 18:106–14 (January–February 1951).
Ross, Alan. Introduction to *The Complete Works of Nathanael West*.
Sanford, John. "Nathanael West," *Screen Writer*, 2:10–13 (December 1946).
Troy, William. "Four Newer Novelists," *Nation*, 136:672–73 (June 14, 1933).
Williams, William Carlos. "Sordid? Good God!" *Contempo*, 3:5, 8 (July 25, 1933).
———. Review of *The Day of the Locust*, *Tomorrow*, 10:58–59 (November 1950).
Wilson, Edmund. "Postscript," *The Boys in the Back Room*. San Francisco: Colt Press, 1951.

ABOUT THE AUTHORS

About the Authors

LOUIS AUCHINCLOSS is a prolific novelist and critic as well as a partner in a New York law firm. Among his recent works are *The House of Five Talents, Portrait in Brownstone,* and *Powers of Attorney.*

MARK SCHORER, professor of English at the University of California, Berkeley, is the author of three novels, many short stories, works of literary criticism, and *Sinclair Lewis: An American Life.*

CHARLES E. SHAIN, president of Connecticut College, was formerly a professor of English and American Studies at Carleton College, Northfield, Minnesota. He has contributed articles to various journals.

WILLIAM VAN O'CONNOR has written many volumes of literary criticism and a collection of short stories and has edited several textbooks. He is a professor of English at the University of California, Davis.

PHILIP YOUNG is a professor of American literature at the Pennsylvania State University. He is the author of the book-length study *Ernest Hemingway* and of numerous critical articles.

C. HUGH HOLMAN is Kenan professor of English and dean of the Graduate School at the University of North Carolina. He is co-author of *The Development of American Literary Criticism* and has edited several volumes.

STANLEY EDGAR HYMAN, staff writer for the *New Yorker* and book critic of the *New Leader*, was a member of the literature faculty at Bennington College. Among his books are *The Tangled Bank*, *Poetry and Criticism*, and *The Promised End*.

INDEX

Index

Absalom, Absalom!, 8, 135, 138–40, 149
"Absolution," 110
Across the River and into the Trees, 166–68, 169, 174
Adams, Nick (fictional character), 143, 154–59, 160, 161, 165, 168, 170, 178, 183, 184–86
Adventures of Huckleberry Finn, The, 148, 176, 182–86
Africa, 25, 163, 164, 170, 174
"After Holbein," 40–41
Afternoon of an Author, 109
Age of Innocence, The, 32–34, 35, 44
Aiken, Conrad, 120
Alexander the Great, 36
Alger, Horatio, 86
"All Souls," 24
All the Sad Young Men, 109
"Alpine Idyll, An," 157
Altamont (fictional city), 195, 196, 201
Ambassadors, The, 34
American Academy of Arts and Letters, 66, 75
American Adam, The, 77–78
"American Fear of Literature, The," 66
American Mercury, 64
American Tragedy, The, 108
American Writers Congress, 231
Americana, 229
Americans and American society, attitudes toward: of Edith Wharton, 17, 22, 28–29, 30–31, 37–38, 39–40, 44–45; of Lewis, 50, 52, 53, 59, 64–65, 66, 67–68, 71–72, 76–80; of Fitzgerald, 95, 99–102, 107–8; of Hemingway, 186–88; of Wolfe, 190, 192, 208, 210, 217–

18, 220, 223–24; of West, 248–49, 255–59. *See also* Society and social classes
Americans in Europe, literary theme: Edith Wharton's use of, 22, 27, 28–29, 31, 32, 34, 35–36, 39, 41, 42–43, 43–44; Lewis' use of, 65; Fitzgerald's use of, 111, 112; Hemingway's use of, 160, 165, 166, 167, 185–87; Wolfe's use of, 201
Anderson, Sherwood, 66, 75, 76, 120, 121, 122, 141, 159, 177, 178, 190
Andrews, Wayne, 14
"Angel at the Grave, The," 15
"Angel on the Porch, An," 191
Ann Vickers, 69–70
Antaeus (Of Time and the River), 192, 208
Anti-Saloon League, 62
Arabian Nights, 257
Archer, Newland (fictional character), 33–34
Arnold, Matthew, 110, 113
Arrowsmith, Martin (fictional character), 57, 58, 64
Arrowsmith, 57–59, 65
As I Lay Dying, 128–31, 144, 151, 152
Asheville, N.C.: Wolfe's literary use of, 193, 195, 206; Wolfe's roots in, 195, 196; residents indignant at portrayal by Wolfe, 199
Ashley, Lady Brett (fictional character), 142, 160
Aswell, Edward C., 203, 204, 205, 206, 207, 208
Atkinson, Brooks, 231
Austen, Jane, 8
"Autre Temps," 31–32, 38

287

Babbitt, George F. (fictional character), 53, 54, 55, 56, 57, 64, 65, 71, 100
Babbitt, Irving, 75
Babbitt, 42, 52–57, 59, 65
"Babylon Revisited," 111
Baker, Carlos, 170
Baker, George Pierce, 194, 197
Balsan, Consuelo Vanderbilt, 20
Baptists, 133, 236
Barkley, Catherine (fictional character), 142, 162, 167
"Barn Burning," 149, 151
Barnes, Jake (fictional character), 142, 160
Bart, Lily (fictional character), 17–19, 26, 28, 29, 36
"Battler, The," 155
Baudelaire, Charles, 228
"Bear, The," 146–47
Beardsley, Aubrey, 121
Beautiful and Damned, The, 99, 102–4, 109, 178
Bergson, Henri, 216, 218
Berlin, 63, 67
"Bernice Bobs Her Hair," 99
Bernstein, Mrs. Aline, 198, 199
Berry, Walter, 20–22, 41
Bethel Merriday, 73
"Bewitched," 25
Bierce, Ambrose, 152, 179
Big-game hunting, literary use by Hemingway, 158, 163, 178
"Big Two-Hearted River," 156, 157
Bishop, John Peale, 89, 96, 97, 105
Blaine, Amory (fictional character), 95, 96, 97, 102
Boni and Liveright, 159, 160
Book of Common Prayer, 153
Boom Town, 200, 221
Boston, bans *Elmer Gantry*, 62
Boston *Transcript*, 62
"Bottle of Perrier, A," 25
Bourget, Paul, 16, 23, 30
Brave New World, 72
Brontë, Emily, 8, 9
Brooke, Rupert, 90
Brooklyn, N.Y., 191, 199, 202, 220, 222
Brooks, Van Wyck, 19
Brothers Karamazov, The, 128
Broughton, Rhoda, 13, 14
Brown, Charles Brockden, 152, 185
Brown University, 227–28, 229

Bryant, William Cullen, 13
Buccaneers, The, 43–44
Buchanan, Daisy Fay (fictional character), 5, 91, 93, 94, 106–8, 109
Bulfinch, Thomas, 243
Bullfighting, literary use by Hemingway, 158, 160, 163–64, 175
"Bunner Sisters, The," 26
Burden, Joanna, 3, 133, 135
Burgum, Edwin Berry, 221
Burns, Robert, 194
"Business Deal," 229
Businessman in fiction: in Edith Wharton's work, 22–23, 37–38, 39–40; in Lewis' work, 51, 53, 54–55, 69, 70–71
Butler, Samuel, 90, 97

Caldwell, Erskine, 228
California: Lewis in, 48; West's literary use of, 229, 251, 256, 257, 258, 259–61; West in, 230–31
Camus, Albert, 123
Carew, Thomas, 194
Carmel, Calif., 48
Carolina Playmakers, 194, 197
Carraway, Nick (fictional character), 107, 113
Casements, 228, 229
Cass Timberlane, 73–74
Castro, Fidel, 175
Cather, Willa, 8, 114
Cerf, Bennett, 199
Chapel Hill, N.C., 193, 194, 197
Characterization, in novels, 4–7: by Edith Wharton, 4, 16, 34; by Faulkner, 5, 6–7, 125–26, 128, 131, 136–37, 151; by Hemingway, 5, 153, 154, 158; by Fitzgerald, 5, 93–94, 102–3; by Wolfe, 5, 219–20; by West, 5, 236–39, 251–53, 258; by Lewis, 79–80. *See also* Hero, Heroine
"Chickamauga," 206
"Child by Tiger, The," 191
Children, The, 34, 41–42
Christianity: Faulkner's acceptance of Christian moral code, 124–25, 150; Hemingway's use of Christian symbolism, 169; West's use of Christian imagery and ideas, 233, 234, 239, 240, 244
Christmas, Joe (fictional character), 3, 133–35, 139

Church, Margaret, 216
Cincinnati, Ohio, setting of *Babbitt*, 52
Civil War, 13, 17, 118, 119, 139, 140, 155, 200
Clemens, Samuel L., *see* Twain, Mark
Coates, Robert M., 249
Code and code hero, in Hemingway, 142, 158–59, 164, 168–69, 178–79, 187. *See also* Hero
Coleridge, Samuel Taylor, 115, 147, 194
Collected Stories (Faulkner), 149
Columbia Pictures, 231
Communists: in Lewis' fiction, 72; in Fitzgerald's fiction, 116; West's sympathy with, 231; in West's fiction, 247
Compson family (fictional), 6–7, 120, 125–28
Conrad, Joseph, 8, 105, 106, 125, 151, 152, 177
Contact, 229, 259
Contact Publishing Company, 142
Contempo, 229, 231
Cool Million, A, 230, 231, 246–50, 251
Coolidge, Calvin, 111
Cooper, James Fenimore, 152
Cowley, Malcolm, 75, 109, 123, 126
Cozzens, James Gould, 80
Crack-Up, The, 86, 114
Crane, Stephen, 125, 176–77, 179
Crime and Punishment, 128
"Cross Country Snow," 157
Crucial Instances, 15
Cuba, 164, 168, 172, 173, 175
Custom of the Country, The, 28–29
"Cut-Glass Bowl, The," 100

"Daisy Miller," 25
"Dalyrimple Goes Wrong," 100
"Dangerous Summer, The," 175
Dark Laughter, 159
Dartmouth College, 72
Day of the Locust, The, 231, 251–62
Death, theme in Hemingway's work, 154–55, 157, 163–64, 166, 175, 179, 183, 188
Death in the Afternoon, 163–64
Death the Proud Brother, 200, 202
Decoration of Houses, The, 11
"Dejection," 115
De Kruif, Paul, 57–58
"Delta Autumn," 147
Democratic Vistas, 221

Depression, 65, 69, 220, 222
Descent of Man, The, 16
De Voto, Bernard, 58–59, 203
"Diamond as Big as the Ritz, The," 101–2
Dickens, Charles, 6, 8, 9, 116
"Dilettante, The," 16, 19
Disenchanted, The, 115
Diver, Dr. Richard (fictional character), 112–13, 114
"Doctor and the Doctor's Wife, The," 155
Dr. Martino, 149
Dodsworth, Samuel (fictional character), 54, 63, 64
Dodsworth, 51, 63–65, 69, 75
Donne, John, 165
Doran publishing house, 49
Dos Passos, John, 9, 98, 101, 116, 151
Dostoevski, Feodor, 128, 226
Double-Dealer, 121
Doughty, Charles Montagu, 234
Doyle, Fay (fictional character), 236, 238–39, 242
Doyle, Peter (fictional character), 236, 238–39, 241, 242, 261
Dramatic adaptations: of Faulkner's *Requiem for a Nun*, 123; of West's *Miss Lonelyhearts*, 231–32. *See also* Motion pictures, Theater
Dream Life of Balso Snell, The, 228, 229, 230, 232–35, 236, 246
Dreiser, Theodore, 7, 55, 66, 76, 101, 108, 151
Drunkard's Holiday, The, 108
"Dry September," 149, 151
Dublin, 9

Ecclesiastes, book of, 161
Eliot, George, 9, 16, 35
Eliot, T. S., 8, 114, 137
Elmer Gantry, 59–63
"End of Something, The," 155
England: Lewis in, 58; Fitzgeralds in, 104; Hemingway in, 172; West's books published in, 232
Esquire, 82, 114, 116, 207
Ethan Frome, 25–26, 44
Eugénie, Empress of France, 13
Europe: Edith Wharton's sojourns in, 11, 13, 14, 29–31, 35; Edith Wharton's literary use of, 15, 22, 27, 28–29, 32,

35, 39, 41, 42–43, 43–44; literary theme of Americans in, 22, 27, 28–29, 31, 32, 34, 35–36, 39, 41, 42–43, 43–44, 65, 111, 112, 160, 165, 166, 167, 185–87, 201; reaction to Lewis' work in, 52–53, 66, 67; Lewis travels in, 58, 63, 69; Lewis' literary use of, 63, 78; Fitzgeralds travel in, 104, 105, 109; Fitzgerald's literary use of, 111, 112; Faulkner travels in, 121, 123; Hemingway's literary use of, 160, 162, 165, 166, 167, 185–86; Hemingway travels in, 171–72, 174; Wolfe travels in, 198, 199; Wolfe's literary use of, 201, 205; West travels in, 228
Euthanasia, 23
Eve of Saint Agnes, The, 89
"Eyes, The," 23–24

Fable, A, 120, 149–50, 151
Fadiman, Clifton, on Dodsworth, 53–54
Falkner, J. W. T., 120
Falkner, Maud Butler, 119
Falkner, Murray C., 119
Falkner, William C., 119
Farewell to Arms, A, 4, 142–43, 156, 161–63, 165, 167, 176, 181
Farrell, James T., 228
"Fathers and Sons," 157, 182
Faulkner, Estelle Oldham, 122
Faulkner, William, 8, 79, 80: good at story beginnings, 4; diversified characters of, 5, 6–7, 125–26, 128, 131, 136–37, 151; literary world of, 118–19; literary use of South, 118–19, 120, 122, 124, 128, 133, 138, 141, 142, 148, 149, 150, 152; autobiographical basis of fiction, 119, 122, 150; family background, 119–20; early years and schooling, 120–21; poetry of, 121; literary style of, 121–22, 123–24, 125–26, 128, 137–38, 139–40, 145–46, 151; marriage of, 122; receives Nobel Prize, 123, 148; receives Pulitzer prizes, 123; death of, 123; critical assessment of, 123–24, 150–52; acceptance of Christian moral code, 124–25, 150; position of Negro in novels of, 134, 138–39, 146–47, 148, 150; compared with Hemingway, 141–43; in "tall tale" tradition, 145–46; as short

story writer, 149; on Thomas Wolfe, 208; on writer's responsibility, 211
   WORKS: Absalom, Absalom!, 8, 135, 138–40, 149; As I Lay Dying, 128–31, 144, 151, 152; "Barn Burning," 149, 151; "The Bear," 146–47; Collected Stories, 149; "Delta Autumn," 147; Dr. Martino, 149; "Dry September," 149, 151; A Fable, 120, 149–50, 151; "The Fire and the Hearth," 147; "Go Down, Moses," 147–48; Go Down, Moses, 146–48; The Hamlet, 144–46, 150, 151, 152; Intruder in the Dust, 147, 148; Knight's Gambit, 148–49; Light in August, 4, 133–35, 137, 151; The Mansion, 150; The Marble Faun, 119, 121; "Mirrors of Chartres Street," 121; Mosquitoes, 122; "The Old People," 147; "Pantaloon in Black," 147; Portable Faulkner, 123; Pylon, 135–38, 151; "Red Leaves," 149; The Reivers, 123, 150; Requiem for a Nun, 123, 149; "A Rose for Emily," 149; Sanctuary, 123, 131–33, 149, 150, 152; Sartoris, 120, 122, 126, 132; Soldiers' Pay, 121–22, 142; The Sound and the Fury, 6–7, 8, 120, 122, 125–28, 131, 151; "That Evening Sun," 149; These Thirteen, 149; The Town, 123, 150; The Unvanquished, 120, 140–41, 146; "Was," 147; "Wash," 149; The Wild Palms, 142–44
Faulkner at Nagano, 133, 136
Fay, Monsignor Sigourney, 85
Fifth Column, The, 165
"Fifty Grand," 158
Finn, Huckleberry (fictional character), and Hemingway hero, 183–86
"Fire and the Hearth, The," 147
Fitzgerald, Annabel, 100
Fitzgerald, Frances Scott (daughter of F. Scott Fitzgerald), 89, 98, 104, 109, 111
Fitzgerald, F. Scott, 8, 9, 65, 79, 80, 177, 178, 224, 230, 246: rise and fall of personal and professional fortunes, 81–82; problem with alcohol, 81, 94; critical assessment of work, 82, 99, 116, 117; autobiographical basis of fiction, 82, 86–87, 91, 94, 96, 97, 104, 109, 110, 111, 117; attitude toward money, 82–84, 93, 101, 105, 107–8, 109; and Hem-

ingway, 82–83, 114; birth and early years, 85–88; Catholic background of, 85–86; short stories of, 86–87, 98–99, 109–10; early writing, 87–88; writing for theater, 88, 90, 104; at Princeton, 88–90; letters to daughter, 89, 98–99, 109; on writing, 89; service during World War I, 90; courts Zelda Sayre, 91–92; literary style of, 91, 97, 115, 117; earnings of, 92, 98, 109, 114, 115; attitude toward women, 91–94; satire in work of, 96–97, 101–2; popular success of, 98, 104; own summation of personal legend, 109; "the crack-up," 114–15

WORKS: "Absolution," 110; *Afternoon of an Author*, 109; *All the Sad Young Men*, 109; "Babylon Revisited," 111; *The Beautiful and Damned*, 99, 102–4, 109, 178; "Bernice Bobs Her Hair," 99; *The Crack-Up*, 86, 114; "The Cut-Glass Bowl," 100; "Dalyrimple Goes Wrong," 100; "The Diamond as Big as the Ritz," 101–2; *Flappers and Philosophers*, 99; *The Great Gatsby,* 5, 81, 85, 91, 94, 99, 104, 105–8, 109, 113, 116; "The Ice Palace," 92, 100; "The Jelly-Bean," 99–100; *The Last Tycoon*, 94, 116–17; "The Lees of Happiness," 100; "The Lost Decade," 116; "May Day," 100–1; "The Off-Shore Pirate," 100; "One Trip Abroad," 111; "The Rich Boy," 110; "The Scandal Detectives," 87; *The Stories of F. Scott Fitzgerald*, 109; *Tales of the Jazz Age*, 99; *Taps at Reveille*, 109, 114; *Tender Is the Night*, 85, 111–14, 116; *This Side of Paradise*, 81, 85, 88, 90, 92, 94–97, 99; *The Vegetable*, 104; "Winter Dreams," 86, 109–10; *The World's Fair*, 108
Fitzgerald, Zelda Sayre, 81, 84, 90–94, 100, 104, 108, 111–12
Five Came Back, 230
Flappers and Philosophers, 99
Flaubert, Gustave, 226
"Flight of the Rocket, The" (*The Beautiful and Damned*), 102
For Whom the Bell Tolls, 157, 165–66, 167, 175
Ford, Ford Madox, 8, 125, 177, 181

Forster, E. M., 4
47 Workshop, 194, 197
"Four Lost Men, The," 202
France, 72: Edith Wharton lives in, 11, 13, 35; Edith Wharton's literary use of, 22, 27, 28–29; *French Ways and Their Meaning*, 30; Edith Wharton's wartime work for, 31; Fitzgeralds in, 104, 105, 109; Faulkner in, 121, 123; recognition of Faulkner's work in, 123; Faulkner's literary use of, 149; Hemingway's literary use of, 160; Hemingway in, 172, 173; West in, 228; influence of West's fiction in, 232
Franco, Francisco, 175
Franklin, Benjamin, 106
Free Air, 50
French Ways and Their Meaning, 30
Freud, Sigmund, 243
From Death to Morning, 189, 200, 202
Frost, Robert, 120, 124
Fruit of the Tree, The, 22–23

"Gambler, the Nun and the Radio, The," 158–59
Gant, Ben (fictional character), 193, 214, 219
Gant, Eliza Pentland (fictional character), 193, 196, 200, 214, 219
Gant, Eugene (fictional character), 196, 198–99, 200, 201, 205, 209, 213, 215, 219
Gant, W. O. (fictional character), 193, 196, 214, 215, 219
Gantry, Elmer (fictional character), 59–60, 61, 63
Gatsby, Jay (fictional character), 5, 91, 93, 106–8, 109, 110, 112, 114
Gauss, Christian, 90
Gay, Walter, 27
Gellhorn, Martha, 172
Georgia Scenes, 146
Germany, 205, 206, 220, 221
Ghost stories, by Edith Wharton, 23–25
Ghosts, 25, 44
Gideon Planish, 73
Glasgow, Ellen, 45
Glimpses of the Moon, The, 35–37
"Go Down, Moses," 147–48
Go Down, Moses, 146–48
God-Seeker, The, 75
Gods Arrive, The, 42

Goethe, Johann Wolfgang von, 42
Gopher Prairie, Minn. (fictional city), 51
Gorki, Maxim, 249
Graham, Sheilah, 110, 115
Graham, Tom (Sinclair Lewis), 49
Great Depression, 65, 69, 220, 222
Great Expectations, 9
Great Gatsby, The, 5, 81, 85, 91, 93, 94, 99, 104, 105–8, 109, 113, 116, 246
Great Neck, L.I., 104–5, 115
Greater Inclination, The, 15
Greeley, Horace, 229
Green Hills of Africa, 163–64
Greene, Graham, 131
Greener, Faye (fictional character), 251–53, 254, 255, 258, 259, 262
Greenlaw, Edwin A., 194
Guggenheim Foundation, 199, 208, 230

Hackett, Tod (fictional character), 251–62 passim
Hamlet, The, 144–46, 150, 151, 152
Hammett, Dashiell, 228
Hanover, N.H., 115
Hanrahan, Gene Z., 170
Harcourt, Alfred, 67
Harcourt, Brace, and Company, 67, 68
Harding, Warren G., 163
Hardy, Thomas, 9
Harper and Brothers, 192, 203
Harris, George W., 146
Harvard University, 194, 197, 201, 207
Hawthorne, Nathaniel, 8, 58, 101, 127, 133, 152, 167, 179, 185, 194
Hearst, William Randolph, 247
Hearst's International, 98
Hegel, Georg, 194
Helicon Hall, 48
Hemingway, Clarence Edmonds (Ernest Hemingway's father), 155, 170
Hemingway, Ernest, 7, 8, 9, 76, 79, 80, 103, 124, 246: good at story beginnings, 4; autobiographical basis of fiction, 5, 158, 163, 168–69; and Fitzgerald, 82–83, 114; compared with Faulkner, 141–43; literary style of, 153, 161, 162, 168, 171, 176, 177, 180–82; literary hero of, 153–59, 160, 163, 165, 166, 167–68, 175, 184–86; influence on other writers, 153, 180; violence in works of, 154–55, 180, 183–84,
187–88; death of, 155, 175; major themes in work of, 159; in Spanish civil war, 165; uses Christian symbolism, 169; financial success of, 170; health of, 170, 171, 173, 174, 175; birth and early years of, 170–71; as reporter and correspondent, 171, 172–73, 176; in World War I, 171–72, 173; marriages of, 172; nonliterary exploits, 172; in World War II, 172–73, 174; last years of, 173, 175; psychological explanation of his preoccupations, 174–75; receives Nobel Prize, 176; compared with Stephen Crane, 176–77; as poet, 177; influences of other writers on, 177–80; compared with Twain, 182–86; literary world of, 187–88; compared with Wolfe, 190
  WORKS: Across the River and into the Trees, 166–68, 169, 174; "An Alpine Idyll," 157; "The Battler," 155; "Big Two-Hearted River," 156, 157; "Cross Country Snow," 157; "The Dangerous Summer," 175; Death in the Afternoon, 163–64; "The Doctor and the Doctor's Wife," 155; "The End of Something," 155; A Farewell to Arms, 4, 142–43, 156, 161–63, 165, 167, 176, 181; "Fathers and Sons," 157, 182; The Fifth Column, 165; "Fifty Grand," 158; For Whom the Bell Tolls, 157, 165–66, 167, 175; "The Gambler, the Nun and the Radio," 158–59; Green Hills of Africa, 163–64; "In Another Country," 157; In Our Time, 153, 155, 162, 177; "Indian Camp," 154–55, 178; "The Killers," 156, 157; "The Light of the World," 156–57; Men without Women, 156; "My Old Man," 177, 178; "Now I Lay Me," 157; The Old Man and the Sea, 159, 168–70, 181; "Out of Season," 177, 178; "The Short Happy Life of Francis Macomber," 158, 178–79; "The Snows of Kilimanjaro," 82, 170, 178, 179; The Sun Also Rises, 103–4, 142, 157, 160–61, 172, 246; "The Three-Day Blow," 155; Three Stories and Ten Poems, 142, 177, 178; To Have and Have Not, 164–65, 179; The Torrents of Spring, 159; "The Undefeated," 158; "Up in Michigan,"

177, 178; "A Very Short Story," 162; "A Way You'll Never Be," 157; *The Wild Years*, 170; *Winner Take Nothing*, 156
Hemingway, Mary Welsh, 172
Henry, Frederic (fictional character), 142, 156, 161–63, 167, 168
Henry Esmond, 105
Hermit and the Wild Woman, The, 23
Hero, fictional: Edith Wharton's, 16, 19–20, 22, 23, 33, 34, 36, 39, 41, 42–43; Lewis', 54, 55, 57, 59–60, 64, 70; Fitzgerald's, 93, 102–3, 112–13, 114, 116–17; Hemingway's, 153–59, 160, 163, 165, 166, 167–68, 175, 184–86; Wolfe's, 190, 201, 204, 205, 219; West's, 236–37, 246, 251
Heroine, fictional: Edith Wharton's, 17–19, 26, 27, 28–29, 31–32, 36–37, 38–39, 40, 42; Lewis', 51, 58, 69–70; Fitzgerald's, 91–92, 93–94; Hemingway's, 167; West's, 251–53, 258
Hike and the Aeroplane, 49
Hills Beyond, The, 189, 192, 206–7
Hitler, Adolf, 71, 249
Hobby, Pat (fictional character), 116
Hoffman, Frederick, 54
Hollywood, Calif., 100, 110: Fitzgerald in, 114–15; Fitzgerald's literary use of, 116–17; Faulkner in, 123; West's literary use of, 229, 251, 256, 257, 258, 259–61; West in, 230–31
Homosexuality, 157, 241–43, 245, 250, 261
"Hound of Darkness, The," 209
House of Mirth, The, 16–20, 22, 26, 36, 44
"House of the Far and Lost, The," 200
House of the Seven Gables, The, 127
Howells, William Dean, 55, 66
Huckleberry Finn, 148, 176, 182–86
Hudson River Bracketed, 42
Humor and comic literary elements, 132, 145–46, 234, 246–48, 257, 258, 260–61, 262. *See also* Satire
Hürtgen Forest, 173
Hunt, Richard Morris, 17
Huxley, Aldous, 72
Huysmans, J. K., 228

I Stole a Million, 230
"I Want to Know Why," 178

"Ice Palace, The," 92, 100
"In Another Country," 157
In Our Time, 142, 153, 155, 162, 177
"Indian Camp," 154–55, 178
Innocents, The, 49
Intruder in the Dust, 147, 148
Irving, Washington, 13
It Can't Happen Here, 71–72
Italian Villas and Their Gardens, 11
Italy: Edith Wharton's visits to, 13; Edith Wharton's literary use of, 15, 35; Faulkner in, 121; Hemingway's literary use of, 162, 167; Hemingway in, 171–72, 174, 182

Jack, Esther (fictional character), 189, 198, 201, 205, 214
James, Henry, 8, 9, 28, 55, 124, 125, 128, 151, 152, 185, 226: and rendering of character, 5, 6; friend of Edith Wharton's, 11; experiences similar to Edith Wharton's, 13, 25; Jamesian qualities in Edith Wharton's work, 15, 16, 22, 37; description of Newport, 17; attitude toward Berry, 21; criticism of *Custom of the Country*, 29; work of contrasted with Edith Wharton's, 30, 34–35, 44; Edith Wharton's comment on, 38; influence on Fitzgerald, 105, 111
James, William, 236
Japan, 123
Jazz Age, 95, 99, 100, 101
Jefferson, Miss. (fictional city), 118, 129, 132, 133, 135, 138, 144, 149
"Jelly-Bean, The," 99–100
Job, The, 50
Johnson, Eastman, 33
Johnson, Pamela Hansford, 221
Johnson, Dr. Samuel, 193
Jones, Edith Newbold, *see* Wharton, Edith
Jones, George Frederic, 12
Jones, Lucretia Stevens Rhinelander, 12
Jonson, Ben, 194
Jordan, Robert (fictional character), 157, 165–66
Journey Down, The, 198
Joyce, James, 9, 125, 151, 152, 179, 198, 200, 228
Jude the Obscure, 9
Jurgen, 228

Kansas City, Mo.: field of research for *Elmer Gantry*, 59; bans book, 62; Hemingway in, 171
Kansas City *Star*, 171
Kazin, Alfred, 80, 180
Keats, John, 89, 115
Kenmore Hotel, 228
Kennicott, Carol (fictional character), 51, 58, 64
Key, Francis Scott, 85
Key West, Fla., 172
"Killers, The," 156, 157
King, Alexander, 229
Kingsblood Royal, 74–75
Kipling, Rudyard, 47
Knight's Gambit, 148–49
Koch, Frederick, 194
Kruif, Paul de, *see* De Kruif, Paul
Krutch, Joseph Wood, 80
Kussy, Bella, 220

"Lady's Maid's Bell, The," 24
Lake Como, 35
Lardner, Ring, 105, 171, 177
Last Tycoon, The, 94, 116–17
"Launcelot," 47
Lawrence, D. H., 9, 82, 93, 117, 179
Leaves of Grass, 211, 213
Leclerc, Jean, 173
"Lees of Happiness, The," 100
Lenox, Mass., 22, 26, 29
Leskov, Nikolai S., 249
Letters of Thomas Wolfe, The, 209
Lewis, Claude, 51
Lewis, Edwin J., 46, 51
Lewis, Grace Hegger, 49
Lewis, Michael (Sinclair Lewis' younger son), 65, 68
Lewis, R. W. B., 77–78
Lewis, Sinclair, 8, 84, 151, 198: dedicates *Babbitt* to Edith Wharton, 42; birth and schooling, 46, 48; early writing, 47–50; poetry of, 47; marriage to Grace Hegger, 49; writes for slick magazines, 49; public reaction to books of, 50, 52–53, 56–57, 58–59, 60, 62–63; satire in work of, 50–51, 55–56, 57, 58, 59, 63, 64, 70, 73, 78; literary style of, 50–51, 55–56, 61–62, 64, 79–80; attitude toward Americans and American society, 50, 52, 53, 59, 64–66, 67–68, 71–72, 76–80; chronicler

of middle class, 50–51, 52, 53, 55, 64–65, 70–71, 72, 76, 80; method of work, 51–52; businessmen in novels of, 51, 53, 54–55, 69, 70–71; literary use of Middle West, 51, 52, 57, 64–65, 75; comparison with Babbitt, 54, 57; literary hero of, 54, 55, 57, 59–60, 64, 70; travels in Europe, 58, 63, 69; refuses Pulitzer Prize, 59; dedicates *Elmer Gantry* to Mencken, 63; marriage to Dorothy Thompson, 64; *Dodsworth* as turning point in career of, 65; and Nobel Prize, 65–66, 67, 68, 75, 76, 199; children of, 65, 68; breaks with Harcourt, 67; declining years, 68–69; interest in actresses and theater, 69, 73; death of, 69, 75; relationship with Dorothy Thompson, 69–70, 71; critical estimate of, 75–80; helps young writers, 76; influence on American literature, 79; Wolfe bases character on, 206; influence on Wolfe, 220
WORKS: "The American Fear of Literature," 66; *Ann Vickers*, 69–70; *Arrowsmith*, 57–59, 65; *Babbitt*, 42, 52–57, 59, 65; *Bethel Merriday*, 73; *Cass Timberlane*, 73–74; *Dodsworth*, 51, 63–65, 69, 75; *Elmer Gantry*, 59–63; *Free Air*, 50; *Gideon Planish*, 73; *The God-Seeker*, 75; *Hike and the Aeroplane*, 49; *The Innocents*, 49; *It Can't Happen Here*, 71–72; *The Job*, 50; *Kingsblood Royal*, 74–75; "Launcelot," 47; *Main Street*, 48, 50–51, 59, 65, 70; "The Man Who Knew Coolidge," 64; *The Man Who Knew Coolidge*, 65; *Mantrap*, 59; "Nature, Inc.," 49; *Our Mr. Wrenn*, 49; *The Prodigal Parents*, 72, 73; *The Trail of the Hawk*, 49; *Work of Art*, 70–71; *World So Wide*, 75
Lewis, Wells (Sinclair Lewis' older son), 68
Liber Brunensis, 228
Libya Hill (fictional city), 195, 206, 221
Liebling, A. J., 235
Light, James F., 235
Light in August, 4, 133–35, 137, 151
"Light of the World, The," 156–57
Lindsay, Vachel, 177
Little Review, 141

Liveright, Horace, 229. *See also* Boni and Liveright
Lock, R. H., 29
London, Jack, 48, 55, 66, 179
London, 9, 30, 43, 64, 198
Long, Huey, 71
"Long Run, The," 21
Longfellow, Henry Wadsworth, 13
Longstreet, A. B., 145
Look Homeward, Angel, 76, 189, 193, 194, 196, 198, 199, 201, 208, 209, 210, 213, 219, 220, 225
"Lost Boy, The," 191, 206, 217
"Lost Decade, The," 116
"Lost generation," 122, 157, 160, 161
Lowes, John Livingston, 194, 197
Lubbock, Percy, 11, 21, 22, 30, 35
Luxembourg, 173

Machen, Arthur, 228
McKenney, Eileen (Mrs. Nathanael West), 231
McKenney, Ruth, 231
Mackenzie, Compton, 90
Madame de Treymes, 22, 37
Mademoiselle Cœur-Brisé, 232
Magazines, *see* Popular magazines
Mahoney, Jeremiah, 227
Main Street, 48, 50–51, 59, 65, 70
Malraux, André, 123
Maltese Falcon, The, 228
"Man Who Knew Coolidge, The," 64
Man Who Knew Coolidge, The, 65
Mannerhouse, 207
Manners, Lady Diana, 100
Mansion, The, 150
Mantrap, 59
Marble Faun, The, 119, 121
Marne, The, 31
Marquand, John, 80
"May Day," 100–1
Mayo Clinic, 175
Medical profession: Lewis' fictional treatment of, 57–58; Fitzgerald's fictional treatment of, 112–13; Hemingway's fictional treatment of, 154–55
Melville, Herman, 8, 13, 152, 167, 194
Melville, Whyte, 13
Men without Women, 156
Mencken, H. L., 53, 102, 103, 105; *Elmer Gantry* dedicated to, 63
Meredith, George, 91

Methodists and Methodist Church, 60, 62, 133
Metro-Goldwyn-Mayer, 200
Metropolitan Magazine, 104
Michigan: Hemingway's literary use of, 170, 171, 184; Hemingway in, 170, 172
Middle West (U.S.): Edith Wharton's attitude toward, 28, 31; Edith Wharton's literary use of, 42; Lewis' roots in, 46, 57, 68; Lewis' literary use of, 51, 52, 57, 64–65, 75; Fitzgerald's roots in, 84, 85; Fitzgerald's literary use of, 84, 100–1, 107, 109; Hemingway's literary use of, 156, 170, 171, 184; Hemingway's roots in, 170, 172; West's literary use of, 251
Milan, 162, 172
Minnesota: Lewis' roots in, 46, 68; Lewis' literary use of, 51, 75; Fitzgerald's roots in, 84; Fitzgerald's literary use of, 84, 100, 109. *See also* St. Paul
"Mirrors of Chartres Street," 121
"Miss Lonelyhearts" (fictional character), 236–46, 261, 262
Miss Lonelyhearts, 229, 230, 231, 235–46, 251, 254, 261, 263
"Miss Mary Pask," 25
Mississippi: Faulkner's literary use of, 118–19, 128, 133, 138, 142, 149, 150, 152; Faulkner's roots in, 119–20, 121, 123, 150
Mississippi River, 183
Mitchell, Dr. S. Weir, 14
Mizener, Arthur, 81, 89, 93, 109
Montgomery, Ala., 84, 90, 91, 92
Moran of the Lady Letty, 179
Morris, Lloyd, 79
Mosquitoes, 122
Mother's Recompense, The, 34, 38–39
Motion pictures: adaptation of *Elmer Gantry* for, 60; Fitzgerald's stories sold to, 98, 109; Fitzgerald's literary use of, 108, 113, 116–17; Fitzgerald works on, 114–15; Faulkner works on, 123; Wolfe refuses to work on, 200; West's work sold to, 230, 231, 232; West works on, 230, 231; West's literary use of, 251, 260
My Mortal Enemy, 8

"My Old Man," 177, 178
My Sister Eileen, 231

Nathan, George Jean, 105
"Nature, Inc.," 49
Negro in literature: in Lewis' work, 74–75; in Faulkner's work, 134, 138–39, 146–47, 148, 150
New American Literature, The, 75
New England, Edith Wharton's literary use of, 25–26
New Humanism, 65, 75
New Masses, 65
New Orleans: Faulkner in, 121, 141; Faulkner's literary use of, 122, 135–36, 137, 139
New Orleans *Times-Picayune,* 121
New Statesman, 56
New York City, 9: Edith Wharton's roots in, 12, 13–14, 29, 31, 45; Edith Wharton's literary use of, 17, 18, 22, 28, 30, 32–33, 35, 38, 40, 42, 43, 44; Lewis in, 48, 49; Fitzgerald in, 92, 104, 116; Fitzgerald's literary use of, 97, 101, 110; Faulkner in, 121, 123; Wolfe in, 197, 198; Wolfe's literary use of, 201, 205; West's roots in, 226, 228, 230; West's use of, 245
New York *Times,* 104
New York *Tribune,* 104
New York University, 62, 198, 199
Newman School, 86, 87, 97
Newport, R.I., 12, 14, 17, 20
Nietzsche, Friedrich, 103, 228
Nigger of the Narcissus, The, 105
1984, 72
"No Door," 200
No Door, 192, 200
Noailles, Madame de, 45
Nobel Prize for Literature: to Lewis, 65–66, 67, 68, 75, 76, 199; to Faulkner, 123, 148; to Hemingway, 176
Norma, 13
Norris, Frank, 101, 179
"Now I Lay Me," 157

Oak Park, Ill., 170, 171
"Occurrence at Owl Creek Bridge, An," 179
"October Fair, The," 200, 208
Odo of Cluny, 235
O'Donnell, George Marion, 141

Of Time and the River, 189, 192, 197, 198, 200, 201, 203, 204, 205, 209, 210, 213, 214, 215, 217, 219, 221
"Off-Shore Pirate, The," 100
O'Hara, John, 54, 80
Old Man and the Sea, The, 159, 168–70, 181
Old New York, 35
"Old People, The," 147
"One Trip Abroad," 111
"Only the Dead Know Brooklyn," 191, 202
Oregon, 230, 231
Origo, Iris, 45
Orwell, George, 72
Our Mr. Wrenn, 49
"Out of Season," 177, 178
Oxford, Miss.: Faulkner's literary use of, 119; Faulkner's roots in, 119–20, 121, 123, 150. *See also* Jefferson, Miss.

Panama, 48
"Pantaloon in Black," 147
Paris, 11, 35, 45, 109, 111, 160, 172, 173, 228
Parkman, Francis, 13
Party at Jack's, The, 192, 221
Patch, Anthony (fictional character), 102–4, 106, 114
Pattee, Fred L., 75
"Pelican, The," 15
Perelman, S. J., 228, 229
Perkins, Maxwell E.: Fitzgerald's editor, 94, 98, 99, 106, 108, 110; Hemingway's editor, 161; Wolfe's editor, 192, 198, 199, 200–1, 203, 208, 209, 210, 211, 214, 221, 222
Pfeiffer, Pauline, 172
Pfister, Karin, 218
Phillips, David Graham, 55
Pictorial Review, 35
Pius IX, Pope, 85
Placi, Carlo, 45
Plaza Hotel, 84
Poe, Edgar Allan, 81, 152, 167, 194
Poetry: Edith Wharton's, 12, 14, 15; Lewis', 47; Fitzgerald's, 88; Faulkner's, 121; Hemingway's, 177; West's, 228
Poincaré, Raymond, 31
"Pomegranate Seed," 24–25
Poole, Ernest, 55

Popular magazines, writing for: by Edith Wharton, 35; by Lewis, 49; by Fitzgerald, 98; by Faulkner, 141; by Wolfe, 191, 199, 200, 206; by West, 230
Portable Faulkner, 123, 126
Portrait of Bascom Hawke, A, 191–92, 199
Pound, Ezra, 120, 177
Presbyterians, 133
Prescott, William H., 13
Princeton University: Fitzgerald at, 85, 88–90; Fitzgerald's literary use of, 97
Prodigal Parents, The, 72, 73
Professor's House, The, 8
Proust, Marcel, 18, 33, 45, 216, 218
Publishing houses: Lewis works in, 49; Lewis' relations with Harcourt, 67; Fitzgerald's relations with Scribner's, 90, 92, 114; Faulkner and Harrison Smith, 131; Hemingway changes publishers, 159–60; Wolfe's relations with, 192, 198–99, 203; West's relations with, 229, 231
Pulitzer Prize: Sinclair Lewis refuses, 59; to William Faulkner, 123
Pylon, 135–38, 151

Race problem: Lewis on, 74–75; Faulkner on, 139, 147, 148
Raskolnikov (fictional character), 128
Reading: Edith Wharton's, 13; Fitzgerald's, 90; West's, 228
Red Badge of Courage, The, 179
"Red Leaves," 149
Rednecks, 120, 128, 144
Reef, The, 27–28, 35
Reign of Terror, 16
Reivers, The, 123, 150
Religion: treatment by Lewis, 53, 59–63; treatment by Faulkner, 133–34. *See also* Christianity
"Rembrandt, The," 15
Renan, Ernest, 97
Republic Studios, 230
Requiem for a Nun, 123, 149
Reynolds, Quentin, 227
"Rich Boy, The," 110
Richardson, Hadley, 172, 177
Richelieu, Cardinal Armand, 30
Rimbaud, Arthur, 228
Ritz Hotel, 173

Riviera, 35, 39, 105, 108, 113
RKO Radio, 230
Road to Xanadu, The, 194
Roberts, J. M., 197
Roberts, Leo, 62–63
Roberts, Margaret, 193–94, 197
Rockefeller Institute, 57
Rockwell, Norman, 249
"Roman Fever," 24
Romantic Egoist, The (*This Side of Paradise*), 90
Rome, 94
Romola, 16
Roosevelt, Theodore, 34
"Rose for Emily, A," 149
Rubin, Louis D., Jr., 210

St. Paul, Minn.: influence on Fitzgerald, 84; Fitzgerald's birth in, 85; Fitzgerald's literary use of, 86, 87, 100, 109; Fitzgerald's plays produced in, 88; Fitzgerald returns to, 92, 104
St. Raphaël, 105
Salinger, J. D., 167
Salome (Strauss), 25
Sanctuary (Faulkner), 123, 131–33, 149, 150, 152
Sanctuary (Wharton), 16
Sanford, John, 227
Santiago (fictional character), 159, 168–70
Sartoris family (fictional), 120, 122, 140–41
Sartoris, 120, 122, 126, 132
Sartre, Jean-Paul, 123
Satire, in literary works: of Edith Wharton, 17; of Lewis, 50–51, 55–56, 57, 58, 59, 64, 70, 73, 78; of Fitzgerald, 96–97, 101–2; of Faulkner, 122, 132, 146, 150; of Hemingway, 159; of Wolfe, 197, 198; of West, 247–49
Saturday Evening Post, 49, 86, 87, 98, 105, 109, 110, 111, 191, 249
Saturday Review, 232
Sauk Centre, Minn., 46, 48, 68, 71, 152
Save Me the Waltz, 111
Sayre, Zelda, *see* Fitzgerald, Zelda Sayre
"Scandal Detectives, The," 87
Scarlet Letter, The, 167, 179
Schnee Eifel, 173
Schulberg, Budd, 115
Scott, Sir Walter, 194

Screen Writers Guild, 231
Scribner's (Charles Scribner's Sons), 90, 92, 98, 99, 159, 160, 192, 198, 200, 203, 208
Scribner's Magazine, 98, 199, 200
Sea Wolf, The, 179
Seager, Allan, 260
Selden, Lawrence (fictional character), 18–19, 36
Seldes, Gilbert, 56
Sexuality and sexual imagery, in literary works: of Lewis, 60; of Faulkner, 131–32, 143; of West, 234, 237–38, 239, 241–43, 245, 247, 250, 252–53, 258, 259, 260, 261–62
Shakespeare, William, 19, 194
Shaw, George Bernard, 90
Shell shock, 156, 175
Shelley, Percy Bysshe, 38
Shepard, Alice, 230
Sherwood Anderson and Other Creoles, 121
"Short Happy Life of Francis Macomber, The," 158, 178–79
Short Novels of Thomas Wolfe, The, 200
Shrike, Mary (fictional character), 236, 237–38, 241, 242, 254
Shrike, William (fictional character), 236, 237, 240, 241, 242, 243, 244, 245, 246
Sibon, Marcelle, 232
Simpson, Homer (fictional character), 251, 252, 254–55, 257, 258, 259, 261
Sinclair, Upton, 48, 55, 66
Sinister Street, 90
Smart Set, 98
Smith, Harrison, 131
Snopes family (fictional), 132, 141, 144–46, 150
"Snows of Kilimanjaro, The," 82, 170, 178, 179
Society and social classes, 32–33: Edith Wharton concerned with, 18–19, 26, 27–28, 44–45; Lewis as chronicler of middle class, 50–51, 52, 53, 55, 64–65, 70–71, 72, 76, 80; Fitzgerald and wealthy, 82–84, 88, 100, 102–3, 107–8, 110; Faulkner held not centrally concerned with aristocrats, 124, 141; treated by Wolfe, 194, 195–96, 221–22; treated by West, 249, 256–57.

See also Americans and American society
Soldiers' Pay, 121–22, 142
"Some Notes on Miss Lonelyhearts," 236, 243
"Some Notes on Violence," 259
Son at the Front, A, 31
Sound and the Fury, The, 6–7, 8, 120, 122, 125–28, 131, 151
Soupault, Philippe, 232
South (U.S.): Zelda Fitzgerald from, 91; Fitzgerald's literary use of, 100; Faulkner's literary use of, 118–19, 120, 122, 124, 128, 133, 138, 141, 142, 148, 149, 150, 152; Faulkner's roots in, 119–20, 121, 123, 150; Wolfe's literary use of, 193, 195, 206; Wolfe's roots in, 195–96, 197, 221
Spain, 7, 164, 165, 166, 175, 231
Spanish civil war, 165–66
Spengler, Oswald, 248
Spirit of Culver, 230
Spokesmen, 75
Spratling, William, 121
Stahr, Monroe (fictional character), 116–17
Stein, Gertrude, 122, 160, 161, 172, 177, 178, 179–80
Sterling, George, 48
Stern, Maurice, 226
Sterne, Laurence, 215
Stevens, Wallace, 122, 124
Stockholm, 66
Stone, Phil, 120, 121
Stories of F. Scott Fitzgerald, The, 109
Story of a Novel, The, 199, 202
Strauss, Richard, 25
Strether, Lambert (fictional character), 34
Strong, George Templeton, 34
Sturgis, Howard, 30
Style, literary: of Edith Wharton, 15, 17, 24, 25, 34–35, 35–37; of Lewis, 50–51, 55–56, 61–62, 64, 79–80; of Fitzgerald, 91, 97, 115, 117; of Faulkner, 121–22, 123–24, 125–26, 128, 137–38, 139–40, 145–46, 151; of Hemingway, 153, 161, 162, 168, 171, 176, 177, 180–82; of Wolfe, 190–91, 202, 206, 212–13; of West, 232–33, 234–35, 243–44, 245–46, 248, 250, 256–57, 259, 261
Summer, 26

Summit Avenue, 84, 85, 86
Sun Also Rises, The, 103–4, 142, 157, 160–61, 172, 246
Sun Valley, Idaho, 175
Sunday, Billy, 63
Supernatural, see Ghost stories
Sut Lovingood's Yarns, 146
Sutton Hotel, 228, 229
Sweden, 66, 123
Swedish Academy, 65
Swinburne, Algernon Charles, 47, 90, 121

Tales of Men and Ghosts, 23
Tales of the Jazz Age, 99
Tall tale: Faulkner's contribution to tradition, 145–46, 152; West's use of, 248
Taps at Reveille, 109, 114
Tarkington, Booth, 55
Tender Is the Night, 85, 111–14, 116
Tennyson, Alfred, 47, 90
Tess of the d'Urbervilles, 9
Thackeray, William M., 42
"That Evening Sun," 149
Theater, interest in: Lewis', 69, 73; Fitzgerald's, 88, 90, 104; Hemingway's, 165; Wolfe's, 194, 197, 207; West's, 231. See also Motion pictures
These Thirteen, 149
This Side of Paradise, 81, 85, 88, 90, 92, 94–97, 99
Thompson, Dorothy (Mrs. Sinclair Lewis), 63–64, 68, 70, 71, 73
Thoreau, Henry David, 77, 78
"Three-Day Blow, The," 155
Three Stories and Ten Poems, 142, 177, 178
Tiger, The, 90
To Have and Have Not, 164–65, 179
Tolstoi, Leo, 226
Toronto Star, 170, 172
Torrents of Spring, The, 159
Totalitarianism, 71–72, 249
Town, The, 123, 150
Tracy, Lee, 230
Trail of the Hawk, The, 49
Transatlantic, 142
Triangle Club, 88, 90
Tristram Shandy, 215
Tufts University, 227
Turgenev, Ivan, 177

Twain, Mark, 58, 77, 146, 176, 190: comparison with Hemingway, 182–86
Twentieth Century-Fox, 230
Twilight Sleep, 32, 39–40

Ulysses, 179, 198
"Undefeated, The," 158
United Front, 72
Universal-International Pictures, 230
University of Mississippi, 120, 121
University of North Carolina, 194, 197
University of Virginia, 123
Unvanquished, The, 120, 140–41, 146
"Up in Michigan," 177, 178
Upjohn, Richard, 17

Valley of Decision, The, 15–16, 23
Van Dyke, Henry, 75
Vanity Fair, 105
Varieties of Religious Experience, The, 236
Vassar College, 89, 109
Vegetable, The, 104
Verlaine, Paul, 228
"Very Short Story, A," 162
Village Virus, The (Main Street), 48
Violence, theme of in American literature: in Faulkner, 139, 141; in Hemingway, 154–55, 180, 183–84, 187–88; in West, 236, 243, 244, 246, 249–50, 255, 259, 261–62
Vogue, 49
Voltaire, 63, 97

Walden, 77–78
War: Edith Wharton's literary use of, 31; Faulkner's literary use of, 120, 140; Hemingway's literary use of, 156, 157, 160, 161–63, 165–66, 177, 187–88
Warren, Nicole (fictional character), 94, 112–13
Warren, Robert Penn, 123–24, 163, 203
"Was," 147
"Wash," 149
Watkins, Floyd C., 193
"Way You'll Never Be, A," 157
Web and the Rock, The, 189, 191, 198, 201, 205, 210, 212, 218, 219
Web of Earth, The, 191, 200, 202, 213, 215

Webber, George (fictional character), 204, 205–6, 214, 215, 219
Weinstein, Anna Wallenstein, 226, 229
Weinstein, Hinda, 226
Weinstein, Laura (Mrs. S. J. Perelman), 226, 228, 229, 230
Weinstein, Max, 226
Weinstein, Nathan, *see* West, Nathanael
Welcome to Our City, 207
Wells, H. G., 78, 90, 198
Wescott, Glenway, 95
Wessel, Horst, 249
West, Nathanael, 8: characterization in novels of, 5, 236–39, 251–53, 258; birth and schooling, 226–27; at Brown University, 227–28; attitude toward Jewishness, 227–28, 229, 233–34; works in hotels, 228; changes name, 229; sales of books, 229, 231; edits magazines, 229; engaged, 230; in Hollywood, 230–31; Communist sympathies of, 231; marriage of, 231; death of, 231; influence on French fiction, 232; critical evaluation of, 232, 234, 235, 246, 250, 262, 263; literary style of, 232–33, 234–35, 243–44, 245–46, 248, 250, 256–57, 259, 261; use of Christianity in work of, 233, 234, 239, 240, 244; use of sexuality and sexual imagery, 234, 237–38, 239, 241–43, 245, 247, 250, 252–53, 258, 259, 260, 261–62; violence as theme in work of, 236, 243, 244, 246, 249–50, 255, 259, 261–62; theme of human suffering, 239–40
WORKS: "Business Deal," 229; *A Cool Million*, 230, 231, 246–50, 251; *The Day of the Locust*, 231, 251–62; *The Dream Life of Balso Snell*, 228, 229, 230, 232–35, 236, 246; *Miss Lonelyhearts*, 229, 230, 231, 235–46, 251, 254, 261, 262, 263; "Some Notes on Miss Lonelyhearts," 236, 243; "Some Notes on Violence," 259
West, Rebecca, on *Babbitt*, 56
West (U.S.), 19: Nathanael West's literary use of, 229, 251, 256, 257, 258, 259–61; Nathanael West in, 230–31. *See also* Middle West
Westport, Conn., 104
Wharton, Edith, 4, 8, 55, 66, 114: cultivation of, 11–12; poetry of, 12, 14, 15; early reading of, 12–13; roots in New York, 12, 13–14, 29, 31, 45; sojourns in Europe, 13, 14, 29–31, 35; marriage of, 14; early writings of, 14; literary use of Europe, 15, 22, 27, 28–29, 32, 35, 39, 41, 42–43, 43–44; literary style and form of, 15, 17, 24, 25, 34–35, 35–37; political and social conservatism of, 16, 27–28, 39–40, 43; influence of Bourget on, 16, 23; influence of James on, 16, 22, 23, 34–35; "hero" of, 16, 19–20, 22, 23, 33, 34, 36, 39, 41, 42–43; literary use of New York, 17, 18, 22, 28, 30, 32–33, 35, 38, 40, 42, 43, 44; satire in work of, 17; attitude toward Americans and American society, 17, 22, 28–29, 30–31, 37–38, 39–40, 44–45; relationship with husband, 20, 29; relationship with Berry, 20–22, 41; experiment in novel of reform, 22–23; ghost stories of, 23–25; divorce of, 30; friends of, 30; decorated by Poincaré, 31; lapse into slick fiction, 35–37; literary use of Middle West, 42; Lewis dedicates *Babbitt* to, 42; critical assessment of, 44–45; death of, 45
WORKS: "After Holbein," 40–41; *The Age of Innocence*, 32–34, 35, 44; "All Souls," 24; "The Angel at the Grave," 15; "Autre Temps," 31–32, 38; "Bewitched," 25; "A Bottle of Perrier," 25; *The Buccaneers*, 43–44; "The Bunner Sisters," 26; *The Children*, 34, 41–42; *Crucial Instances*, 15; *The Custom of the Country*, 28–29; *The Decoration of Houses*, 11; *The Descent of Man*, 16; "The Dilettante," 16, 19; *Ethan Frome*, 25–26, 44; "The Eyes," 23–24; *French Ways and Their Meaning*, 30; *The Fruit of the Tree*, 22–23; *Ghosts*, 25, 44; *The Glimpses of the Moon*, 35–37; *The Gods Arrive*, 42; *The Greater Inclination*, 15; *The Hermit and the Wild Woman*, 23; *The House of Mirth*, 16–20, 22, 26, 36, 44; *Hudson River Bracketed*, 42; *Italian Villas and Their Gardens*, 11; "The Lady's Maid's Bell," 24; "The Long Run," 21; *Madame de Treymes*, 22, 37; *The*

Marne, 31; "Miss Mary Pask," 25; *The Mother's Recompense*, 34, 38–39; *Old New York*, 35; "The Pelican," 15; "Pomegranate Seed," 24–25; *The Reef*, 27–28, 35; "The Rembrandt," 15; "Roman Fever," 24; *Sanctuary*, 16; *A Son at the Front*, 31; *Summer*, 26; *Tales of Men and Ghosts*, 23; *Twilight Sleep*, 32, 39–40; *The Valley of Decision*, 15–16, 23; *Xingu*, 21, 31

Wharton, Edward Robbins, 14, 20, 29
Wheelock, John Hall, 208
Whipple, T. K., 75, 79
Whitman, Walt, 56, 58, 66, 77, 190, 201, 211, 213, 221–22, 223, 224
Wild Palms, The, 142–44
Wild Years, The, 170
Williams, Horace, 194, 195
Williams, William Carlos, 229
Wilson, Edmund, 12, 14, 84, 85, 89, 97, 98, 105, 114, 116, 180
Wilson, Woodrow, 163
Winner Take Nothing, 156
"Winter Dreams," 86, 109–10
Wolfe, Ben, 193, 196
Wolfe, Julia Elizabeth Westall, 193, 196
Wolfe, Mabel, 196
Wolfe, Thomas, 8: autobiographical basis of fiction, 5, 189, 190, 192–93, 201, 202, 209, 210, 211–12, 219, 224, 225; "discovered" by Lewis, 76, 199; pattern of contrasts in work of, 189–95, 211, 215, 225; themes in work of, 190, 213–19; literary style of, 190–91, 202, 206, 212–13; structural problems of, 191–92, 206, 210, 224; as short story writer, 191, 224; influence of teachers on, 193–94; interest in theater, 194, 197, 207; roots in South, 195–96, 197, 221; birth and early years, 195–97; literary world of, 195–96; teaches at New York University, 198; affair with Mrs. Bernstein, 198, 199; relations with Perkins, 199, 200–1, 203, 209–11, 214; critical assessment of, 202–3, 208, 210, 212, 224–25; changes publishers, 203; illness and death, 204–5; causes of failings as writer, 211, 223–24; skill in characterization, 219–20; social criticism in work of, 220–22

WORKS: "An Angel on the Porch," 191; *Boom Town*, 200, 221; "Chickamauga," 206; "The Child by Tiger," 191; *Death the Proud Brother*, 200, 202; "The Four Lost Men," 202; *From Death to Morning*, 189, 200, 202; *The Hills Beyond*, 189, 192, 206–7; "The House of the Far and Lost," 200; *The Letters of Thomas Wolfe*, 209; *Look Homeward, Angel*, 76, 189, 193, 194, 196, 198, 199, 201, 208, 209, 210, 213, 219, 220, 225; "The Lost Boy," 191, 206, 217; *Mannerhouse*, 207; "No Door," 200; *No Door*, 192, 200; "The October Fair," 200, 208; *Of Time and the River*, 189, 192, 197, 198, 200, 201, 203, 204, 205, 209, 210, 213, 214, 215, 217, 219, 221; "Only the Dead Know Brooklyn," 191, 202; *The Party at Jack's*, 192, 221; *A Portrait of Bascom Hawke*, 191–92, 199; *The Short Novels of Thomas Wolfe*, 200; *The Story of a Novel*, 199, 202; *The Web and the Rock*, 189, 191, 198, 201, 205, 210, 212, 218, 219; *The Web of Earth*, 191, 200, 202, 213, 215; *Welcome to Our City*, 207; *You Can't Go Home Again*, 189, 192, 195, 199, 200, 205–6, 210, 219, 221, 222

Wolfe, William Oliver, 193, 196
Woodward, C. Vann, 222
Woolf, Virginia, 9
Wordsworth, William, 115, 194, 215
Work of Art, 70–71
World, literary, 7–8, 9: of Edith Wharton, 17, 44–45; of Lewis, 52, 60, 80; of Faulkner, 118–19, 151–52; of Hemingway, 187–88; of Wolfe, 195–96; of West, 262
World So Wide, 75
World War I, 55, 69, 88, 118: Edith Wharton during, 31; Edith Wharton's literary use of, 31; Fitzgerald's service during, 90; Faulkner's service during, 120; Faulkner's literary use of, 120; Hemingway's literary use of, 156, 157, 160, 161–63; Hemingway in, 171–72, 173
World War II, 72, 118: Lewis' son killed in, 68; Hemingway in, 166, 172–73, 174
World's Fair, The, 108

Wuthering Heights, 8, 9

Xingu, 21, 31

Yale College and University, 45, 46, 47, 48
Yale Literary Magazine, 47, 48

Yoknapatawpha County, Miss. (fictional), 118, 138
You Can't Go Home Again, 189, 192, 195, 199, 200, 205–6, 210, 219, 221, 222

Zenith (fictional city), 52, 54, 57
Zola, Émile, 42